Thank you...

... for purchasing this copy of Writing for Literacy for ages 7-8. We hope that you find our worksheets, teachers' notes and display materials helpful as part of your programme of literacy activities.

This Writing for Literacy book is part of our growing range of educational titles. Most of our books are individual workbooks but, due to popular demand, we are now introducing a greater number of photocopiable titles especially for teachers. You may like to look out for:

WRITING FOR LITERACY for ages 5-7, 8-9, 9-10, 10-11

SPELLING FOR LITERACY for ages 5-7, 7-8, 8-9, 9-10, 10-11

NUMERACY TODAY for ages 5-7, 7-9, 9-11

HOMEWORK TODAY for ages 7-8, 8-9, 9-10, 10-11

BEST HANDWRITING for ages 7-11

To find details of our other publications, please visit our website: **www.andrewbrodie.co.uk**

...ications

Suggestions for using this book ...

We have examined carefully the current national policies for teaching literacy. In writing this book we have included activities at **word level**, **sentence level** and **text level**, to be used as part of your programme of teaching. Within the teachers' notes we have provided some guidance as to extra resources that you may wish to use.

We have created thirty units of work that can be used at your discretion across the school year, though we have indicated a suggested term for each unit. To enable you to incorporate the units effectively into your teaching we make suggestions as to other materials that work well with our activities - particular traditional tales, for example.

Each unit consists of four sheets:

Sheet A consists of teachers' notes, providing full guidance for the three activity sheets. Extra resources you may need are also listed here.
As you may well choose to use the unit as part of your programme of activities we also provide a box for you to list other ideas, ready for next time you use the unit.

Sheet B is the first activity sheet for each unit. It frequently includes word level work.

Sheet C often features sentence level work, though may well include word level or text level activities.

Sheet D provides the culmination for each unit. It will often be useful as a reminder sheet, perhaps to enlarge to go on the wall or to be copied on to an OHP transparency. In this way it provides an excellent focus for class or group discussion. In some units Sheet D includes a frame for extended writing.

We also include some extra writing frames, together with a useful reminder sheet for pupils at the very end of the book.

Thank you...

... for purchasing this copy of Writing for Literacy for ages 5-7. We hope that you find our worksheets, teachers' notes and display materials helpful as part of your programme of literacy activities.

Please note that photocopies can only be made for use by the purchasing institution. Supplying copies to other schools, institutions or individuals breaches the copyright licence. Thank you for your help in this.

This Writing for Literacy book is part of our growing range of educational titles. Most of our books are individual workbooks but, due to popular demand, we are now introducing a greater number of photocopiable titles especially for teachers. You may like to look out for:

WRITING FOR LITERACY for ages 7-8, 8-9, 9-10, 10-11

SPELLING FOR LITERACY for ages 5-7, 7-8, 8-9, 9-10, 10-11

NUMERACY TODAY for ages 5-7, 7-9, 9-11

HOMEWORK TODAY for ages 7-8, 8-9, 9-10, 10-11

BEST HANDWRITING for ages 7-11

To find details of our other publications, please visit our website: **www.andrewbrodie.co.uk**

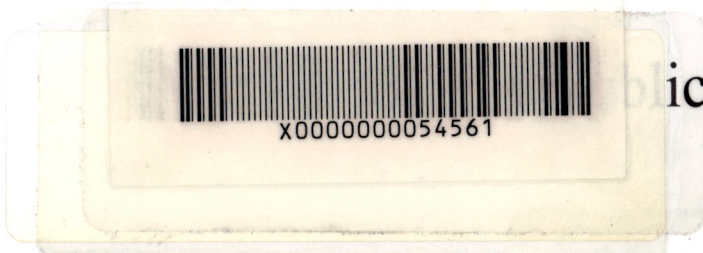

ications

Suggestions for using this book ...

We have examined carefully the current national policies for teaching literacy. In writing this book we have included activities at **word level**, **sentence level** and **text level**, to be used as part of your programme of teaching. Within the teachers' notes we have provided some guidance as to extra resources that you may wish to use.

We have created thirty-nine units of work that can be used at your discretion across Year One and Year Two, though we have indicated a suggested term for each unit. Six units per term are provided for Year One and seven units per term for Year Two. This allows you the freedom to extend and consolidate areas covered and to do writing work around festivals, trips, etc. To enable you to incorporate the units effectively into your teaching we make suggestions as to other materials that work well with our activities.

Each unit consists of four pages:

Sheet A consists of teachers' notes, providing full guidance for the three activity sheets. Extra resources you may need are also listed here.
As you may well choose to use the unit as part of your programme of activities we also provide a box for you to list other ideas, ready for next time you use the unit.

Sheet B is the first activity sheet for each unit. It frequently includes word level work.

Sheet C often features sentence level work, though may well include word level or text level activities.

Sheet D provides the culmination for each unit. It will often be useful as a reminder sheet, perhaps to enlarge to go on the wall or to be copied on to an OHP transparency. In this way it provides an excellent focus for class or group discussion. In some units Sheet D includes a frame for extended writing.

We also include some extra writing frames, together with a useful reminder sheet for pupils, at the very end of the book.

Contents ...

● Year 1, Term 1

Unit 1	B	Spelling and handwriting based on 'a'
	C	Joining parts of words together to label pictures
	D	Completing 'sensible sentences' using word boxes
Unit 2	B	Spelling and handwriting based on 'e'
	C	Cutting out words to assemble complete sentences
	D	Adding missing punctuation
Unit 3	B	Spelling and handwriting based on 'i' and 'o'
	C	Captioning pictures
	D	Writing about recent experiences
Unit 4	B	Spelling and handwriting based on 'u'
	C	Choosing rhyming words
	D	Listing classroom items
● Unit 5	B	Spelling and handwriting based on 'A' and 'E'
	C	Changing two words around to make sensible sentences
	D	Instructions for booklet creation
Unit 6	B	Spelling and handwriting based on 'T' and 'B'
	C	Captioning artwork, etc
	D	Writing frame for instructions

● Year 1, Term 2

Unit 7	B	Spelling and handwriting based on 'bl'
	C	Adding capital letters and full stops
	D	Playing with rhymes
Unit 8	B	Spelling and handwriting based on 'sc'
	C	Making a wall story or class book
	D	Writing about a pet
● Unit 9	B	Spelling and handwriting based on 'sp'
	C	Labelling 'Vog the Amazing Alien'
	D	Punctuation, prediction and story writing exercise
Unit 10	B	Spelling and handwriting based on 'sl'
	C	Writing variations of 'Little Red Riding Hood'
	D	Frames for pictures and captions on the subject of homes
Unit 11	B	Spelling and handwriting based on 'mp'
	C	Labelling a picture of the parrot
	D	Questions about the parrot
Unit 12	B	Spelling and handwriting based on 'ch'
	C	Rewriting the caption for a picture
	D	Instructions for a story writing exercise

●

© Andrew Brodie Publications ✓ PO Box 23, Wellington, Somerset, TA21 8YX ✓ www.andrewbrodie.co.uk

Year 1, Term 3

Unit 13	B	Using capital letters at the start of the words 'Mr', 'Mrs' and 'Miss'
	C	Writing about part of story of 'Goldilocks and the Three Bears'
	D	Writing a story from the start provided
Unit 14	B	Spelling and handwriting based on 'oo'
	C	Adding words to sentences to make them sensible
	D	Adding to a simple poem
Unit 15	B	Spelling and handwriting based on 'st'
	C	Formation of question marks and their use
	D	Writing alternate lines of a poem about water
Unit 16	B	Spelling and handwriting based on 'ea'
	C	Instructions for making a class book about toys
	D	Frame for producing a class book about toys
Unit 17	B	Spelling and handwriting based on 'oa'
	C	Thinking of questions
	D	Writing answers to captions in boxes
Unit 18	B	Spelling and handwriting based on 'ay' and 'ai'
	C	Writing about a day out
	D	Instructions for a booklet about something that has happened

Year 2, Term 1

Unit 19	B	Spelling based on 'oo'
	C	Sequencing language
	D	Instructions for a piece of writing about school holidays
Unit 20	B	Spelling based on 'ar'
	C	Reading with expression
	D	Sequencing words and story writing
Unit 21	B	Spelling based on 'oy' and 'oi'
	C	Correcting a story
	D	Using rhythm and rhyme to write new lines of poetry
Unit 22	B	Spelling based on 'ow'
	C	Arranging a story in sequence
	D	Writing instructions for a simple task
Unit 23	B	Spelling based on 'ou'
	C	Revision of use of capital letters
	D	Rewriting jumbled instructions
Unit 24	B	Spelling based on 'air'
	C	Continuing a sequence of directional instructions
	D	Drawing a new map and writing instructions for its use
Unit 25	B	Spelling high frequency words
	C	Instructions for writing a story
	D	Writing frame for use with Sheet C

© Andrew Brodie Publications ✓ PO Box 23, Wellington, Somerset, TA21 8YX ✓ www.andrewbrodie.co.uk

Year 2, Term 2

Unit 26	B	Spelling based on 'ur' words
	C	Identification of speech marks
●	D	Pictures and frame for use with Sheet C

Unit 27	B	Compound words
	C	Past and present verbs
	D	Commas and lists

Unit 28	B	Spelling based on 'ore' words
	C	Word association for colour words
	D	Writing frame for a two verse poem based on colour

Unit 29	B	Syllables
	C	Story of 'The Two Jays'
	D	Writing ideas based on the story on Sheet C

Unit 30	B	Spelling different letter groups which give the same sound
	C	Describing characters
	D	Making a poster about one of the two Jays

● Unit 31	B	Antonyms
	C	Introduction to definitions
	D	Creating a class dictionary

Unit 32	B	Work on the prefixes 'un' and 'dis'
	C	Simple flow chart showing morning routine
	D	Frame for pupils to produce own flow chart

Year 2, Term 3

Unit 33	B	Different spellings that can produce the sounds 'ay' and 'ee'
	C	Making questions from statements
	D	Writing a book review

Unit 34	B	Different spellings that can produce the sounds 'i' and 'oh'
	C	Pairing verbs into past and present tenses
	D	Frame for story writing

● Unit 35	B	Using the suffixes 'ful' and 'ly'
	C	Use of terms 'heading', 'subheading' and 'picture'
	D	Finding out information about other creatures

Unit 36	B	Using and collecting synonyms
	C	Simple factual writing
	D	Adding adjectives

Unit 37	B	Syllables and synonyms
	C	Commas and lists
	D	Producing a class anthology of poems

Unit 38	B	Spelling work on months of the year
	C	Alliteration
	D	Tongue-twisters

Unit 39	B	Spelling of common colour words
●	C	Instruction sheet for story writing
	D	Frame for use with Sheet C

© Andrew Brodie Publications ✓ PO Box 23, Wellington, Somerset, TA21 8YX ✓ www.andrewbrodie.co.uk

● Teachers' Notes

✓ This unit incorporates work on the sentence level requirement to ensure that a written text makes sense, and the requirement at text level to use phonological skills and sight vocabulary knowledge ✓ to aid the accurate spelling of words.

✓ **Sheet B** Letter formation of *a*, and correctly copying a word and matching to the appropriate picture.

✓ **Sheet C** Joining two parts of words to enable pictures to be correctly labelled.

✓ **Sheet D** Inserting correct words into sentences to make 'sensible sentences'.

Use this box to write your own notes ready for the next time you use this unit.

© Andrew Brodie Publications ✓ PO Box 23, Wellington, Somerset, TA21 8YX ✓ www.andrewbrodie.co.uk

● **Word/text level work**

Name: Date:

> Go over my letters, and do some more of your own.

ȧ a a a

> Copy each word ...

> ... and draw a line to the correct picture.

cat

van

rat

bat

● **Word/text level work**

Name: Date:

My words have been cut in two.

Join the parts and label the pictures.

hou

sch   og   ig

d   ok   se   c   lo

d   ool   at

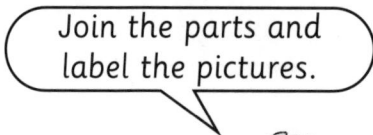

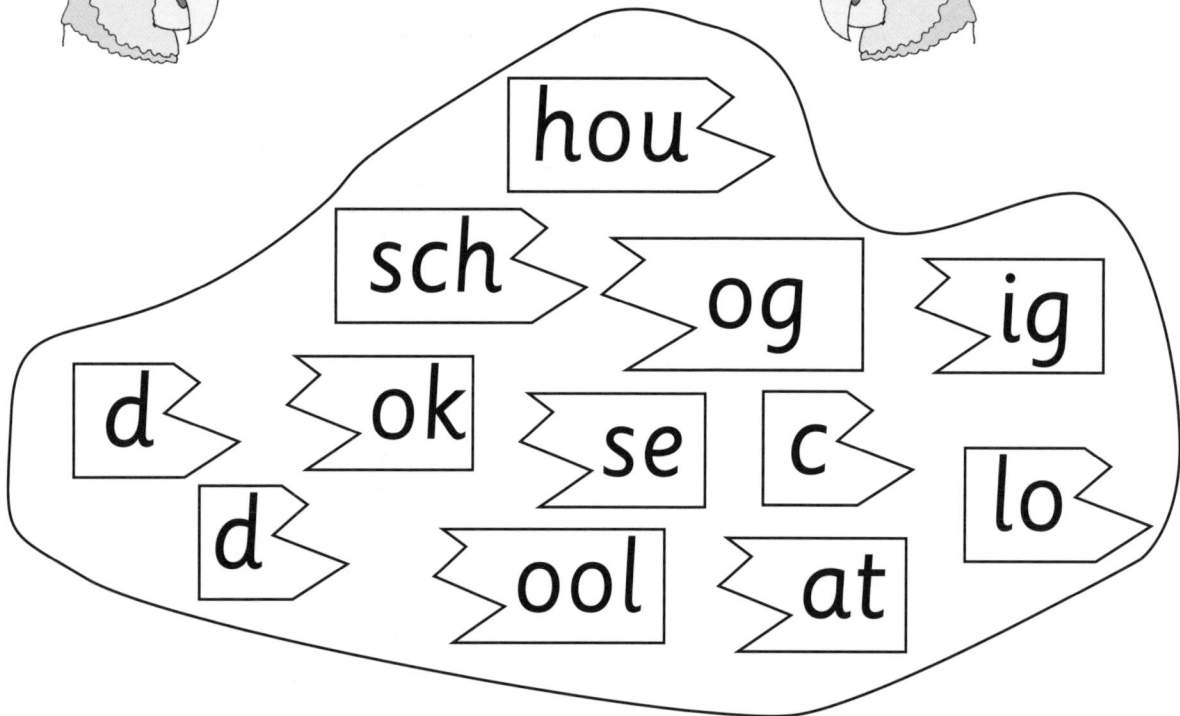

Make the broken parts into words, and match them with the pictures.

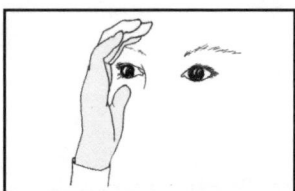

© Andrew Brodie Publications ✓ PO Box 23, Wellington, Somerset, TA21 8YX ✓ www.andrewbrodie.co.uk

Name: Date:

Put a word from the box into each sentence.

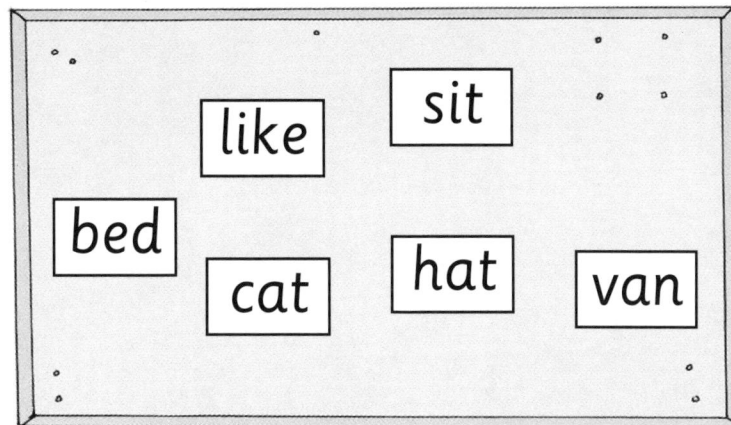

like
sit
bed
cat
hat
van

My _ _ _ sleeps in a basket.

The _ _ _ went along the road.

I _ _ _ _ to play in the garden.

My _ _ _ is in my bedroom.

I have a _ _ _ on my head.

You can _ _ _ on a chair.

Draw a picture of a hen on a hat.

● Teachers' Notes

✓ This unit, with handwriting and spelling, covers sentence level requirements to use the term 'sentence' correctly and to recognise capital letters and full stops. It also tackles the fact that a line of writing is not necessarily a sentence and asks pupils to begin to use full stops.

✓ **Sheet B** Handwriting and spelling based on the letter *e* and its short vowel sound.

✓ **Sheet C** This sheet is designed for cutting out the word boxes and assembling in the correct order - each sentence can then be glued or copied into individual writing books.
You will notice that each sentence has differently framed words to avoid confusion.

✓ **Sheet D** This sheet can be used individually to put in the missing full stops and capital letters (Once, She, The) before copying, or can be copied onto an OHP for group use.

Use this box to write your own notes ready for the next time you use this unit.

Name: Date:

Go over my letters.

e e e e

✏ Copy each word.   Draw a line to the
                                       correct picture.

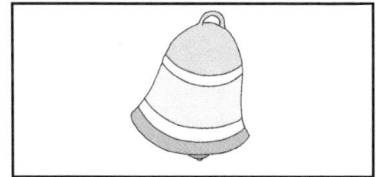

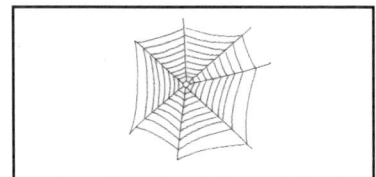

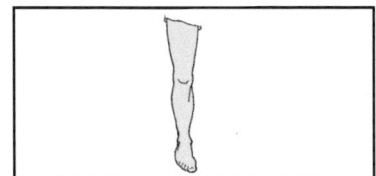

web

bed

net

leg

bell

● **Sentence level work**

Name: Date:

Jumbled sentences

My sentences are in a muddle.

Cut out the words and put them in the right order.

tree.	little	A	in
bird	landed	a	

with	leaves	and	It
made	twigs.	nest	a

You can <u>glue</u> or <u>copy</u> the sentences into your writing book.

© Andrew Brodie Publications ✓ PO Box 23, Wellington, Somerset, TA21 8YX ✓ www.andrewbrodie.co.uk

Name: Date:

I have written a story ...

... but I forgot 3 capital letters and 3 full stops.

✍ Write the story in your book.

✍ Don't forget the capital letters and full stops.

> once upon a time a little girl went for a walk she met a big green monster the little girl shouted "boo" and frightened the monster away

Draw a picture to go with the story.

© Andrew Brodie Publications ✓ PO Box 23, Wellington, Somerset, TA21 8YX ✓ www.andrewbrodie.co.uk

● Teachers' Notes

✓ This unit covers spelling and handwriting requirements at word and text level. There is also sentence level work on writing captions (in the form of a simple sentence) to pictures and text level work based on personal experience and family stories.

✓ **Resources**   Shared reading (Big Book) fiction based on 'real' and familiar experiences, e.g. shopping, going to school and holidays.

✓ **Sheet B**   Short vowel sounds *i* and *o*, and handwriting exercises.

✓ **Sheet C**   Captioning pictures - an important part of this work is the opportunity for pupils to read captions to each other.

✓ **Sheet D**   Writing frame asking the children to write about something that has happened to them - this should be linked to this week's shared reading.

Use this box to write your own notes ready for the next time you use this unit.

© Andrew Brodie Publications ✓ PO Box 23, Wellington, Somerset, TA21 8YX ✓ www.andrewbrodie.co.uk

● Word and text level work

Name: Date:

Go over my letters.

Choose the correct word for each picture.

pot   bin   dog

six

fox   pig

_ _ _

_ _ _

_ _ _

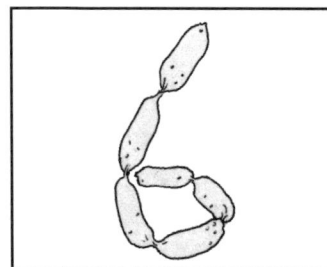

_ _ _

_ _ _

_ _ _

© Andrew Brodie Publications ✓ PO Box 23, Wellington, Somerset, TA21 8YX ✓ www.andrewbrodie.co.uk

● **Sentence level work**

Name: Date:

Write a sentence to put with each picture.

Read your sentences to a friend.

Text level work

Name: Date:

Think about the book your class has been looking at.

Write about something that has happened to you.

✏ Draw a picture too.

© Andrew Brodie Publications ✓ PO Box 23, Wellington, Somerset, TA21 8YX ✓ www.andrewbrodie.co.uk

● Teachers' Notes

✓　This unit deals with the text level requirements to use rhyming words and to make lists. It also deals with word and text level spelling and writing.

✓　**Resources**　Big Book materials including simple rhymes and 'patterned' stories would be useful. Examples of using lists.

✓　**Sheet B**　Spelling and handwriting based on short vowel sound *u*.

✓　**Sheet C**　Pairs of rhyming words and using these to complete lines.

✓　**Sheet D**　Lists: for the best use of this work, a preparatory class/group session on classroom toys and games is a necessity. The teacher (or other classroom adult) will need to provide a bank of appropriate words for listing. The results of this may link with maths work on data collection.

Use this box to write your own notes ready for the next time you use this unit.

© Andrew Brodie Publications ✓ PO Box 23, Wellington, Somerset, TA21 8YX ✓ www.andrewbrodie.co.uk

Name: Date:

Go over my letters.

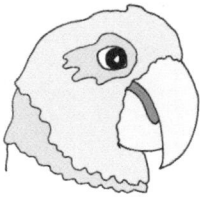

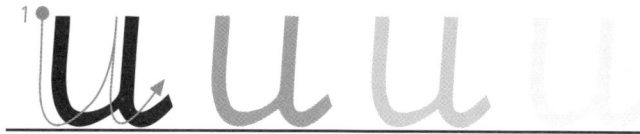

^{1}u u u u

Read and write the words.

run	mum	bug

hug	cup	mud

✎ Label the pictures.

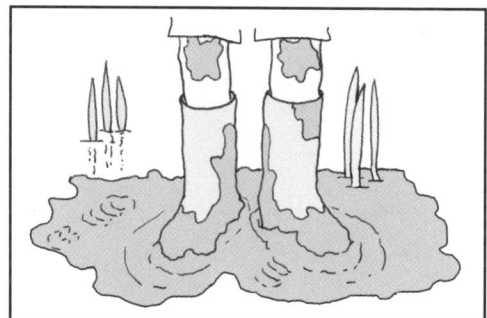

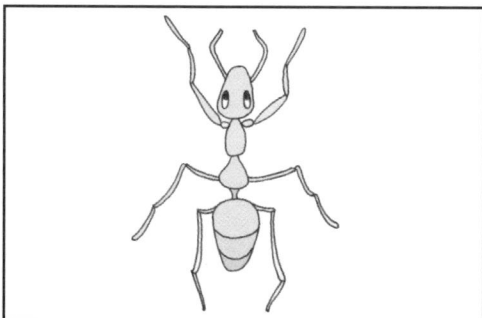

● **Word and text level work**

Name: Date:

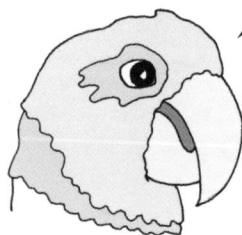

Look in the box to find a word to rhyme with each word here.

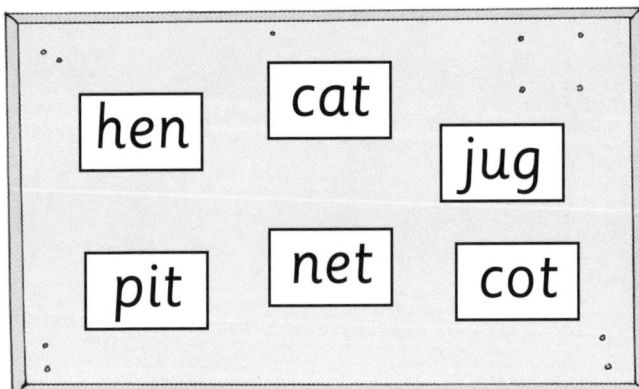

hen   cat   jug

pit   net   cot

mat ....   pot ....

pen ....   get ....

sit ....   mug ....

✏ Finish the lines of this rhyme.

I sat on a mat,

And I stroked my _ _ _ .

I have a pet hen,

Who can write with a _ _ _ .

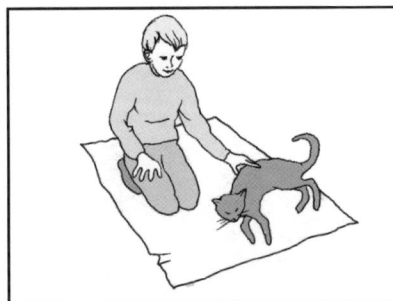

Name: Date:

Make a list of your six favourite classroom toys.

1. _____

2. _____

3. _____

4. _____

5. _____

6. _____

Draw and label your very favourite classroom toy here.

● Teachers' Notes

✓ This unit works on formation of capital letters, checking sentences to make sure they make sense, and text level work on making a story book.

✓ **Resources** Story books (Big Books) written in clear sentences. (Please try to ensure the book does not always finish a sentence at the end of a line.)

✓ **Sheet B** Formation of capital *A* and capital *E*.

✓ **Sheet C** Changing two words around to make a sentence make sense.

✓ **Sheet D** This is an instructional sheet for enlarging or copying to an OHP transparency for group use. The resulting work can be produced on a story book frame found at the back of this publication. This frame provides a cover plus three writing frames.

Use this box to write your own notes ready for the next time you use this unit.

● Word and sentence level work

Name: Date:

These are capital letters.

We always find a capital letter at the beginning of a sentence.

✏ Write over these letters.

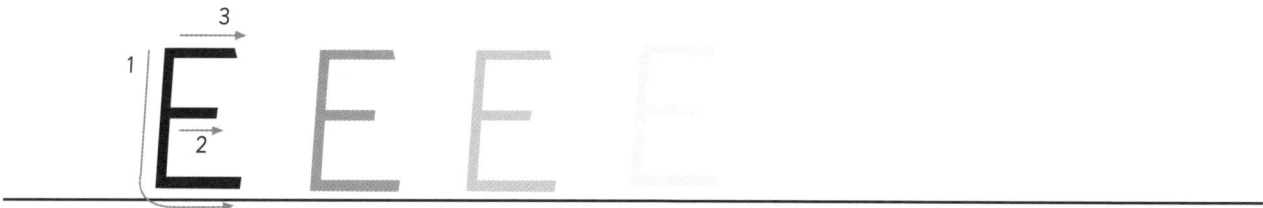

A A A A A

E E E E E

✏ Read and copy these silly sentences.

Elephants eat empty eggs.

All alligators are amazing.

● **Sentence level work**

Name: Date:

My sentences are muddled.

Swap two words in each sentence to help me.

The first one has been done for you.

I like eat to dinner.
I like to eat dinner.

A tree is in garden. the

boy. The played outside

A picture on is the wall.

I like to lemonade drink.

© Andrew Brodie Publications ✔ PO Box 23, Wellington, Somerset, TA21 8YX ✔ www.andrewbrodie.co.uk

Name: Date:

Read these instructions ...

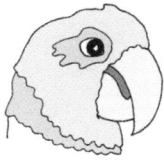

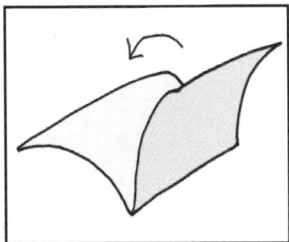

1. Fold your paper in half to make a booklet.

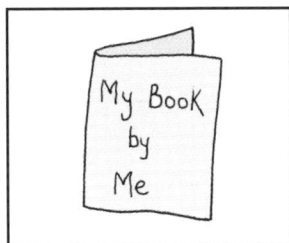

2. Put the title and author's name on the front cover.

My Book by Me

3. Put one or two sentences and a picture on each page.

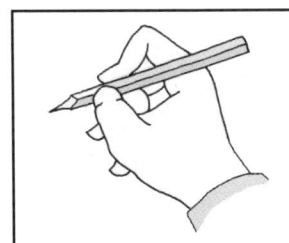

4. Use your best writing so your friends can read your story too.

You have made a story book.

● Teachers' Notes

✓ In addition to word and sentence level work based on capital letters, this unit tackles the text level requirement to write simple labels, captions and instructions for classroom display.

✓ **Resources** Simple instructional texts and examples of labels/captions on displayed work.

✓ **Sheet B** Capitals T and B, and their use alongside their lower case counterparts.

✓ **Sheet C** Label frames suitable for captioning art work, building toy constructions and other examples of children's work. Children should be encouraged to write in a large, clear, bold print, and to have their spellings checked before writing for display.

✓ **Sheet D** Frame for instructions.
Suggestions include: washing hands after visiting the toilet, rules for role play areas, instructions for use and storage of classroom equipment.

Use this box to write your own notes ready for the next time you use this unit.

Name: Date:

Here are some more capital letters to write.

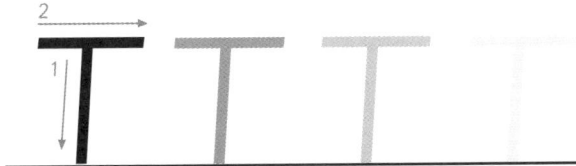

T T T T

B B B B

Carefully read and copy these silly sentences.

Toast tastes terrific.

Billy burst his blue balloon.

● **Text level work**

Name: Date:

Use these frames to write labels
to use in your classroom.

Cut out your
labels with care!

© Andrew Brodie Publications ✓ PO Box 23, Wellington, Somerset, TA21 8YX ✓ www.andrewbrodie.co.uk

Name: Date:

Use this frame to write some instructions.

Have you used capitals and full stops?

● Teachers' Notes

✓ In addition to work on spelling and handwriting, this unit tackles text level work on rhyming patterns and sentence level work on the use of capital letters and full stops.

✓ **Resources** Big Book texts with rhyming poems. Any text written in clear sentences - try not to choose texts with full stops at ends of lines.

✓ **Sheet B** Spelling and handwriting based on *bl*.

✓ **Sheet C** Rewriting three sentences adding the appropriate capital letters and full stops. (This sheet is also suitable for enlargement for group use, followed by writing completed in books.) The illustration is requested to check understanding of the text.

✓ **Sheet D** This introduces 'playing with rhymes', and is suitable for other extension work in the classroom.

Use this box to write your own notes ready for the next time you use this unit.

© Andrew Brodie Publications ✓ PO Box 23, Wellington, Somerset, TA21 8YX ✓ www.andrewbrodie.co.uk

● Word and text level work

Name: Date:

Go over my letters ...

bl bl bl bl

... and colour the stars.

black

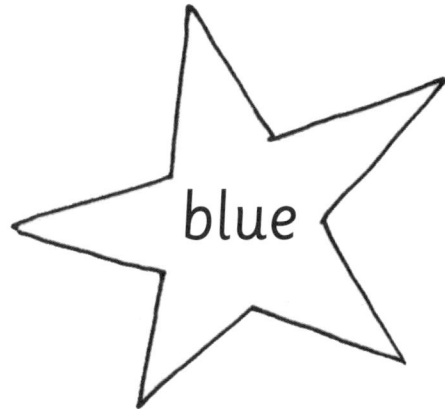
blue

Choose the correct
word for each picture.

blade

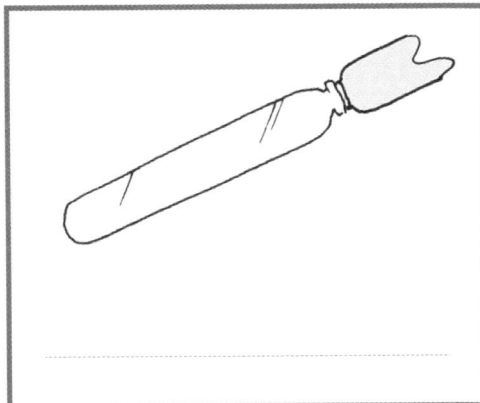

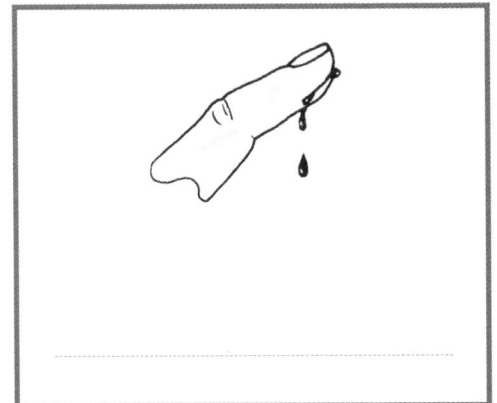

blow

blossom

blood

● **Sentence and text level work**

Name: Date:

Rewrite the three sentences.

Put in the capital letters and full stops.

one day two children went

to play in the garden they

played hide and seek for a

long time at twelve o'clock

they went indoors for dinner

Draw a picture to go with the writing.

© Andrew Brodie Publications ✓ PO Box 23, Wellington, Somerset, TA21 8YX ✓ www.andrewbrodie.co.uk

Name: Date:

Let's change some rhymes you know.

Choose the best words from the box to make new rhymes.

flew   floor

tea   fell

me

Ding dong bell,
Pussy tripped and _ _ _ _ .

One, two, my bird _ _ _ _ .
Three, four, stamp on the _ _ _ _ _ .

Little Miss Muffet
Sat on a tuffet
Drinking a cup of _ _ _ .
Down came a spider
And sat down beside her
And said, "Is there any for _ _ ?"

Can you change some other rhymes you know?

© Andrew Brodie Publications ✓ PO Box 23, Wellington, Somerset, TA21 8YX ✓ www.andrewbrodie.co.uk

● Teachers' Notes

✓ In addition to spelling and handwriting, this unit looks at the text level requirements to present information based on pupils' own experiences, and to use captions to present main incidents of a story plot.

✓ **Resources** Story suitable for wall story or class book. Simple informational texts on familiar subjects.

✓ **Sheet B** Spelling and writing based on *sc*.
N.B. Making both letters the same height will need to be emphasised.

✓ **Sheet C** This is a frame designed for making a wall story or class book of a known story.
N.B. Upper right hand speech bubble needs the title of the story you have chosen to use.

✓ **Sheet D** Frame for information and writing about a pet.

Use this box to write your own notes ready for the next time you use this unit.

© Andrew Brodie Publications ✓ PO Box 23, Wellington, Somerset, TA21 8YX ✓ www.andrewbrodie.co.uk

● Word and text level work

Name: Date:

Go over my letters.

SC SC SC SC

Write the correct word under each picture.

screw   scarf   scooter   scales

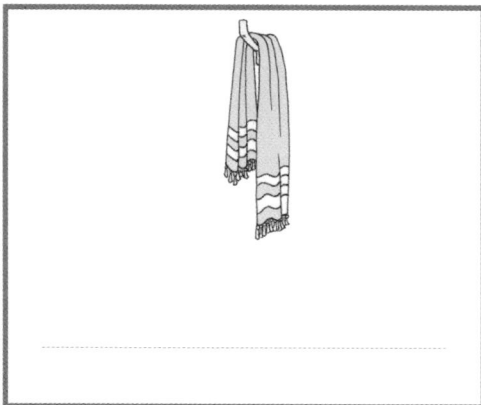

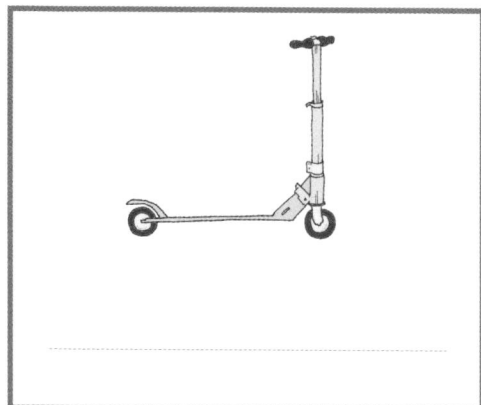

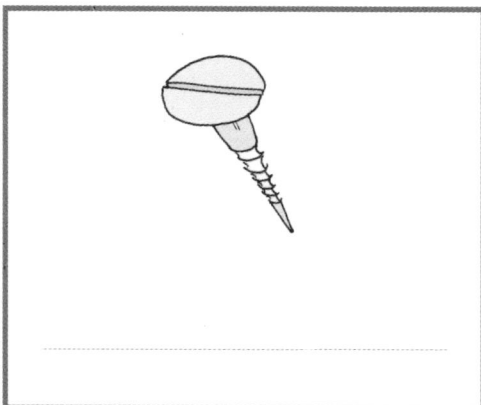

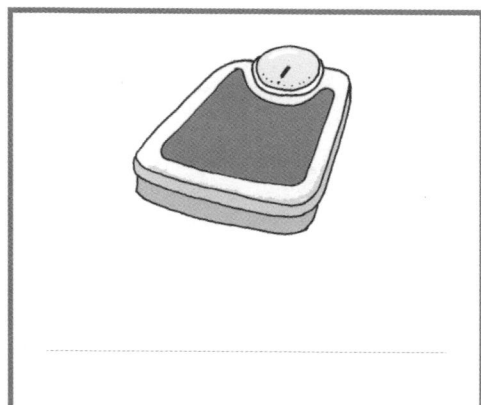

● **Text level work**

Name: Date:

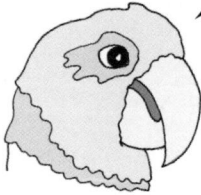 Draw a picture and write a sentence about ...

... the story of

Page

Name: Date:

Draw a picture
of a pet.

Write three sentences
about that sort of pet.

● Teachers' Notes

✓   In addition to spelling and handwriting, this unit covers sentence level requirements to use capital letter for pronoun "i" and for the beginning of names and the text level requirement to label drawings or diagrams.

✓   **Resources**   Any simple, clear examples of labelled pictures (linked to Sheet C). Texts showing pronoun "I" and with names of people and/or places, to show use of capital letters.

✓   **Sheet B**   Spelling and handwriting based on *sp*.
N.B. Emphasis on *s* and *p* reaching same height and tail on letter *p* being below the line.

✓   **Sheet C**   Six labelling lines have been prepared so that children can, if they wish, add extra features to label. (This should be encouraged and completed ideas shared with the group.)

✓   **Sheet D**   This is written as an instructional sheet for enlargement or transfer to an OHP transparency. In addition to punctuation, it is a tool for prediction and story writing.

Use this box to write your own notes ready for the next time you use this unit.

© Andrew Brodie Publications ✓ PO Box 23, Wellington, Somerset, TA21 8YX ✓ www.andrewbrodie.co.uk

Name: Date:

Go over my
letters with care.

sp sp sp sp

Read and write all the 'sp' words.

spill	spade	spider

spot	spin	spell

Draw a spider
with a spade.

Can you think of any more
'sp' words?

A spider with a spade

© Andrew Brodie Publications ✓ PO Box 23, Wellington, Somerset, TA21 8YX ✓ www.andrewbrodie.co.uk

● **Text level work**

Name: Date:

Read this carefully.

Vog the Amazing Alien

Vog was an amazing alien. He came from a planet far away. Vog was very blue with six green arms and his eyes were at the top of tall yellow stalks. When he smiled, which he did a lot, you could see his four round red teeth.

Draw Vog. Label your picture.

Vog

Name: Date:

The word I is always a capital letter.

Write this story in your book putting in capital letters and full stops.

my best friend is called
abigail one day abigail and
i had an exciting adventure
we were out for a walk
when i saw something very
strange

What do you think happened next?

Could you finish the story?

● Teachers' Notes

✓ In addition to spelling and handwriting, this unit covers the text level requirements to present information in simple sentences and to use known stories to structure own writing.

✓ **Resources** Information on homes (this could be human or animal homes), to link to Sheet D.
- The story of 'Little Red Riding Hood'

✓ **Sheet B** Spelling and handwriting *sl*. Again there is the need to emphasise the differing heights of these two letters.

✓ **Sheet C** This is a writing frame (with space in the lower right-hand corner for pupil illustrations), for a variation on the 'Little Red Riding Hood' story. There is scope for an imaginative story here - though the class will need a chance to discuss a variety of ideas.

✓ **Sheet D** Frames for pictures and captions on the subject of homes.

Use this box to write your own notes ready for the next time you use this unit.

© Andrew Brodie Publications ✓ PO Box 23, Wellington, Somerset, TA21 8YX ✓ www.andrewbrodie.co.uk

Name: Date:

Go over my writing.

sl sl sl sl

✏ Choose a word from the box to label each picture.

slipper	slug
slam	sleep
	sledge

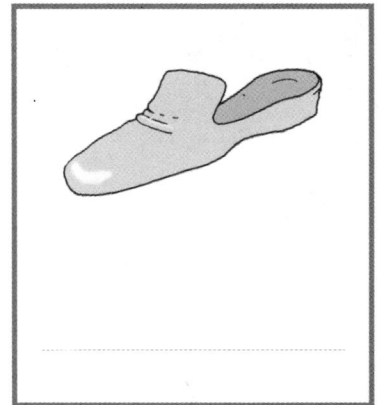

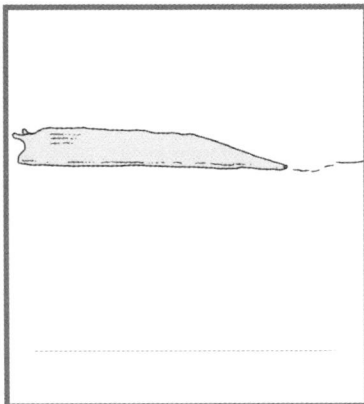

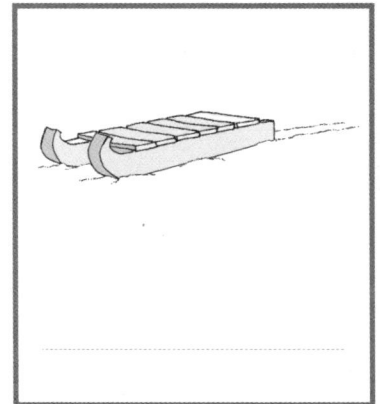

✏ Copy the sentence and draw the picture.

The slow slug slid down the slope.

© Andrew Brodie Publications ✓ PO Box 23, Wellington, Somerset, TA21 8YX ✓ www.andrewbrodie.co.uk

● **Text level work**

What else could happen to Little Red Riding Hood in the forest?

Name: Date:

Draw four different sorts of home.

Write a sentence about each one.

1.

2.

3.

4.

◎ Teachers' Notes

✓ In addition to spelling and handwriting, this unit covers the text level requirements to label pictures and diagrams, and to write simple questions.

✓ **Resources** Examples of labelled pictures and diagrams. Large pictures suitable for pupils to ask questions about.

✓ **Sheet B** Spelling and writing based around *mp* at the end of a word. The emphasis will need to be on the tail of the *p* hanging below the line.

✓ **Sheet C** *N.B.* Extra words have been put in the word box that will not be needed.

✓ **Sheet D** This is a good opportunity to point out the 'question mark and its function'. You could ask the children to colour the picture, to make up some questions, then to ask a friend to make up some answers. The questions and answers they think of may provide a good focus for your plenary.

Use this box to write your own notes ready for the next time you use this unit.

© Andrew Brodie Publications ✓ PO Box 23, Wellington, Somerset, TA21 8YX ✓ www.andrewbrodie.co.uk

Name: Date:

Go over my writing.

mp mp mp mp

Carefully copy each of the words.

| camp | limp | bump |
| stamp | lamp | jump |

Label each picture.

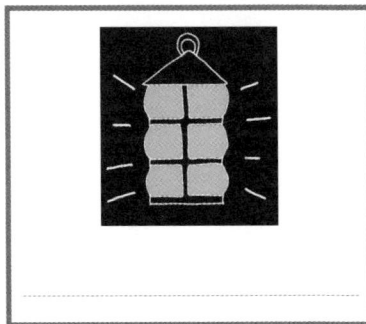

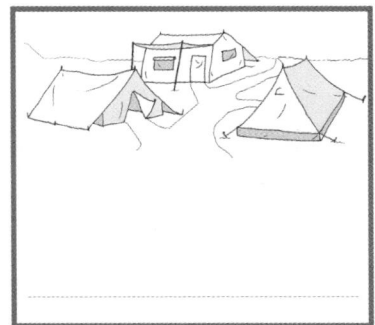

● **Text level work**

Name: Date:

Choose words from the box to label this picture of me.

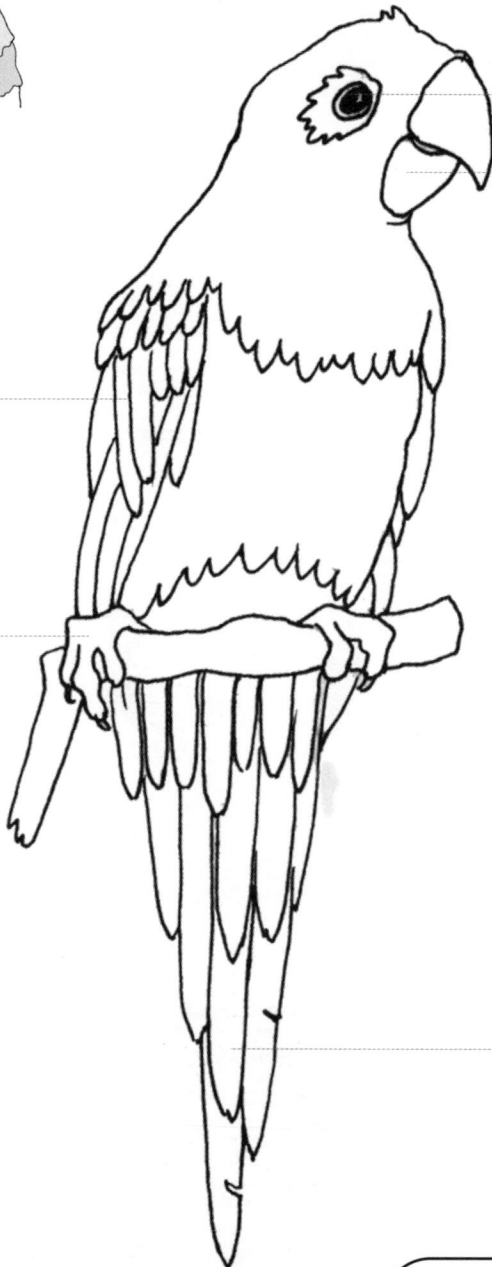

Now colour me in.

claws	eye	bones
feathers	chin	arms
tail	beak	

Name: Date:

Here are some questions you could ask about me.

What is the parrot called?

How old is the parrot?

Where does the parrot live?

✎ Now make up some questions about this picture.

© Andrew Brodie Publications ✓ PO Box 23, Wellington, Somerset, TA21 8YX ✓ www.andrewbrodie.co.uk

● Teachers' Notes

✓ This unit, in addition to spelling and handwriting, covers the requirements to write extended captions and to consolidate the writing composition requirements for the term with a story.

✓ **Resources** Any story texts. Examples of pictures with extended captions. *N.B.* Sheet C can be linked to art work.

✓ **Sheet B** Spelling and handwriting based on *ch* as a word ending. ('Church' is included because it has *ch* at the beginning and end.)

✓ **Sheet C** This can be used (after class discussion) as an individual work sheet, or you may wish to enlarge or copy to an OHP for whole class teaching. In this case you may wish to copy only the frame at the bottom of the page, for captioning art work or class displays.

✓ **Sheet D** The booklet writing frame at the end of the book is ideal for this task. Using this frame to compare pupils' results with the same frame from last term can help provide you with clear evidence of progress within writing.

Use this box to write your own notes ready for the next time you use this unit.

Name: Date:

Go over my writing.

ch ch ch ch

Label this picture with words from the word box.

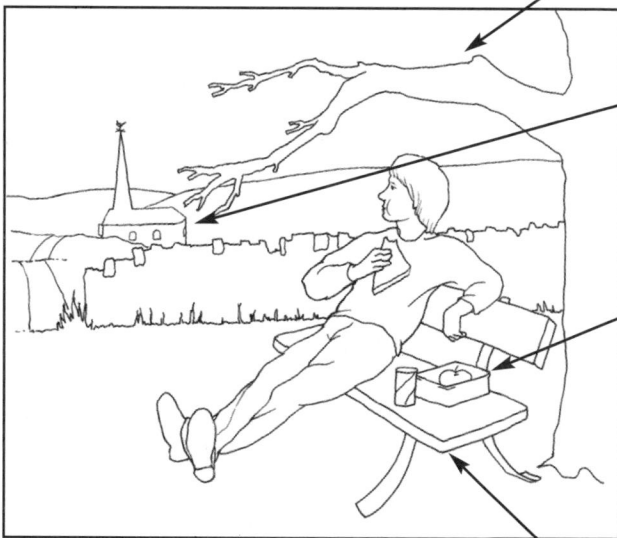

crunch	munch	lunch
church		bunch
bench		branch

Now carefully colour the picture.

● **Text level work**

Name: Date:

This is a boring caption for such a good picture.

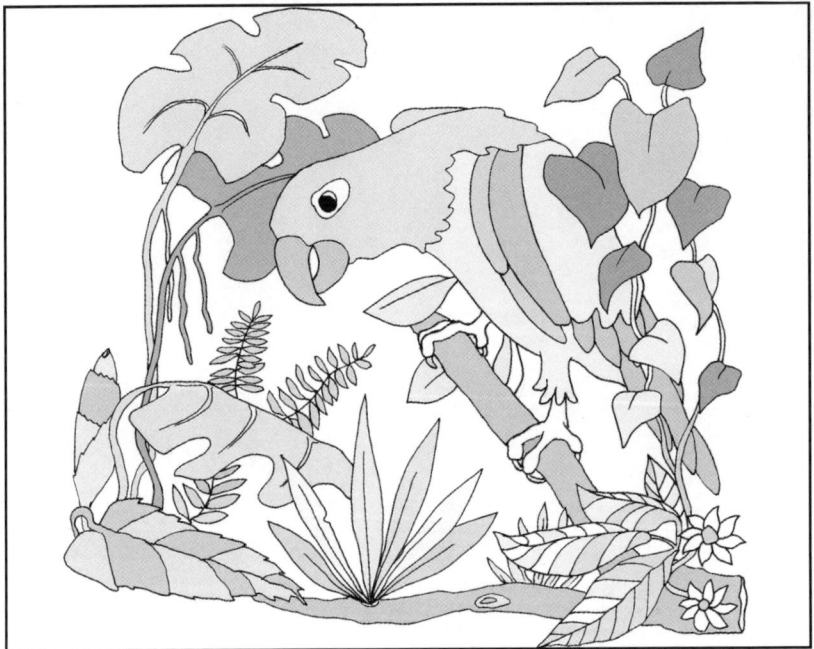

Parrot

You could write a far more interesting one in here.

✎ Use this frame to write a good caption for a picture or painting you have done.

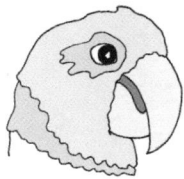

Let's write a story.

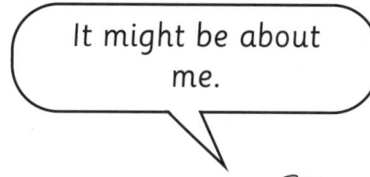

It might be about me.

✐ Write a story for your friends to read.

✐ Make it like a book.

✐ It could be a story you know, or one you make up yourself.

✐ Give it a beginning, a middle and an end.

✐ Put the title and your name on the front cover.

✐ Enjoy writing and illustrating your story.

© Andrew Brodie Publications ✓ PO Box 23, Wellington, Somerset, TA21 8YX ✓ www.andrewbrodie.co.uk

● Teachers' Notes

✓ In addition to spelling and handwriting, this unit looks at writing significant incidents from stories, and works on story settings.

✓ **Resources** Story of 'Goldilocks and the Three Bears'
Examples of simple story settings.

✓ **Sheet B** This sheet provides the opportunity to focus on using capital letters to start names, as well as the more obvious use of a capital at the beginnings of *Mr, Mrs* and *Miss*.

✓ **Sheet C** In preparation for this task, the class/group should have discussed parts of the story to enable pupils to write about one event in the tale.
You may wish to use writing books instead of the writing frame provided.

✓ **Sheet D** It is important to look at a range of simple story settings with the class/group. Children should be clear about the fact that they are going to copy the given setting into their books and use this as the beginning of an imaginative story. You may wish to enlarge this sheet for group use.

Use this box to write your own notes ready for the next time you use this unit.

Name: Date:

Go over my writing.

Mr Mr Mr

Mrs Mrs Mrs

Miss Miss Miss

The man's name was _ _ Brown.

The little girl was called _ _ _ _ Natasha Black.

The married lady was called _ _ _ Green.

© Andrew Brodie Publications ✔ PO Box 23, Wellington, Somerset, TA21 8YX ✔ www.andrewbrodie.co.uk

● **Text level work**

Name: Date:

Write about your favourite part of the story.

Goldilocks and the Three Bears

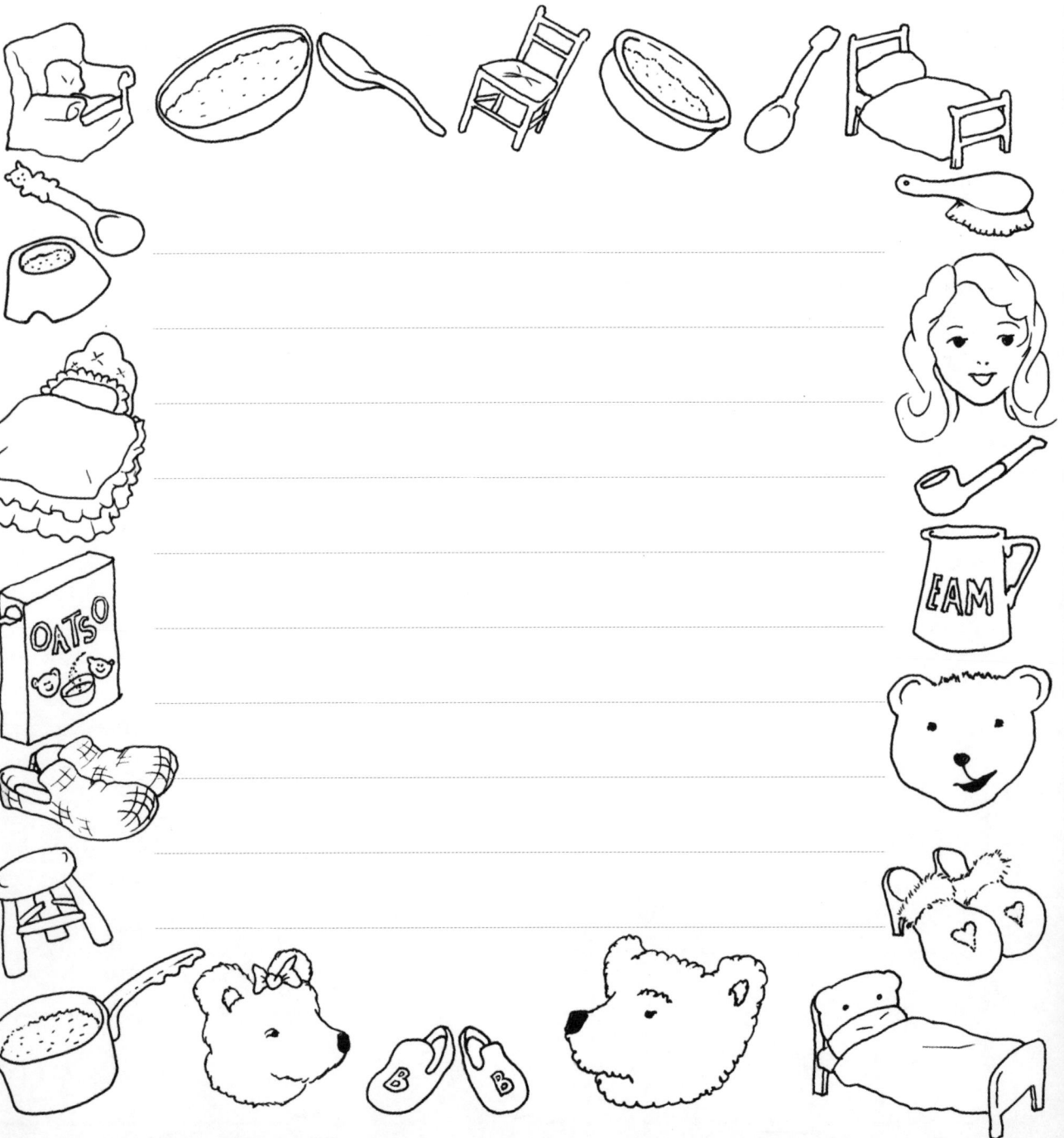

© Andrew Brodie Publications ✓ PO Box 23, Wellington, Somerset, TA21 8YX ✓ www.andrewbrodie.co.uk

Name: Date:

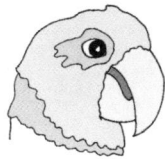

Here is the beginning of a story.

Once upon a time, in a far-away land, a little cottage stood in the middle of a large forest.

Who might be in the story? What will happen next?

Write the whole story in your writing book.

● Teachers' Notes

✓ In addition to spelling and handwriting, this unit covers work on sentences and using a poem to develop writing skills.

✓ **Resources** Range of poems, rhyming and non-rhyming, with accent on simple descriptions.

✓ **Sheet B** *oo* as in 'moon' and 'soon'.

✓ **Sheet C** Adding words to sentences to make sense.

✓ **Sheet D** Children have a simple poem to read, enjoy and discuss.
They are then asked to invent their own line for each verse.
This is simple if they understand they need:
  a) the name of a food,
  b) *is* or *are*,
  c) a word to describe the food.
Other possibilities are:
  1) Change 'Hot chocolate' to a different drink,
  2) Substitute someone else for 'Gran',
  3) Substitute cakes for other food,
  4) The most able might wish to try writing another verse.

Use this box to write your own notes ready for the next time you use this unit.

© Andrew Brodie Publications ✓ PO Box 23, Wellington, Somerset, TA21 8YX ✓ www.andrewbrodie.co.uk

Name: _____   Date: _____

Carefully copy the letters
then the words.

OO OO OO OO OO OO

tools	room	school	moon

tooth	soon	boot	fool

Label the pictures.

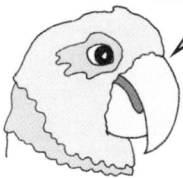

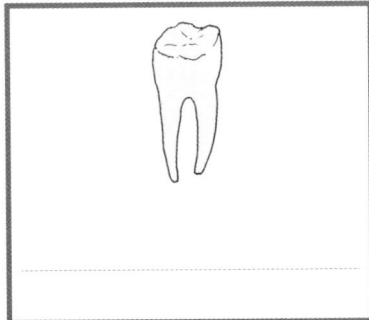

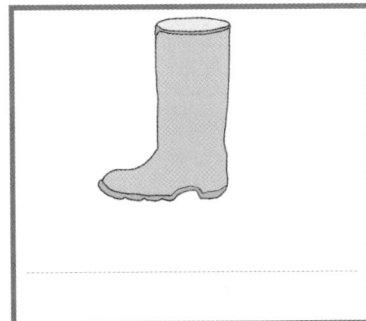

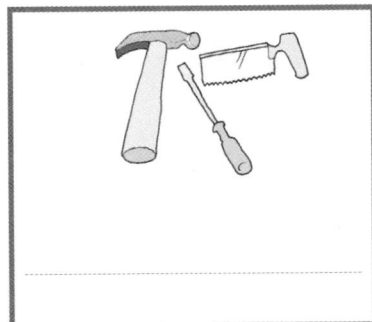

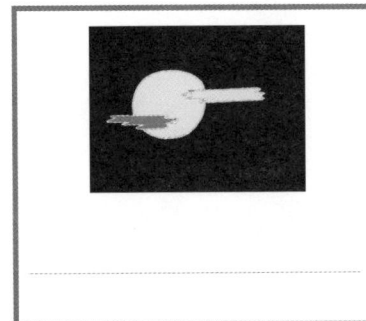

● **Sentence level work**

Name: Date:

There is a word missing from each sentence.

Choose a word from the box to help you write each sentence correctly.

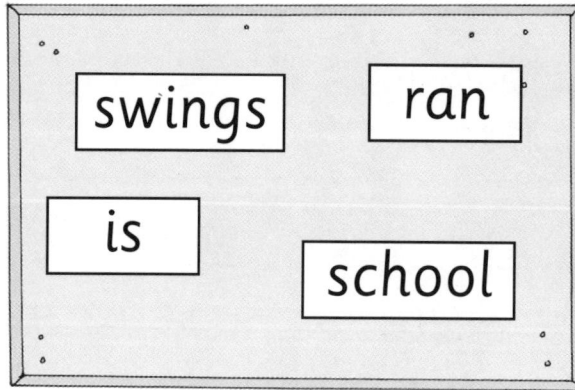

swings   ran

is

school

The dog across the grass.

My sister a girl.

I like to play on the.

I came to on the bus.

Name: Date:

Read this poem.

Spaghetti is slithery,
Tomatoes are red.
Hot chocolate is tasty,
To drink before bed.

Mashed potato is fluffy,
Cabbages are green.
My Gran makes the best cakes
You ever have seen.

Help me to write it again.
Describe your favourite foods
at the beginning of each verse.

_____ ,

Tomatoes are red.
Hot chocolate is tasty,
To drink before bed.

_____ ,

Cabbages are green.
My Gran makes the best cakes
You ever have seen.

© Andrew Brodie Publications ✓ PO Box 23, Wellington, Somerset, TA21 8YX ✓ www.andrewbrodie.co.uk

● Teachers' Notes

✓ In addition to spelling and handwriting, this unit covers the sentence level requirement for pupils to use question marks appropriately and the text level requirement for them to compose their own poetic sentences.

✓ **Resources** Any texts with examples of questions.
A selection of descriptive poems.

✓ **Sheet B** Spelling and handwriting based on *st* word ending.

✓ **Sheet C** Formation of question marks and their use.

✓ **Sheet D** Writing alternate lines in a poem about water. The emphasis should be on using a descriptive poetic style of language.

Use this box to write your own notes ready for the next time you use this unit.

Name: Date:

Go over my letters.

st st st st

chest	rest	vest	best

last	fast	past	mast

post	most	dust	list

✏ Label this picture.

● **Sentence level work**

Name: Date:

A question mark is put at the end of a question.

Go over these, and do some more of your own.

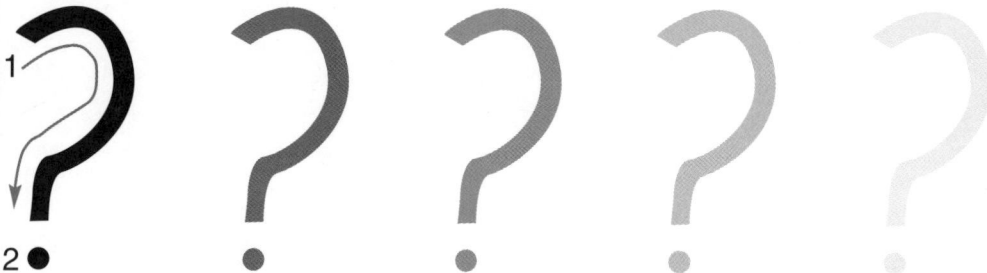

1 ? ? ? ? ?
2 ●

Put a <u>question</u> <u>mark</u> or a <u>full</u> <u>stop</u> at the end of each sentence.

<u>I like chips</u>

<u>Why is the sea cold</u>

<u>Do you want to play with me</u>

<u>There is a banana on the table</u>

<u>Is there a banana on the table</u>

<u>My toe hurts</u>

<u>Where are my shoes</u>

<u>What is your name</u>

Name: Date:

You can choose words from the box to help you write a poem.

stream	waves

drip   wet   swim

cold   drip   paddle

sea   river

Water

splish splash

splish splash

splish, splash, splosh.

● Teachers' Notes

✓   In addition to spelling and handwriting, this unit covers the text level requirement to use the features of a non-fiction book to make a class book.

✓   **Resources**   Non-fiction books/texts about toys.

✓   **Sheet B**   Spelling and handwriting based around *ea* (making a long 'ee' sound).

✓   **Sheet C**   Suitable for enlarging or copying with OHP.
    This is an instructional sheet for making a class book about toys.
    It encourages children to think/find out about toys in the past (linking with QCA History planning) as well as the modern toys that most children will already be knowledgeable about.

✓   **Sheet D**   Writing frame for making a class book.
    The circle at the base is for ordering pages.
    The frame encourages one labelled diagram and two captioned pictures. Children should be encouraged to produce extended, explanatory captions.

Use this box to write your own notes ready for the next time you use this unit.

© Andrew Brodie Publications ✓ PO Box 23, Wellington, Somerset, TA21 8YX ✓ www.andrewbrodie.co.uk

● Word and text level work

Name: Date:

Go over my letters with care.

ea ea ea ea ea

Read and copy these words.

tea	team	meat	seat

steam	stream	leaf	read

sea	flea	clean	beans

Label each picture.

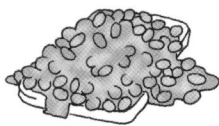

Draw a man on a seat, eating beans and meat for tea.

© Andrew Brodie Publications ✓ PO Box 23, Wellington, Somerset, TA21 8YX ✓ www.andrewbrodie.co.uk

● **Text level work**

Name: Date:

You are going to make a class book.

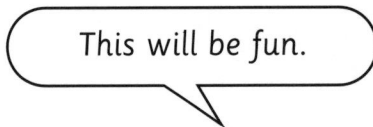

This will be fun.

🖉 Your book will be about toys.

🖉 You know all about the toys you play with.

🖉 Find out about toys from long ago.

🖉 What did your parents play with?

🖉 What did your grandparents play with?

🖉 You will each make one page for the book.

🖉 Your page will have one labelled diagram.

🖉 Your page will have two pictures with clear captions.

🖉 Each page will have a number.

🖉 Enjoy making your page!

© Andrew Brodie Publications ✓ PO Box 23, Wellington, Somerset, TA21 8YX ✓ www.andrewbrodie.co.uk

● **Text level work**

YEAR	Term	UNIT	Sheet
1	3	16	D

Name: Date:

© Andrew Brodie Publications ✓ PO Box 23, Wellington, Somerset, TA21 8YX ✓ www.andrewbrodie.co.uk

● Teachers' Notes

✓ In addition to spelling and handwriting, this unit covers the text level requirements for pupils to write questions prior to reading for information, and to then present their findings.

✓ **Resources** Texts on the topic you choose for children to investigate.

✓ **Sheet B** Spelling and handwriting with *oa* (as in 'boat', 'moat', etc).

✓ **Sheet C** Sheet for children to write questions.
N.B. Speech bubble, top left, leaves a space for you to select the topic. This is done in order for you to link literary work to other areas of the curriculum; or a topic of interest in your school/classroom at the time. You may wish to reinforce the use of question marks.

✓ **Sheet D** Writing frames - linked to question on Sheet C - for answers to be written for captioning use. These might be used to caption classroom display work.

Use this box to write your own notes ready for the next time you use this unit.

© Andrew Brodie Publications ✓ PO Box 23, Wellington, Somerset, TA21 8YX ✓ www.andrewbrodie.co.uk

Name: Date:

Go over the letters.

oa *oa* *oa* *oa*

coat

stoat

moat   foal

boat   goat

Choose a word from the box to label each picture.

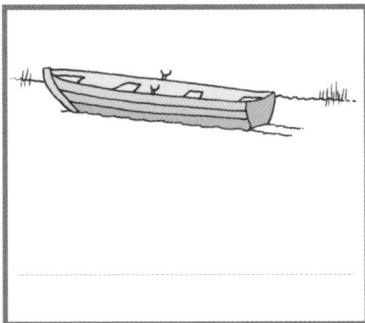

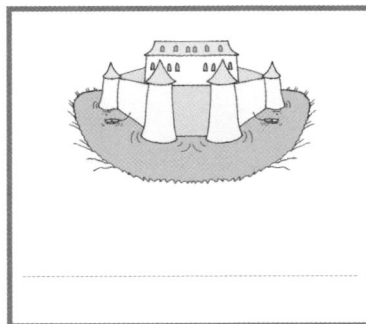

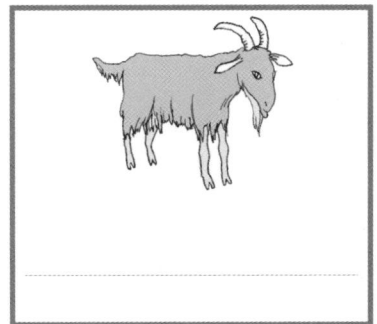

● **Sentence and text level work**

Name: Date:

Think of some questions about _____

Remember your question marks.

Write your questions here.

1.

2.

3.

4.

5.

Now use books to find the answers to your questions.

Name: _____ Date: _____

Use what you have found out to write captions in the frames below.

You can use these to label pictures or a display.

● Teachers' Notes

✔ In addition to spelling and handwriting, this unit covers work on the text level requirement to write a simple account of a personal experience and incorporates the opportunity to do a piece of writing particularly for assessment purposes.

✔ **Resources** No specific requirements for this unit.

✔ **Sheet B** Spelling and handwriting based on *ay* and *ai*.

✔ **Sheet C** A writing frame to recount a day out - this could be linked to a class outing.

✔ **Sheet D** Instructional sheet suitable for enlarging or copying for use with an OHP.
This again makes use of the booklet writing frame at the end of this publication and provides for monitoring pupil progress.

Use this box to write your own notes ready for the next time you use this unit.

© Andrew Brodie Publications ✔ PO Box 23, Wellington, Somerset, TA21 8YX ✔ www.andrewbrodie.co.uk

Name: Date:

Go over my letters.

ay ay ay ay

ai ai ai ai

play	paint

brain	train	rails

stain	away

Choose words from the box to fill the spaces.

1. My _ _ _ _ _ is in my head.

2. I am going _ _ _ _ for a holiday.

3. A _ _ _ _ _ runs on _ _ _ _ _ .

4. The _ _ _ _ _ made a _ _ _ _ _ on my jumper.

5. I am going to _ _ _ _ with my friend.

© Andrew Brodie Publications ✓ PO Box 23, Wellington, Somerset, TA21 8YX ✓ www.andrewbrodie.co.uk

● **Text level work**

Name: Date:

Write about a day out that you have enjoyed.

Remember to write in clear sentences.

© Andrew Brodie Publications ✓ PO Box 23, Wellington, Somerset, TA21 8YX ✓ www.andrewbrodie.co.uk

Name: Date:

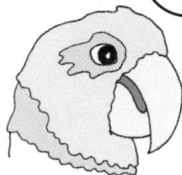

You are going to make a booklet.

✐ Write a story about something that has happened to you.

✐ Remember to put a title and your name on the front cover.

✐ Write in clear sentences.

✐ Make sure that each sentence makes sense.

✐ Make your writing exciting.

✐ Illustrate your story with care.

✐ Enjoy reading each other's stories.

● Teachers' Notes

✓ In addition to spelling and word level work on vowels and consonants, this unit covers the requirements (sentence and text level) to use sequencing language and the text level requirement to use story structure to write about one's own experiences.

✓ **Resources** Fictional texts to look at ways to begin and end a story, and to note sequencing language.

✓ **Sheet B** Spelling *oo* as in 'book', 'look'; vowels and consonants.

✓ **Sheet C** Sequencing language.

✓ **Sheet D** Instructional sheet (for enlargement or copying for use with an OHP), for discussion before writing.
Preliminary whole class work on simple effective ways to 'set out' their writing and to conclude it, is an important part of this work.
Children should be encouraged to read each other's work as part of the "checking your work" process.
An incident from the holidays has been chosen for this work as it is the first unit of the term and holidays will still be freshly in pupils' minds. This of course could be changed to suit individual purposes.

Use this box to write your own notes ready for the next time you use this unit.

© Andrew Brodie Publications ✓ PO Box 23, Wellington, Somerset, TA21 8YX ✓ www.andrewbrodie.co.uk

Name: Date:

Copy these words with care.

took	book	shook	wood	hood

cook	stood	look	crook	nook

Which vowel is found in all the words? ☐

Write the eleven consonants in the words.

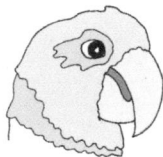

☐ ☐ ☐ ☐ ☐ ☐ ☐ ☐ ☐ ☐ ☐

Choose one of the oo words
to fill each of the spaces.

I _ _ _ _ a _ _ _ _ from the library.

A raincoat may have a _ _ _ _ to keep your head dry.

Some tables are made from _ _ _ _ .

The boy _ _ _ _ _ at the bus stop and waited for the bus.

Write the five oo words you did not use.

© Andrew Brodie Publications ✓ PO Box 23, Wellington, Somerset, TA21 8YX ✓ www.andrewbrodie.co.uk

Name: _____ Date: _____

The words in the box help you to know when things happen.

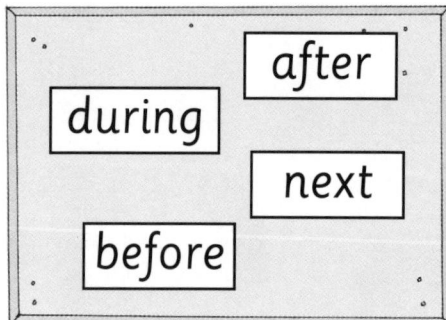

after
during
next
before

Use any one of the words in each of the spaces.

1. Clean your teeth _ _ _ _ _ _ you go to bed.

2. This Monday is the 1st of October, so
_ _ _ _ Monday will be the 8th of October.

3. Wash your hands _ _ _ _ _ you have been to the toilet.

4. Listen carefully _ _ _ _ _ _ your lessons.

Here are three more 'time' words.

next   **then**   **meanwhile**

Write a sentence for each word.

_____

_____

_____

_____

Name: Date:

> Write about something that happened to you in the school holiday.

✎ Make your writing as interesting as a really good story.

✎ Give your work a title.

✎ Give your writing a clear beginning, middle and end.

✎ Use interesting describing words.

✎ Try to use words like meanwhile, during, after, before and next to show when things happened.

✎ Check your work as you go along.
Does it make sense?
Have you used capital letters and full stops?
Are your words spelt correctly?
Is your writing neat?

✎ Illustrate your work.

✎ Most importantly …

> … enjoy your writing.

© Andrew Brodie Publications ✓ PO Box 23, Wellington, Somerset, TA21 8YX ✓ www.andrewbrodie.co.uk

● **Teachers' Notes**

✓ In addition to spelling work this unit covers the requirement to pay attention to commas and exclamation marks when reading aloud, and further consolidates use of sequencing words within a writing task.

✓ **Resources** Suitable fiction texts for work on commas, exclamation marks and sequencing words.

✓ **Sheet B** Work on *ar* words.

✓ **Sheet C** Inserting commas and reading resulting sentences with expression.
Reading exclamations with expression.
This is very suited to sharing of ideas within a whole class plenary.

✓ **Sheet D** Using sequencing words within story writing.
Ensure pupils 'choose' a story to write (or an incident from personal experience), before beginning the task.
You may wish to give your pupils a wider <u>choice</u> of sequencing words, but it may be unwise to ask them to <u>use</u> more than about four within one piece of writing.

Use this box to write your own notes ready for the next time you use this unit.

Name: Date:

Copy and read these ar words.

car	carpet	bar	star	card

sharp	park	garden	far	farm

shark	lark	mark	market	arch

Choose one of the **ar** words to match each clue.

1. A type of bird. _ _ _ _

2. Find this is in the sky. _ _ _ _

3. Buy your fruit and vegetables here. _ _ _ _ _ _

4. Keep this in your garage. _ _ _

5. Animals might be here. _ _ _ _

Make up a clue for each word.

shark

garden

carpet

© Andrew Brodie Publications ✓ PO Box 23, Wellington, Somerset, TA21 8YX ✓ www.andrewbrodie.co.uk

● **Sentence level work**

Name: Date:

Put a comma in each sentence ...

... then read the sentence aloud, with expression.

✳ The monster was enormous but luckily it was very friendly.

✳ The mouse crept silently through the grass then suddenly an owl swooped down and took it.

✳ I go horse riding on Saturdays and on Sundays I visit my grandparents.

✳ Father bear said "Who has been eating my porridge?"

✳ The boy watched for a while then he went to join in with the game.

Read these phrases with expression.

The exclamation marks should help you.

Oh no !

Never !

Whatever next !

Goodness me !

Name: Date:

✎ Choose a story you know well.

✎ Write the story.

✎ You <u>must</u> use the words from the word box in your story.

later   suddenly   during   next

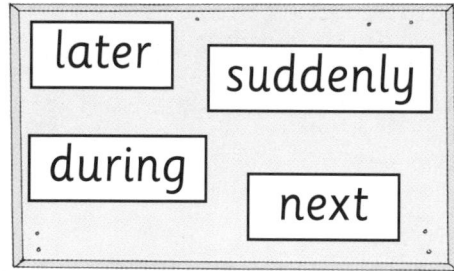

Remember to give your story a title.

In your story <u>underline</u> the words from the word box.

● Teachers' Notes

✓ In addition to spelling work, this unit covers the sentence level requirement to reread writing for sense and punctuation, and text level poetry work based on simple structures and substituting own ideas.

✓ **Resources** Poems, both rhyming and non-rhyming; traditional and modern. Look for rhythm of poetry, layout and line lengths.

✓ **Sheet B** Words with *oy* and *oi*.

✓ **Sheet C** This sheet is for use at three levels.
A: Lower attainers may only work on corrections on the sheet.
B: Medium attaining pupils may also be asked to rewrite the story correctly in writing books.
C: Higher attaining pupils may also be asked to consider writing a better ending to the story: i.e. miss out "So he did", and conclude the story from "I would rather eat you".

✓ **Sheet D** Poetry - using rhyme and rhythm. Substitute alternate lines of poem.
Rhyming words are given to aid this. Children need to understand the lines should be short to help the rhythmic feel of the poem. (Soft clapping or tapping to final poems will help pupils to understand rhythm.).

Use this box to write your own notes ready for the next time you use this unit.

Name: Date:

oy and oi can sound the same.

boy	oil	foil

toy	coil	coin

royal	soil	noise

enjoy	boil	voice

Label each picture correctly.

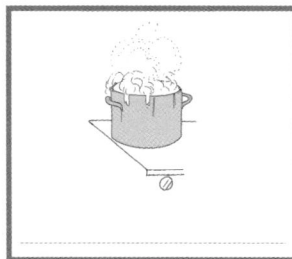

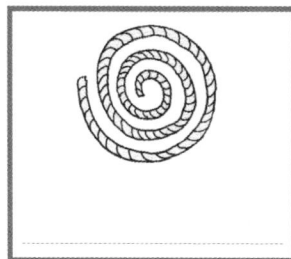

Write a silly sentence. Use as many "oy" or "oi" words as you can.

Draw a picture to go with your sentence, on the back of this sheet.

● **Sentence level work**

Name: Date:

> Read this carefully.

O ne day a girl little went for a walk in the woods   She watched the birds flying and she flowers picked   You can imagine her surprise when she met a very brown bear large
"I am rather hungry," said the bear
"Would you like a piece of my chocolate?" the replied girl
"No thank you," said the bear, "I would rather eat you"
So he did !

> Oh dear, some of the words are muddled …

> … and the full stops are missing.

<u>On the paper:</u>
    🖉 Underline the muddled words and put in the full stops.

<u>In your writing books:</u>
    🖉 Give the story a title.
    🖉 Write the story again with the words in the correct order and the full stops in the right places.
    🖉 Illustrate the story.

<u>An extra task:</u>
    🖉 Could you write a better ending to the story?

Name: Date:

Read this rhyming poem.

Invent some new lines - use the rhyming words at the bottom of the page to help you.

One <u>two</u>
Buckle my <u>shoe</u>

Three <u>four</u>
Knock at the <u>door</u>

Five <u>six</u>
Pick up <u>sticks</u>

Seven <u>eight</u>
Lay them <u>straight</u>

Nine <u>ten</u>
A big fat <u>hen</u>

One <u>two</u>

....

Three <u>four</u>

....

Five <u>six</u>

....

Seven <u>eight</u>

....

Nine <u>ten</u>

....

Look at the rhyming words.

Here are some rhyming ideas to help you to write your version of the same poem.

Read your poems to each other.

two	stew, flu, blue, clue, boo
four	poor, paw, store, core, shore
six	licks, mix, tricks, kicks, bricks
eight	mate, late, bait, gate, fete
ten	Ben, then, men, pen, den

© Andrew Brodie Publications ✓ PO Box 23, Wellington, Somerset, TA21 8YX ✓ www.andrewbrodie.co.uk

✓ In addition to spelling, this unit covers work on the sentence level requirement to use simple organisational devices and at text level, to write simple instructions.

✓ **Resources** Examples of simple written instructions, especially any that also use boxes, arrows, diagrams, etc.

✓ **Sheet B** Spelling based on *ow* as in 'cow', 'town'.

✓ **Sheet C** Inserting arrows and numbers to picture story of 'Goldilocks'. This is also suitable for cutting out and sticking in writing books in correct order. If this is done you may also wish pupils to caption the pictures.

✓ **Sheet D** *N.B.* Space on top left speech bubble for teacher to choose topic for instructions. This enables you to select most appropriate work for your class or groups within the class. Suitable topics could include:
- making a sandwich/drink,
- washing hands,
- the way to school,
- playing a game,
- tidying up.

Use this box to write your own notes ready for the next time you use this unit.

Name: Date:

Copy these **ow** words.

cow	crowd	frown

down	clown	flowers	brown

towel	owl	town	shower	now

Label these pictures correctly.

A _ _ _ under a _ _ _ _ _ _ .

A _ _ _ _ _ _ with a _ _ _ _ _ .

A _ _ _ _ _ _ carrying _ _ _ _ _ _ _ _ .

An _ _ _ with a _ _ _ _ _ .

Which four **ow** words didn't you use?

● **Sentence level work**

Name: Date:

My picture story is
in a muddle.

Number the boxes to show the
order they should be in.

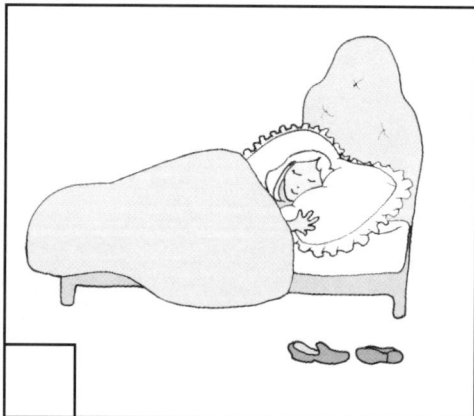

Name: Date:

How do you

_____

_____ ?

Can you tell me by writing
five simple instructions?

1. _____

_____

2. _____

_____

3. _____

_____

4. _____

_____

5. _____

_____

Draw a picture
here to go with
your instructions.

© Andrew Brodie Publications ✓ PO Box 23, Wellington, Somerset, TA21 8YX ✓ www.andrewbrodie.co.uk

● Teachers' Notes

✓ In addition to spelling work, this unit covers the sentence level requirement to revise use of capital letters and text level work on ordering instructions, and using diagrams.

✓ **Resources** Examples of ordered instructions, for example recipes, construction toy instructions, etc.

✓ **Sheet B** Spelling work based on *ou* as in 'pound'.

✓ **Sheet C** Revision of use of capital letters.

✓ **Sheet D** Children are asked to rewrite and number a set of jumbled instructions. This clearly shows that some instructions need to be in the correct order to make sense.
An additional activity could then be to ask pupils to write numbered instructions for another everyday task, and to put simple diagrams with them.

Use this box to write your own notes ready for the next time you use this unit.

© Andrew Brodie Publications ✓ PO Box 23, Wellington, Somerset, TA21 8YX ✓ www.andrewbrodie.co.uk

Name: Date:

Read and copy each word carefully.

mouse	house	blouse	mouth	count

shout	loud	about	out	bound

thousand	around	found	pound	round

Label each picture.

Now write a silly sentence using at least four **ou** words.

Draw a picture to go with your sentence.

© Andrew Brodie Publications ✓ PO Box 23, Wellington, Somerset, TA21 8YX ✓ www.andrewbrodie.co.uk

● **Sentence level work**

Name: Date:

Remember to use capital letters when you need to.

Use capital letters for the beginning of —
  ➤ sentences.
  ➤ titles.
  ➤ names of people and places.
  ➤ days of the week.
  ➤ months of the year.

Rewrite these sentences, with the capital letters that are needed.

1. my sister natasha goes swimming every monday.

2. the title is goldilocks and the three bears.

3. at three o'clock on tuesday the plane leaves london.

4. it arrives in hong kong at ten o'clock wednesday morning.

● Text level work

Name: Date:

Rewrite the following instructions in the correct order.

How to make a jam sandwich

You will need:
    2 slices of bread,
    butter or margarine,
    jam.

Number your instructions.

The diagrams will help you.

○ Enjoy eating your sandwich.

○ Put the second slice on the top.

○ Spread butter onto one side of each piece of bread.

○ Cut the sandwich into four pieces.

○ Spread jam, on top of butter, on one of the slices.

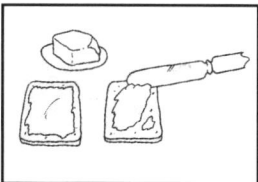   ○ _____

   ○ _____

   ○ _____

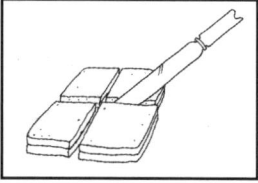   ○ _____

   ○ _____

● Teachers' Notes

✓ In addition to spelling, this unit looks at both writing and following simple instructions.

✓ **Resources** Appropriate instructional diagrams.

✓ **Sheet B** Spelling work based on *air*.

✓ **Sheet C** Continuing a sequence of directional instructions.
N.B. Point out the brief impersonal language used for instructions.

✓ **Sheet D** This work needs whole class/group preparatory work - including offering ideas for the order of work:
   a) decide route,
   b) add pictures to grid,
   c) mark start point,
   d) write instructions.
Tell pupils <u>NOT</u> to mark route on map - their partner can do that by following correctly written instructions.
Encourage pupils to choose a topic of interest to them for their grid, and to enjoy presenting it well.

Use this box to write your own notes ready for the next time you use this unit.

© Andrew Brodie Publications ✓ PO Box 23, Wellington, Somerset, TA21 8YX ✓ www.andrewbrodie.co.uk

Name: Date:

Read and copy these words with care.

| fair | hair | chair |

| fairy | hairy | pair |

| unfair | stairs | lair |

Write the missing word in each sentence.

1. The fox lives in his _ _ _ _ .

2. I go up the _ _ _ _ _ _ to my bedroom.

3. A _ _ _ _ _ has four legs.

4. I wear a _ _ _ _ of trousers.

5. There are lots of rides at the _ _ _ _ .

Write a silly air sentence here.

● **Text level work**

Name: _____   Date: _____

Help me swim to the underwater treasure chest.

up

left —— right

down

START

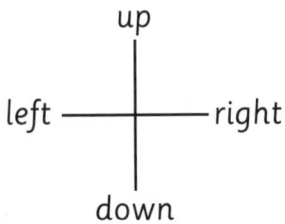

Complete the instructions below.

a. Begin at START.

b. Move up one square.

c. Move right two squares.

d. _____

e. _____

f. _____

g. _____

h. _____

i. _____

j. _____

You have found it!

© Andrew Brodie Publications ✓ PO Box 23, Wellington, Somerset, TA21 8YX ✓ www.andrewbrodie.co.uk

Name: Date:

You can make a map ...

... and write directions for a friend to follow.

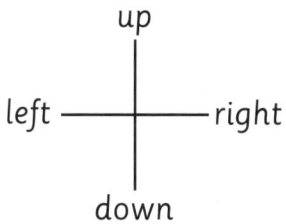

up

left ——|—— right

down

Put letters or numbers with your instructions.

● **Teachers' Notes**

✓ In addition to spelling, this unit provides a writing task for consolidation or/and assessment purposes based on previous learning this term.

✓ **Sheet B** Spelling – high frequency words.

✓ **Sheet C** An instructional sheet for possible enlargement or copying for use with an OHP.
This invites pupils to write a story – but without limiting choice. You may wish to offer a focus for the writing or allow freedom of choice.
Sheet C reminds pupils of some of the literacy points they have worked on this term.
The added challenge is suitable for ensuring the use of sequencing words, and making higher attaining pupils think carefully about how to incorporate given words into their writing.

✓ **Sheet D** This is an optional writing frame on which to produce the writing task set on Sheet C.

Use this box to write your own notes ready for the next time you use this unit.

© Andrew Brodie Publications ✓ PO Box 23, Wellington, Somerset, TA21 8YX ✓ www.andrewbrodie.co.uk

Name: Date:

> Read and copy these everyday words.

> It is important to be able to spell them correctly.

colour words	question words	other words
blue	what	because
yellow	where	they
brown	when	people
white	how	school
purple	which	these
green	why	would
black	who	should

Write the missing vowels in these sentences.

1) The bl _ ck and wh_te cow stood in a field.

2) Wh _ is wearing that gr _ _ n and bl _ _ hat?

3) Wh _ n will th _ y go to sch _ _ l?

4) Wh _ re are you going?

5) Wh _ ch p _ _ pl _ like p _ rple ice cream?

Fill in the consonants and colour the stars with the correct colours.

_ _ ue ☆   _ e _ _ o _ ☆

_ _ a _ _ ☆   _ _ e e _ ☆

_ _ o _ _ ☆   _ _ i _ e ☆

It's time to write a story.

✎ You are going to write a story.

✎ Give your story a title.

✎ Give your story a beginning, middle and end.

✎ Write in clear sentences.

✎ Use capital letters when you need to.

✎ Use full stops and question marks when you need to.

✎ Spell words carefully.

✎ Check that your work makes sense.

✎ Use interesting describing words.

✎ Illustrate your work.

✎ You may want to decorate the edge of the writing frame.

✎ Most importantly … … enjoy your writing.

<u>An added challenge</u>
See if you can include the ten words below in your story:

before   later   so   they   people

stood   yellow   where   because   during

Name: Date:

● Teachers' Notes

✓ In addition to spelling, this unit covers the sentence and text level requirements to identify and understand speech marks and to investigate other ways of presenting speech.

✓ **Resources** Texts containing speech, both in conventional speech marks and in speech bubbles.

✓ **Sheet B** Spelling based on *ur*. Rhyming word 'learn' is also included to encourage discussion on different ways of writing the same sound.

✓ **Sheets C/D** Linked sheets asking children to identify speech marks and to show their understanding of these by putting the speech into the speech bubbles provided on Sheet D.
Pupils are also asked to predict what might have been said next.
This activity could lead to children writing their own speech bubble picture stories.

Use this box to write your own notes ready for the next time you use this unit.

© Andrew Brodie Publications ✓ PO Box 23, Wellington, Somerset, TA21 8YX ✓ www.andrewbrodie.co.uk

● Word/text level work

Name: Date:

Read and copy these words.

Put a ring round the odd one out.

burn	curve	curl	learn

fur	curtains	purple	nurse

purpose	hurt	turn	return

Label the pictures correctly.

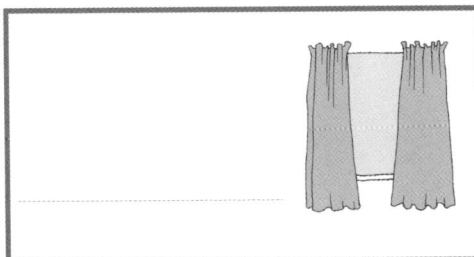

Write a silly sentence using as many **ur** words as you can.

Read this story carefully.

Kit Koala was clinging to a branch in his usual dozy way. He had just had a huge meal of eucalyptus leaves, (his favourite food), and was looking forward to a nice long nap. Suddenly Rob Roo bounced right into the tree Kit was on.

"Oh my goodness," said Kit. "Is it an earthquake?"

"Sorry," squeaked Rob, "I bounced too high and hit your tree".

Kit liked to talk to Rob when he wasn't eating or sleeping, so he slowly climbed down from his branch to find out where his friend was going in such a rush.

Write the words Kit and Rob said, in the speech bubbles in picture 1 on the worksheet.

In picture 2, use the speech bubbles to write what you think Rob and Kit might have said next.

© Andrew Brodie Publications ✓ PO Box 23, Wellington, Somerset, TA21 8YX ✓ www.andrewbrodie.co.uk

Name: Date:

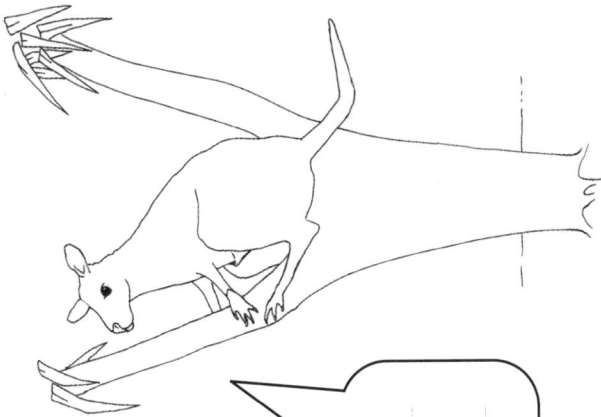

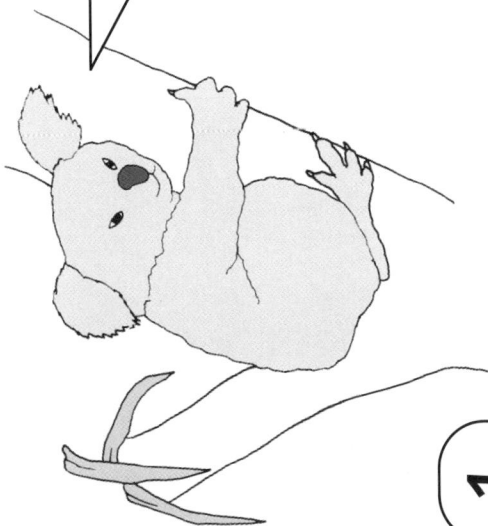

1

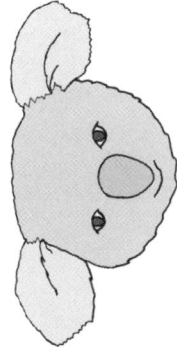

2

© Andrew Brodie Publications ✓ PO Box 23, Wellington, Somerset, TA21 8YX ✓ www.andrewbrodie.co.uk

● Teachers' Notes

✓ In addition to word level work to aid spelling, this unit covers the sentence level requirements to use commas in lists and to understand past and present tenses of verbs.

✓ **Resources** Texts suitable for showing grammatical agreement, verbs, adverbs, lists.

✓ **Sheet B** Compound words. It is important that pupils realise that seeing compound words as two (or more) smaller words is an aid to spelling.

✓ **Sheet C** The focus of this sheet is sorting verbs into past and present tenses.

✓ **Sheet D** Putting commas in lists.
The hardest of the sentences on the sheet is the one with phrases rather than words within the sentence – this could be a focus for class discussion.
The children's own sentences could form a good starting point for a plenary.

Use this box to write your own notes ready for the next time you use this unit.

Name: Date:

Compound words

Some words are made up from two smaller words.

Knowing this can help you to spell those words.

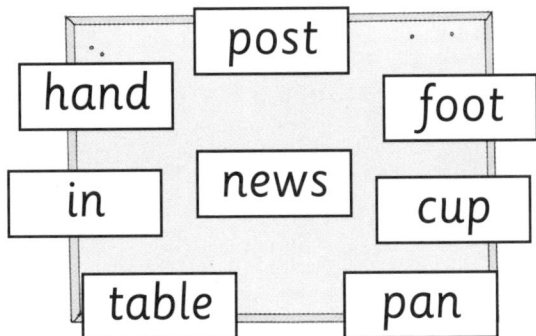

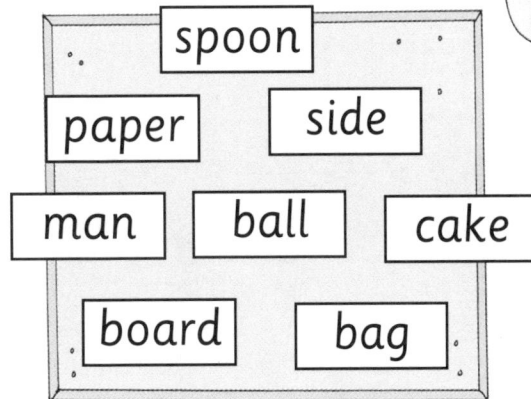

post

hand

foot

in news cup

table pan

spoon

paper side

man ball cake

board bag

Use the words from the boxes to make eight compound words..

1. ....

2. ....

3. ....

4. ....

5. ....

6. ....

7. ....

8. ....

Work on your own or with a friend.

Write eight more compound words.

Use books to help you.

1. ....

2. ....

3. ....

4. ....

5. ....

6. ....

7. ....

8. ....

© Andrew Brodie Publications ✓ PO Box 23, Wellington, Somerset, TA21 8YX ✓ www.andrewbrodie.co.uk

● **Sentence level work**

Name: Date:

Look at these words.

Put them into pairs of 'present' and 'past'.

swim   laugh   swam

walk   ran   find

found   catch   walked

run

caught   laughed

Present   Past   Present   Past

swim   swam

Did you know that 'doing' words are called verbs?

See how many verbs you can think of.

Write them on the back of this sheet.

Name: Date:

> Commas can be used to separate items in a list.

> Cod, haddock, tuna, mackerel and plaice are all types of fish.

> Did you notice that no comma was needed before 'and'?

Put commas in these lists.

At the zoo I saw tigers elephants kangaroos monkeys and penguins.

Red orange yellow green blue indigo and violet are the colours of the rainbow.

Please put knives forks spoons plates and mugs on the table.

Spain France Italy Germany and Belgium are all European countries.

Today I fed the fish cut the grass picked some flowers cleaned the floor and cooked dinner.

Make up a sentence with a list in.
Remember to put in the commas.
Read your sentence to a friend.

● **Teachers' Notes**

✓ In addition to spelling work, this unit covers work on the poetry writing requirement for this term.

✓ **Resources** Poetry, particularly descriptive, non-rhyming poems.

✓ **Sheet B** *ore* words with 'war' and 'floor'.

✓ **Sheet C** Designed for children to jot words and phrases about colours, ideally as part of whole class teaching.

Another colour should be chosen for 'shared writing' of jotted words and phrases. (Choose a colour less likely to be chosen by individual children).

Pupils can be encouraged to make extra colour 'pots' on the back of the sheet if time allows.

✓ **Sheet D** Writing frame for a two verse colour poem (one colour per verse).

Again as part of whole class teaching the joint jottings that have been done could be turned into a verse.

Pupils should be encouraged to draft, and then helped to lay out their work correctly before writing their work in the writing frame.

Discuss the impact that the colour and subject of illustrations may have on the finished poems.

Use this box to write your own notes ready for the next time you use this unit.

© Andrew Brodie Publications ✓ PO Box 23, Wellington, Somerset, TA21 8YX ✓ www.andrewbrodie.co.uk

Name: Date:

Read and copy these **ore** words.

core	snore	floor	explore

war	snore	store	tore

more	sore	score	before

Which two words are the odd ones out?

Write a sentence to say why they are the odd ones out.

Label the pictures.

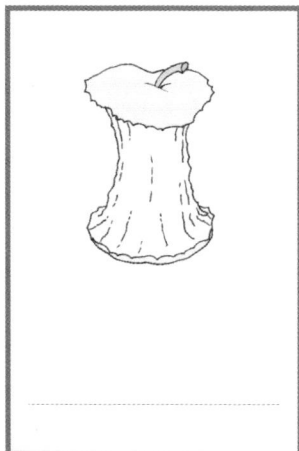

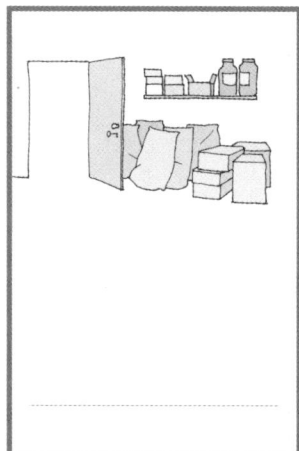

Use books to find some more **ore** words. Write them on the back of the sheet.

● **Text level work**

Name: Date:

The very best poems can come from single words or phrases.

Think of some words or phrases that each of these colours make you think of.

I have started the first one for you.

SILVER

fish swimming

stars at night

shiny

gleam

BLUE

RED

Now choose a colour of your own.

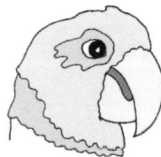

Name: Date:

Use the frame to write a colour poem.
Write two verses.
Choose one colour for each verse.

It is a good idea to plan
your work first.

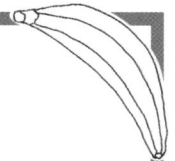
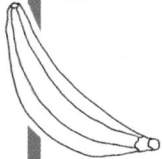

Colours

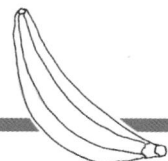

Illustrate your poems with care.

© Andrew Brodie Publications ✓ PO Box 23, Wellington, Somerset, TA21 8YX ✓ www.andrewbrodie.co.uk

● Teachers' Notes

✓   In addition to word level work on syllables, this unit has work on the text level requirement to use story settings from reading.

✓   **Resources**   Stories with clear settings. Any texts for looking at syllables within words.

✓   **Sheet B**   Syllables.

✓   **Sheet C**   Story in school playground setting.
      This is suitable for enlarging or copying for use with an OHP, to enable class/group use.
      Discuss with pupils, are there two children with the same name in your class? – What problems can this cause?

✓   **Sheet D**   Instructional sheet – writing ideas.
      You may wish to limit choice.
      You may wish to make a class book of stories.
      N.B. Jay and Jay are also used in the next unit. You may wish to do Sheets C/D Unit 30 before this work.

Use this box to write your own notes ready for the next time you use this unit.

© Andrew Brodie Publications ✓ PO Box 23, Wellington, Somerset, TA21 8YX ✓ www.andrewbrodie.co.uk

Name: Date:

> Syllables are the 'sounds' or 'beats' that make up a word.

$$\underline{fi}\underline{sh} = 1 \text{ syllable}$$

$$\underline{par}\underline{rot} = 2 \text{ syllables}$$

$$\underline{el}\underline{e}\underline{phant} = 3 \text{ syllables}$$

Pack the words from the house into the boxes below.

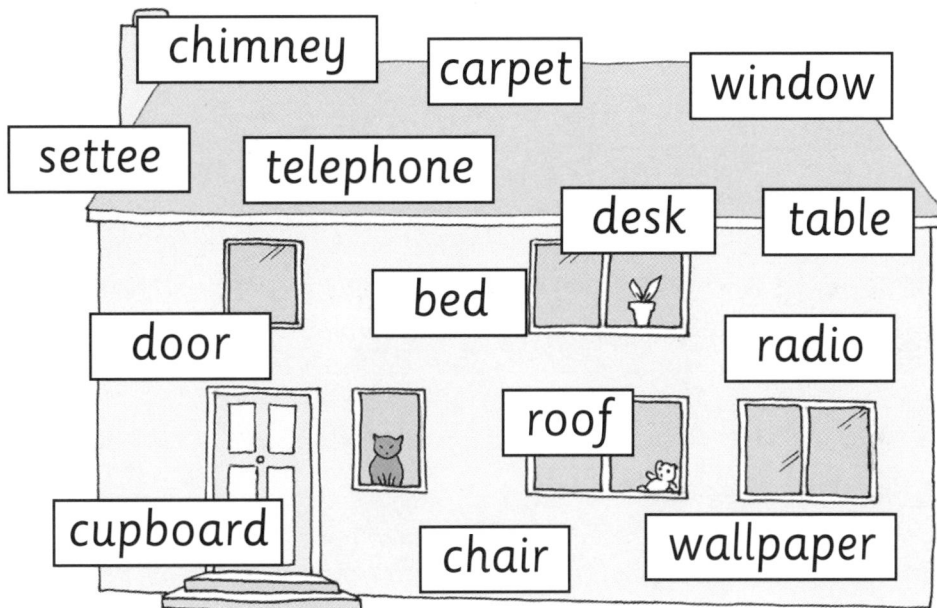

chimney   carpet   window

settee   telephone

desk   table

bed

door

radio

roof

cupboard   chair   wallpaper

1 syllable	2 syllables	3 syllables

Read this story.

The Two Jays

The playground was a large bustling place, full of children laughing and playing. They all seemed very happy to be there, knowing each other and greeting their friends. All that is, except Jay.

Jay had just arrived at the school and was feeling very lonely, frightened and very very new. He had a new school uniform, a new school bag, a new pair of trainers for PE and a new lunch box.

A whistle blew and all the children became quiet and formed neat lines. Jay was feeling empty and alone; he didn't know where to go. He could feel tears forming in his eyes. He tried to blink them away and then wiped his face with his sleeve, his very new sleeve.

"Hi," a voice said cheerfully. It was another boy about his own age. "You must be Jay."

"Yes," replied Jay, surprised that someone seemed to know him.

"Our teacher told us you were starting today," said the other boy, "and it's my job to make sure you have a friend for the day. By the way, my name's Jay."

"So is mine," said Jay and they both laughed.

By the end of the day they were best of friends and soon became known as "The Two Jays". Jay knew then that he was going to be very happy at his new school.

Do you remember your first day at school?

© Andrew Brodie Publications ✓ PO Box 23, Wellington, Somerset, TA21 8YX ✓ www.andrewbrodie.co.uk

Name: Date:

I wonder what adventures happened to the two Jays.

What is your school playground like?

Here are some writing ideas from the 'Two Jays' story.

> Write a story about a first playtime in your school playground.

> Write a different sort of story set in a school playground.

> Write about an adventure that the two Jays might have had after they became good friends.

✐ Give your writing a title.

✐ Write in clear sentences.

✐ Present your writing neatly.

✐ Illustrate your work.

✐ Most importantly…

… enjoy your writing.

© Andrew Brodie Publications ✓ PO Box 23, Wellington, Somerset, TA21 8YX ✓ www.andrewbrodie.co.uk

✓ In addition to spelling, this unit covers a text level requirement to create character profiles.

✓ **Resources** Texts with character profiles.

✓ **Sheet B** Spelling. This sheet is a good starting point for investigating different letter groups that can give the same sound.

✓ **Sheet C** Children are asked to write about the characters of the two Jays.
At this stage they are probably carrying visual images of the Jays without realising it. So encourage pupils to describe what they can already 'see in their heads'. Discuss possible character points too, before pupils do this work.

✓ **Sheet D** Encourage children to include mini pictures – perhaps Jay's favourite toys, particular skills and interests, etc. Help the children to build a rounded character.
N.B. In the original text there is no clue as to the Jays' ethnic origin in order to allow complete freedom.

Use this box to write your own notes ready for the next time you use this unit.

© Andrew Brodie Publications ✓ PO Box 23, Wellington, Somerset, TA21 8YX ✓ www.andrewbrodie.co.uk

Name: Date:

The rhyming words below have three different spellings.
Write them in the correct boxes.

My shirt will have a tear
It will need a repair
It happened at the fair
And gave me a scare

A bear ate a pear
He sat on the stair
Perhaps he will share
His chocolate square

I saw a sight that made me stare
A chair floating in the air

Do all the words
with ear rhyme
with square?

are	air	ear

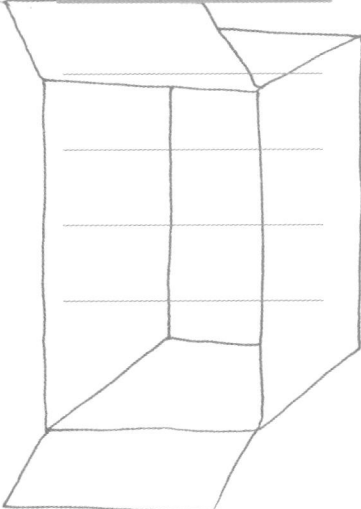
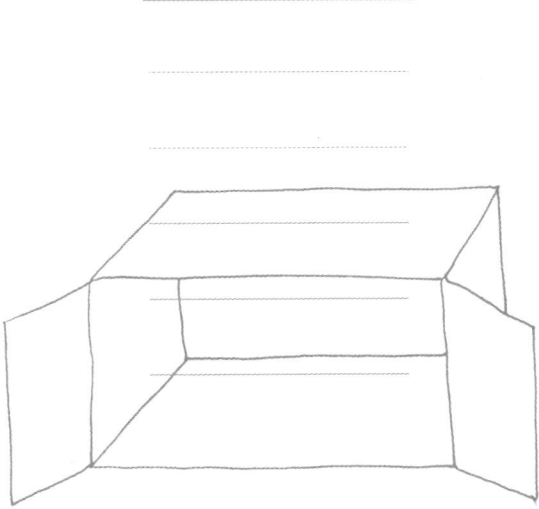
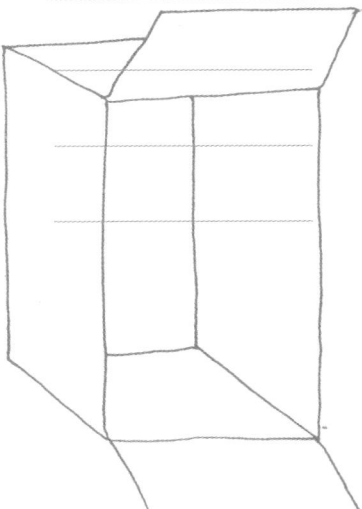

● **Text level work**

Name: Date:

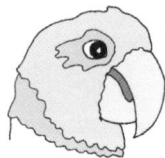

What do you think the
two Jays are like?

Think about their appearances
and their characteristics.

Use the two columns to write about the two Jays.

Think of interesting details.

You may want to give them last names.

<u>Jay</u>   <u>Jay</u>

© Andrew Brodie Publications ✓ PO Box 23, Wellington, Somerset, TA21 8YX ✓ www.andrewbrodie.co.uk

● Text level work

Name: Date:

- ● Make a poster about one of the Jays.

- ● Put a picture in the middle.

- ● Put other interesting words, phrases and pictures in to help others to know all about him.

© Andrew Brodie Publications ✓ PO Box 23, Wellington, Somerset, TA21 8YX ✓ www.andrewbrodie.co.uk

✓ In addition to word level work on antonyms, this unit tackles work on the text level requirement to make class dictionaries or glossaries.

✓ **Resources** Examples of dictionaries and glossaries.

✓ **Sheet B** Antonyms. Self-explanatory worksheet suitable for individual work.
Last item on worksheet is a good starting point for group discussion and for checking understanding of 'opposites'.

✓ **Sheet C** An introduction to writing definitions in clear sentences.

✓ **Sheet D** This sheet is designed to be used with any particular topic work being undertaken with the class. Each child is asked to write 3 good definitions. These can then be cut out and organised alphabetically within a class book or wall display. You will probably wish to select the exact words each child will write about.

Use this box to write your own notes ready for the next time you use this unit.

© Andrew Brodie Publications ✓ PO Box 23, Wellington, Somerset, TA21 8YX ✓ www.andrewbrodie.co.uk

Name: Date:

Opposites

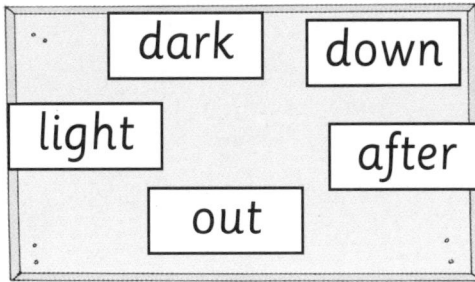

Label the pictures with words from the box.

up _____

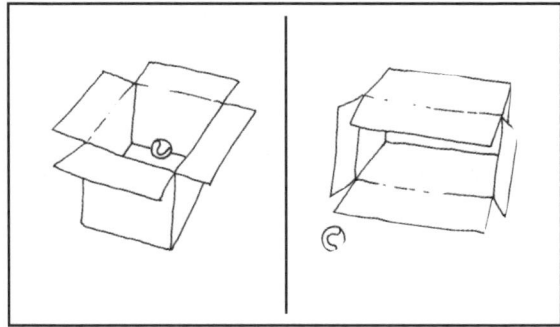

in _____

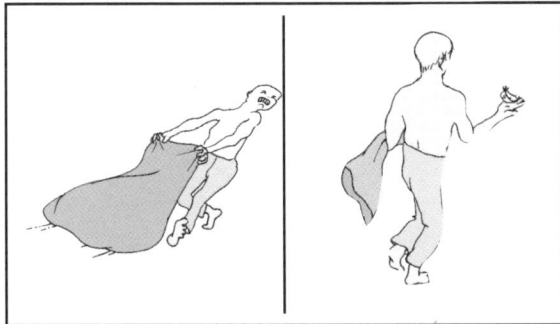

heavy _____

light _____

before _____

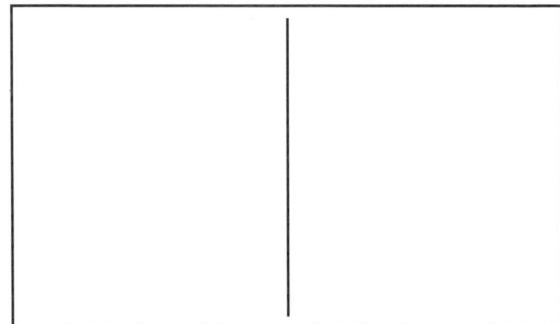

Think of your own opposites for this one. Spell the words correctly.

Alphabetical Animals

Arrange the animal names in alphabetical order.

fox   koala   goat   mouse   elephant   beaver

Use a dictionary or information book to help you write a definition of each one.

Word	Definition

● **Text level work**

Name: Date:

You are going to find out about 3 things.

They will be part of a dictionary.

1

2

3

© Andrew Brodie Publications ✓ PO Box 23, Wellington, Somerset, TA21 8YX ✓ www.andrewbrodie.co.uk

● Teachers' Notes

✓   In addition to spelling, this unit has work on the requirements to produce simple flow charts or diagrams that explain a process.

✓   **Resources**   Examples of flow charts and instructional diagrams. Sheet C

✓   **Sheet B**   Work on the prefixes *un* and *dis*, looking at how they change the meanings of words.

✓   **Sheet C**   This sheet is for enlarging or copying for use with an OHP.
It shows a simple flow chart and a simple set of diagrams showing a typical morning, getting ready for school.
It is important to discuss your pupils' own version of this process.
There will be many differences – e.g. feeding pets, daily worship, varying orders of events, etc.

✓   **Sheet D**   This is a frame for pupils to produce their own six stage flow chart of their morning and diagrams of the same.
You may wish some children to produce only a set of instructions or only a set of diagrams.

Use this box to write your own notes ready for the next time you use this unit.

© Andrew Brodie Publications ✓ PO Box 23, Wellington, Somerset, TA21 8YX ✓ www.andrewbrodie.co.uk

Name: _____ Date: _____

un or dis

Use the underlined words with un or dis before them...

... to make new words.

✳ It is not <u>fair</u>, it is _ _ _ _ _ _ .

✳ I will not <u>do</u> it, I will _ _ _ _ it.

✳ When you get on a ship you <u>embark</u>, when you get off it, you _ _ _ _ _ _ _ _ _ .

✳ Something that has not been <u>said</u> is _ _ _ _ _ _ .

✳ Putting things together is <u>connecting</u> them; taking them apart is _ _ _ _ _ _ _ _ _ _ _ _ _ _ .

✳ I am not <u>able</u> to go to your party, so I am _ _ _ _ _ _ to go to it.

✳ If you are not <u>certain</u>, you are _ _ _ _ _ _ _ _ _ _ .

✳ Are you <u>comfortable</u>, or _ _ _ _ _ _ _ _ _ _ _ _ _ _ ?

What do you think un and dis mean?

Share your ideas with a friend.

© Andrew Brodie Publications ✓ PO Box 23, Wellington, Somerset, TA21 8YX ✓ www.andrewbrodie.co.uk

● **Text level work**

Name: Date:

Here is a flow chart showing how Jaz the alien gets ready for school each day...

... and here are some pictures to show the same thing.

START

First I get out of bed.

↓

I have a wash.

↓

I get dressed.

↓

I have breakfast.

↓

I get my school bag ready.

↓

I go to school.

END

Name: Date:

What do you do each
morning before school?

Make a flow chart, and a
set of diagrams about it.

START

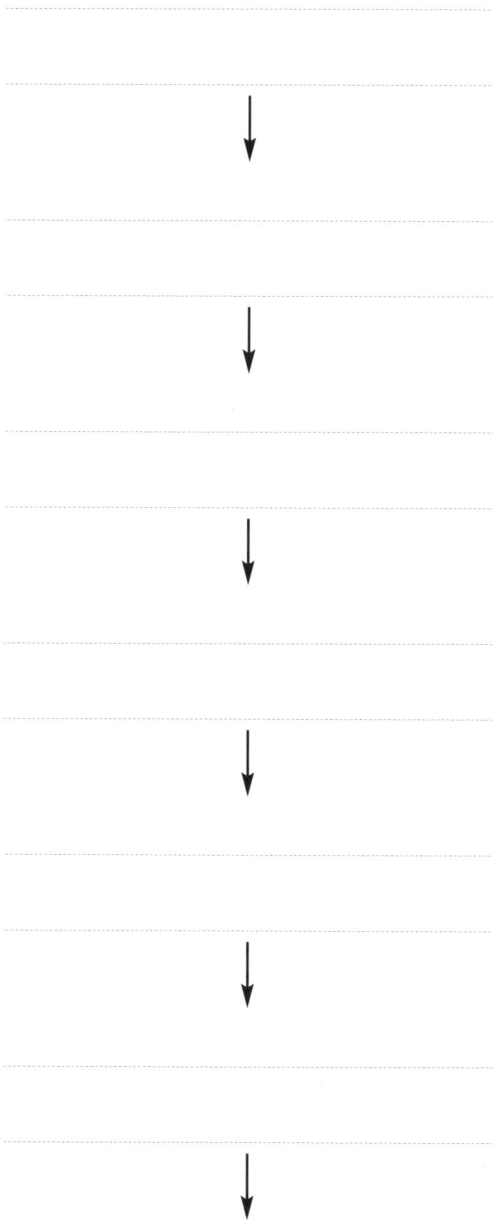

END

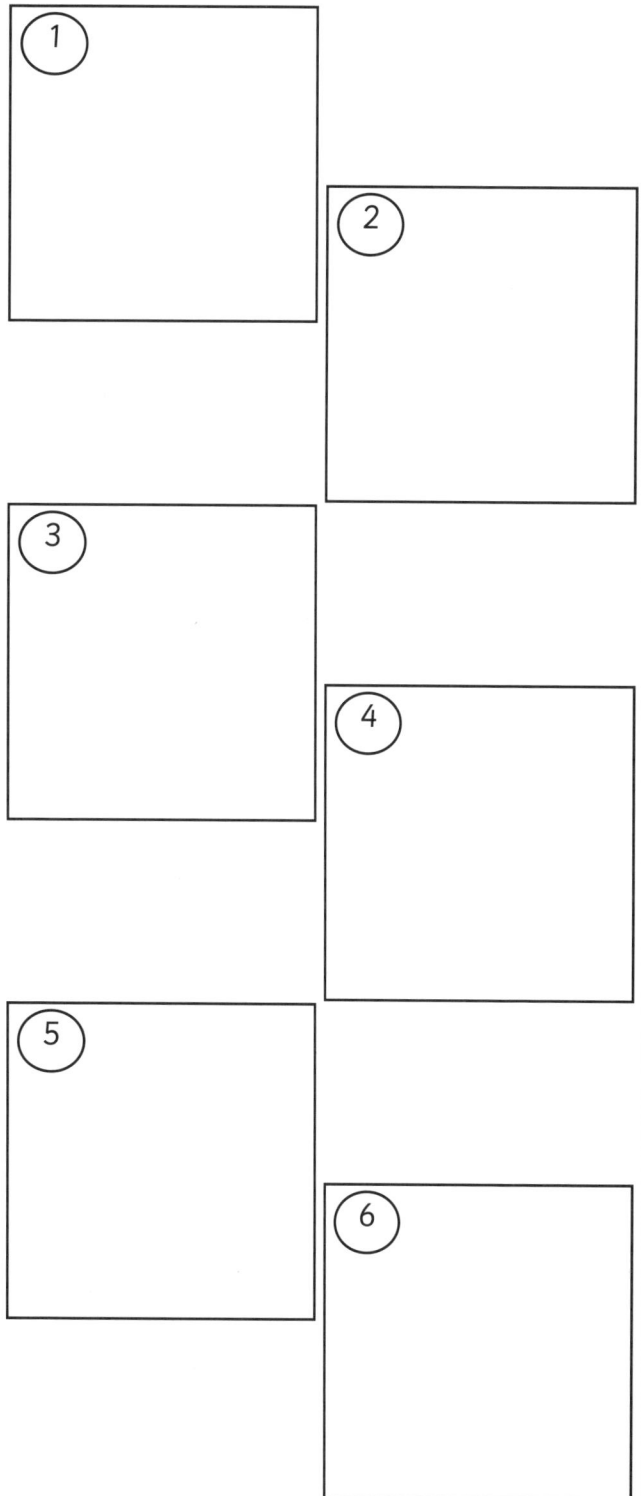

● Teachers' Notes

✓ In addition to word level spelling work, this unit looks at the sentence level requirement to turn statements into questions and the text level requirement to write a book review.

✓ **Resources** A selection of book reviews.
Samples of 'whole sentences'.

✓ **Sheet B** Word level work looking at a variety of spellings that can produce the sounds *ay* and *ee*.

✓ **Sheet C** Looking at statements and making questions from them.
e.g. <u>My pen is black</u> as a question might be <u>What colour is your pen?</u> or <u>Is your pen black?</u>
It is important for pupils to realise that there might be more than one correct way to make a question from a statement.

✓ **Sheet D** Book reviews – simple instructions and writing frame.
Cutting guide provided in case you wish to display this work.

Use this box to write your own notes ready for the next time you use this unit.

© Andrew Brodie Publications ✓ PO Box 23, Wellington, Somerset, TA21 8YX ✓ www.andrewbrodie.co.uk

● Word level work

YEAR 2 Term 3 UNIT 33 Sheet B

Name: Date:

Read the words in the box.

lay   skate   feel   late
cheese   male
kneel   tail   shield   please
field   tray   east
train   meal   meet
mail   steal   eight   stay

Sort them into words with the same sound in.

ay sound

ee sound

© Andrew Brodie Publications ✓ PO Box 23, Wellington, Somerset, TA21 8YX ✓ www.andrewbrodie.co.uk

● **Sentence level work**

Name: Date:

Read the statements below.

See if you can change them into questions.

Make each question a complete sentence.
The first one has been done for you.

1. The dog ran quickly across the grass.

   How did the dog run across the grass?

2. My feet fit into size 13 shoes.

3. It takes me twenty minutes to travel to school.

4. My cat is black.

5. My favourite game is football.

6. My friend's name is Kit.

Did you remember to put a question mark at the end of each question?

Name: Date:

✍ Choose a book you have read recently.

✍ Remember to write the title, author and publisher.

✍ If it is a fiction book, say a small amount about the plot of the story.

✍ Tell the reader what you really liked or didn't like about it.

✍ Say what age reader you think the book is best for.

✍ Say what you thought of the illustrations.

Use this frame to write a book review.

Book title   Author

Publisher

© Andrew Brodie Publications ✓ PO Box 23, Wellington, Somerset, TA21 8YX ✓ www.andrewbrodie.co.uk

● Teachers' Notes

✓ In addition to word level spelling work, this unit looks at the sentence level requirements to use the past tense of verbs for narration and incorporates this into a text level writing task.

✓ **Resources** Examples of stories written as a narrative. These can be used to pick out verbs and to note the need for grammatical agreement – e.g. he was, they were.

✓ **Sheet B** This sheet looks at a variety of ways within words that the sounds 'i' and 'oh' are made.

✓ **Sheet C** This sheet asks for verbs to be paired into past and present tenses.
It is important to ensure that pupils understand the term 'verb'.

✓ **Sheet D** This extends and consolidates work on Sheet C by asking pupils to write a story.
The subject matter has not been specified, as it will depend on what is happening in your class at the time.
Some title suggestions are:
- 'When I got lost'
- 'My favourite story'
- 'A holiday adventure'
Or, of course, you could leave the subject matter free for the pupils to choose.

Use this box to write your own notes ready for the next time you use this unit.

● Word level work

Name: Date:

Read the words in the box.

float   cry   phone

might   sty   close   buy

high   crow   soul   bite

slow   roll   moan   pie

blow   file   fly   nine

Sort them into words with the same sounds.

i sounds

oh sounds

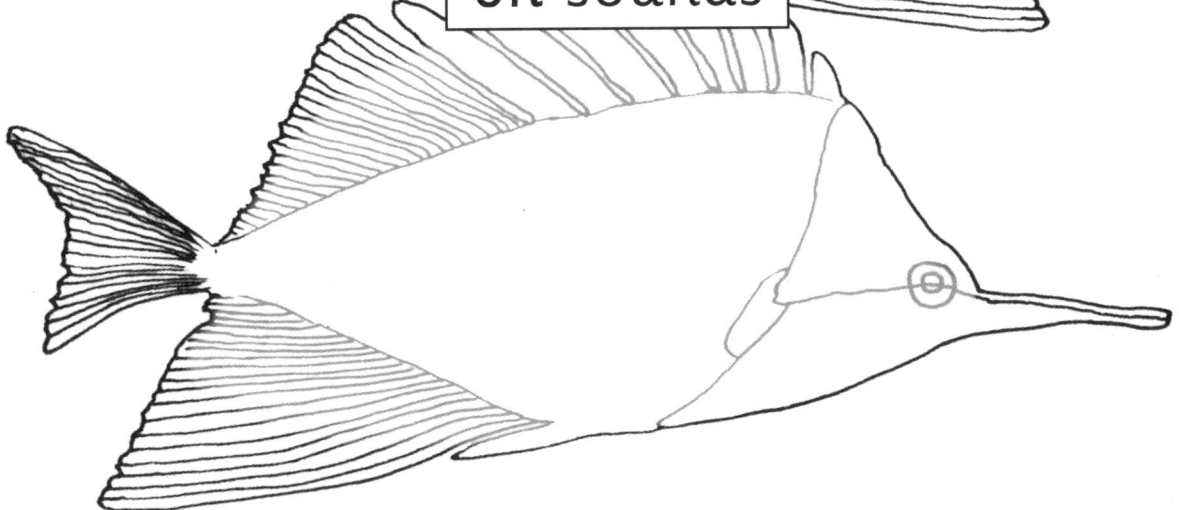

Name: Date:

The 'present tense' is when things are happening now.

The 'past tense' shows that things have already happened.

<u>go</u> = present tense

<u>went</u> = past tense

Put these verbs (doing words) into present and past tense pairs.

The first pair has been done for you.

see   fling   trot

catch   ran   bought

laugh   buy   am

flung   saw   trotted   went

caught   run   laughed

go   was

Present	Past	Present	Past
go	went		

Think of some more verb pairs of your own on the back of the sheet.

Name: Date:

This is a story writing page.

Oh good, I like writing stories.

✏ Write a really good short story.

✏ Your teacher will help you with some story writing ideas.

✏ Write your story in the past tense.

© Andrew Brodie Publications ✓ PO Box 23, Wellington, Somerset, TA21 8YX ✓ www.andrewbrodie.co.uk

● Teachers' Notes

✓   In addition to word level spelling work, this unit covers work on the text level requirement of non-fiction texts using conventional devices such as subheadings, etc. Implicit in this unit is the need to write notes from information texts, hence also helping to cover that text level requirement.

✓   **Resources**   A range of non-fiction texts, particularly those with information on animals, insects, birds, fish, etc.

✓   **Sheet B**   This introduces the suffixes *ful* and *ly*.
Whilst the worksheet does not introduce the term suffix, you may wish to do so.

✓   **Sheet C**   This is a group/class instructional sheet. It is suitable for enlarging or copying for use with an OHP.
This sheet encourages discussion of the terms 'subheading', 'heading', 'diagram'; and has spaces for labelling these for use as visual reminders.
The lower part of the sheet introduces the task requirements for Sheet D.
Pupils should be asked to find their information, making simple notes, before being given the writing frame for Sheet D.

✓   **Sheet D**   This asks children to find information to make their own 'creature' sheets.
The layout of the writing frame is designed to encourage children to use the devices noted on Sheet C, and to present their work in the manner of non-fiction texts.

Use this box to write your own notes ready for the next time you use this unit.

© Andrew Brodie Publications ✓ PO Box 23, Wellington, Somerset, TA21 8YX ✓ www.andrewbrodie.co.uk

Name: Date:

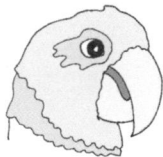

ful and ly are often at the ends of words.

Fill in the spaces in the sentences,
by adding ful or ly to the underlined words.

If I am full of <u>hope</u> you could say I am very

_ _ _ _ _ _ _ .

She helped in a very <u>kind</u> way. She did it

_ _ _ _ _ _ .

Something done in a <u>cruel</u> way is done

_ _ _ _ _ _ _ .

Someone who likes to <u>play</u> could be called

_ _ _ _ _ _ _ .

Add ful or ly to each of these.

week _ _   wonder _ _ _   pain _ _ _

ful _ _   real _ _

thought _ _ _   slow _ _   friend _ _

proper _ _   care _ _ _

● **Text level work**

Name: _____   Date: _____

Read this information
about fish.

Fish

There are many different kinds of fish. Fish live in water, breathe through gills and use their fins to move through the water.
Most fish have scales covering their bodies, and all fish have bones (a skeleton) inside them.

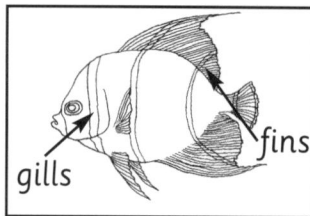

gills   fins

Colourful fish

Some fish are very colourful. They use their colours to help them survive. Sometimes spots or stripes provide camouflage.

Flat fish

Fish that live on the sea bed are often flat, so that they can lie unseen on the bottom.

Label these things.

Diagram	Heading	Subheading

Use the next sheet to write an information page of your own.

Use headings and subheadings, and draw some clearly labelled diagrams.

Perhaps you can find out about a type of living creature.

Name: Date:

● Teachers' Notes

✓   This unit contains word level work on using synonyms, text level work on writing simple non-chronological reports and consolidation work on using adjectives to improve writing.

✓   **Resources**   Factual texts on a variety of creatures.
                               Fictional texts to show good use of adjectives.

✓   **Sheet B**   Using and collecting synonyms. This sheet also encourages the use of the thesaurus.

✓   **Sheet C**   An introduction to simple factual writing. The task set at the bottom of the sheet invites pupils to write a report of their own.
                    Whilst medium attaining pupils might reasonably write about six facts, lower attainers could be asked to write four important facts and high attainers eight or more.
                    Encourage pupils to find the information, and write notes, from reference books, before selecting which facts to choose for their reports.

✓   **Sheet D**   Adding adjectives – pupils should be encouraged to read the whole text before adding any adjectives, and not to use any adjective more than once.

Use this box to write your own notes ready for the next time you use this unit.

Name: Date:

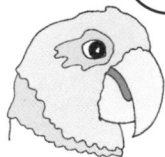

Thinking of interesting words ...

... helps to make your writing more interesting.

For each of the words below, choose three words from the box that mean the same thing.

miserable	gloomy	tiny
huge	little	enormous
merry	large	unhappy
cheerful	miniature	joyful

happy

sad

big

small

On the back think of some words that mean nearly the same thing as ...

quiet   puzzle   break

You can use a thesaurus to help you.

● **Word level work**

Name: Date:

We are going to practise writing simple information.

Our information will only be a few important facts, in short sentences.

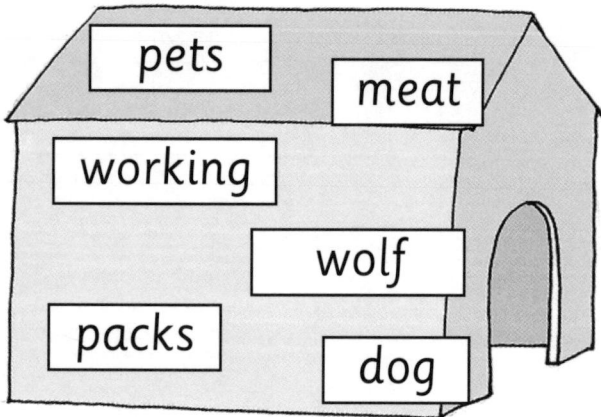

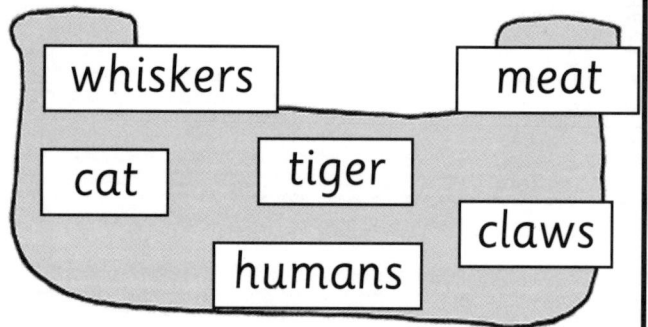

pets

meat

working

wolf

packs

dog

whiskers

meat

cat

tiger

claws

humans

There are many different types of _ _ _ .

Many people keep dogs as _ _ _ _ .

Pet dogs of today are all descendants of the _ _ _ _ .

Some dogs are used as _ _ _ _ _ _ _ dogs.

Dogs eat _ _ _ _ .

In the wild, dogs live in groups called _ _ _ _ _ .

There are many different types of _ _ _ .

All cats have _ _ _ _ _ _ .

All cats have _ _ _ _ _ _ _ _ _ to help them feel things.

Cats are _ _ _ _ eaters.

The largest cat in the cat family is the _ _ _ _ _ .

In the dark cats can see very much better than _ _ _ _ _ _ .

In your book write a simple report about another sort of animal.

Name: Date:

Adjectives are describing words.

Nouns are naming words.

✐ Make this writing more interesting by adding adjectives before the nouns.

✐ Do not use any adjective more than once.

✐ Use a dictionary to make sure your words are spelt correctly.

✐ Read through the whole text before choosing your adjectives.

There was once a _____ mountain where a group of _____ giants lived. The giants lived in _____ caves, where they slept all day, and woke up at night. Each evening the giants would go to the edges of their _____ homes and look out over the _____ trees and down to the humans' _____ village. Luckily they were _____ giants, and spent their nights planting crops, picking _____ fruit and singing _____ songs.

● **Teachers' Notes**

✓ This unit has word level consolidation work on syllables and synonyms, sentence level consolidation of use of commas in lists and word/text level poetry work.

✓ **Resources** A range of poetry for discussion of poets, rhythm, rhyme, adjectives, etc.

✓ **Sheet B** This uses colour words to complete a task on syllables and synonyms.

✓ **Sheet C** Inserting commas in lists.
These lists are not single word lists, so pupils will have to be more careful to read for meaning to complete these correctly.

✓ **Sheet D** Writing frames, with cutting guide, to allow a class anthology of favourite poems to be produced.
It is important that pupils are given the opportunity to use poems they have written themselves if they wish to. This helps them to begin to think of themselves as genuine poets.

Use this box to write your own notes ready for the next time you use this unit.

Name: Date:

Syllables and synonyms

All these words are about colours.

blue   red

lavender   pink   cherry   navy

turquoise   ruby   purple

violet   scarlet   burgundy

sapphire   mauve   crimson

Sort the words into the same number of syllables.

one

two

three

Now sort the words again according to their colour.

red

blue

purple

● **Sentence level work**

Name: Date:

Remember that items in a list ...

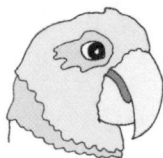

... are separated by commas.

Put commas in the lists below.
Remember that you do not need a comma between the last two items on the list.

Wrist watches church clocks grandfather clocks sand timers and sundials are all used to tell the time.

My favourite snacks are cheese on toast banana sandwiches bowls of cereal and chocolate cake.

Aeroplanes hot air balloons and helicopters can all be used to fly in.

The Three Little Pigs The Ugly Duckling Jack and the Beanstalk and Cinderella are all famous fairy tales.

Greyhounds terriers poodles and spaniels are all types of dog.

Hammer head sharks blue whales dolphins sea urchins and seaweed are all found in the ocean.

Name: Date:

✏ Use the frame below to write your favourite poem.

✏ It could be a poem you already know, or one you have written yourself.

✏ Use your best handwriting and make sure each word is spelt correctly.

✏ Illustrate your work as well as you can.

● Teachers' Notes

✓ In addition to word level spelling work, this unit has text level work on alliteration and tongue-twisters.

✓ **Resources** Examples of alliteration (often found within poetry) and tongue-twisters.

✓ **Sheet B** Spelling work on months of the year.
This is also a good sheet to use as a reminder of the need for a capital letter to begin proper nouns.

✓ **Sheet C** Work on alliteration.
Writing frames and cutting lines allow for easy classroom display.

✓ **Sheet D** Writing tongue-twisters.
This is a natural progression from the alliteration work, and again is suitable for classroom display.

Use this box to write your own notes ready for the next time you use this unit.

© Andrew Brodie Publications ✓ PO Box 23, Wellington, Somerset, TA21 8YX ✓ www.andrewbrodie.co.uk

Months of the Year

Remember the names of months must all begin...

... with a capital letter.

Carefully copy the names of the months:

1. January   2. February   3. March

4. April   5. May   6. June

7. July   8. August   9. September

10. October   11. November   12. December

Pick the correct months to complete each sentence.

1. The first month of the year is called _ _ _ _ _ _ _ _ .

2. The last month of the year is called _ _ _ _ _ _ _ _ _ .

3. The two months that follow March are _ _ _ _ _ and _ _ _ .

4. My birthday is in _ _ _ _ _ _ _ _ _ _ _ _ _ .

5. _ _ _ _ _ _ _ _ is the month before November.

6. _ _ _ _ _ _ _ is the eighth month of the year.

● **Text level work**

Name: Date:

When words begin with the same sound …

… it is called alliteration.

Look at these examples of animal alliteration.

<u>D</u>esmond the <u>d</u>ozy <u>d</u>og <u>d</u>oesn't <u>d</u>ig.

A <u>g</u>oat <u>g</u>obbles <u>g</u>rapefruit <u>g</u>ladly.

Use the frames below to write some more animal alliterations.

Name: Date:

Read these tongue-twisters
with a friend.

How quickly can you
repeat each one?

Red leather, yellow leather.

Sally sells sea shells on the seashore.

Round the rugged rock the
ragged rascal ran.

Did you notice the alliteration in the last two?
What do you think makes a good tongue-twister?

Write two really good tongue-twisters.
Share them with your friends.

_____

_____

_____

_____

● Teachers' Notes

✓ In addition to word level spelling work, this unit looks at the requirement to write a substantial story.

✓ **Resources** Fictional texts.

✓ **Sheet B** Spelling of common colour words.

✓ **Sheet C** Instructional sheet, suitable for enlarging or copying for use with an OHP, for group/class work.
This is an important sheet as it reminds the pupils of many aspects of story writing covered during Year Two.

✓ **Sheet D** The frame for the story writing.
This can be free choice of story, or you may wish to give pupils a particular theme.
This frame is designed to be suitable to use as both a front sheet and continuation sheet.

Use this box to write your own notes ready for the next time you use this unit.

© Andrew Brodie Publications ✓ PO Box 23, Wellington, Somerset, TA21 8YX ✓ www.andrewbrodie.co.uk

Name: Date:

Colour the pictures and copy the words.

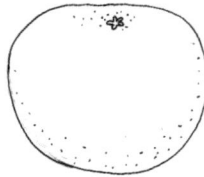

pink	orange	white

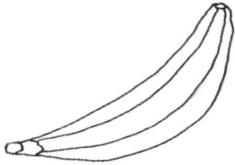

yellow	brown	green

Now draw pictures for these words.

red	black	blue	purple

Use the back of the sheet to try spelling all ten of these colour words.

© Andrew Brodie Publications ✓ PO Box 23, Wellington, Somerset, TA21 8YX ✓ www.andrewbrodie.co.uk

Oh good, it's time to write a story.

You are going to write a really good story on the sheet provided.

✎ You may need to use some extra sheets.

✎ Think about some of your favourite stories.

✎ What is it that makes you enjoy them?

✎ Think of a title for your story.

✎ Remember to use the past tense when you need to.

✎ Use interesting adjectives (describing words) to describe your nouns (naming words).

✎ Begin your story well, with a good 'setting'.

✎ Check your work as you go along.

✎ Use a dictionary to check spellings.

✎ Use a thesaurus to find interesting synonyms.

✎ Present your writing neatly.

✎ Illustrate your work well.

✎ Most importantly ...

... enjoy your writing.

© Andrew Brodie Publications ✓ PO Box 23, Wellington, Somerset, TA21 8YX ✓ www.andrewbrodie.co.uk

Name: Date:

✐ Use this frame to write your story.
✐ Put page numbers in the circles at the bottoms of the pages.

◯

© Andrew Brodie Publications ✓ PO Box 23, Wellington, Somerset, TA21 8YX ✓ www.andrewbrodie.co.uk

Writing frames ...

The following pages can be photocopied (both sides) to fold into a simple booklet. The small parrots at the top of the 'cover' are to help with the correct orientation of the booklet. Lines on the front cover are for the title and author.

This frame is suitable for any story writing activities. The three 'pages' following the cover allow for any story to have a clear beginnning, middle and end. There is adequate space for about two sentences and an illustration on each page.

We hope that you find this useful, particularly during Year One.

by

1

4

2

3

8 mm writing guide

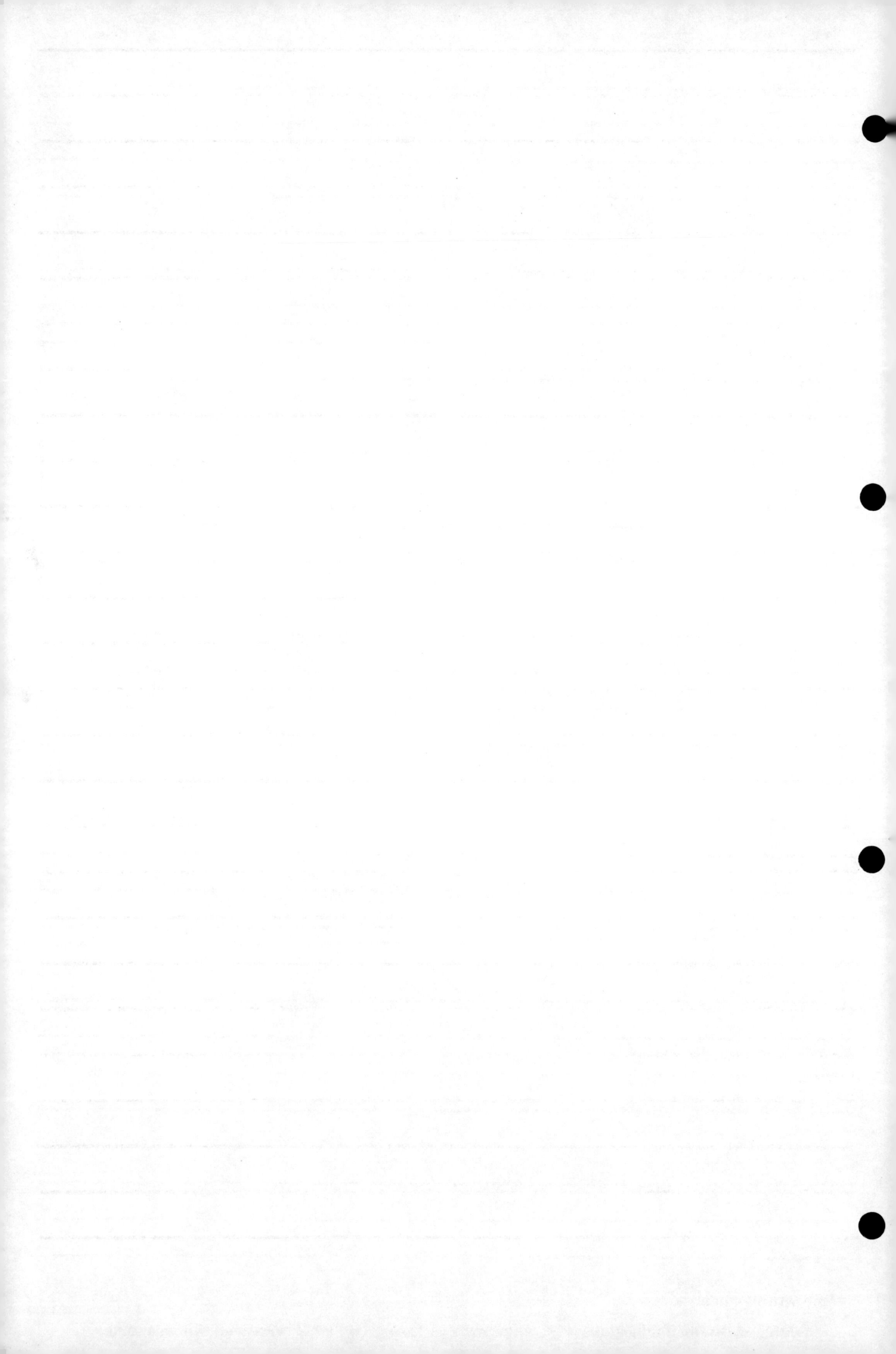

10 mm writing guide

© Andrew Brodie Publications ✓ PO Box 23, Wellington, Somerset, TA21 8YX ✓ www.andrewbrodie.co.uk

Contents ...

Term 1

Unit 1   B   Vocabulary development
        C   Verb use
        D   Story writing: Two story starts provided

Unit 2   B   Speech bubbles
        C   Speech marks
        D   Dialogue writing

Unit 3   B   Writing descriptions of places
        C   Verb tenses
        D   Story writing using a description of a place

Unit 4   B   Story beginnings and endings
        C   Changing verbs in sentences
        D   Writing a short story

Unit 5   B   Writing in sentences
        C   Paragraph breaks
        D   Story writing

Unit 6   B   Question marks and exclamation marks
        C   Preparation for writing a play script
        D   Writing a play script

Unit 7   B   Looking for unusual words
        C   Descriptive words
        D   Writing a poem

Unit 8   B   Shape writing
        C   Describing colours
        D   Shape poems

Unit 9   B   Commas in lists
        C   Reading comprehension about pets
        D   Making a poster about pets

Unit 10   B   Alphabetical order and definitions
        C   Key facts about 'our' school
        D   Writing about 'our' school

© Andrew Brodie Publications ✓ PO Box 23, Wellington, Somerset, TA21 8YX ✓ www.andrewbrodie.co.uk

Term 2

Unit 11	B	Extracting the main points from the story of the Emperor's New Cloth
	C	Making a story board
	D	Rewriting the original story
Unit 12	B	Listing adjectives
	C	Using adjectives to make writing more interesting
	D	Making a poster about a character
Unit 13	B	Singular and plural nouns
	C	Planning a fable
	D	Writing a fable
Unit 14	B	More singular and plural nouns
	C	Familiar phrases
	D	Writing a sequel to the story of Chicken Licken
Unit 15	B	Collective nouns
	C	Writing an alternative ending to well known rhymes
	D	Writing a new verse for a poem
Unit 16	B	Consolidation work on singular and plural
	C	More nouns – nouns that do not change
	D	Presenting a recipe
Unit 17	B	Deleting unnecessary words from sentences
	C	Inserting commas
	D	Writing instructions for having a bath or shower
Unit 18	B	Capital letters
	C	Grammatical agreement
	D	Writing instructions
Unit 19	B	Headlines
	C	Points for and against a topic
	D	Drawing diagrams
Unit 20	B	Spelling and definitions
	C	Preparation for making a board game
	D	Making a board game

© Andrew Brodie Publications ✓ PO Box 23, Wellington, Somerset, TA21 8YX ✓ www.andrewbrodie.co.uk

Term 3

Unit 21	B	Basic pronouns
	C	Dividing a story into episodes
	D	Writing the episodes of the story

Unit 22	B	Personal and possessive pronouns
	C	Creating moods with words and phrases
	D	Writing a first person account of a chosen story

Unit 23	B	Grammatical agreement
	C	Story planning
	D	Story writing

Unit 24	B	Presenting dialogue
	C	Laying out information for a book review
	D	Writing a book review

Unit 25	B	Conjunctions
	C	Onomatopoeia and alliteration
	D	Poetry writing

Unit 26	B	Sequences of events
	C	Planning a letter
	D	Letter writing frame

Unit 27	B	Using commas
	C	Writing notes and messages
	D	Letter writing

Unit 28	B	Alphabetical order
	C	Giving information on 'My Favourite Sports'
	D	Making a poster

Unit 29	B	Presenting an incident as a short story
	C	Presenting the same incident as a letter
	D	Presenting the same incident as a newspaper article

Unit 30	B	Summarising a passage
	C	Writing notes
	D	Translating notes into detailed writing

© Andrew Brodie Publications ✓ PO Box 23, Wellington, Somerset, TA21 8YX ✓ www.andrewbrodie.co.uk

● Teachers' Notes

✓   This unit incorporates **word level** and **sentence level** work on verbs and **text level** writing work using 'brainstorming' to generate ideas.

✓   **Sheet B**   is particularly suitable for children working with partners or in small groups. It features vocabulary development exercises where pupils find interesting words to go with particular settings. Searching for words in this way can help when children are adding details to descriptions when writing their own stories.

✓   **Sheet C**   features finding interesting verbs to use in place of other common words, again to enrich the quality of children's writing.

✓   **Sheet D**   This unit culminates in story writing around the subject of holidays. This subject has been selected as it is likely that this work will take place early in the autumn term.

Use this box to write your own notes ready for the next time you use this unit.

© Andrew Brodie Publications ✓ PO Box 23, Wellington, Somerset, TA21 8YX ✓ www.andrewbrodie.co.uk

Name: Date:

Have you had a holiday?

No, I just went for days out.

Think about a holiday you have had. If you haven't had a holiday, think about some days out that you have enjoyed.

Look at the large words below. Think of some words to go with each large word. We have done some for you.

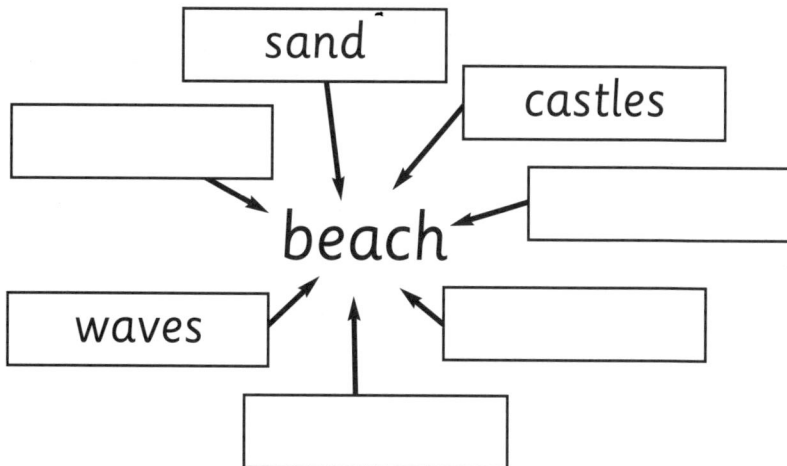

sand

castles

beach

waves

We have only given you four spaces for words to go with 'beach'.

If you can think of any more, write them down as well.

grass

field

cricket

Can you think of any more to go with 'field'?

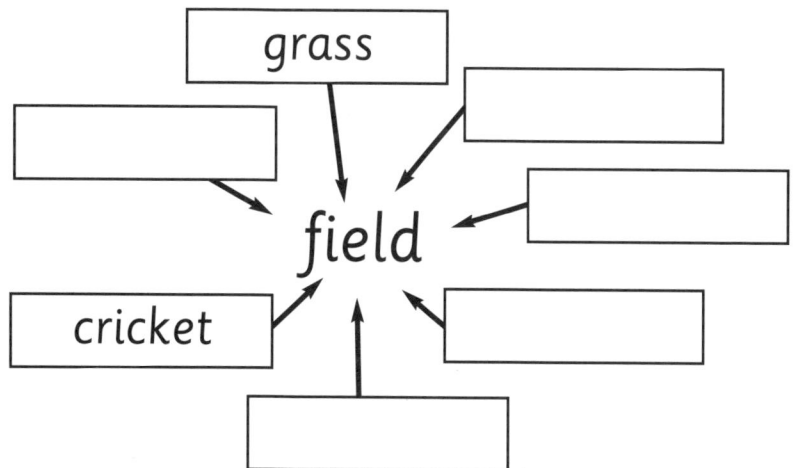

Now try to 'brainstorm' some words to go with these words and write them on the back of the sheet:

barbecue   fairground

● **Word and sentence level work**

Name: Date:

Using verbs.

> Most verbs are 'doing' words.

> Every sentence needs at least one verb.

Some verbs are much more interesting than others.

Look at each of these verbs below.

Can you think of three more interesting words that mean the same, or nearly the same, for each one?

You could use a thesaurus to help you.
The first one has been done for you.

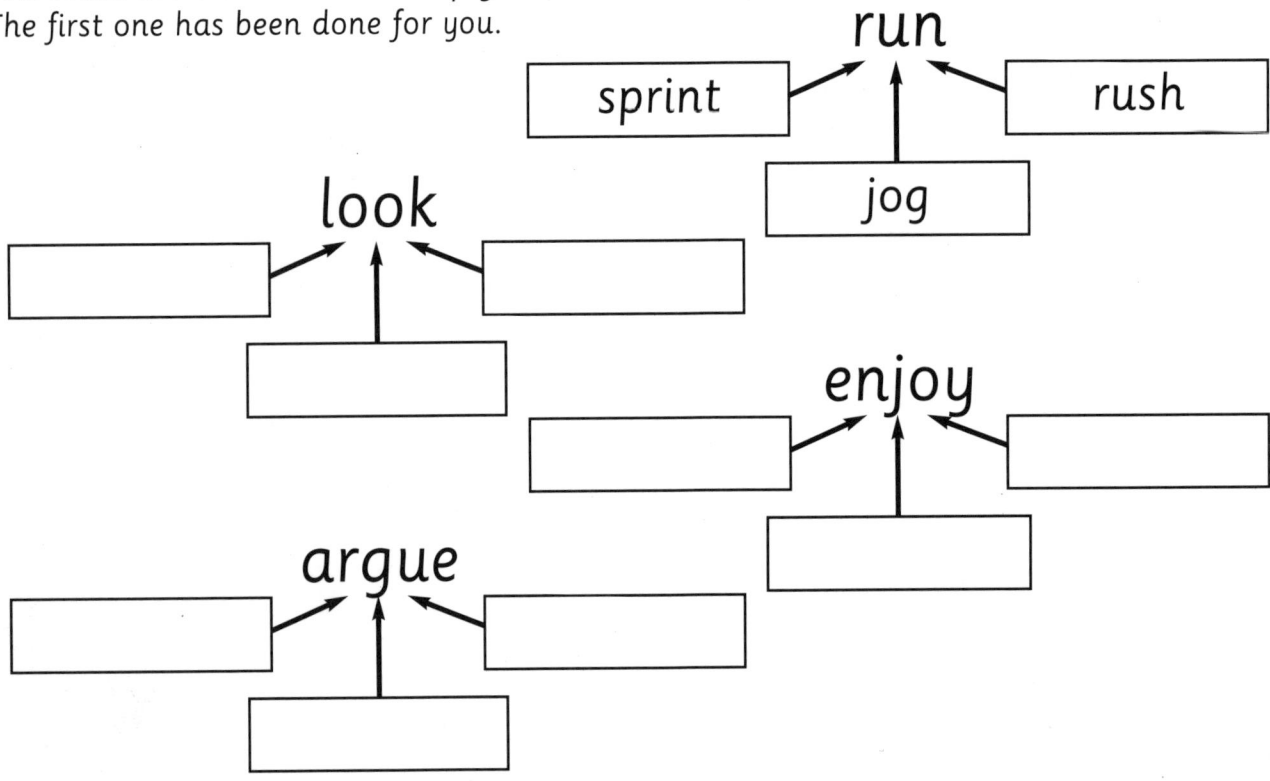

run

sprint		rush

jog

look

enjoy

argue

Look at the sentence below.
Think of an interesting verb to fill each gap.

1. The boy had [   ] a great day at the beach.

2. He was in a hurry so he [   ] all the way home.

3. The two girls could not agree so they [   ] for a long time.

© Andrew Brodie Publications ✓ PO Box 23, Wellington, Somerset, TA21 8YX ✓ www.andrewbrodie.co.uk

Name: Date:

Read these two short passages. Each one could be the start of a story.

Story start number 1

The children were very excited. They were off to the seaside for a holiday. Paul, who was nearly eight, was looking forward to the scariest rides at the fairground. His little sister, Chloe, wanted to build a fantastic sandcastle on the beach.
They got up really early. It was five o'clock in the morning when they loaded everything into the car ready for the long drive to the coast......

Story start number 2

Barbecues are usually good fun. But not when your dad singes the sausages, burns the burgers and, worst of all, sets the barbecue up in an empty field that turns out not to be empty at all!
Here's how all our problems started......

Choose one of the story beginnings.

Copy it into your book and continue the story.

When you write your part of the story, try to use the most interesting verbs you can think of. The 'brainstorming' of verbs that you have done already should help you.

You may change the names of the characters if you wish to.

Remember to make up a good title for your story.

© Andrew Brodie Publications ✓ PO Box 23, Wellington, Somerset, TA21 8YX ✓ www.andrewbrodie.co.uk

● **Teachers' Notes**

✓   The work in this unit incorporates text level work on presentation of dialogue and writing own passages of dialogue.

Resources: To make optimum use of this unit, you will need to use a range of stories, etc. in which dialogue is used. The children will need to see a range of ways to present speech in writing.

✓   **Sheet B**   Using speech bubbles to present simple dialogue.

✓   **Sheet C**   Using speech marks to present simple dialogue. The children will need to be taught the main conventions for presenting speech:

Always start with speech marks, then a capital letter.

Only put speech marks for what is actually said. You could ask two pupils to have a short conversation for the rest of the class to listen to. (This could start with something simple such as "How are you?") Write the conversation on the board or on the OHP for everybody to see - demonstrate that the speech marks only go with the words spoken:

"How are you?" asked Sidney.

The closing speech marks are never alone. They always need a full stop, a comma, a question mark or an exclamation mark.

When a different person speaks, a new line is started.

✓   **Sheet D**   Pupils should be encouraged to read their own work to the group/class, both to celebrate each pupil's ideas and to develop expressive reading.

Use this box to write your own notes ready for the next time you use this unit.

Name: Date:

Speech Bubbles.

Do you know this story?

What do you think Cinderella and the Prince are saying?

In the speech bubbles, write the words that you think are being said. Keep your writing small and neat to fit in.

Draw another speech bubble picture from the Cinderella story on the back of this sheet.
Remember to write the words being spoken in your speech bubble.

© Andrew Brodie Publications ✓ PO Box 23, Wellington, Somerset, TA21 8YX ✓ www.andrewbrodie.co.uk

● **Sentence level work**

Name: Date:

Speech Marks.

Continue the picture story below.
Use speech marks to show what the characters are saying.

"Oh good," said Martyn, "I love coming to the beach."
"I hope I can go for a paddle," laughed his sister Jasmine.

When we write what people are saying to each other…

…it is called dialogue.

On the back of this sheet, draw another picture of what the children did during the day. Write what they said. Remember to use speech marks.

© Andrew Brodie Publications ✓ PO Box 23, Wellington, Somerset, TA21 8YX ✓ www.andrewbrodie.co.uk

Name: Date:

Writing A Dialogue.

In your writing book write an interesting dialogue.

Remember what you have learned about using speech marks.

You may choose from one of the ideas below.

✎   A conversation between best friends who are arguing about what to play in the playground.

or

✎   A conversation between two or three friends visiting a fairground.

or

✎   A conversation between some characters in your favourite story or TV programme.

Remember...

Your work is about using speech marks.
You do not have to write a whole story.
Make your work interesting.
Practise reading your dialogue aloud with lots of expression.

If you are pleased with what you have written...

...your teacher may let you read it to the class.

● Teachers' Notes

✓ This unit includes writing composition work on writing short descriptions of familiar places. It also looks at the use of verbs and their tenses in sentences. Finally, these two aspects are combined into a story writing activity.

✓ **Sheet B** You might like to present this example to the children before they attempt their own descriptions:

My Lounge
My lounge is quite long and thin. It has pale green walls with framed pictures and family photographs. There is a fireplace along one wall, so the whole family enjoy blazing log fires in the winter.

✓ **Sheet C** The words the children should underline are:

Sentence 2	enjoyed
Sentence 3	was
Sentence 4	pretended, was, played
Sentence 5	ate

✓ **Sheet D** The children should be encouraged to make use of one of their descriptions created on Sheet B. This should form the start of a story, creating a setting. You may like to present them with an adapted version of the description of a lounge:

My Old Lounge
My old house had a lounge which was quite long and thin. It had green walls with framed pictures and family photographs. There was a fireplace along one wall and when we lived there we enjoyed blazing log fires in the winter.

You could now discuss how a story could be created to take place in this setting, before they try to start their own story.

Use this box to write your own notes ready for the next time you use this unit.

© Andrew Brodie Publications ✓ PO Box 23, Wellington, Somerset, TA21 8YX ✓ www.andrewbrodie.co.uk

Name: Date:

Writing descriptions of known places.

Descriptions are often used in story settings.

They can be quite short but full of interesting detail.

Use the boxes below to write descriptions.

Each description need only be two or three sentences.

My Bedroom

_____

_____

_____

_____

The Playground

_____

_____

_____

_____

My Favourite Place

_____

_____

_____

_____

Name: Date:

Using Verb Tenses.

Stories are usually written in the past tense.

That is because they happened in the past.

Change these sentences from the present to the past tense.
Underline the verb. Remember to write neatly.
The first one has been done for you.

1. The family live in a large old house.
   The family lived in a large old house.

2. The twins enjoy playing in the garden.

_____

3. In the garden there is an old tree house near a pond.

_____

_____

4. The children often pretend the tree house is an old ship, and play 'pirates' in it.

_____

_____

5. They sometimes eat a picnic tea there.

_____

● Text and sentence level work

Name: Date:

✎   Choose <u>one</u> of the descriptions you have written, about your **bedroom**, the **playground** or your *favourite place*.

✎   Use it to write the beginning of a story. Write the story in the past tense.

✎   You may have to add to your description or change it in some ways.

✎   When you have finished, practise reading your story to a friend.

✎   If you have time you could carry on to write the rest of your story.

© Andrew Brodie Publications ✓ PO Box 23, Wellington, Somerset, TA21 8YX ✓ www.andrewbrodie.co.uk

● Teachers' Notes

✓ This unit deals with aspects of the national literacy strategy concerning beginnings and endings of stories, looking at how changing a verb has an impact on a sentence and writing a whole story focussing on the teaching points covered so far this term. Sharing ideas and reading aloud can be important aspects of this unit.

✓ **Sheet B** A useful research activity. Children examine fiction books looking for beginnings and endings. A class discussion of what they find could be very useful. One conclusion that may be reached is that the 'traditional' beginnings and endings are actually quite rare. Writers try to start and end stories with some originality!

✓ **Sheet C** An exercise on choosing interesting verbs to enliven sentences. Try to encourage the children to transfer this aspect of their learning to their own story writing. Sheet D will provide an opportunity for them to consider the structure and content of an original story of their own.

✓ **Sheet D** is designed to be used either in independent work, or as part of whole class teaching. It can be photocopied on to an OHP transparency as a focus for discussion. It allows children the opportunity to share their ideas if used in a whole class setting, as well as giving them some important visual reminders to aid their work.

Use this box to write your own notes ready for the next time you use this unit.

© Andrew Brodie Publications ✓ PO Box 23, Wellington, Somerset, TA21 8YX ✓ www.andrewbrodie.co.uk

Name: Date:

Story beginnings and endings.

Working with a friend, collect the most interesting story beginnings and story endings that you can find.

We have done the first one for you.

You can find more if you look in lots of different books.

Story beginnings

Once upon a time.

_____

_____

_____

_____

_____

_____

_____

Story endings

They all lived happily ever after.

_____

_____

_____

_____

_____

_____

Underline the beginning and the end that you think are the best.

© Andrew Brodie Publications ✓ PO Box 23, Wellington, Somerset, TA21 8YX ✓ www.andrewbrodie.co.uk

Name: Date:

Changing verbs in sentences.

Every sentence has at least one verb.

Choosing your verbs carefully can help to make your writing more interesting.

✎   Neatly rewrite the following sentences.

✎   Replace each underlined verb with a new one that you like better.

1. The dog <u>ran</u> across the garden.

_____

2. They <u>looked</u> at the picture.

_____

3. The boy <u>went</u> along the road.

_____

4. The sports car <u>went</u> along the motorway.

_____

5. I <u>like</u> going to parties.

_____

6. The terrified girl <u>said</u> "Help".

_____

✎   Why do you think your verbs make the sentences more interesting?

✎   Share your ideas with your friends.

Name: Date:

Writing a short story.

✐   Use your writing book to write a story.

✐   Who will be in your story?

_____

_____

✐   What will happen to them?

_____

_____

✐   How will your story begin? Write the first sentence below.

_____

_____

✐   Remember to tell your story in the <u>past</u> tense.

✐   Use speech marks in dialogue.

✐   Write in clear sentences.

✐   Use interesting verbs.

✐   How will your story end? Write an idea for the last sentence:

_____

_____

✐   What will the title of your story be?

_____

Now enjoy writing
your story.

© Andrew Brodie Publications ✓ PO Box 23, Wellington, Somerset, TA21 8YX ✓ www.andrewbrodie.co.uk

● Teachers' Notes

✓ This unit works on sentence and text level work on sentences and paragraphs.
Some whole class work should look at paragraphing this week.

✓ **Sheet B**   It may be preferable for some children to insert full stops and capital letters in the given text before attempting to rewrite it.

Full stops occur in:
Line 1 after the word **lost.**
Line 2 after the word **her.**
Line 4 after the word **scared.**
Line 5 after the word **help.**
Line 6 after the word **department.**
Line 7 after the word **mother.**

✓ **Sheet C**   Children could discuss the text and mark on it where each paragraph break is. We suggest that paragraph one ends after the word **home** and that paragraph two ends after the word **evening**.

There are possibilities here for shared writing to complete the story, or of course, individual work.

✓ **Sheet D**   The use of paragraphs is a difficult thing to learn. By limiting the story here to three paragraphs, the children are able to gain confidence in using paragraphs to create sections in their story writing.

Use this box to write your own notes ready for the next time you use this unit.

© Andrew Brodie Publications ✓ PO Box 23, Wellington, Somerset, TA21 8YX ✓ www.andrewbrodie.co.uk

Name: Date:

Writing in sentences.

> Sentences begin with a capital letter...

> ...and finish with a full stop.

✎   The writer of the passage below forgot to write in clear sentences.

✎   Rewrite it carefully, putting in the missing capital letters and full stops.

✎   Reading aloud may help you to put the full stops in the correct place.

Sophie was lost she had been shopping with her mother and somehow she had lost sight of her at first she thought that she would see her mother again at any moment but after a while she began to be scared she wandered around the shop unsure who to go to for help suddenly there was an announcement asking Sophie Richards to meet her mother in the toy department what a relief it was to see her mother

---

✎   Did you put in all eight full stops?
✎   Did you begin each sentence with a capital letter?

● **Text level work**

Name: Date:

- This is the beginning of the story of a rather naughty dog.
- The writer should have written it in three clear paragraphs.
- Decide where each paragraph should start.
- Now write it correctly in your writing book.

Winston was a very large, very loveable and very mischievous Old English Sheepdog. He was a grey and white bundle of energy, and left a trail of trouble wherever he went. His owners first saw him at a rescue centre; he badly needed a loving new home. On the first day in his new home he raced round the garden barking loudly as if to tell everyone who would listen that he had arrived. Winston enjoyed his first dinner from his shiny new bowl and curled up comfortably in front of the fire during the evening. The first sign of trouble came at bedtime. He was shown his soft new bed tucked cosily in the corner of the kitchen. His people went upstairs to their bedrooms. Winston didn't like being alone in this new place. He wanted to be near his new family. They made him feel safe.

What do you think happened next in the story?

Share your ideas with a friend.
Think of a title for the story.

© Andrew Brodie Publications ✓ PO Box 23, Wellington, Somerset, TA21 8YX ✓ www.andrewbrodie.co.uk

Name: Date:

Writing a story.

Plan your story with care ...

...before you write it in your book.

Your job is to write a short story, just using three paragraphs.

Decide what will happen in each paragraph before you start writing.

Here are some ideas of things you may want to write about.

A troublesome pet, like Winston.

A lost child or pet.

A mountain adventure.

A forest adventure.

A time travelling story.

… or perhaps you have got another good idea of your own.

✎ Remember to split your work into paragraphs.
✎ Write some ideas for your three paragraphs here:

1 _____

2 _____

3 _____

✎ Don't forget to give your story a title.
✎ You can illustrate your story.
✎ Read your story aloud to some of your friends.

© Andrew Brodie Publications ✓ PO Box 23, Wellington, Somerset, TA21 8YX ✓ www.andrewbrodie.co.uk

● Teachers' Notes

✓ This unit covers sentence level work on exclamation marks and question marks, and text level work on writing play scripts.

✓ **Resources** To use this unit effectively you will need samples of play scripts for whole class work/shared reading.

✓ **Sheet B** This task ensures understanding of questions marks and exclamation marks.

✓ **Sheet C** Completing this task will give children a good start ready to write a play script.

✓ **Sheet D** **Writing a play script**
This is an instruction and reminder sheet as an aid to play script writing work. You may wish to enlarge or copy for use with OHP when working with the whole class.
Higher ability children could be encouraged to include stage directions, etc., in their script.

Use this box to write your own notes ready for the next time you use this unit.

© Andrew Brodie Publications ✓ PO Box 23, Wellington, Somerset, TA21 8YX ✓ www.andrewbrodie.co.uk

Name: Date:

Instead of just a full stop you may need a question mark (?).

Or an exclamation mark (!).

On each of the phrases and sentences below, decide whether to use a question mark (?) or an exclamation mark (!) or just a full stop.

Is it really for me

Oh no

Where is the bus stop

My house is over there

Why won't the car start

Wow

Which mug is mine

Your mug is the blue one

REMEMBER: We use an exclamation mark where somebody ...

... shouts!   or   ... makes a strong statement!

Now write 2 questions and 2 exclamations below.

_____

_____

_____

_____

_____

Name: Date:

Three Little Pigs – Speech Bubble Story.

This is the beginning of the story of the Three Little Pigs.
What would the characters be saying in the pictures.

Name: Date:

Writing a play script.

✎ Use the words from your Three Little Pigs sheet, to begin a Three Little Pigs play script.

✎ Can you write the whole story as a play?

✎ Remember to list your characters at the beginning. You might need to include a narrator to tell parts of the story.

✎ Present your work very neatly so that you can perform your play with your friends.

> Write each character's name in a left-hand margin…

> …so it doesn't get muddled with the words being spoken.

This could be how your play script starts:

Mummy Pig: Build yourselves a house each. Keep a look out for the wolf, he's very dangerous.

Three Pigs: We will mother. Don't worry about us.

Narrator: The first little pig meets a man carrying some hay.

Pig One: Please sir, can I buy your hay?

Man: Yes, that will be three pounds.

© Andrew Brodie Publications ✓ PO Box 23, Wellington, Somerset, TA21 8YX ✓ www.andrewbrodie.co.uk

● Teachers' Notes

✓ For this unit on the requirement to write short poems, descriptions and word patterns, you will need to look at a range of poems for whole class teaching. Look in particular for poems with repeating words or lines. The children will need access to poetry books to complete the task on sheet B.

It is important that pupils know their target is to describe **not** to rhyme. It may be useful to find out what your pupils think a poem is. One definition that works very well with children is to describe a poem as being 'a picture made from words'.

✓ **Sheet B**   Before the children start this sheet you may like to show them a poem, picking out interesting words and phrases with them. Which particular words and phrases help the poem to be effective? After they have listed their own twenty words or phrases, the results of this work can be put to good use in whole class teaching.

✓ **Sheet C**   This is another task to promote the sharing/collecting of ideas by the whole group. The last two words on the list (sadness and coldness) are a little more challenging than the others.

✓ **Sheet D**   This task is ideal for making a class book or display to celebrate the children's work. You may wish to limit the subject matter of the poems or use the subjects from sheet C.

Use this box to write your own notes ready for the next time you use this unit.

© Andrew Brodie Publications ✓ PO Box 23, Wellington, Somerset, TA21 8YX ✓ www.andrewbrodie.co.uk

Name: Date:

This task is even more fun …

… if you work with a friend.

Find a poetry book to look through.

Use the poems to help you find some interesting or unusual words or phrases.

Choose the ones that you think sound the best or most interesting.

Write your 20 favourites in the box below.

Underline your two favourites.

© Andrew Brodie Publications ✔ PO Box 23, Wellington, Somerset, TA21 8YX ✔ www.andrewbrodie.co.uk

● **Word and text level work**

Name: Date:

Think of the best words or phrases to describe each of the things below.

We have put some ideas for the first ones for you …

… but you might want to think of something even better.

Apple   green, crispy

Black cat   sleek, furry

Snow

Sand

Flowers

Rain

Clouds

Spaghetti

Sadness

Coldness

Name: Date:

✏ Look at these examples of poems that use a repeating line.
They have some good descriptive words or phrases.

Fish
Brilliant colours,
In the water,
I love to watch fish swim.
Through weeds,
Under lily pads,
I love to watch fish swim.
Moving quickly,
Flashing past,
I love to watch fish swim.
Gliding, turning,
Tails swishing,
I love to watch fish swim.

Fire
The fire is a monster waving in the air.
The flames spit and crackle.
Fire is a dragon's breath.
The flames spit and crackle.
Rich, beautiful, flickering colours.
The flames spit and crackle.
Sparks and smoke rising into the sky.
The flames spit and crackle.

✏ Now make up your own poem with a repeating line.

✏ Do a rough draft first so that you can change it if you want to.

Now write a best
copy. You may
want to illustrate
it too.

● Teachers' Notes

✓   This unit focuses on text level work, writing calligrams and shape poems.

✓   **Sheet B**   Children for whom presentation of writing is a difficulty may gain more from this task by exploring fonts on the computer.

✓   **Sheet C**   Some introductory work on words to describe a range of colours will enhance this task.

✓   **Sheet D**   This sheet comprises examples of shape poems to be used as a starting point for pupils' own ideas You may wish to copy this for use on an OHP.
Topics producing excellent results include nature, the fairground and food.

✓   All tasks within this unit could be used to produce some excellent display work for the classroom.

Use this box to write your own notes ready for the next time you use this unit.

© Andrew Brodie Publications ✓ PO Box 23, Wellington, Somerset, TA21 8YX ✓ www.andrewbrodie.co.uk

Name: Date:

Shape poems.

✎   Your teacher will tell you whether to do this work in
      a book or on paper for displaying.

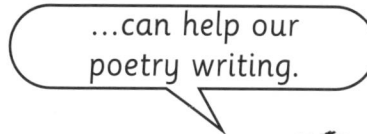

Sometimes what
our words look
like...

...can help our
poetry writing.

W a v e s
Think of some words to describe waves.
Write them in wavy writing.

Bubbles. Bubbles. Bubbles. Bubbles.
Think of some words to describe bubbles.
Write each word inside a bubble, or in bubble writing.

Tall and Thin
Think of some things that are tall and thin.
Write them in tall thin writing.

scary
Think of some scary words and invent a 'scary'
style of writing to write them in.

✎   Now make your favourite words into a poem.

✎   Will you write all the words in special writing or only the important ones?

You choose – after all the poem belongs to YOU!

© Andrew Brodie Publications ✓ PO Box 23, Wellington, Somerset, TA21 8YX ✓ www.andrewbrodie.co.uk

● **Word and text level work**

Name: Date:

Red

Orange

Yellow

Green

Blue

Indigo

Violet

How many words can you think of to describe each colour of the rainbow?

Write them on your rainbow to make a rainbow poem.

Name: Date:

Look at these examples of simple shape poems.

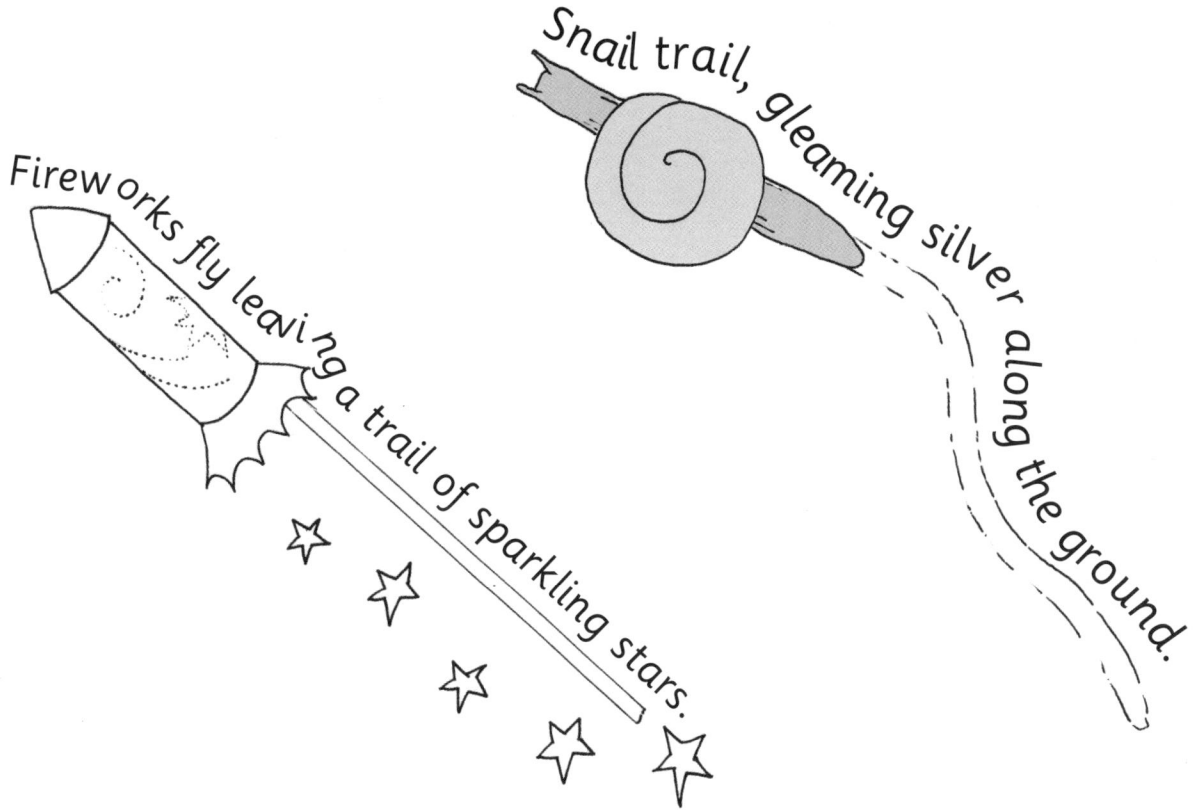

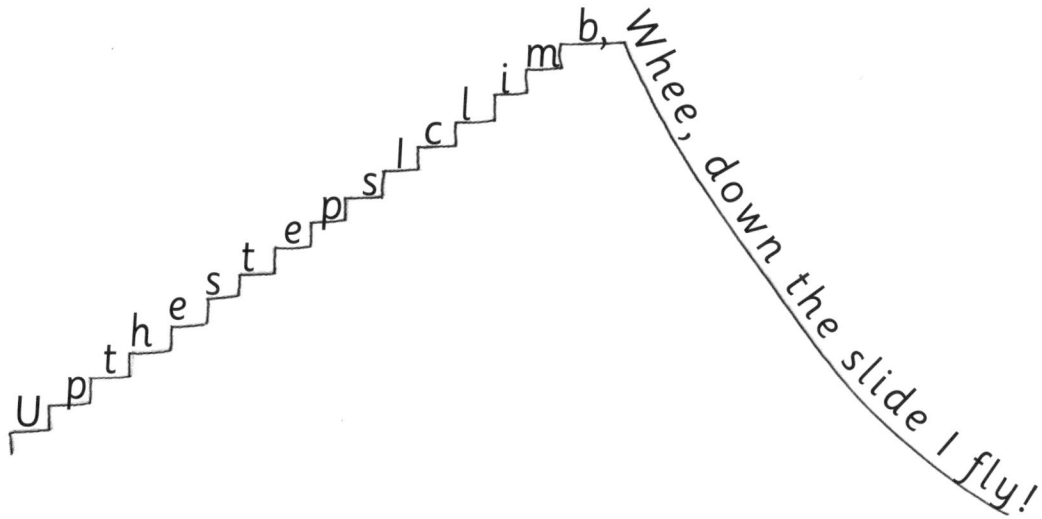

Snail trail, gleaming silver along the ground.

Fireworks fly leaving a trail of sparkling stars.

Up the steps I climb, Whee, down the slide I fly!

Try writing some shape poems of your own.

Remember to use interesting adjectives.

● Teachers' Notes

✓ This unit covers sentence level work on using commas to separate items in a list. It also tackles text level work on extracting information from texts.

✓ **Sheet B** Exercises on commas.

✓ **Sheet C/D** These sheets are based on information work about Pets. This has been chosen as most primary schools have a range of books/big books on this subject, and it is a topic that interests the majority of girls and boys.

✓ **Sheet D** You will need a range of books/leaflets etc. on a variety of pets to make optimum use of this work.
You may wish the children to work in pairs or small groups on this task.
This work can lead to effective factual material written by the children, being displayed in the classroom.
It is important to ensure children understand the need to check their facts, as at this age children may make generalisations based on their previous experience with one animal.

Use this box to write your own notes ready for the next time you use this unit.

Using Commas in Lists.

✎   When you are writing a list of things, use a comma after each item to separate it from the next.

✎   The last two items are usually separated by the word **and** instead of a comma.

> Read this example aloud.

I like to eat apples, peas, bananas, grapes and peaches.

> Now it's your turn to put commas in the lists below.

1. To make a cake you need flour sugar milk eggs and butter.

_____

_____

2. Cows sheep rabbits dogs and cats are all mammals.

_____

_____

3. Gardening reading music football and painting are all popular hobbies.

_____

_____

4. Flutes oboes saxophones clarinets and trombones are all played in a wind band.

_____

_____

5. Beethoven Mozart Schubert and Elgar are famous composers.

_____

✎   On the back of this sheet, write four interesting sentences with lists in them.

● **Word and text level work**

Name: Date:

Looking After Dogs.

My favourite subject! Please read carefully.

Dogs can make wonderful pets but it is important to look after them properly. All dogs need regular feeding, grooming and exercise to keep them healthy, and of course they need a great deal of loving attention.

There are many different breeds of dog in all sorts of sizes. The smallest types of dog are known as 'toy' or 'miniature' dogs and can be less than 30 centimetres tall. The largest dogs can be very big, and they need a great deal of exercise.

✎ Write down the four key words that explain about caring for a pet dog.

_____   _____

_____   _____

✎ Which two words in the text are used to describe very small breeds of dog?

_____   _____

✎ Use an information book to find out about the different breeds (types) of dog. Name eight breeds of dog below.

_____   _____

_____   _____

_____   _____

_____   _____

✎ Which is your favourite type of dog?   ✎   Which is your least favourite?

_____   _____

Name: Date:

Caring For a Pet.

Make an information poster or booklet about caring for a pet.

Choose a pet to find out about.

Use information books to help you.

Here are some pets to choose from.

dogs   hamsters   gerbils
          cats   rats   rabbits
fish   birds   guinea pigs

✎   Remember to put any information into your own words. Do not
    just copy from a book.

✎   Do not just guess things – always check your facts.

✎   Any lists in your work will need commas to separate the items.

✎   Use illustrations and charts to help you to present your work well.

✎   Your finished work should help other people to know how to
    care for a pet.

✎   If you are making a poster your writing should be very clear,
    bold and easy to read. You will need to write with very big,
    careful handwriting.

© Andrew Brodie Publications ✓ PO Box 23, Wellington, Somerset, TA21 8YX ✓ www.andrewbrodie.co.uk

● Teachers' Notes

✓ It is important (as with unit 9) to use factual texts during the week and to consider their layout, use of language, etc.

This unit comprises three linked tasks covering requirement to write a simple non-chronological report based on the pupils' own experiences. It also helps them to organise their ideas using notes and key facts.

Most schools have pupils moving during the year, so this unit culminates in a very real task, the results of which can be used to help new pupils to feel welcomed at any time during the year.

✓ **Sheet B** Word level work. Alphabetical order and using a dictionary.

✓ **Sheet C** Key facts about 'our school'.

✓ **Sheet D** Organising the most relevant facts to produce a report about the school, the target audience for this being any new pupil.

Use this box to write your own notes ready for the next time you use this unit.

Name: Date:

These words and phrases are all about things you have in your school.

Read them aloud.

teachers   pupils   games and toys
classrooms   big books   pencils
assembly   playtime   office

✎   Arrange the words into alphabetical order.
     Beside each one write a definition for it.
     You may need a dictionary to help you.

1. _____

2. _____

3. _____

4. _____

5. _____

6. _____

7. _____

8. _____

9. _____

● **Word, sentence and text level work**

Name: Date:

✎   What do you think a new pupil coming to your school needs to know about?

✎   Use the lines below to write down the most important things.

✎   You may not need all the lines.

✎   Your list might include short sentences, phrases or just key words.

_____

_____

_____

_____

_____

_____

_____

_____

_____

_____

_____

Compare your list with one of your friends.

Do you need to change your list or add to it?

Name: Date:

Writing About Your School.

✎ You are going to write a report about your school so that a new pupil would feel welcomed, and would learn some important things about your school.

✎ Call your writing 'Our School'.

✎ Use your ideas and notes from the last work sheet (Sheet C).

✎ Decide which order to use your ideas in.

✎ Write in good clear sentences.

✎ Remember to include everything a new pupil will need to know.

Did you remember to say what your school is called?

And what time you begin each day?

© Andrew Brodie Publications ✓ PO Box 23, Wellington, Somerset, TA21 8YX ✓ www.andrewbrodie.co.uk

● Teachers' Notes

✓ Any version available of the tale of 'The Emperor's New Clothes' would help make use of this unit.
The story on Sheet B could be enlarged for group reading.

✓ **Sheet B** This sheet is best used enlarged due to the amount of writing on it. The work to be done from this could be done in a class or group session, or as independent work.
This version of the story is ideal for class work on adjectives and the impact they have on the writing.

✓ **Sheet C** This covers the requirement to make a story board to remind pupils of the key points in the tale. (The story has been written in 5 paragraphs to help children pick out 5 key features for sheets B and C.)

✓ **Sheet D** The story writing should reflect children's own ideas. They should refer to either their story boards or key points, with no access to the full story.
Encourage embellishments to add interest, good use of interesting verbs and adjectives and a traditional beginning and ending to their story.

Use this box to write your own notes ready for the next time you use this unit.

© Andrew Brodie Publications ✓ PO Box 23, Wellington, Somerset, TA21 8YX ✓ www.andrewbrodie.co.uk

Name: Date:

The Emperor's New Clothes.

> Read this story carefully.

Once, many years ago, in a far off land there lived an emperor who loved to wear the finest clothes. Each day he wore something new, and before going out, would strut up and down in front of the mirror admiring himself. He was exceedingly vain.

One day some weavers arrived at the palace asking to be allowed to show the emperor some marvellous new magical clothing they had invented. They showed him first some magnificent threads in brilliant golds and silvers, and explained that when it was woven into cloth, only intelligent people would see its true splendour. Stupid people would see nothing.

The emperor, being a very vain man, couldn't wait to have some spectacular new clothes made from the cloth that would be woven from the magical thread. He paid them a fortune in gold (100 bags of gold to be exact) for his new outfit, and arranged for it to be ready for him to wear at a grand parade.

The great day came, the weavers returned to the palace carefully carrying the emperor's new clothes. To his horror, as they helped him dress, he realised he could see nothing. This must mean, he thought, that he was really quite stupid. Being a vain man he couldn't admit this, so as usual he admired himself in front of the mirror, telling the weavers how delighted he was with his wonderful new outfit. All his courtiers agreed with him, as they too could see nothing but were too afraid to be thought of as stupid.

At 2.00pm the parade began. A large crowd had gathered and the emperor walked proudly along the street. People clapped and cheered, saying how splendid he looked, all of course too afraid to say that they could see nothing! Suddenly everything changed. A small child in the crowd pointed at the emperor and shouted, "Look, the emperor has forgotten his clothes!" A murmur rippled through the crowd. The murmur grew to a chuckle as everyone realised that the emperor really was naked (well almost – luckily he had on his usual, and quite real, boxer shorts). The most embarrassed person there, was of course the emperor who was never again to be so vain and foolish. And the weavers? As you have probably guessed they were long gone, busy spending the gold (all 100 bags of it) that the emperor had paid them for absolutely nothing.

✐   In your book write five key points to help you to remember the main things that happened in the story.

✐   You could write sentences, phrases or key words.

✐   If you have time, make a list of all the adjectives (describing words) used in the story.

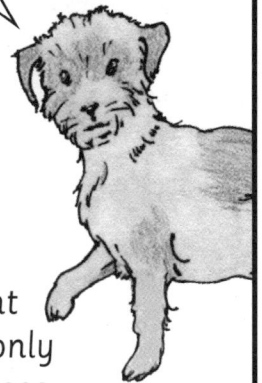

© Andrew Brodie Publications ✓ PO Box 23, Wellington, Somerset, TA21 8YX ✓ www.andrewbrodie.co.uk

● **Word level work**

Name: Date:

This page is about 'The Emperors New Clothes' again.

✐ Writing the key points in a story is a good way to help you remember it, or to plan a new piece of writing.

✐ Another way to help you to plan out a story is to draw a set of pictures about it. (This is called making a story board).

✐ Make an 'Emperor's New Clothes' story board in the frames below.

1.

2.

3.

4.

5.

✐ Talk to a friend about the details in your pictures that would help you to write a really interesting version of the story.

Name: Date:

The Emperor's New Clothes - an illustrated story.

Now it's your turn to do some writing.

✐   You are going to write your own version of 'The Emperor's New Clothes'. You can draw pictures so that it becomes an illustrated story.

✐   Use your key points or your story board to help you.

✐   You can make the story yours by making changes or adding things to the story but without changing the important parts of it.

✐   Remember that interesting adjectives and verbs will make your writing more exciting.

✐   You might want to write a draft first so that you can change parts of the story to make your final work even better.

✐   When you have finished and checked your work, read it to a friend, or ask a friend to read it to you so you can listen to it.

✐   Colour your illustrations really carefully. Good pictures make a big difference to a story. People are more likely to read your story if it looks good, so you will need to use your best handwriting as well.

✐   **Most importantly - enjoy your writing.**

© Andrew Brodie Publications ✓ PO Box 23, Wellington, Somerset, TA21 8YX ✓ www.andrewbrodie.co.uk

● Teachers' Notes

✓ This unit deals with using adjectives (sentence level) and with the requirement to create character portraits.

✓ **Resources** Big Books and other fiction books containing character portraits will need to be used as part of whole class teaching.

✓ **Sheet B** This task encourages pupils to use more interesting adjectives than they may have done in the past. It is linked to physical and behavioural aspects of a character.

✓ **Sheet C** This sheet demonstrates the importance of using adjectives and encourages the use of interesting ones.

✓ **Sheet D** To make best use of this sheet you need to prepare for it by working with the children on the type of character they are describing.

Choices to be made: young/old
attractive/ugly
cheerful/grumpy
male/female etc.

Once these choices have been made the pupils should be encouraged to add as much detail as possible to their posters, and to ensure that they include enough character points as well as physical details.

Use this box to write your own notes ready for the next time you use this unit.

Name: Date:

Using Adjectives.

Try to find at least three interesting adjectives to describe each of the following things.

(These are about looks)

A person's eyes – _____ _____ _____ _____

A person's nose – _____ _____ _____ _____

A person's mouth – _____ _____ _____ _____

A person's ears – _____ _____ _____ _____

A person's hair – _____ _____ _____ _____

(These are about character)

A sulky person – _____ _____ _____ _____

A happy person – _____ _____ _____ _____

A good friend – _____ _____ _____ _____

Now use some of those words to describe someone you like.
You only need to write two or three good sentences.

_____

_____

_____

On the back of this
sheet, draw the person
you have described.

_____

_____

● Word, sentence and text level work

Name: Date:

Using Adjectives.

Read this description of my friend.

My friend is tall with dark, curly hair. She is a good friend to have and is nice to play with in the playground. Her eyes are brown and she usually wears gold earrings. She is a happy girl who laughs a lot and tells jokes. I am lucky to have such a good friend.

✎   Now see which adjectives have been added to make the description more interesting:

My friend is quite tall and has long, dark, curly hair. She is a good friend to have and is nice to play with in the school playground. Her eyes are dark brown and she usually wears gold earrings. She is a happy girl who laughs a lot and tells funny jokes. I am lucky to have such a good friend.

✎   Now write a description of your own friend. Try to use interesting adjectives. See if your description can be better than the one I have written.

Name: Date:

Make a poster about a character of your choice.
Draw a picture, then write words or short phrases around the picture. These
should describe the character you have drawn.
Use this sheet or a large piece of paper.

> Draw your character in the centre frame.

> Have you used some excellent adjectives?

© Andrew Brodie Publications ✓ PO Box 23, Wellington, Somerset, TA21 8YX ✓ www.andrewbrodie.co.uk

✓ Resources needed for this unit are a range of fables (Aesop's Fables are ideal) and other traditional tales enabling you to explore the typical story themes:

Good triumphs over evil (as in Snow White over wicked step mother).

The weak or gentle over the strong or fierce (as in Aesop's Sun and Wind fable.).

✓ **Sheet B** Word level. This looks at singular and plural nouns, then requires children to change sentences from singular to plural. Inevitably they will therefore need to change some of the verbs to ensure 'grammatical agreement' within the sentences. For example:

My leg hurts. ➔ **Our legs hurt.**

✓ **Sheet C** Shared reading of traditional tales and fables will help the children when they come to tackle this sheet. Class discussions of morals within stories will guide the children in developing ideas for their own stories with morals. They will need reminding of the story of 'The Hare and the Tortoise' and this provides a valuable opportunity for considering their own attitudes towards others.

✓ **Sheet D** An instructional sheet that you may wish to use with an OHP, or to enlarge for group use.

Use this box to write your own notes ready for the next time you use this unit.

© Andrew Brodie Publications ✓ PO Box 23, Wellington, Somerset, TA21 8YX ✓ www.andrewbrodie.co.uk

Name: Date:

Singular and Plural.

Singular means **one**, plural means **more than one**.

See if you can make these singular nouns into plurals.

I have done the first one for you.

Singular	Plural	Singular	Plural
cat	cats	car	
banana		carpet	
house		pencil	
book		table	
cup		picture	

✎   Now see if you can rewrite these sentences, changing them from singular to plural.

1. The dog likes going for a walk.

    _____

2. I am going to dig a big hole on the beach.

    _____

3. The clock is striking 7 o'clock.

    _____

4. My leg hurts.

    _____

5. Cut out the picture with a pair of sharp scissors.

    _____

✎   Underline the words you had to change.
    What do you notice about them?
    Discuss this with a friend.

© Andrew Brodie Publications ✓ PO Box 23, Wellington, Somerset, TA21 8YX ✓ www.andrewbrodie.co.uk

● **Sentence and text level work**

Name: Date:

A fable is a story with a moral. The most famous fables were written by a man called Aesop. Aesop was a slave in Greece, many years ago.

The story of 'The Hare and the Tortoise' was written by Aesop.
What is the moral of this story?

_____

_____

_____

_____

Have you read some of Aesop's fables?

My favourite is 'The Sun and the Wind'.

✎   Think about some characters that you could put in a fable of your own.

_____   _____   _____

✎   Think of a title for your writing.

_____

✎   What would be the 'moral' at the end of your fable?

_____

_____

✎   What are the 5 or 6 key points in the story?

_____

_____

_____

_____

Writing a fable.

> Now you are going to write down your fable.

Points to Remember:

✐ Describe your characters well.

✐ Use your key points to help you write each section of your story.

✐ Don't forget to put the 'moral' of the tale at the end of it.

✐ You may want to do a rough draft first so that you can make changes.

✐ Present your finished work neatly and check it carefully.

✐ Enjoy reading your stories to each other.

> You could make a class book of fables.

● Teachers' Notes

✓ You will need the story of 'Chicken Licken' to help with text level work. (See Sheet D notes).

This unit covers more work on singular and plural nouns (sentence level). It also covers the text level requirement to identify familiar phrases and expressions for well known stories, and asks the children to write a sequel to a well known tale.

It is important to ensure the children understand the term 'sequel' to complete the text level work successfully.

In Unit 13 children changed words from the singular to the plural. In this unit the reverse process occurs.

✓ **Sheet B**   Work on changing from plural to singular. This applies firstly to words and then to sentences.

✓ **Sheet C**   This encourages children to investigate familiar phrases found in well known stories.

✓ **Sheet D**   An instructional sheet for use with an OHP or enlargement for group work. This sheet is based on 'Chicken Licken', so this story will be an important part of your whole class teaching this week. This story has been selected due to its general availability in primary schools and its suitability to the task. There are also variations of the story to be found in a variety of modern publications. Use of these would also be beneficial.

In the event of 'Chicken Licken' being unavailable, 'The Gingerbread Man' or 'The Billy Goats Gruff' would be suitable texts to use, though you would need to make appropriate changes to sheet D.

Use this box to write your own notes ready for the next time you use this unit.

Name: Date:

Singular and Plural.

Remember that plural means more than one and singular means only one.

✎   Write the single noun by each of these plurals. Take care with the spelling.
      Some plurals have 's' and others have 'es' on the end.
      The first one has been done for you.

Plural	Singular	Plural	Singular
potatoes	potato	telephones	
walls		rulers	
ponds		chairs	
buildings		carrots	
tomatoes		cakes	

✎   Now change these sentences from plural to singular.

1. My cats like to sleep in the sun.

   _____

2. Lots of fish were swimming in the pond.

   _____

3. I walked over hills and through valleys.

   _____

4. The gates were closed.

   _____

5. We ate all the cakes.

   _____

✎   Underline all the words you needed to change.

✎   Did you notice that you needed to change some of the verbs as well as the nouns?

✎   Read your new sentences to a friend. Do the sentences still make sense?

© Andrew Brodie Publications ✓ PO Box 23, Wellington, Somerset, TA21 8YX ✓ www.andrewbrodie.co.uk

● Text and word level work

Familiar Phrases.

✐ On this page there are some very well known words from some very well known stories.

✐ Read each phrase and write which story you think it comes from.

✐ The first one has been done for you.

Words: I'll huff and I'll puff and I'll blow your house down.

Story: The Three Little Pigs.

Words: We're going to tell the king the sky has fallen down.

Story: _____

Words: I'm a troll, fol-de-rol, and I'll eat you for my supper.

Story: _____

Words: Fee fi fo fum.

Story: _____

Words: Mirror mirror on the wall,

                Who is the fairest one of all?

Story: _____

Now you write down some well known story words.

Can your friends work out which stories they are from?

_____

_____

_____

© Andrew Brodie Publications ✓ PO Box 23, Wellington, Somerset, TA21 8YX ✓ www.andrewbrodie.co.uk

Name: Date:

> Do you know the story of Chicken Licken?

> He was rather a silly little chick.

You are about to write a sequel to the Chicken Licken story.

Things to Think About:

1. A repeating line to replace telling 'the king that the sky is falling down'.

2. Some rhyming names for Chicken Licken's friends.

3. What might alarm Chicken Licken? It won't be the sky falling this time.

4. How will the story end?

Remember:

✎   List your characters.

✎   Write down the key points in your story.

✎   Do a rough draft of your full story.

✎   Read it to a friend. Can your friend suggest any improvements?

✎   Write your final story.

✎   Present it with care.

✎   You may want to illustrate your story.

✎   Share your story with your friends.

● Teachers' Notes

✓ This unit covers work on collective nouns (sentence level) and the text level requirement to write new verses for poems, paying attention to rhythms, etc.

Resources for this unit should include a range of poems, both traditional nursery rhymes and more up to date verses.

✓ **Sheet B** Work on collective nouns, including the requirement for pupils to invent their own.

✓ **Sheet C** This has examples of a variety of alternative endings to 'Jack and Jill'. Children are then asked to invent endings to Hickory Dickory Dock. It would be useful to explore rhythm and line lengths in whole class teaching, before pupils work on this sheet.

This sheet may be used to work on, or work could be done in books enabling enlargement of copying for OHP use, for the whole group.

✓ **Sheet D** This work invites children to make new verses for known poems. This sheet is instructional, for enlargement or OHP use.

Use this box to write your own notes ready for the next time you use this unit.

© Andrew Brodie Publications ✓ PO Box 23, Wellington, Somerset, TA21 8YX ✓ www.andrewbrodie.co.uk

Name: Date:

Collective Nouns.

Collective nouns are words used to describe a group of things.
There are many well known collective nouns.

Choose collective nouns from the box
to complete the phrases.

A _____ of flowers.

A _____ of cows.

A _____ of sheep.

A _____ of cards.

A _____ of geese.

A _____ of ships.

flight   pack
         shoal   lots
bunch   fleet
   flock   giggle
gaggle   many
      brood   herd

Take care.
You don't need all
the words.

Now have some fun <u>inventing</u> some collective nouns
of your own to put in the spaces below.

A _____ of trumpets.

A _____ of windmills.

A _____ of teachers.

A _____ of doughnuts.

A _____ of footballers.

A _____ of chairs.

✐   Share your ideas with your friends.

© Andrew Brodie Publications ✓ PO Box 23, Wellington, Somerset, TA21 8YX ✓ www.andrewbrodie.co.uk

● **Word and text level work**

Name: Date:

Look at these poems. They all have the same
well known beginning, but then look what happens.

Jack and Jill went up the hill,
To fetch a pail of water.
Jack tripped up and broke his cup.
And Jill fell over with laughter.

Jack and Jill went up the hill,
To eat their curds and whey.
Then Jill said to Jack
"Are you sure we're in the right play?"

Jack and Jill went up the hill,
To fetch a pail of water.
Jack fell down and broke his crown
And Jill said 'This is no time for games'.

Here is the beginning of another well known poem.

Can you think of a new ending?

Hickory Dickory Dock

The mouse ran _____

_____

_____

_____

_____

_____

Name: Date:

Writing a new verse for a poem.

I like writing poems.

You will need some poetry books to help you with this task.

1.   ✐   Find a short poem (or one verse of a longer one) that you like.

     ✐   Read it aloud.

     ✐   Listen to the rhythm of the poem.

     ✐   Look at the length of the lines.

     ✐   Does the poem rhyme?

2.   ✐   Try to write a new verse for your poem.

     ✐   Work in rough first, then you can make changes if you need to.

     ✐   Write the original poem in your book (or on paper) in your

          best writing.

     ✐   Now add the new verse to your poem.

     ✐   You may want to illustrate your work.

3.   ✐   Share your poem with your friends.

● Teachers' Notes

✓ **Resources** needed for optimum use of this unit include recipes and similarly laid out instructions.
The unit covers the requirement to pick out long words and phrases from a text (text level). It also includes more sentence level work on Nouns.

✓ **Sheet B** Consolidation work on singular and plural.

✓ **Sheet C** Nouns that do not change in plural form.

✓ **Sheet D** Picking out key words/phrases from text.
Organising facts in the form of a recipe.
Ideally each child or pair of children should have a copy of this sheet, though their written work will need to be completed in a book or on other paper.
To make this task more meaningful, children might be given the opportunity at some time to make these biscuits.

Use this box to write your own notes ready for the next time you use this unit.

© Andrew Brodie Publications ✓ PO Box 23, Wellington, Somerset, TA21 8YX ✓ www.andrewbrodie.co.uk

Name: Date:

In the box below there are twenty nouns. Ten are singular and ten are plural.
Sort them into pairs. The first one has been done for you.

jelly	loaves	party	bush	geese	parties
houses	potato	elf	house	toy	ears	loaf
toys	bushes	ear	goose	elves	jellies	potatoes

jelly   ⟶   jellies

Now think of eight more
singular and plural pairs.

● **Word and sentence level work**

Name: Date:

More Nouns.

🖉   There are some nouns that do not change their spelling whether they are singular or plural.

🖉   You can have one pair of **scissors** or six pairs of scissors. The word **scissors** stays the same.

🖉   Other nouns that do not change when they become plural include **trousers** and **sheep**.

🖉   See if you can find three more nouns that do not change.

> Work with a friend.

> Write your nouns below.

_____   _____   _____

🖉   Put each noun into two short phrases or sentences, one singular (I have a pet sheep) and one plural (Thirty sheep are in a field).

© Andrew Brodie Publications ✓ PO Box 23, Wellington, Somerset, TA21 8YX ✓ www.andrewbrodie.co.uk

Name: Date:

Read these instructions carefully.

Biscuits.

To make about 25 small biscuits you must follow these instructions. Firstly take 200 grams of self-raising flour and put it into a bowl. Rub 125 grams of butter into the flour. Add 100 grams of sugar to the mixture. Mix it to a stiff dough with an egg that you have beaten. Next put the mixture into a polythene bag and put it in the fridge to let it get cold. It can stay there for about half an hour (30 minutes). Get it out again and use a rolling pin to roll it until it is quite thin. Use a round biscuit cutter to cut about 25 biscuits. Now grease some baking trays. Put your biscuits onto the trays, prick them with a fork and cook them for about 15 minutes. Remove them from the oven very carefully, with an adult's help. After 2 or 3 minutes put them on a wire rack to cool. Now they are ready to eat. Yum!

What a muddly way of writing a recipe!

Can you do better?

✐ Write it again, but as a well presented recipe.

✐ Underline the ingredients and all the key points in the method.

✐ List the ingredients.

✐ Write the method with numbered instructions.

✐ Do not use words you do not need.

✐ If you are lucky you may get a chance to make some biscuits using your improved recipe.

© Andrew Brodie Publications ✓ PO Box 23, Wellington, Somerset, TA21 8YX ✓ www.andrewbrodie.co.uk

● Teachers' Notes

✓ This unit focuses on the sentence level requirements to put commas in sentences and to experiment with deleting words from sentences. It also looks at text level work on writing instructions.

✓ In your whole class teaching resources this week you will need:
(a) reading materials to investigate using commas in sentences;
(b) instructional texts with bullet points.

✓ **Sheet B** This looks at deleting unnecessary words from sentences.

✓ **Sheet C** Inserting commas into sentences.

✓ **Sheet D** The topic of having a bath or shower has been chosen for this work as it is something that should be familiar to all children, but each child will produce a slightly different list of instructions.

Use this box to write your own notes ready for the next time you use this unit.

© Andrew Brodie Publications ✓ PO Box 23, Wellington, Somerset, TA21 8YX ✓ www.andrewbrodie.co.uk

Removing unnecessary words.

The sentences below all have unnecessary words in them.

Underline the words that are not needed.

Rewrite the sentences without the extra words.

The first one has been done for you.
You may need to change the order of words in sentence 5.

1. My friends are playing games <u>because</u> so that they don't get bored.

   <u>My friends are playing games so that they don't get bored.</u>

2. My best friend Paul, he is eight today.

   _____

3. I like tomatoes and carrots and beans and peas.

   _____

4. In my house the windows of my house are all square.

   _____

5. My tie has two colours of stripes, red and blue.

   _____

Discuss your answers with a friend.

Did you both remove the same words?

© Andrew Brodie Publications ✓ PO Box 23, Wellington, Somerset, TA21 8YX ✓ www.andrewbrodie.co.uk

● **Sentence level work**

Name: Date:

Putting commas into sentences.

A comma is sometimes put before a joining word.

And, but, or, so, then and **because** are all joining words.

Commas are used to split a sentence into parts.
They help you to read with expression.

Put commas before the joining words in the following sentences.

1. I would like to go out to play but it is too wet.

2. Would you like to go to the beach or would you rather visit the zoo?

3. There was a robbery so the police were called.

4. First she turned on the light then she started to read her book.

5. I like chocolate but I don't eat it too often.

6. He wanted a new computer game so he saved all his pocket money.

7. She didn't really like board games because she didn't always understand the rules.

Now read the sentences aloud pausing briefly at the comma.

Did you know joining words are also called conjunctions?

© Andrew Brodie Publications ✓ PO Box 23, Wellington, Somerset, TA21 8YX ✓ www.andrewbrodie.co.uk

Name: Date:

Writing instructions.

Write a clear list of instructions for having a bath ...

... or having a shower.

Write the instructions clearly.

Put the title at the top.

Use either numbers or bullet points.

● Teachers' Notes

✓ This unit covers word level work on the use of capital letters and sentence level work on grammatical agreement. The text level work concerns instructional writing.

✓ **Resources** needed include examples of writing in the first, second and third person, to show how these are used in different types of text. (e.g. diary = 1st person, instructions = 2nd person, narrative = 3rd person.)

Also needed are pictures of routes, etc, that children can turn into written or oral instructions. Here is a sample map which could be enlarged:

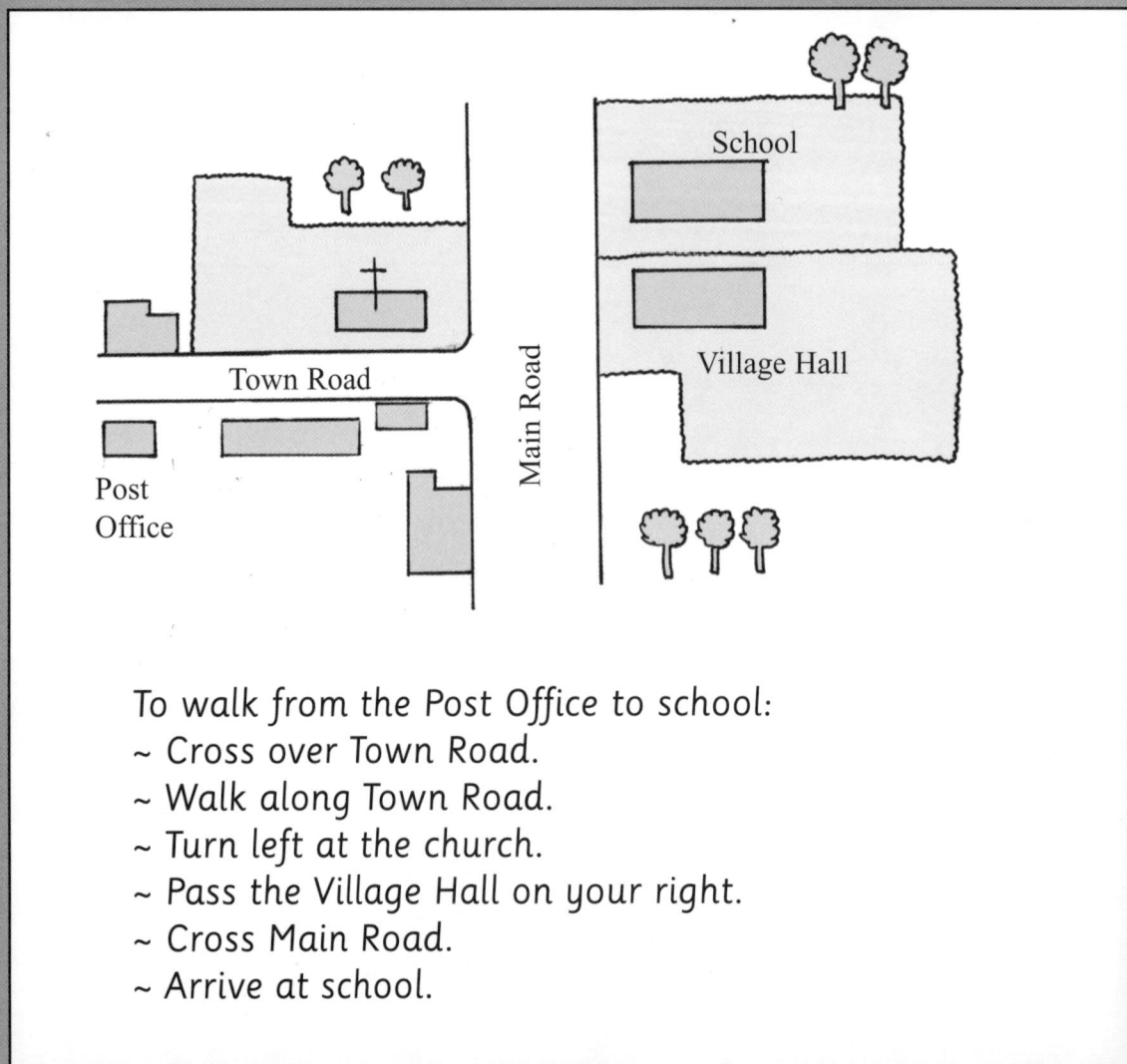

School

Village Hall

Town Road

Main Road

Post Office

To walk from the Post Office to school:
~ Cross over Town Road.
~ Walk along Town Road.
~ Turn left at the church.
~ Pass the Village Hall on your right.
~ Cross Main Road.
~ Arrive at school.

✓ **Sheet B** Adding capitals; introducing the term 'proper noun'.

✓ **Sheet C** Grammatical agreement.

✓ **Sheet D** Writing instructions from a picture, using left, right, forwards and a selection of landmarks.

Name: Date:

Capital letters.

Capital letters are used at the start of sentences.

Capital letters are sometimes used at the start of new lines of poetry.

Capital letters are used at the start of the names of:

people;

places;

days of the week;

months of the year.

> Naming words that need capital letters are called proper nouns.

Rewrite the sentences below,
putting in capital letters where they are needed.
We have done the first one for you.

1. blackpool, torquay and lowestoft are all seaside towns.

   Blackpool, Torquay and Lowestoft are all seaside towns.

2. joseph's birthday is on thursday july 10th.

   _____

3. i am going to visit london with my friends zak and lee.

   _____

4. the weather is usually cold in january.

   _____

5. thirty days has september,
   april, june and november.

   _____

   _____

© Andrew Brodie Publications ✓ PO Box 23, Wellington, Somerset, TA21 8YX ✓ www.andrewbrodie.co.uk

● **Word and sentence level work**

Name: Date:

Grammatical agreement.

Some words go together well …

… and some words never go together.

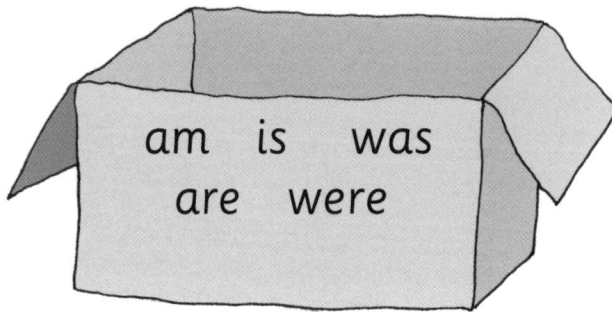

am   is   was
are   were

Choose the correct word from the box to fit into each sentence.

1. I _____ going shopping.

2. The children _____ having a party tomorrow.

3. When I saw them they _____ walking along the road.

4. It _____ going to be cold today.

5. It _____ quite warm yesterday.

6. Next Sunday I _____ going swimming.

7. Yesterday I _____ watching television.

Discuss your answers with a friend.

Which words did you use when things happened in the past?

_____

_____

Name: Date:

Writing instructions.

Can you write instructions to take the dog to find his bone?

He must stay on the pathways until he reaches the bone.

Only use the words that are really needed.

Did you help me to find my bone?

● Teachers' Notes

✓ This unit focuses on ways of taking notes and considering what are the most important points in a text. It also looks at drawing diagrams to aid instructions.

✓ **Resources** Newspaper articles with headlines; examples of lists, notes, instructions, reminders, etc. Instructional diagrams are useful too (origami books are good for these!).

✓ **Sheet B** This encourages the discussion of key points of text by asking children to invent a headline. Paired work is ideal for this.

✓ **Sheet C** This asks children to work in pairs or small groups to list points for or against a topic. You may wish to use a topic that is more relevant to your school situation.

✓ **Sheet D** A set of diagrams to help a child know how to clean their teeth.

Use this box to write your own notes ready for the next time you use this unit.

Name: Date:

Headlines.

Read the articles on this page and invent a good headline for each one.

You can work with a friend to do this.

Sooty the black cat had a lucky escape yesterday when firemen rescued her from the top of a tall chimney. She had been stuck there for several hours before the fire brigade was called.

Last night Sooty was glad to be at home enjoying her tin of tuna.

Mr and Mrs Ferris, owners of Dylan the dog, had a lucky find yesterday. Dylan was busy digging a hole in the garden when he unearthed the gold necklace that Mrs Ferris had lost more than ten years ago.

"I was overjoyed," she said, "when Dylan's frantic digging resulted in my necklace appearing."

"We will be burying an enormous bone for him tomorrow," added Mr Ferris.

Two hundred passengers arriving in Spain for their holiday discovered that their suitcases had all been put on the wrong flight. The holiday-makers were most upset when they realised that their cases had been sent to America by mistake and they had no fresh clothes to wear.

A spokesman for the holiday company said they would all be bought some new clothes and their own suitcases would join them in Spain within 24 hours.

The alarm was raised yesterday when an air-bed with what looked like a child on it was seen floating in the sea off the coast of Norfolk. The lifeboat was launched but, to everyone's relief, the air-bed passenger turned out to be a seal!

Mr R S Cue, a spokesman for the coastguard, said, "It was funny this time, but everyone should be aware of the dangers of using air-beds in the sea."

© Andrew Brodie Publications ✓ PO Box 23, Wellington, Somerset, TA21 8YX ✓ www.andrewbrodie.co.uk

● **Text level work**

Name: Date:

Should people keep pet dogs in flats?

Discuss this with a friend. You might think of reasons **for** keeping pet dogs in flats and you might think of reasons **against** keeping pet dogs in flats.
List your reasons in the two columns below.

<u>For</u>	<u>Against</u>

Did you think of more reasons **for** ...

... or more reasons **against**?

© Andrew Brodie Publications ✓ PO Box 23, Wellington, Somerset, TA21 8YX ✓ www.andrewbrodie.co.uk

Name: Date:

Using diagrams to give instructions.

Use diagrams to help show a young child how to clean their teeth.

You may need to number and label your diagrams.

Make your diagrams clear and simple.

①

○

○

○

○

Use the back of the sheet if you need more boxes.

● Teachers' Notes

✓ The main focus of this unit concerns writing instructions.

✓ **Resources** Dictionaries for Sheet B;
A range of instructions from classroom games, to look at and discuss their merits;
Card, counters, etc. (see Sheet D).

✓ **Sheet B** This work consolidates the spelling and meaning of some of the words encountered in literacy work this term. Encourage children to write definitions in sentences with due regard to punctuation.

✓ **Sheet C** This prepares children for the main Sheet D task. Children should be encouraged to use a fairly easy game to avoid over-complex rules and instructions. Also remind pupils to avoid lengthy sentences and unnecessary words.

✓ **Sheet D** A real task - to make the most of this, stout card, etc., suitable for game making should be available. Inevitably extra time will be needed for this to be successful. The need to keep the rules simple must be stressed to the children.

Use this box to write your own notes ready for the next time you use this unit.

Name: Date:

Word spellings and definitions.

Look at each set of words.
Pick the one that is spelled correctly.
Write it and put a definition beside it.

You will need a dictionary to help you.

I have done the first one for you.

1. digram   (diagram)   diagramme

diagram   A set of pictures that show how something works.

2. sentense   sentence   centense

_____   _____

3. hedline   headlin   headline

_____   _____

4. commer   comma   komma

_____   _____

5. dictionary   dicshunary   dikshionary

_____   _____

● **Sentence and text level work**

Name: Date:

Board games.

Think of a board game you know how to play.   Why do you like it?

Write the name of the game and a clear set of instructions for how to play it.

Now work with a
friend or two …

… and begin to invent
a new board game.

Name: Date:

Making a board game.

I like board games.

This should be fun.

☆ Working with a friend, invent a new board game that could be played in the classroom.

☆ Make your game and try playing it.

☆ Write a clear set of instructions so that other people can play your game.

Remember:

☆ Your game should be attractive.

☆ You should be able to make it from things that are available in the classroom.

☆ Plan it all before you start making it.

☆ List what players will need to use, e.g. dice, counters.

☆ Write clear instructions and rules in the correct order.

☆ Try not to make your game too complicated.

☆ Now everyone can enjoy playing your game. ☆

● Teachers' Notes

✓ This unit has sentence level work on introducing understanding and use of pronouns. It looks at planning episodes of a story.

✓ **Resources** 'Big book' version of 'Jack and the Beanstalk'. Use this for work both on pronouns and on story episodes. You could refer to chapters of books and episodes from TV serials to help pupils to understand the concept of making a story into a sequence of episodes.
Sheets C and D can be amended, if you wish, to use a different story.

✓ **Sheet B** This has work on using some basic pronouns. As an extension activity pupils could be asked to find sentences with pronouns in their own reading books.

✓ **Sheet C** Children are asked to complete a grid dividing 'Jack and the Beanstalk' into five episodes. You could suggest:
Episode 1 - Burying beans and the beanstalk growing.
Episode 2 - The first trip up the beanstalk.
Episode 3 - The second trip up the beanstalk.
Episode 4 - The final trip up the beanstalk.
Episode 5 - Chopping down the beanstalk and end of tale.

✓ **Sheet D** This is an instructional sheet and could also be used for any other story you wish to use.
Depending on the time you are able to devote to this work, you may wish the pupils to write the whole story in episodes or you may ask them to write just one episode.

Use this box to write your own notes ready for the next time you use this unit.

Name: Date:

Pronouns.

A pronoun is a word we can use in place of a noun.

It helps to make our writing less repetitive.

Look at this example:

My friend Peter likes reading and <u>Peter</u> likes playing football.

My friend Peter likes reading and <u>he</u> likes playing football.

Rewrite the following sentences, replacing the underlined nouns with pronouns from the Pronoun Box.

they   she
he   it

1. Cedric went shopping and <u>Cedric</u> bought a game.

_____

2. The girls played outside, then <u>the girls</u> went home for tea.

_____

3. The building is very tall, so <u>the building</u> has a lift to reach the top.

_____

4. Sophia walked along the road and then <u>Sophia</u> crossed to the other side.

_____

_____

5. I like pens and pencils. <u>Pens and pencils</u> come in all sorts of colours.

_____

_____

● **Sentence and text level work**

Name: Date:

Jack and the Beanstalk.

Have you heard the story of 'Jack and the Beanstalk'?

Can you divide it into five episodes?

✏ Decide how to split the story into five clear sections.

✏ The sections can be called chapters or episodes.

✏ In the frame below, write the key points of each episode.

✏ You can use <u>sentences</u>, <u>phrases</u> or just <u>key words</u>.

Episode 1	_____
Episode 2	_____
Episode 3	_____
Episode 4	_____
Episode 5	_____

✏ On the back of the sheet, or in your book, write a short 'character portrait' of three of the characters in the story.

Name: Date:

Now it is your turn to write each episode of your story.

☆ Write the title of your story first.

☆ Start Episode One with a clear beginning and write your story setting with care.

☆ Remember to give each episode a title or number.

☆ Use your character portraits to help you to introduce each of the main characters.

☆ Try to make the end of each chapter so exciting that the reader wants to find out what will happen next.

☆ Use the most interesting verbs and adjectives you can think of to make your story as exciting as possible.

☆ Help each other by reading each other's work and suggesting improvements.

☆ You may want to illustrate your work.

Most importantly…

… enjoy your writing.

● Teachers' Notes

✓ This unit tackles sentence level grammar points on pronouns. These need to be further studied as a part of whole class teaching. The main points to look at should be personal and possessive pronouns and the first, second and third person usage of pronouns - examples are given on Sheet B.

Text level work is on first person accounts of incidents and language to create 'mood'.

✓ **Resources** Fiction with examples of settings, moods, suspense, etc. and fiction using first person accounts.

✓ **Sheet B** Using personal and possessive pronouns.

Personal pronouns: him, her, it, she, he, I, me, we, us, you, they, them.
Possessive pronouns: my, mine, our, ours, his, hers, its, your, yours, their, theirs.
Extension: finding sentences with first, second and third person pronouns.
First person: I, me, we, us.
Second person: you.
Third person: he, him, she, her, they, them.

✓ **Sheet C** Words and phrases to create moods. Ideal for paired or small group work.

✓ **Sheet D** Using the writing frame provided (or using exercise books) writing a first person account of a chosen story.

Use this box to write your own notes ready for the next time you use this unit.

© Andrew Brodie Publications ✓ PO Box 23, Wellington, Somerset, TA21 8YX ✓ www.andrewbrodie.co.uk

Name: Date:

Pronouns.

☆   Some pronouns are called <u>personal</u> because they are about <u>who</u> or <u>what</u> is being referred to.

☆   Some pronouns are called <u>possessive</u> because they are about <u>the possessor</u> (or owner) of what is being referred to.

☆   Look at these examples: I am tidying my bedroom.

                            He is tidying his bedroom.

I and he are personal pronouns.

My and his are possessive pronouns.

In the following sentences, underline the personal pronouns in red and the possessive pronouns in blue.

1.   The banana in the fridge is mine.

2.   Fred is a dog. He likes long walks.

3.   Whose turn is it, mine or yours?

4.   We are going shopping, then we will cook tea.

5.   They said the football was theirs.

6.   I like them.   7.   Will you play with us today?

8.   Does this game belong to them?

On the back of this sheet write three sentences.
One must include a first person pronoun: I, me, we, us.
One must include a second person pronoun: you.
One must include a third person pronoun: he, him, she, her, they, them.

● **Word and text level work**

Name: Date:

Mood.

☆ The words and phrases we use can help to create the 'mood' or 'feel' of our writing.

☆ Working with a friend, fill the boxes below with some really good words and phrases to match the mood shown.

☆ You may need to look in some books to help you with ideas.

<u>Eerie quietness</u>	<u>Calm and peaceful</u>

<u>Gradually becoming more and more scared</u>	<u>Sadness</u>

Share your ideas with your friends.

You could make a class 'mood bank'.

© Andrew Brodie Publications ✔ PO Box 23, Wellington, Somerset, TA21 8YX ✔ www.andrewbrodie.co.uk

Name: Date:

Think of a story
you know.

Pretend you are the main
character in the story.

✎   Writing a story in the first person can be a bit like writing a very exciting diary.

✎   Use the frame below to write a story, or part of a story.

✎   Choose a story you know well and write it as if it happened to you.

✎   Continue on the back of the sheet if you need to.

● Teachers' Notes

✓ This unit deals with sentence level work on grammatical agreement between pronouns and verbs, and text level work on planning and writing an extended story.

✓ **Resources** Stories divided into chapters.
'Paper booklets' for writing task (see Sheet D).

✓ **Sheet B** Children should be encouraged to think about the verb 'to be' as it is not obvious to them that it is a verb.

✓ **Sheet C** Emphasis should be placed on the fact that each 'key point' will be the basis of a whole 'chapter' of the story.

✓ **Sheet D** An instructional sheet for enlarging or putting on an OHP for group use.

Children will need reminding about organising their writing into paragraphs within each chapter.

This extended writing task may take several sessions to complete well.

Use this box to write your own notes ready for the next time you use this unit.

● Word level work

| YEAR 3 | Term 3 | UNIT 23 | Sheet B |

Name: Date:

Grammatical Agreement.

The first column of the table below shows a list of pronouns.

The other columns all contain verbs.

Your job is to fill in the correct forms of the verbs to go with the pronouns.

We have done the first verb to show you what to do.

Pronouns	Verbs				
	go	walk	like	sing	climb
I	go				
you	go				
he	goes				
she	goes				
we	go				
they	go				

Did you notice a pattern in the verbs?

Choose a verb from the table to put in each of the sentences below.

1. I like to ____ for a _____ with my dog.

2. My best friend is Mike. He _____ to _____ trees.

3. They will _____ at the concert tonight.

4. We ____ to the hall and we _____ in assembly every day.

5. Do you _____ chocolate?

6. He _____ football and she _____ rugby.

3

● **Text level work**

Name: Date:

Story Planning.

Do you remember how you planned your 'Jack and the Beanstalk' story?

Now you are going to plan a story of your own.

✏ Think of the sort of story you like.

✏ Decide what will happen in your story.

✏ What will your characters be like?

✏ Write the title of your story here: _____

Chapter 1	_____
Chapter 2	_____
Chapter 3	_____
Chapter 4	_____
Chapter 5	_____

© Andrew Brodie Publications ✓ PO Box 23, Wellington, Somerset, TA21 8YX ✓ www.andrewbrodie.co.uk

Name: Date:

Writing your story.

☆ You are going to use your plan to help you write your story.

☆ You must put your title at the beginning.

☆ Your story must be in clear chapters.

☆ Your story will be written on folded paper so that it can be made into a book.

Remember:

☆ Draft your work first.

☆ Use character portraits and interesting settings.

☆ Use interesting words to create the mood of each chapter.

☆ Write each chapter in clear paragraphs.

☆ Use illustrations.

☆ Your finished work must be written very carefully so that other people can read your book.

☆ Most importantly - **enjoy your writing**.

You are the author of this story ...

... so remember to put your name on the front cover with the title.

© Andrew Brodie Publications ✓ PO Box 23, Wellington, Somerset, TA21 8YX ✓ www.andrewbrodie.co.uk

● Teachers' Notes

✓ This unit looks at the conventions of writing dialogue, and writing a book review for a specified audience.

✓ **Resources** Book extracts showing ways of presenting dialogue. A selection of sample book reviews. (In addition to resources normally found in schools, newspapers and magazines are a good source of book reviews.)

✓ **Sheet B** Exercises on the presentation of dialogue.

✓ **Sheet C** Grid to lay out information on a book, ready for writing a review. You will need to guide children on their choice of books and on who their review audience might be.

✓ **Sheet D** Instructional sheet, for enlarging or use with an OHP, for group or class use.

Use this box to write your own notes ready for the next time you use this unit.

© Andrew Brodie Publications ✓ PO Box 23, Wellington, Somerset, TA21 8YX ✓ www.andrewbrodie.co.uk

Name: Date:

Dialogue.

Rewrite the dialogue below, putting in the missing punctuation and setting out the writing correctly.

Remember to use speech marks.

Start a new line whenever someone starts speaking.

Why can't I play outside with my friends? asked Jim. Because it's not safe, said Mum for the third time that day. She was getting quite annoyed that Jim would not accept this. But it's not fair, everyone else is allowed to, whined Jim, still trying to wear his mother down. I'm sure it isn't everybody, replied Mum. Those who are there are much older than you. You are not playing outside and that's final.

© Andrew Brodie Publications ✓ PO Box 23, Wellington, Somerset, TA21 8YX ✓ www.andrewbrodie.co.uk

● **Text level work**

Name: Date:

Use your reading book …

… or choose another book you know.

✎   Use the book you have chosen, to fill in all the information on the chart below.

✎   Work very carefully because you will need this chart ready to write a book review.

Book title:

Author:

Publisher:

Reason for choosing this book:

Characters in the book:

What the book is about:

What I think of the illustrations:

Who, I think, would like to read this book:

Other comments:

© Andrew Brodie Publications ✓ PO Box 23, Wellington, Somerset, TA21 8YX ✓ www.andrewbrodie.co.uk

Name: Date:

Writing a book review.

☆   You are going to use the plan you have made, to write a really interesting book review.

☆   Your review should help a reader to decide whether they would enjoy the book.

☆   It should also tell a new reader what sort of book it is. Is it funny or serious? Is it about people or animals? Does it have a happy ending? (But don't say what actually happens in the end - the reader has to find that out!)

☆   It is important to include all the important details that will help someone to find the book. Don't forget to write the title, the name of the author and the name of the publisher.

Will your review help me to choose a book?

Important:

☆   Before you begin, decide who you are writing your review for. A book review for a five year old child would be quite different from a book review for a ten year old child.

☆   Have fun!

© Andrew Brodie Publications ✓ PO Box 23, Wellington, Somerset, TA21 8YX ✓ www.andrewbrodie.co.uk

● Teachers' Notes

✓ This unit covers sentence level work on the use of conjunctions, and text level poetry work using onomatopoeia and alliteration.

✓ **Resources** Texts showing a wide range of conjunctions.
Poetry with distinctive rhythms, as well as poetry with clear examples of onomatopoeia and alliteration.

✓ **Sheet B** An exercise on putting conjunctions in sentences.

✓ **Sheet C** Working on alliteration and onomatopoeia.

✓ **Sheet D** Instructions and a writing frame for writing a poem. The choice of subject for the poem has been left for the teacher to decide or to offer guidance on.

Simple poems with a regular beat can be clapped along with to help understanding of rhythm in poetry.

Use this box to write your own notes ready for the next time you use this unit.

© Andrew Brodie Publications ✓ PO Box 23, Wellington, Somerset, TA21 8YX ✓ www.andrewbrodie.co.uk

Name: Date:

Conjunctions.   Conjunctions are joining words.

> Just using **and, but** and **then** can get rather boring

> Try using **so, if, while, when, since, though** or **however.**

Use the lines below to write six sentences.

Use a different conjunction in each sentence.

1. _____

2. _____

3. _____

4. _____

5. _____

6. _____

Did you remember to put commas where they were needed?

Read your sentences to your friends.

● **Word and text level work**

Name: Date:

Onomatopoeia and alliteration.

Onomatopoeia sounds like on-o-mat-o-pee-a.

Sounds crazy to me.

Words like **hiss** sound like what they are describing.

This is called onomatopoeia.

Work alone or with a friend to find ten more words that sound like what they are describing.

_____   _____

_____   _____

_____   _____

_____   _____

_____   _____

Alliteration is where we use words beginning with the same sound.

For example: Giggling girls gathering grapes.

Write six alliterative phrases.

_____

_____

_____

_____

Name: Date:

Poetry writing.

Write a poem in the frame below.

Try to use onomatopoeia or alliteration.

● Teachers' Notes

✓ This unit includes sentence level work on words and phrases used to sequence events, and text level work on writing letters.

✓ **Resources** Texts including a variety of sequencing words. Examples of letters, some formal and some informal. Also ensure that pupils see samples of letters written on the computer - some children may use the computer to write their own letter, instead of using the Sheet D writing frame.

✓ **Sheet B** Work on sequencing words.

✓ **Sheet C** Instructional sheet on planning a letter. The topic of the letter has been deliberately excluded, to allow you to guide pupils' work according to what is relevant in the class at the time. It is important to write real letters to make this task meaningful. The letter can be drafted on paper or in writing books. Suitable topics include:

Thank you letters, perhaps after a school fete or after a visitor has been into school.

Letters requesting information, perhaps linked to local geography and history work.

Letters to politicians.

Invitations.

✓ **Sheet D** This is a letter writing frame. It has been printed boldly so that it can be placed behind a sheet of plain paper, attached with paper clips or a clipboard.

Use this box to write your own notes ready for the next time you use this unit.

Name: Date:

Putting events in order - a **sequence** of events.

> Words like first and **next** ...

> ... help you to know the sequence of events in a piece of writing.

Look for the words in this text that help you to know the order in which things happen - the sequence of events.

Underline the words you find.

A special day on holiday

The first thing that Davy did that day was to go for a long walk. Meanwhile his parents made breakfast.

Later on that morning the family all enjoyed a swim, after which they had a game of tennis. Shortly before midday they were ready for a picnic lunch.

Finally, after a happy afternoon on the beach, the family went indoors for the evening.

Write the words that you found:

_____   _____

_____   _____

_____   _____

> Did you find all six words?

● **Text level work**

Name: Date:

Planning a letter.

Who will you write to?

Why are you writing? The first paragraph of your letter should include a sentence or two about why you are writing.

The middle paragraph, or paragraphs, should include the main points of your letter.

The final paragraph should 'round off' your letter.

Set your letter out as shown below.

You write **Dear** and a name here.

Write your own address at the top right.

The date goes under your address.

This is where you start writing.

On this line you could put: love from, best wishes from Yours sincerely, or Yours faithfully,.

Your name goes here.

Now use some paper or a new page of your writing book to write a letter.

© Andrew Brodie Publications ✓ PO Box 23, Wellington, Somerset, TA21 8YX ✓ www.andrewbrodie.co.uk

_____

_____

_____

_____

_____

_____

_____

_____

_____

_____

_____

_____

_____

_____

_____

_____

_____

_____

_____

_____

_____

_____

_____

_____

_____

_____

_____

© Andrew Brodie Publications ✓ PO Box 23, Wellington, Somerset, TA21 8YX ✓ www.andrewbrodie.co.uk

● Teachers' Notes

✓ This unit focuses on the text level requirement of awareness of uses of commas in sentences, and text level work on writing notes and messages. Within this, pupils should be given the opportunity to use ICT to produce their notes and messages. Use of email could be helpful in this context.

✓ **Resources** A variety of types of messages, particularly those in note form rather than formal prose.

Texts showing ways of using commas. It is important to talk about commas used to interrupt a sentence where there is no conventional conjunction. For example:

My best friend, who lives just down the road, calls at my house every day.

These are bracketing commas and usually, but not always, appear in pairs. Note that the phrase between the commas can be missed out and the sentence still makes sense.

✓ **Sheet B** Exercise on commas.

✓ **Sheet C** Writing messages in note form.

✓ **Sheet D** Writing an imaginary letter to a favourite author. This is to consolidate work on presentation of letters, setting them out in clear paragraphs. This is an instructional sheet designed to be enlarged for display or to be shown on an OHP.

Use this box to write your own notes ready for the next time you use this unit.

Name: Date:

Using commas.

Commas are used instead of writing **and** or **or** in lists ...

... and to separate parts of a sentence.

Put the missing commas into the sentences below.

The number in brackets tells you how many commas should be in the sentence.

(3) For tea we had lettuce tomato cucumber cheese and bread.

(1) Today I might go to school in the car but if the rain stops I will walk.

(2) My best friend who lives just down the road calls at my house every day.

(1) Most of the class wanted to go out and play football while a few said they would prefer to stay inside.

(1) Do you like strawberry ice-cream or is vanilla your favourite?

(2) Bradley's dog a large golden labrador loved long walks on the beach.

(2) At school today we have literacy numeracy history and art.

Read your sentences aloud, pausing briefly at each comma.

Now try writing two sentences of your own. The first sentence should contain a list of things you would like to do. The second sentence should use one comma or two commas to separate parts of the sentence.

_____

_____

_____

_____

● **Text level work**

Name: Date:

Writing notes and messages.

We often need to write short notes to other people.

We do not need to write long sentences for these.

This note was written by a child who had taken a telephone message for his mother.

Mum,
Aunty Jill rang.
Ring her. Urgent.

Nick

Use this box to write a message arranging to play with your best friend at the weekend.

Remember to arrange time and place.

In the next box write yourself a reminder note about the things you need to remember at school this week.

Name: Date:

Letter writing.

☆ Plan and write an imaginary letter to one of your favourite authors.

☆ Remember how to set out your letter.

☆ You could write this letter on a clean page of your book, or use a letter writing frame behind some plain paper.

☆ Write your letter in three clear paragraphs.

☆ Write your letter in three clear paragraphs:

Paragraph One - tell the author why you are writing.

Paragraph Two - the main points of the letter. You may want the author to know why you particularly like his other books.

Paragraph Three - a finishing off paragraph.

☆ The author is not one of your friends so you might finish the letter with:

Yours sincerely,   or   Best wishes,

© Andrew Brodie Publications ✓ PO Box 23, Wellington, Somerset, TA21 8YX ✓ www.andrewbrodie.co.uk

● Teachers' Notes

✓ This unit is centred around the text level requirement to present alphabetically ordered informational texts.

✓ **Resources** Whole class texts ordered alphabetically.
Dictionaries.
Reference books.

✓ **Sheet B** Sorting into alphabetical order by first and second letters.

✓ **Sheet C** Linked by topic to Sheet B, this asks children to present information alphabetically. It is important to ensure children understand that they are to present facts and not opinions.

✓ **Sheet D** Instructional sheet regarding making an informational text in booklet or poster form. Children should be encouraged to use reference skills to find accurate information.

Use this box to write your own notes ready for the next time you use this unit.

© Andrew Brodie Publications ✓ PO Box 23, Wellington, Somerset, TA21 8YX ✓ www.andrewbrodie.co.uk

Name: _____ Date: _____

Alphabetical order.   Sort the sports below into alphabetical order.

If more than one item begins with the same letter ...

... look at the second letter.

gymnastics

skiing

rowing

cricket

hockey

rugby

swimming

judo

tennis

football

archery

badminton

1. _____

2. _____

3. _____

4. _____

5. _____

6. _____

7. _____

8. _____

9. _____

10. _____

Write the names of six more sports:

_____ _____ _____

_____ _____ _____

Now write them again, in alphabetical order:

_____ _____ _____

_____ _____ _____

● **Sentence and text level work**

Name: Date:

My favourite sports.

Make an information sheet about your three favourite sports. ✓

List them in alphabetical order.

Write two or three clear sentences about each sport.

> I support Norwich City does not help the reader understand the sport

> A football team has eleven players is more helpful information.

1. _____

_____

_____

_____

_____

_____

2. _____

_____

_____

_____

_____

3. _____

_____

_____

_____

Name: Date:

Giving information.

Design a poster to give
people information.

Choose an
interesting subject.

☆   First of all, decide what your poster will be about.

☆   Use information books to make sure you are writing
     accurate facts.

☆   Make your poster look attractive so that people want to
     read it. Pictures will help.

☆   Use very neat writing, with large, clear lettering.

☆   Your choice of subject is important. It could be something
     that particularly interests you, or it could be connected
     with work you are doing at school.

Most importantly …
Enjoy your writing.

● Teachers' Notes

✓   This unit deals with the text level requirement to recount the same incident in a variety of ways.

✓   **Resources**   Any text suited to being presented as a story, a letter or a news report.

Sheets B, C and D are interlinked and all work from the same chosen topic.

Preparatory whole class work on choosing a subject to write about needs to be done before starting on Sheets B, C or D.

✓   **Sheet B**   Presenting an incident as a short story. Choice of subject could be a topical news item, a well-known tale or an incident from the pupils' own experiences, such as a holiday or a day out.

✓   **Sheet C**   Presenting the same incident as a letter. This could be a letter to a friend about the incident or a letter written from one character in the incident to another. The letter is particularly appropriate if the chosen incident is outside the pupils' own experience.

✓   **Sheet D**   Presenting the incident as a newspaper report.

Whilst all the sheets are produced with writing frames, you may prefer to use them as instructional sheets, with the children writing in their books.

Some pupils may present their work using a word processor.

Use this box to write your own notes ready for the next time you use this unit.

© Andrew Brodie Publications ✓ PO Box 23, Wellington, Somerset, TA21 8YX ✓ www.andrewbrodie.co.uk

Name: Date:

A special incident.

> Your teacher has talked about a special incident to write about.

> Remember to give your writing a title.

In the writing frame below, write about the incident as a really good short story. Try to use interesting words that make the story exciting for people to read.

A letter about the special incident.

This could be a really exciting letter. Tell somebody about the special thing that has happened. Make it sound amazingly interesting.

Name: Date:

A newspaper report.

Think about the incident you have written about this week.

Pretend you are a newspaper reporter. Write a report for the local newspaper.

Remember to write an eye-catching headline - you want people to read your story.

● Teachers' Notes

✓   This unit addresses the text level requirements to summarise a passage of writing, and to revise work on note-taking.

✓   **Resources**   Children should have access to a range of books about various creatures.

✓   **Sheet B**   Summarising a passage. Lower attainers may need a simplified text - one about an animal, bird or insect would be appropriate.

✓   **Sheet C**   When children have found a range of resources and chosen a creature to find out about, they should have a limited time (perhaps 10 to 15 minutes) in which to jot down their notes.

✓   **Sheet D**   Pupils should write about the creature that they have researched by referring to their own notes and <u>not</u> looking back at their source materials. This is quite a challenge and will demonstrate the effectiveness of their notes to the children.

Use this box to write your own notes ready for the next time you use this unit.

Name: _____ Date: _____

Weather.

Do you ever watch the weather forecast?

Everyone is interested in the weather. Weather forecasts can be heard on the radio or seen on television or read in the newspapers every day. Why is there this interest? The farmer needs to know when to harvest his crops and the sailor needs to know when it is safe to go to sea.

Different types of weather can be experienced in different regions of the world. It is extremely cold the nearer you go towards the North or South Poles, whereas you can be sure of warmth near the equator. Some weather conditions can cause terrible disasters. Flash floods, long droughts, hurricanes and tornadoes can all cause huge problems and even loss of life.

Over millions of years, the world's weather patterns have been changing. Now scientists are anxiously trying to forecast the effects of global warming. Let us hope that they do not forecast too many disasters.

Try to summarise what the text is all about. Use only two or three sentences.

● **Text level work**

Name: Date:

Notes about a creature.

By looking in books, find out about a creature that interests you. It could be a bird, an insect, a spider or any other type of animal.

It could be a dog like me!

Read about the creature you have chosen.

Look at pictures of it. Find out as much as you can.

In the frame below, write some **notes** that will help you remember your creature. You only need to write key words and phrases.

Do not write full sentences. These are notes only.

Draw a simple picture or diagram.

Name: Date:

Writing in detail about your chosen creature.

Use the creature notes you made to help you to write about the creature.

This time you need to use good, clear sentences. You should include accurate information about your creature.

You may wish to draw a detailed picture of your creature.

Most importantly …

… enjoy your writing.

Name: Date:

Writing prompt sheet

The chart below can be photocopied and used with all units as it provides a prompt sheet for all writing activities.

A copy could be stuck into the front of each child's exercise book for use throughout the year.

REMINDERS FOR WRITING

Don't forget:

... to write your name on your work

... to write the date for all new pieces of work

... to use your best handwriting

... to present your work neatly

... to follow all instructions about your work

... to use capital letters and full stops in the correct places

... to use interesting words

... to check your work through carefully

ENJOY YOUR WORK

© Andrew Brodie Publications ✓ PO Box 23, Wellington, Somerset, TA21 8YX ✓ www.andrewbrodie.co.uk

Starting Out
Foundation Stage Mathematics

 Sheila Ebbutt, Fran Mosley and Carole Skinner

a BEAM Education publication

BEAM Education

BEAM Education is a specialist mathematics education publisher, dedicated to promoting the teaching and learning of mathematics as interesting, challenging and enjoyable.

BEAM materials cover teaching and learning needs from the age of 3 to 14. They deal with many of the classroom concerns voiced by teachers of mathematics, and offer practical support and help. BEAM materials include more than 80 publications, as well as a comprehensive range of mathematical games and equipment.

BEAM services include consultancy for companies, institutions and government, and a programme of courses and in-service training for schools, early years settings and local education authorities.

BEAM is an acknowledged expert in the field of mathematics education.

BEAM Education Tel 020 7684 3323
Maze Workshops Fax 020 7684 3334
72a Southgate Road Email info@beam.co.uk
London N1 3JT www.beam.co.uk

Acknowledgements

We are grateful for the contributions of the many members of the Early Childhood Mathematics Group (ECMG) who provided valuable feedback and suggestions at various times. These have helped shape the structure and content of *Starting Out: Foundation Stage Mathematics*.

The ECMG is a working group of the Association of Teachers of Mathematics.

Our thanks also go to:
Dr Sue Gifford, University of Surrey Roehampton
Anna Skinner for planning documents
Manor Park Primary School, Sutton
Minchinhampton Primary School, Gloucestershire
Ridgeway Primary and Nursery School, Croydon
St Bede's Primary School, Redbridge
Surbiton Hill Nursery School, Kingston upon Thames
Whitmore Primary School, Hackney

Published by BEAM Education.
© BEAM Education 2003. All rights reserved.
ISBN 1 903142 00 8
British Library Cataloguing-in-Publication-Data. Data available.
Edited by Henrietta Preston. Designed by Roger Marks.
Photography by Dee Johnston, Sally Greenhill and Len Cross. Additional photography by BEAM.
Qualifications and Curriculum Authority copyright material is reproduced under the terms of HMSO Guidance Note 8.

Foreword

Our understanding of how young children learn about mathematics has grown a lot in recent years; this has raised expectations for children and for those who work with them. Young children's interest in learning about number, for example, is now celebrated and fostered: the new *Curriculum guidance for the foundation stage* in England states that children should "enjoy using and experimenting with numbers". This official statement of intent, linking enjoyment and mathematics, presents a challenge, albeit a welcome one, to those of you whose own mathematics education may have been associated with quite different emotions. The range and diversity of the early years mathematics curriculum also presents a challenge in, for example, encouraging children to experiment with symmetry and measuring, although they may not fully understand either yet. To support children doing this, you need to know where the mathematics is leading, as well as what you might realistically expect young children to learn from it.

You also need to be aware of those things that children have to consciously learn that we can hardly imagine not knowing, like whether it is morning or afternoon and whether or not you have had your dinner yet! Many complex skills that challenge young children, such as those involved in counting, are subconscious for us as adults. Making the necessary skills and knowledge accessible to young children requires a good understanding of how children learn and some creative thinking. Spotting when children are engaging with mathematical ideas and assessing what they have learned from them also requires subtlety and skill, as young children may not be able to verbalise the experience. Therefore, although young children may be engaging with mathematical ideas at a very simple level, teaching them requires a great deal of knowledge and sensitivity, as well as a fund of practical and stimulating activities.

Starting Out offers a real support in meeting the challenges of teaching Foundation Stage mathematics and of helping children become mathematically confident and competent. It draws on the experience of many practitioners' mathematical work with young children, and the expertise of the BEAM team. The result is an extremely accessible resource that encapsulates current best practice and should help everyone to enjoy mathematics in the Foundation Stage.

Dr Sue Gifford

Senior Lecturer
University of Surrey Roehampton

Preface

This is an exciting period for everyone involved in working with young children. For the first time, children aged 3 to 5 have a statutory curriculum in England; a change that has brought both benefits and challenges for practitioners. *Starting Out: Foundation Stage Mathematics* is designed to help you implement the mathematical development section of the curriculum, make the most of its benefits and rise to its challenges.

Starting Out brings together our knowledge of the holistic way in which children learn, the organisational features of early years settings, and the mathematical ideas that are key to the Foundation Stage, and focuses on how to introduce an exciting maths curriculum that incorporates child-initiated play and adult-led activities. *Starting Out* also demonstrates what the maths provision looks like in action. The ideas, activities and suggestions within this publication will help you enhance children's sense of themselves as capable mathematicians and competent learners.

In writing *Starting Out* we aimed to support practitioners in providing a maths curriculum that is meaningful to the children, develops their creative thinking, and gives practitioners and children opportunities for success.

Carole Skinner

BEAM Education

Contents

Introduction   6

How to use this book   8

Section 1: Numbers as labels and for counting

Say and use number names in order in familiar contexts   10

Count reliably up to ten everyday objects   18

Recognise numerals 1 to 9   26

Use developing mathematical ideas and methods to solve practical problems   34

Section 2: Calculating

In practical activities and discussion begin to use the vocabulary involved in addition, subtraction and comparing numbers   42

Beginning to relate addition to combining two groups of objects and subtraction to "taking away"   50

Find one more or one less than a number from 1 to 10   58

Use developing mathematical ideas and methods to solve practical problems   66

Section 3: Shape, space and measures

Use language such as "greater", "smaller", "heavier" or "lighter" to compare quantities   74

Talk about, recognise and recreate simple patterns   82

Use language such as "circle" or "bigger" to describe the shape and size of solid and flat shapes   90

Use everyday words to describe position   98

Use developing mathematical ideas and methods to solve practical problems   106

Section 4: Planning, assessment and resources

Planning for success   114
   exemplar plans   116

Assessment activities   120
Resources
   numbers as labels and for counting   126

   calculating   127

   shape, space and measure   128

Most useful mathematical learning at the Foundation Stage arises from play that enables children to develop mathematical understanding and gain confidence in their abilities, almost as a by-product of having fun.

Anyone who has worked with children of this age will know that they have their own ideas about what they want. They are capable of great concentration, unquenchable curiosity, wonderful imagination and seemingly irrational determination. These qualities will help them learn if we can capture their imagination and attention by providing a stimulating and well-balanced environment.

Starting from where children are

Mathematics learning for 3-, 4- and 5-year-olds should draw upon what they have already experienced at home. It is important to find out what children know and are interested in and to use this as a starting point for activities.

Children progress at different rates. Some find learning easy, and need broad and challenging situations to deepen their understanding; others require a lot of support. All children, however, need to meet mathematical ideas in many different situations, and to meet them at a level that suits them.

To help you do this:

build on what happens in the children's everyday lives and show that what matters to them matters to you too	*For example, if it snows, adapt the plans for the morning: make snow people and talk about which one is tallest, fattest or widest.*
observe what children do and say, then use this information to provide further activities	*For example, a practitioner working with children who were fascinated by circles, spirals and rotation set up a hands-on exhibition of turning objects. This included egg whisks, screws and screwdrivers, taps, and table-top mincers to feed dough into. The group used the exhibition to generate a lot of discussion.*
develop a partnership with parents and carers	*Share your maths plans for the term with parents and carers. Discuss with them the ways in which they can support the child's mathematical development.*
build on children's successes to inspire confidence in their ability to be mathematical problem solvers	*Identify children's successes with them and help them to reflect on what they have achieved.*

Mathematics provision in the nursery

Set up a mathematically rich environment where children will experience mathematical ideas in a purposeful way.

Provide:

>> interesting and varied resources: number tracks for the floor; calculators and large wooden or plastic numerals; dice and dominoes; construction materials; regular and irregular shapes (2D and 3D); real-life measuring instruments such as weighing scales, clocks, calendars and watches, rulers, tape measures and height charts; mathematical games and puzzles; collections of interesting objects such as "square things"; and books about numbers or shapes

>> mathematical displays that children help create, or can interact with, such as: portraits of the children made from sticky shapes; a collection of twenty very small things that fit in a matchbox; or a pattern frieze

>> stimulating and challenging activities that are relevant to the children's lives, with a broad range in which to explore mathematics

>> an insight into how we as adults use mathematical skills each day: show children the charts we make; let them see us counting the chairs; or weighing the ingredients for dough

>> situations in which children can themselves use these skills: helping count the trikes; laying the table; or tidying up

Talking with children

In order to develop children's mathematical learning in an informal and enjoyable way, practitioners should plan when and how to use mathematical language. You and the children should ideally use mathematical language in at least these three different ways:

Discussing relationships

In mathematics, relationships between shapes, positions, sizes and quantities are all important and children need the language to describe and explain these relationships. For example: "Hera is shorter than me", "Daphne has more buttons than me".

Questioning

As children develop a wider range of vocabulary, they are better able to express their curiosity by asking questions, for example: "Why does the picture in the mirror go backwards?"

Predicting and hypothesising

These processes are an important part of true mathematics. Children can learn to ask and answer questions such as: "What would happen if we had more people?", "What might happen if there was another shape to use?" and "Why do these blocks fit better?"

How to use this book

Starting Out: Foundation Stage Mathematics contains four sections. The first three deal with the three areas of mathematical development: number, calculating, and shape, space and measures, and contain chapters on each of the Early Learning Goals. Section four gives advice on planning, and assessment, as well as listing resources for each of the areas of mathematical development. Each section is colour-coded to help you find the information you need, quickly and easily.

Sections 1 to 3

Every chapter consists of four double-page spreads, and follows the same format:

Spread one: About the maths

Read the About the maths pages to find out more about the mathematical skills, knowledge and ideas needed to work towards each of the Early Learning Goals. These pages give a detailed explanation of the mathematics involved, how children learn about this particular aspect of mathematics and how you can promote their learning. Boxed text on the right hand page gives you a feel for the progression children are likely to make in this area of maths during the Foundation Stage.

Spread two: Mathematics provision

These pages provide a selection of child-initiated play and adult-led activities designed to help you help children deepen their understanding of this area of mathematics. The activities include ideas to develop the play and examples of what to say to encourage children to get the most out of each activity. The adult-led activities are divided into yellow, blue, green, grey and pink colour bands to help you relate them to the *Curriculum guidance for the foundation stage* and the *Foundation Stage Profile*. On this spread you'll also find a list of important words and phrases to introduce.

Spread three: Opportunities through the day

Most nursery and reception activities have some mathematical potential. The Opportunities through the day show you how you can bring maths into every area of your setting. Each spread demonstrates engaging activities in four different areas and, over the course of the publication, every area is featured at least once, from the book corner to the outdoor area and from the creative workshop to the water tray.

All activities include a list of resources and suggestions of what to say.

Spread four: Assessing children's development

These pages contain exemplars of children's work, which have been matched with the appropriate stepping stones, Early Learning Goals or objectives.

The format is one you will be familiar with, from the QCA's *Curriculum guidance for the foundation stage* and the *Foundation Stage Profile*. The detailed exemplars are taken from our extensive practical experience.

For more information on assessment and planning, see Section 4.

Section 4

Refer to Section 4 for guidance on summative assessment, advice on planning – including planning for mathematics in daily routines – exemplar plans, and resources listings for each of the three areas of mathematical development.

This chapter is about children learning and saying number names. And about helping children understand that there is a right order in which to say the number names when counting.

Knowing the right order in which to say the number names is as important as knowing the number names themselves: it is almost impossible to count anything successfully unless you know the number names in order. You will notice that children take a while to understand this idea and that many young children think that just saying number names in any order is enough.

Counting successfully is almost impossible if you don't know the number names in order

Some children can recite numbers up to 40 or even 100: this is within the capability of many 5-year-olds and some 4-year-olds. Doing so helps them recognise the tens structure of the number system by spotting the patterns in the number names, and it develops familiarity with them, as well as confidence and positive attitudes. It does not matter that children do not understand all the numbers at this stage.

How children learn about saying number names in order

Lots of children know some number names by the time they are 3 years old. They may know their own age and the ages of people in their family. They may know a bus or door number. Children build on this knowledge by learning additional random number words, such as 4 – the number in their group – or 12 – the number on their T-shirt. They also learn runs of numbers, such as 5, 6, 7, or pairs of number names. Children connect all of these number names together in some sort of order, although it can be a different order every time they count.

Talking, singing, chanting, whispering, reciting, shouting and echoing number counts will help children to learn the number names in the right order. Using their fingers in number rhyme making can help too. Children can become more fluent by exploring the rhythm of counting through making large physical movements, such as hopping or jumping, to accompany number rhymes and songs. Children also learn about number names by acting as apprentices and counting alongside people in a real-life activity or when they are working in the role-play area. And, of course, all the number books you read together and the songs you sing together will also support children's learning.

Helping children learn about saying number names in order

>> Provide collections of appealing and stimulating objects for children to talk about, rearrange and put in order.

>> Discuss with the children what number names they know and create opportunities for them to use number language.

How many balls do you think it will take to fill the bucket?

How many shells can you hold in your hand?

>> Make a feature of numbers in labels around your room, for example: *Look at these 5 paintings of sunflowers*, or *6 aprons hang on these pegs*.

>> Play action games, using hands and feet, as much as possible: *Jump three times then clap your hands.*

>> Make sure that your book corner includes some number picture books; look at the books with the children.

>> Read stories that include number sequences and play finger rhymes such as *One potato, two potato*. Encourage the children to continue the rhyme without you.

>> Sing and dance plenty of number rhymes and songs.

Make a feature of numbers

Singing number rhymes and songs will help children learn about numbers and counting

Progression in saying number names in order

- Child knows some number names

- Child uses some number names spontaneously

- Child joins in with a number rhyme or song

- Child attempts to count along with an adult

- Child can say number sequences to 5 and later to 10, with numbers in the correct order

- Child begins to be able to say number sequence backwards, from 5 or 10 to zero

- Child begins to say the number sequence beyond 10

- Child can say the number that comes after any number up to 9 or even higher

Mathematics provision

Child-initiated play

Important words and phrases

number, zero, one, two, three… to twenty and beyond

bigger, greater, smaller

order

first, second, third… to tenth

last, last but one, next, between, before, after

Children take turns to add their animal to the line

Robot numbers

Turn a role-play area into a "robot repair workshop". Resource with battery-operated toys that have push-button numbers, as well as robots made by the children. Pre-record a tape with counting numbers in a robotic voice for the children to listen to. Develop the play by encouraging the children to pretend to be robots, robot operators and repairers.

Following the trail (outside)

Provide the children with cut-out paper numbers to use to create a number chase in the outdoor area. Show the children how to lay a trail of the same number by sticking the numbers on the wall or scattering them on the ground. Develop the play by supporting the children in describing to others which numbers they are going to follow on the trail.

Get ready to jump

Make a loudhailer from a cardboard cone or use a pretend microphone. Encourage the children to take it in turns to count "One, two, three, jump", through the loudhailer as their friend jumps from one hoop into another and another.

Carry on counting

Make a recording studio with a tape recorder, blank tape, headphones and some pretend or real microphones. Encourage the children to record themselves counting and provide ready-made tapes of children and adults counting in a range of languages. Develop the play by providing "recording cards" to rehearse with: a child takes a card with a single digit on it and either counts up to that number or counts on from that number to 10.

"How to" display

Take three or four photographs during a construction activity or when children are playing a board game or making a book. Give the photographs to the group and suggest that they put the photographs in order and make a "how to…" display. Develop the activity by using "first", "second", "third" and "last" labels.

Adult-led activities

Numbers we know

Discuss with the children the numbers that they know, then ask the group to clap three times and say their favourite number. At the start they all say their number at the same time and then, as the children become more confident, extend the activity by asking children to decide, in pairs, on a number to say after three claps.

Making music

Give each child either a shaker or a drum. Number the drums "one" and the shakers "two". Rehearse making music by telling the children that when you say their number you want them to strike or shake their instrument. Conduct the orchestra by calling out a string of numbers to make music. Extend the activity by adding a third instrument and encouraging the children to make up strings of numbers to compose a tune.

Off we go

Make a rocket by lining up ten numbered chairs. Children take it in turns to pull a wooden or plastic numeral out of the bag and say that number. They then find that numbered chair and sit down on it. When everyone is sitting on a chair, the group whispers "1, 2, 3, 4, 5, 6, 7, 8, 9, 10, off we go". Extend the activity by calling out the number order for disembarking from the rocket.

That's a 6. I wonder whereabouts that will be on the rocket.

Do you think Sadie's number will be after your number?

Teaching Teddy

Introduce a teddy who has difficulties counting. Ask the children to help you teach Teddy the order of the numbers. Explain that Teddy can count to 10 but that he always misses a number out. Count to 10 several times, each time missing out one of the numbers and asking the children which number Teddy missed that time. Extend the activity by missing out two numbers.

How do you know which number Teddy missed saying?

I wonder which number Teddy will miss saying next time.

How can we help Teddy to remember the numbers?

Guess my number

Pick a number card from a bag; don't show it to the children but give them clues to help them decide what it is.

Provide a large number track to help locate and order the numbers. When the group is confident, extend the activity by choosing pairs of children to pick a secret number for the others to guess; support them in giving clues about it.

When you count, it's next after 3.

It's between 6 and 8.

It's the number before 10.

Count on

Give each child a plastic counting animal and ask them to sit in a circle. Tell the children that they are going to take turns to add their animal to a line in the centre of the circle, as fast as they can, while everyone counts how many there are. Explain that they have one minute to make as long a line as possible. Only when the child whose turn it was is back in their place can the next child take their turn.

I wonder if we'll be able to line up fifteen animals before the sand runs out.

What number would you have said next?

13

Opportunities through the day

Book corner

Resources

Number books, counting books, rhyme and song books

Large laminated pictures to go with songs and rhymes

Soft toys and puppets as characters in stories containing numbers

Activities

Make a class number book using photographs of the children: take photographs of them standing in different sized groups and arrange the photos into a book. Or use them in a wall display.

Act out number rhymes and stories using objects, toys and puppets.

Make an illustrated book of children's favourite number rhymes, using the children's paintings and drawings.

Can you teach Teddy a number rhyme?

How far can you count to?

ICT area

Resources

Tape recorder, tapes of counting rhymes and made tapes of children singing

Blank tapes

Activities

Children say numbers into the tape recorder and play it back to each other, listening and using their fingers to illustrate the numbers being said.

Listen to counting tapes in a range of languages.

Children make a "demo tape" of themselves singing number rhymes, to take home.

I wonder what number comes next.

Shall we say the numbers together?

Outdoor area

Resources

Redundant CDs
Circles of material and glue
Numbered skittles and balls
Planks

Activities

Stick circles of material to CDs. Thread them with string through the centre of the material and then attach them to a fence. Now play "CD Flip": discuss with the children how many discs to flip to the shiny side, and then flip them.

Prop up two planks to create a long skittle alley and line up the numbered skittles at the end of it. Children take it in turns to roll a ball to knock down the skittles and then discuss what number skittles were knocked down.

Have we got enough?

Which numbers did you knock down?

Sand tray

Resources

Sieves
Small pebbles
Small plastic or wooden animals
Hole-making equipment

Activities

Hide some small pebbles in the dry sand tray; scoop up a sieve full of sand and sieve out the pebbles. Discuss how many pebbles are left in the sieve.

Make some holes in the damp sand with a cylinder and fill them with small plastic animals and discuss the number of objects in the holes.

What's your favourite number?

How many have we got?

Assessing children's development

If a child	Then they may be on this step
Mentions numbers they know, in talking with an adult about ages Makes comments about the number of conkers collected so far, saying there are "lots, hundreds" Joins in with number rhymes and songs, but is unsure what number comes next Finds some wooden numerals and takes them to an adult to talk about	Show an interest in numbers and counting Use some number names and number language spontaneously Enjoy joining in with number rhymes and songs Use number words in play Seek out others to share experiences
Looks at a birthday card and talks about people's ages Recites a number rhyme alone with some of the numbers in the correct order Chooses to play with a number game or a game involving dice Talks about which bit of the jigsaw they will do first Says "three" when the large dice lands that way up	Show curiosity about numbers by offering comments or asking questions Use some number names accurately in play Show increasing independence in selecting and carrying out activities
Can play a game where you say a number and they say the next one in sequence Points out errors made by "silly teddy" in counting to 5 or 10 Recites a number rhyme where the numbers go as high as 10, and gets the numbers in the correct order Counts backwards from 5 or more as part of a story	Show increased confidence with numbers by spotting errors in number sequence Say the number after any number up to 9 Begin to count beyond 10 Display high levels of involvement in activities

Jamal said "I can sing 10 little crocodiles, listen… 10 little, 9 little, 8 little, 7 little crocodiles… all swam away"

Grey level

Age 4.11

If a child	Then they may have reached these objectives
Can find the "first" page in the book or point to the "second" doll in the row	Say number names in order
Can say which of two numbers comes first in the number sequence	Order numbers up to 10
Joins in the chanting of number sequences over 10	Continue to be interested, motivated and excited to learn
Counts competently in a language other than English	
Continues a sequence over 10, unsupported	Say and use number names up to 20 with confidence
Recites an entire number rhyme or song where the numbers to 10 go in reverse order, for example, *Ten-in-the-bed* and gets the numbers in the correct order	Sustain involvement and persevere
Says what number comes before or after 8, 12 or 17 without going back to 1 again	

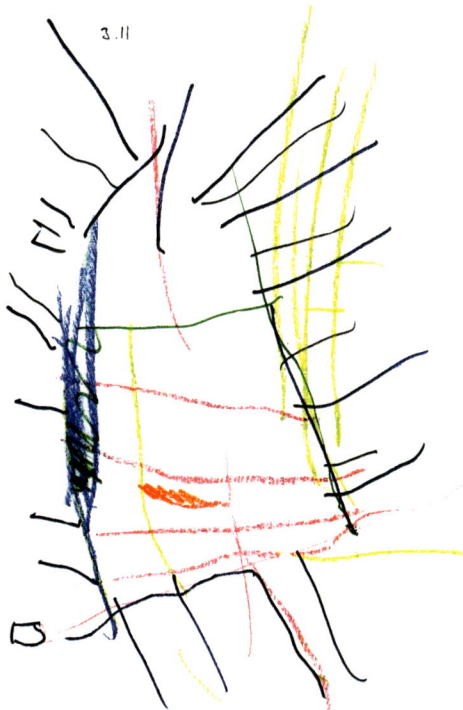

Evie pointed to her drawing and said "Look a spider with lots of legs; hundreds".

Yellow level

Age 3.11

About the maths

This chapter is about ways of helping children move on from just saying the number names in order to being able to count objects.

There are two meanings of counting in early childhood maths. There is saying the number names in order, like counting to 10 when you are playing hide and seek, and there is counting how many objects there are. The second kind of counting requires more understanding and more skill, and as adults we often forget what a complex task this kind of counting is.

Once children know the number names in order, other skills they need to learn are:

>> coordinating saying one number with touching one object at a time

>> separating the objects counted from those not counted

>> recognising a small group of objects without counting

Two concepts that underpin later understanding are that the final number said describes "how many" (cardinality) and that rearranging the objects does not affect the amount (conservation).

How children learn about counting

Children learn to count things through practice so the more often they meet occasions when they need to count, the easier they will find it. When children first start to count, they count things as an activity in itself and not necessarily to answer the question "How many?". It is only later that they understand that the purpose of counting is not just saying the words in order. Counting is often a social activity and, as they begin to learn the sequence of number words, children imitate the behaviour of adults and start to try to coordinate the saying of the words with pointing or touching the objects they are counting. We can help to develop children's understanding of the reasons for counting by saying why we are counting and the result:

Now we've counted the scissors, we'll know if any get lost.

As children develop their counting skills by, for example, learning the sequence to a higher number and not having to physically touch each object, they begin to understand that it doesn't matter which order the objects are counted in and whether they are in a line, a circle or randomly arranged.

As children's counting skills become more sophisticated, you will notice that they self-correct and put in place checking mechanisms. Counting is a very important skill for children to master: children who can count efficiently have a better chance of success in understanding addition and subtraction and the number system.

Many activities in the outdoor environment present opportunities for counting

Children learn that even if objects are rearranged, there will still be the same number of them

Helping children learn about counting objects

Help children learn how to count by modelling how to do it:

>> Touch each object once as you say a number; explain that you are making sure that you don't count any object twice by putting them in a line or a pot or turning them over as you count each one.

Help children understand why we count:

>> At fruit time, count how many pieces there are and discuss whether there is enough for everyone. Check with the children at tidy-up time that all the scissors are back in the tin and that none are lost.

Help children understand counting:

>> Ask children to count out ten counters from a box of 80. That way, they must decide when to stop counting rather than carrying on until the objects run out.

Help children learn that the number of things stays the same when you rearrange them:

>> Count the children in a group and then rearrange them and re-count. Count bricks in a tower, then knock it down and re-count.

>> Count beads in a string and count again from the other end.

>> Provide interesting things to count. These should include objects that need to be counted and can be moved and touched, like beanbags, as well as objects that don't and can't, like leaves on a plant.

Progression in counting reliably up to ten everyday objects

- Child knows some number names

- Child can recite a sequence of number names in the right order

- Child attempts to count objects, but doesn't match one number name with one object

- Child says just one number for each item counted, up to about 3

- Child says the number names and coordinates it with touching the objects, which might be bricks or counters, up to 5 or 10

- Child can count out a given number of objects from a larger collection

- Child shows an understanding that objects are only counted once and that the last number spoken is the number in the set

- Child can count short-lived things, such as sounds, hops or water drips

- Child understands that the order in which the objects are counted doesn't matter and shows that when necessary, they self-correct or check their counting

- Child is very confident in counting sets of objects up to 20

Mathematics provision

> ## Important words and phrases
> **number, zero, one, two, three… to twenty and beyond**
>
> **How many?, none**
>
> **count**
>
> **enough, more, less, guess, estimate**

Animal families (outside)

Set out four different plastic animal families with a shallow tray containing dry bark. Leave the children to set up the animals in groups in the bark. Children will compare the groups using number language and some will count how many each contains. Introduce more animals and extend children's thinking by asking why they have put some of the animals together.

Traffic jam

Provide a "round the block" road system by cutting black paper into strips and making a crossroads. Resource it with small cars and lorries and some traffic lights. Children will begin to line up the cars at the junctions and some will quantify the traffic jams. Introduce a car park drawn in a grid pattern with ten parking spaces.

Five-in-a-bed

Resource this activity with soft toys, the story or songbook and some small wooden beds or cots. Sing *Ten-in-a-bed* but sing it "forwards" by starting with one in a bed and going as far as five, to begin with. Develop the play by introducing the idea of the children deciding how many can be in the bed to start the song.

Come and count table

Set up a table with a selection of interesting things to handle, discuss and count; provide a variety of different sized boxes and containers too. Develop the play by changing containers, making sure some are lidded, and by adding pencils and pads of sticky notes for any children who want to record their counting.

Vote for us

Explain to the children that when we need to make a decision about something, we can all vote to decide what to do. Suggest that together you decide which book to read next at story time. Display three books and set up props for a voting system: enough counters for one for each child and three different boxes to drop them in is one way of doing it. Discuss how you will know which book most children have chosen.

Extend the activity by encouraging children to count and compare how many counters are in each box.

Providing a variety of things to count increases children's interest

Adult-led activities

Button boxes

Collect together five small boxes containing a selection of buttons and beads; the greater the variety the more interesting the children will find the activity. Ask the children to open each box, choose one button or bead from each and arrange them on a felt square. When they have chosen something from each box, talk about and count their collections together. Extend the activity by suggesting that the children choose five buttons from whichever of the boxes that they want to.

Which two buttons do you like the best?

How many buttons did you take from each box?

Froggie circles

Set out plastic bangles flat on the table and give each child a few small frogs. Take it in turns to put one in a bangle circle, until the children have put all the frogs into the circles. Together, count how many frogs are in each circle. Take it in turns to remove two frogs; until the circles are empty. Extend the activity by asking the children to decide how many frogs can sit inside each bangle.

Which frog circle are you going to choose to count?

I wonder if there will be enough frogs to put one in each circle.

Incey Wincey Spider

Collect ten plastic or pipe-cleaner spiders, a spinner or dice, a piece of transparent "drainpipe" made from a drink container with the base cut off, or a tube, and a spider collection box.

Children spin a spinner and pick up that number of spiders. Encourage the children to count the spiders as they post them into the drainpipe and to re-count as spiders emerge from the tube into the collection box. Extend the activity by singing the *Incey Wincey Spider* song and counting the ten spiders together.

How many spiders did you slide down the drainpipe?

Do you think all the spiders have slid down the drainpipe?

Count the chimes

Tap a chime bar a number of times and ask the children to count silently. With their fingers, they keep count of the number of chimes you made and show the total. Now invite a child to make the chimes and do your own finger counting, with exaggerated gestures. Extend the activity by saying a number first or showing a number card and then making the chimes. Ask the group whether the number of chimes that they heard was the same as the number you said.

Josie thinks it was nine chimes. Who else thinks it was nine?

Dinosaur scoop

Each child in the group takes it in turn to use a container top as a scoop. They scoop up some plastic dinosaurs from the dinosaur tub, then each line up their dinosaurs and count how many they scooped. Discuss with the children how many each of them managed to scoop up. Play several rounds and encourage the children to check by counting each other's dinosaur lines or sometimes count together as a group.

Have you scooped more than five?

Will you have still have seven dinosaurs if you rearrange them?

Bear lines

The children will need fifteen bears, cotton reels, or other objects in each of four different colours, as well as a 1–6 dice and a colour dice or spinner.

Explain to the group that the aim is to see which bear line will be the first to be complete with fifteen bears all the same colour.

Children take it in turns to throw both dice and pick up that many bears of the same colour and put them in a line. Keep taking turns and adding to the lines until one line of bears or cotton reels is complete. Extend the activity by using stacking cubes and making towers of twenty cubes all the same colour.

Which colour bear line do you think will be finished first?

I wonder how we can find out how many bears are in that line.

Opportunities through the day

Cooking area

Resources

Plain biscuits, icing sugar, water, small spoons, bowls, sweets or dried fruit to decorate

Activities

Take two biscuits each. Mix together icing sugar and water to make enough paste to top your biscuits. Spread the icing paste on the biscuits. Now take ten sweets or raisins to decorate your biscuits.

How many raisins have you got?

I wonder how we can find out how many more sweets you need to make ten.

Small-world area

Resources

Park and street scene drawn on A3 card
Cars, people, trees and animals
Small boxes or blocks (for houses)

Activities

With a small group of children, arrange a number of cars on the road, people on the pavement and animals in the park. Count and discuss the numbers doing each activity.

How could we make sure that we count all of them?

Would we still have the same number if we rearranged them?

Water tray

Resources

Plastic lids or boats and a collection of plastic bears
Paper fans
A large, shallow water container to be a lake

Activities

Decide on a number and fill the boats with that number of bears. Use the fans to fan the boats across the lake. After the voyage disembark and count the bears. Then change the number of bears in the boat for the next voyage. Or use ten boats and have a different number of passengers in each boat.

Let's all count together.

Will it help if you touch each object as you count?

Construction area

Resources

A wide range of building materials

Activities

Initiate a ten-piece-palace display. Children choose any ten pieces of construction materials, including recycled ones, and build a palace. Photocopy the ten pieces before a child builds with them or lay individual constructions on the photocopier to make a copy to add to the display. Include children's drawings of the ten blocks that they used, as well as photographs of the completed constructions. Develop the idea by constructing a building together, using ten large cartons.

How many pieces have you used so far?

What will you know when you've counted them all?

Assessing children's development

If a child	Then they may be on this step
Uses a string of number words in no particular order when playing Joins in counting activities but does not know the correct number sequence, and does not use a number word for each object counted Brings you one apple when asked to do so	Show an interest in numbers and counting Enjoy joining in with number rhymes and songs Have a positive approach to new experiences
Recognises the number of spots on a card, dice or domino, without counting, up to about 3 Counts out one, two or three spoons and gives them to you, perhaps with support Attempts to count more than three plates, teddies or cherries, using some numbers in the correct order, and pointing (more or less) to one object for each number word	Use some number names accurately in play Willingly attempt to count, with some numbers in the correct order Recognise groups with one, two or three objects Take initiatives and manage developmentally appropriate tasks
Spots an error when "silly teddy" counts out six skittles Counts out seven teddies to give to you Counts five drumbeats Makes four jumps when asked to do so Counts a set of objects such as toy cars, saying one number for each car as they count, and moving the cars aside to avoid counting them twice	Show increased confidence with numbers by spotting errors in techniques of counting objects Count objects by saying one number name for each item Count out objects from a larger group Count actions or objects that cannot be moved Count an irregular arrangement of objects Display high levels of involvement in activities

Discussing his drawing of a visit to a farm, Luke said "It's a cow. See its face and four legs".

Green level

Age 4.11 years

If a child

Uses counting in order to solve simple problems, such as finding out if there are too many children at the water tray

Uses their fingers to represent numbers up to 10

Tells you with confidence that the number of beans hasn't changed just because you moved them closer together, or spread them out

Uses counting in order to solve problems, such as finding out if there are enough pegs for the coats

Counts sounds, people or objects to 20 or even higher

Checks their counting

Counts things they can't see, but know about, such as the number of trikes in the shed, or people in their home

Uses short-cut methods, for example, count the domino spots by starting with the larger number and counting on: "4, 5, 6. There are 6 spots"

Then they may have reached these objectives

Say number names in order

Count reliably up to ten everyday objects

Work as part of a group or class, taking turns and sharing fairly

Count up to 20

Sustain involvement and persevere

Chantelle counted ten sparkly counters and then drew them.

Grey level

Age 5.7

About the maths

This chapter is about ways of helping children read and write numerals.

Written and printed numbers, when they appear as figures, are called numerals or digits.

There are two main kinds of written and printed numerals young children will meet:

>> numerals that are used to name objects such as buses or houses; in these cases names, such as "the Chorley to Preston station bus" or "Dunroamin", could have been used but someone decided that numbers – "the 37 bus" or "number 10", would be easier

>> numerals where the numbers tell you "how many" or "how much", for example, "180 calories per 100 gm" or "2 eggs" or "price £3"

How children learn about numerals

Children meet numerals used in both these ways at home: on birthday cards, microwave ovens, lottery cards, televisions, front doors, and so on. In schools and nurseries they meet even more.

It is important for children that as well as seeing numbers, they hear numbers spoken, and say the words themselves: "I live at number 30", or "I'm four". They also need to write numbers. At first, before they write the "proper" numerals, children often draw pictures or make marks to represent an amount: three lines to represent "3", for example. Only later do they begin to use the everyday symbols we all use.

Helping children learn about numerals

To help children learn about reading numerals:

>> Display numbers for various purposes, and in a variety of ways. This helps children understand how the numerals are used and what they mean.

>> Play games with numeral dice, where the numerals show the number of objects to be collected or given away.

>> Make regular use of calendars, digital clocks and watches, and calculators.

>> Hang a washing line of numbers across the room; remove one number, or swap two over, and challenge children to spot what you've done.

>> Read and look together at picture books about numbers.

>> Play number games involving numerals: board games, number cards, dominoes with numerals instead of spots, number lotto and number jigsaws.

>> Play simple games with large floor and wall number grids, floor number lines and tracks, large number tiles and number friezes, and 100-grids.

>> Have a large supply of plastic or wooden numerals to use as props when singing number rhymes with actions, such as *Five Little Frogs* or *Ten Fat Sausages*, or for recording scores when playing games such as skittles.

>> Provide large, small, rubber, plastic, fluffy or sponge dice with numerals to 3 or to 6. Show children simple games with these or leave them to invent their own.

Before they can write numerals, children make marks or draw pictures to represent them

Progression in recognising numerals 1 to 9 – reading

- Child shows an interest in written or printed numbers
- Child shows curiosity about written numbers and offers comments or asks questions
- Child recognises and names some numerals that have personal significance
- Child recognises and names numerals 1 to 5, then 1 to 9

Progression in recognising numerals 1 to 9 – writing

- Child makes marks, perhaps as part of a picture, and "reads" them as numbers (but usually not consistently)
- Child draws pictures to represent an amount: for example, puts three bears in a box and draws three "bears" on the lid
- Child makes own marks or tallies to record numbers: for example, knocks down three skittles then draws this

  I I I

- Child writes strings of numbers unrelated to any amount, perhaps as part of a picture (these may or may not be in order)

  3 9 0 1 7 2 5 6 7

- Child writes the correct numeral to represent from one to five objects, then up to nine objects, but may reverse some numerals

>> Do measuring activities where you use equipment that shows numerals, such as tape measures, weighing scales, measuring cylinders or stop clocks.

To help children learn about writing numerals:

>> Introduce activities where recording has some meaning for the children: set up outdoor games where they need to keep score, and help them record how many shells, conkers, bottle tops, or crisp packets they have collected.

To help children identify and become familiar with the shape of numerals:

>> Make numerals together out of sandpaper, dough or card covered in glitter; children can wear a blindfold, feel the numbers, and try to identify them.

>> Put wooden numerals in a bag and see if children can identify them by feel alone.

You can also help younger children in the same way as with shared writing:

>> Children offer their own suggestions for recording numbers, and you demonstrate standard ways of doing this. The children then try out any of the suggestions: their own, other children's, or your standard numerals.

Do you know what that number is?

I wonder why that number is there.
(for example, on a road sign)

Can you find a wooden number to tell us how many skittles have fallen over?

That number doesn't look right. I wonder if it is upside down?

Can you find the number on the calculator that shows your age?

Let's write a number to show how many conkers we have collected.

Here are two numbers that look a bit like each other. They are 3 and 5. Can you find a number that looks like the 6?

Have we got all the numbers yet? Let's put them in order and see if any are missing.

Mathematics provision

Child-initiated play

Catching numbers

Put plastic numbers in the water tray or sand tray and give the children sieves and fishing nets to catch them. Provide numbered buckets to sort the catch into.

Scrapbook numbers

Children make a group scrapbook of numerals cut from magazines, newspapers and advertising material. Develop the play by making individual books for each numeral. Some children may want to illustrate the numbers with objects.

Can I help you?

Set up a call-answering service by providing a bank of telephones and lists of telephone numbers. Encourage the children to record an answerphone message such as "To speak to Hannah press 1. To speak to Emmanuel press 2" and so on. Develop the play by providing redundant mobile phones for travelling helplines.

Score (outside)

Resource an outdoor area with beanbags and buckets numbered 1, 2 and 3. Put the relevant wooden or plastic numerals in each bucket for the children to pick up every time they toss a beanbag into that bucket. Develop the play by providing name-tagged sandwich bags for the children to collect their score numbers in.

Number factory shop

Set up a number factory shop and resource with numbers made from different materials, such as corrugated card, cotton or sequinned material, and paper – cut from magazines. Introduce the idea of children being able to go to the shop and buy their favourite number. Encourage them to sort out the numbers for the customers. Develop the play by introducing the idea of using a computer to generate numbers, and set up a writing program which the children can control to produce and print large numbers.

Important words and phrases

number

zero, one, two, three… to twenty and beyond

nought

count, count to, count up to

next, between, before, after

listen, join in, say

Adult-led activities

My numbers book

Support children in making personal number books showing their age, their door number, the number of people in their family, their shoe size, numbers of buses they've seen or car numbers, and any other significant numbers. If appropriate, include numerals in scripts from the child's own culture.

What could we do to find out your shoe size?

Do you have a favourite number?

How do you think we could show that you have two sisters?

Making numbers

Show the children how to press a button on a calculator to get a number to appear on the calculator display. Put out some calculators and number cards and see if the children make connections between the digits they see on the calculator display and those on the number cards. To make these connections easier, use cards with numbers written in the style of light bars, as on a calculator. Develop the activity by providing coloured rods for the children to make the numbers, should they want to.

Racing dinosaurs

Use an unnumbered ten-space track or ten dinosaur footprints cut out from paper and arranged in a line. Choose six different dinosaurs and give each one a number label. The children take it in turns to throw a 1–6 numeral dice and move that numbered dinosaur one space. Keep playing until one of the dinosaurs reaches the end of the track.

Which dinosaur is number 3?

Which dinosaur do you think will reach the end of the track first?

Hunt the numeral

Organise a number hunt in the school or in the local environment. Look for just one number or for any numbers that you can find. Take photographs of the numbers and use them for reminiscence time back in the classroom. Extend the activity by recording the numbers seen.

Did anyone see a number 8 anywhere?

Where do you think the best place to see a number 3 will be?

Number whist

Collect together four sets of 1–10 number cards. Shuffle the cards and deal five to each child in the group, then put the rest face-down on the table. The children pair together any numbers in their hand that are the same and place them on the table. They then take it in turns to take the top card from the centre pile and keep pairing the cards together until all the cards are used. Develop the activity by collecting three cards the same.

Which numbers do you need?

Bingo numbers

Give everyone in the group six number cards and put the same numbered counters into a bag. Take the counters out one at a time and read out the number. If a child has that number, they turn over their card. Keep playing until someone has turned over all of their cards. Extend the activity by asking the children to make up their own bingo cards using numbers up to 20.

Opportunities through the day

Graphics area

Resources

A variety of magazines and newspapers

Nine small containers numbered 1 to 9

Scissors

Long strip of thin card folded to make a zig-zag book

Activities

Ask the children to cut out any numbers they can find in the magazines and sort them into the appropriate numbered containers. Later, use the cut-out numbers to make a group zig-zag number book to use as a wall-display reference book.

Can you see any numbers that you know?

What numbers do you like writing?

Outdoor area

Resources

Magnetic paint, magnetic numerals

Large dice

Plastic numerals, number labels

Activities

Paint magnetic paint on one outside wall. In a small group, children throw a dice and record their scores by placing the relevant magnetic number on the wall. After five throws, everyone discusses the numbers on the wall.

Give each bike and scooter a number label and paint and number parking bays for them. Then park the correct bikes in each bay.

Put giant numbers on PE mats and ask children to jump from one to another, saying the numbers as they land on each mat.

How could you find out what a number 6 looks like?

Sand tray

Resources

Plastic numerals

Wooden numerals

Sticks and feathers

Activities

Bury lots of plastic numerals in the sand and ask children to dig them up. Sort out the numerals that are found into labelled buckets.

Use wooden numerals to make number impressions in the sand.

Give children small individual sand trays to write numerals in, using sticks and feathers.

I wonder what the best way to write an 8 is.

Can you put the numbers in order?

Malleable area

Resources

Dough made by mixing together two cups of flour, one cup of salt and one cup of water

Gravel stones and sequins

Pizza cutters and plastic knives

Metal or plastic number cutters

Activities

Make a long snake with dough and bend it into a numeral. Choose from a range of materials, such as small, coloured gravel stones or large sequins and press them into the numeral.

Make a numeral with dough, pizza cutters and plastic knives.

Press metal number cutters into rolled-out dough.

Is it easy to make a number with straight lines?

What number are you going to make?

If a child	Then they may be on this step
Points out numbers on signs, and tries to name them, or asks what numbers they are Participates in activities involving numerals and pays attention to the numbers	Show an interest in numbers Seek out others to share experiences
Writes several numerals for one amount, for example, writing 123, or 333, for three Looks for a number card to represent the number of cakes they have made Talks about the number of bears in the house when selecting a wooden or plastic numeral	Show curiosity about numbers by offering comments or asking questions Show increasing independence in selecting and carrying out activities
Shows they understand that the number card 8 indicates how many dinosaur models there are Recognises and names some numerals that have importance to them, for example, their age or house number Sorts and matches some digits (wooden, dough, hand-written, printed...) and names them Reads some numerals in contexts such as recipe cards, page numbers and food labels	Recognise some numerals of personal significance Begin to represent numbers using fingers, marks on paper or pictures Recognise numerals 1 to 5, then 1 to 9 Select the correct numeral to represent 1 to 5, then 1 to 9, objects Display high levels of involvement in activities

Amber said "Guess what numbers I've written".

Blue level

Age 4.1

If a child

Then they may have reached these objectives

Presses the right key on the calculator when asked to press "the five" or "seven"

Knows how to write "0", when telling a number story about a fox stealing eggs

Correctly reads numbers on a numeral dice, in a book, or on a sign

Picks out the number they need from a set of numerals even when it is upside down or back to front

Recognise numerals 1 to 9

Order numbers, up to 10

Be confident to try new activities, initiate ideas and speak in a familiar group

Writes the correct numbers on a label or sign or score sheet, up to 20 or more

Correctly writes the numbers in order up to 20, or above, on a number track

Knows which wooden shapes are numerals and which are letters

Writes the number after 5, 12 or 19

Recognise, order and write numerals up to 20

Sustain involvement and persevere

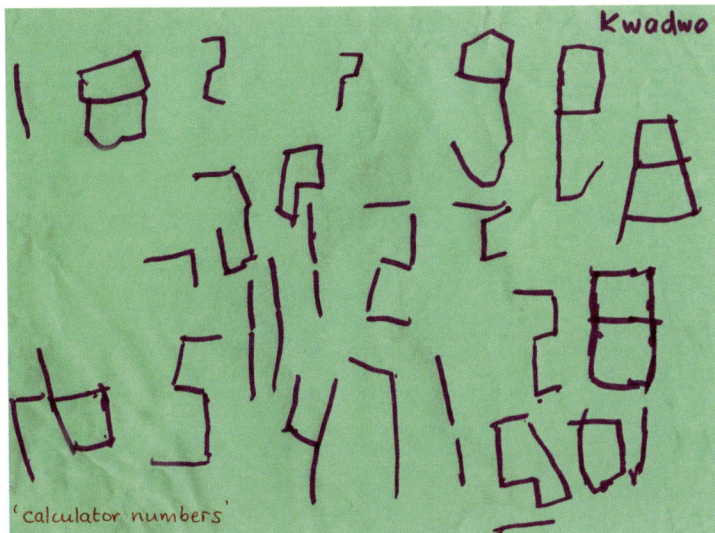

'calculator numbers'

Kwadwo wrote a chart to help his group recognise calculator numbers.

Grey level

Age 5.6

This chapter gives ideas for problem solving involving numbers as labels and for counting.

In the Foundation Stage, mathematical problems are often just everyday events with a mathematical aspect: making sure that everyone has a biscuit; working out how to check that none of the teddies is missing; or deciding the best way to stack the large blocks, for example. Children taking part in these activities are using the maths they know to help them find solutions and are sometimes learning new facts and ideas on the way.

The important point about problem solving is that it involves choices, so children have the opportunity to reason and make decisions.

Children's problem-solving strategies and skills develop through investigating, working on and finding solutions for a wide range of different practical problems. Some will have quick solutions while others will take much of the session time to solve or may even need to be revisited during the course of a week.

It can be helpful to see problem solving as involving two kinds of mathematical understanding: one is learning about some aspect of mathematics such as counting; the other is developing the skills of mathematical reasoning and decision making.

How children learn to solve practical problems using numbers

Children learn to solve practical problems by first recognising that there is a problem and understanding what the problem is. For example, will there be enough fruit for everyone? They then learn to see the possibility of a solution: counting everyone.

Children progress in problem solving by being systematic to some degree: in this case, thinking of a way of making sure that everyone has been counted.

They then begin to see connections: realising that the fruit needs to be counted as well as the people and realising that what they did yesterday, for example, with the toys, is relevant to today's problem with the fruit.

Finally, children need to be persistent and try different approaches: such as estimating the number of apple pieces and the number of children and then sharing the fruit out.

Helping children learn about solving practical problems

>> Create an atmosphere where exploration and "having a go" is seen as more important than getting the right answer.

>> Provide a rich and interesting environment, with plenty of varied activities, and don't make things too easy for the children.

"Do you think there will be enough pieces for everyone?"

>> In your planning include both set-up problems and everyday problems that occur as part of normal activities and involve some kind of number – putting the right number of bulbs in each pot, dealing with money in the "shop", or putting a cup back on each hook.

>> Practise seeing the problem-solving and maths potential in everyday activities, and posing the problem in a way that appeals to – and challenges – the children.

>> Talk with children about what they are doing. Adopt a "softly, softly", wondering approach rather than using too many direct questions:

I wonder if there are enough for everybody to have one…

I'm not sure if we've got three or four lumps of dough.

There should be five red skittles. Shall we see if we have them all?

If the children get stuck, provide prompts:

Show me what you have tried so far.

I wonder if that one comes next.

At the end of the task, you can recap the problem-solving process with the child or the whole group:

Let's tell how you found which number card was missing. First you... then you... And at the end you checked by counting them in order.

Progression in solving practical problems

● Child attempts to tackle problems without much awareness of the likely outcome: for example, when solving a How many…? question, counts randomly

● Child begins to use mathematical skills and knowledge previously acquired: for example, uses tally marks to record a score in a game

● Child begins to be more thorough and systematic: for example, checks that the right number of witches' hats are in the "spooky corner"

● Child begins to use more sophisticated mathematical skills and knowledge: for example, uses numerals to record a score in a game

● Child solves harder problems, in unfamiliar contexts: for example, keeps track of the number of drum beats by putting counters in a pot

● Child relates a problem to others they've solved: for example, remembers that they can put a set of things in order to work out which is missing

● Child uses the mathematics they already know, but in a new context: for example, puts a cup on each hook to see if any are missing

Mathematics provision

Important words and phrases

number

zero, one, two, three… to twenty and beyond

What comes next?

How do you think you'll work it out?

too many, too few, enough, not enough

Water trays have great mathematical potential

Child-initiated play

Filling up

Provide a pile of apple trays (you could get them from a supermarket or market stall) and a bucket of balls. The children will put a ball in each space in the trays and rearrange them. Extend the play by providing a choice of objects to fill the trays.

Stock check

Children dress up in overalls and caps to do the weekly stock-take in an area of the setting.

Develop the play by providing clipboards and pencils for the children to record their stock counts. Some children will suggest counting as a way of knowing if any scissors are missing or to say how many felt-tip-pens should be in the tin.

Some green bottles (outside)

Next to a low wall or shelf, set up the outside water tray, with coloured green water and small plastic bottles, jugs, funnels and number labels.

Develop the play by giving the children numbered bottles and enouraging them to sing the *Ten Green Bottles* song.

Finding out

Collect together a range of different sized boxes and containers. Provide lots of different collections of objects, such as buttons, coloured pasta or fir cones. Give children the opportunity to find out how many different collections of objects fit in a container. Extend the play by adding very large boxes and sticky notes for the children to record their findings on.

Only 10

Provide a selection of empty containers with lids and set the children the challenge of choosing a box and then counting only ten objects into their container. Support the children in producing a display of "Only 10" boxes, such as "only 10 buttons will fit in this box", "only 10 cars will fit in this box", or "only 10 beanbags will fit in this box". Extend the play by providing a suggestion box for children to draw what ten things they think are inside an identified box.

Adult-led activities

Just like mine

Put together two identical collections of objects. Show the children two objects from one of the collections and ask them to find a similar two objects from the other. Extend the activity by covering up the chosen objects so that the children need to remember what was chosen.

Box numbers

Fill five small, lidded boxes with a range of one, two or three items. Ask the children to find two boxes that have the same number of things in.

I wonder if this box has two or three things in it.

Gone missing

Show the children a tray of assorted plastic animals – five of each type, with one missing – and ask for suggestions on how you can find out which one is missing. Extend the activity by removing three animals. Children draw the missing animals.

How do you think you'll work it out?

Take your pick

Put a selection of wooden numerals in a pillowcase and invite pairs of children to take three numerals per person, without looking.

Together they should work out if they have all the numerals to five and, if not, which ones are missing. Change the activity by giving out single-digit number cards and asking which numbers are missing from the sequence.

Which numbers do you think are missing?

Play trams

Collect some small-world characters and set out a line of ten trays as a tram. Put a 1–10 digit card in front of each tray. Ask the children to take turns to throw a 1–6 dice and choose that many characters. They can now decide which carriage their characters want to ride in. Change the activity by using plastic crates and soft toys.

How many characters did you put in carriage 7?

How many ways?

Give the children a pack of 1–20 number cards with some cards missing and ask them to write cards for the missing numbers. Discuss with the children how they solved the problem.

How do you know that 11 is missing?

Opportunities through the day

ICT area

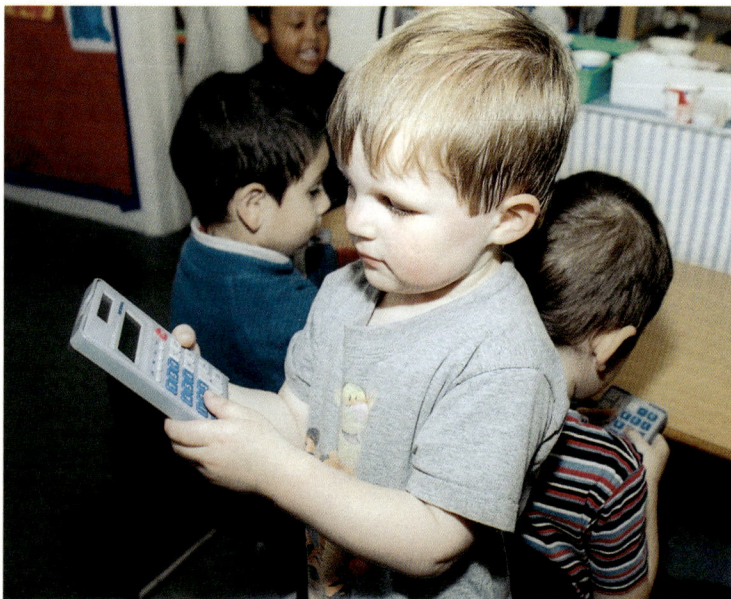

Resources

Number track and number cards
Large calculators
Mobile phones

Activities

Discuss how to turn on a calculator and then make all the numbers from 1 to 8 appear in order.

Choose three number cards in any order and key them into the calculator.

Invent a phone number for Teddy and ring him. Then make a list of the phone numbers for Teddy's friends.

Can you write 5 on the calculator?

Does anyone know Panda's phone number?

Graphics area

Resources

Small loose-leaf folders
Sets of ten sheets of paper
Magazines

Activities

Make a loose-leaf book folder with ten sheets and ask the children to cut out pictures from toy catalogues to make their own number book.

Make sure that there is the right number of pencils, pens and scissors in each container.

What can you write to remind us how many there are?

Can you tell if any pens are missing?

Outdoor area

Resources

Small articles to be priced

Sticky labels

Money

Number mats made from carpet samples with numbers written on them

Activities

Set up the number mats as numbered car boot areas and stick price labels on small items to be "sold".

Discuss how to arrange the small mats to make a trail so that everyone can jump over the mats in number order and everyone can start and finish in the same place.

How much does that cost?

I wonder what number mat we need next.

Creative workshop

Resources

Kitchen roll

Cress seeds

Strawberry plants, and pineapple and carrot tops

Activities

Cut out numbers from thick kitchen roll and sow them with cress seeds. Spray the numbers with water every day, to keep the paper moist.

Grow strawberry plants.

Grow the top of a pineapple and tops of carrots in saucers of water.

Discuss how to keep a diary of the progress of the plants.

How can we check if that has grown?

Will it help if we count them?

Assessing children's development

If a child	Then they may be on this step
Joins in counting activities, but doesn't "know the words" Talks about numerals displayed about the room or outdoors Tries to organise the wooden numerals when they are in a muddle	Show an interest in numbers and counting Use number language in play Show willingness to tackle problems and enjoy self-chosen challenges
Asks what number is chalked on the ground Tries to put right the chalk number that has been partly rubbed out Chooses to look at number books and play with simple number puzzles and equipment Comments that the numbers on the washing line aren't quite right	Show curiosity about numbers by offering comments or asking questions Show an interest in number problems Take the initiative and manage developmentally appropriate tasks
Comments that the numbers on the washing line aren't in the correct order Starts to chalk a "number rocket" on the ground, because the adult hasn't done it yet Continues to make their own "number rocket" even when the adult is available to assist	Show increased confidence with numbers by spotting errors Use own methods to solve a problem Persist for extended periods of time at an activity of their choosing

Emma made her own zig-zag number book.

Green level

Age 4.7

If a child

Then they may have reached these objectives

If a child	Then they may have reached these objectives
Invents a game, with another child, based on characters in a number book Plays a number game in a group, led by an adult Packs a suitcase with enough plates and mugs for a picnic with all the bears	Use developing mathematical ideas and methods to solve practical problems Work as part of a group or class, taking turns and sharing fairly
Uses blank card independently to continue the number sequence on the washing line Counts the number of blocks they have used in their tower and finds a numeral to match Sorts and orders the dominoes according to the total number of their spots	Recognise, count, order and write numerals up to 20 Sustain involvement and persevere, particularly when trying to solve a problem or reach a satisfactory conclusion

Joshua identifies the missing domino.

Grey level

Age 5.9

About the maths

This chapter focuses on the language of calculation and includes ideas for providing children with opportunities to use words that describe calculation situations.

In everyday life, children meet situations that are to do with calculation and comparison, and they are often asked questions such as "How many altogether?" and "Who has the most?"

We use lots of different words to talk about addition and subtraction. The words we choose to use depend on the context. For example, talking with children collecting conkers: "How many have you got altogether?", talking with children playing a game: "Let's add these together to find your total". Working with children using 1p coins in the shop: "How many have you got left?". Children building towers with bricks: "Did you both use the same number of bricks?", "How do you know?".

Alternatively, you may want to compare two amounts and talk about the difference: "You have eight apples and your friend has five apples. When you compare them, who has the most?".

In order to make sense of these experiences, children need to hear, use and begin to understand words such as "more", "add", "take away", "leave", "altogether", "enough", "the same as" and "difference".

How children learn about the vocabulary involved in calculating and comparing

Children learn the language of adding, subtracting and comparing by hearing it in stories and rhymes and meeting it in games

Involve children in developing games that encourage them to use calculating vocabulary

and everyday activities. Children often spontaneously combine or recognise when there is a (numerical) difference between groups of objects during play and, with your encouragement, will discuss what they are doing using words such as "altogether" and "more than".

Helping children learn about the vocabulary involved in calculating and comparing

>> Read stories, sing songs and rhymes, and play games that use the language of number and of adding and taking away. Involve the children in the situations as much as possible by acting out the stories and using props to illustrate what is happening in the rhyme.

>> Draw the children's attention to objects that have a natural partner: cups and saucers, knives and forks, saucepans and lids, and boxes and lids. During play, match them up one-to-one and talk about whether there are the same number of cups and saucers, or too many cups, or too few saucers. This encourages comparing without the need to count.

>> Make sure that children have practical experiences that engage them and that they want to talk about: hunt for leaves, seeds, acorns and conkers. Discuss how many they have altogether and whether they have collected more conkers or more acorns.

>> Play dice games where children collect bricks, shapes or coins and talk about how many they have got and how many more they need.

>> Play more dice games where children eat, spend, or lose cakes or pennies and talk about how many they have to take away and how many they have left.

>> Make use of the opportunities that occur through the day. Look for situations where you can use words such as "add", "take away", "altogether", "more than" and "fewer", and try and show what you mean by counting to demonstrate it.

Using role play is one way children can experience the application of mathematics in daily life

Progression in calculating and comparison vocabulary

● Child begins to join in number rhymes and songs about increasing and decreasing amounts of cats, mice, balloons, and so on

● Child responds to the request to take more conkers or cotton reels or to put some back

● Child may talk about "some left" or "more" in the context of tidying up or playing in the home corner

● Child talks about events in the classroom and in stories, such as: "She's got more than me" or "Two more animals came to tea so then there were five altogether"

● Child notices when two small groups of objects have the same number: for example, comments that they and another child both have two cars. Child comments on numerical totals or differences: for example, says that they have four wheels altogether

● Child explains how to match to find if there is the same number of cups and saucers, or counts both sets of counters to demonstrate the meaning of "total" or how many there are altogether

Mathematics provision

Important words and phrases

more, fewer, less

nearly, the same as, the same number as, not as many as

too many, too few

enough, not enough

add, take away, leave, make, difference between

altogether, total

How many are there altogether? How many are left?

Bouquets-on-line.com

Turn a role-play area into a flower-ordering service. Resource with homemade, artificial or real flowers; vases made from cut-down plastic bottles that have been painted and weighed down with plasticine; labels and price tags; telephone; order pad; note pad; pens and pencils; cash register; card swipe; and a computer, set up with a word-processing package.

Develop the play by encouraging children to enter their bouquet orders on the computer for the assistants to make up. See if they can match the bouquet to the order form (three red flowers, four yellow flowers, and so on). Have a special offer: £1 off the total price.

Yours and mine

Provide a selection of small, interesting baskets, bags or trays and interesting collections of items to fit inside them. Invite the children to select a container and then choose some items to put in it. Encourage them to talk about and compare their container with that of a friend.

Develop the activity by playing "Give again" with two or three children. The children take turns to give one or two things from their collection to the person sitting next to them.

Feed the Hungry Monster

Make a "Hungry Monster" head from a large cardboard box with a hole cut for the mouth, and two different colours of baked play-dough or cardboard biscuits. Provide a number of paper plates for the biscuits. Introduce the children to the biscuits and the hungry monster. Tell them that they have to feed it but remind them that too many biscuits are not good for anyone, so they need to keep a check on how many the monster has eaten at any one feed.

Develop the play by introducing a "feed sheet" on which the children can record how many biscuits they have fed to the monster. Encourage the children to prepare plates of biscuits for the monster by suggesting that today the monster wants vanilla and chocolate biscuits or that today the monster can have plates of four biscuits.

Bike Park entry toll (outside)

Invite the children to make up their own bike challenges and obstacle tracks. Encourage the children to talk about their ideas and discuss the resources they might use. Give the children time to try out and refine their ideas.

Develop the activity by placing all the challenges in a marked out "Bike Park". Provide an entrance, with a "toll box": children toss a token (a counter) into the box as they enter the park. Use the counters to compare how many children used the bike park on different days.

Our Museum

Ask the children to help make collections of interesting objects for "Our Museum". Discuss what might be included: for example, shells, pebbles, dinosaurs, clay bones, and fossils. Provide small dishes or trays for children to make their own collections of items that interest them. Discuss grouping some collections together.

Develop this activity by providing small trays of water for the children to use to see if their items look different when wet.

Organise a rota of museum attendants to sort the collections out at the end of the day.

Adult-led activities

Same!

Play this game with two or three children. Each child has three farm animals in a "stable" or box. They take one, two or three animals in their hands, in secret, and then reveal them at the same time. Encourage children to compare the number of animals in their hands with those in the hands of the other children. Extend the activity by increasing the number of animals to five each and arranging the animals in paired lines to find out if there are the same number of each type.

I wonder if there are the same number of horses and cows.

Waiting for the bus

Play this game with a small group. Put small-world characters in a box and make two bus stops. Pass the box around the group and take it in turns to remove one or two figures from the box and line them up at a bus stop. During the game, discuss which bus stop has the most people waiting in a line. At the end of the game, the bus arrives and all the characters are counted onto the bus, in one go. Extend the activity by throwing a 1–3 dice to decide how many characters to take out of the box.

Spoonfuls

Play this game in pairs. Give each child a bowl of counters in their own colour and a small spoon. Both players take a spoonful of counters and arrange them in a line next to the other player's. They agree who has more and who has fewer and then spin a "more/fewer" spinner to find out which colour line wins the round. Play lots of rounds.

It looks like there are more red counters than yellow ones. We must pair them up carefully though, to check.

I think there are fewer red counters this time; do you?

Do you want the spinner to say "more" or "fewer"?

The Bean Game

Spray-paint twenty butter beans red on one side and leave the other side plain. Play this game in pairs; players have either a white or a red hat and ten beans each. They take turns to shake their ten beans onto the table, and compare the sets by sorting the different colours into two lines, side by side. If there are more reds, the red player wins a brick, if there are more whites, the white player does. If there are the same number, they both win a brick. Extend the activity by changing the rules so that the player with the fewest of their colour beans wins a brick.

Are there more red beans or more white beans?

How can we find out which there are most of?

Dinosaurs love cabbages

A small group of children plant twenty "cabbages" in a "field": green cubes or counters on a sheet of paper. Each child has a cabbage-eating dinosaur. They take turns to roll a 1–3 dice to decide how many cabbages can be eaten this time. Children collect the cabbages until the field is empty. Don't make the game competitive, but compare and discuss amounts as the cabbages are collected. Extend the activity by reading the story *Meg's Eggs* by Helen Nicoll and Jan Pienkowski.

How many will you have altogether when you collect those ones?

The green dinosaur has eaten seven cabbages and the brown one has eaten five. Which dinosaur has eaten the most cabbages?

More or less

Play this game with a large group, in pairs, with 0–10 cards face down and a bag of plastic cubes. Each pair has a voting card with "more" written on one side and "less" on the other. The first pair of children take one handful of cubes, count them and tell the group how many. Then each pair votes on whether or not the next turned over card number will be more or less than the handful of cubes. All the pairs that guessed right collect a cube. Keep taking turns until everyone has won five cubes.

Opportunities through the day

Carpet area

Resources

Two sheets of A3 card, taped together to resemble storybook pages

A collection of interesting objects

Activities

Make up a collective story about finding things and scribe it on to the card, using real objects as illustrations.

Read a story about collecting or losing things such as *Ten in the Bed* (Penny Dale, Walker Books) or *Five Little Ducks* (Ian Beck, Orchard Books).

How many are there altogether?

How many are left?

Role-play area

Resources

Equipment in the home corner for someone coming to tea

Activities

Discuss having an imaginary friend and introduce Teddy, who is coming to tea with his imaginary friend.
Everything that is given to Teddy must be doubled so that there is enough for his friend.

How many more pieces of bread do we need?

I wonder if there are enough apples.

Construction area

Resources

A collection of two different types of small construction material such as Clixi and interconnecting cubes

Polystyrene cups

Activities

Build using the "two cupfuls together and two pieces taken away" technique. Everyone in the group takes a cupful of one of the building materials and then another cupful of the other building material, which they add to their own pile. The children then choose two pieces each to put back in the box, and build with what they have left.

Which bricks have you got more of?

How many pieces did you take away?

Malleable area

Resources

A quantity of two coloured salt-doughs made by mixing together 300 g plain flour, 300 g salt, 1 tablespoon cooking oil and 200 ml water and food colouring

Film canisters

Activities

Use the film canisters as worm holes and make enough worms to put five in each hole. Each hole should contain both colour worms. Discuss how many worms of each colour are in the holes.

Do you need any more?

What would happen if you had fewer?

Assessing children's development

If a child	Then they may be on this step
Talks about the need for "more" of something: "I need more wheels" Comments that two children have the same number: "Holly and me both have two beanbags" Responds to the request to give a few bricks to a friend because they don't have enough	Compare two small groups of objects, saying when they have the same number Begin to accept the needs of others, with support
When asked "Can you give me the tin which has the most pencils in it" offers the right one When matching a set of cup and saucers one-to-one talks about whether there are the same number of each, or what is missing Uses language such as "more" or "some left" to talk about events in the classroom or in role play or a story	Compare two groups of objects, saying whether they have the same number or one group has more or less Take the initiative and manage developmentally appropriate tasks
Finds out if there are more red or more green beads by matching one-to-one or counting Acts out number stories or rhymes using props Responds appropriately, when playing a game, to the question "How many altogether?"	Recognise differences in quantity when comparing sets of objects Respond to the vocabulary involved in addition and subtraction in rhymes and stories Operate independently within the environment

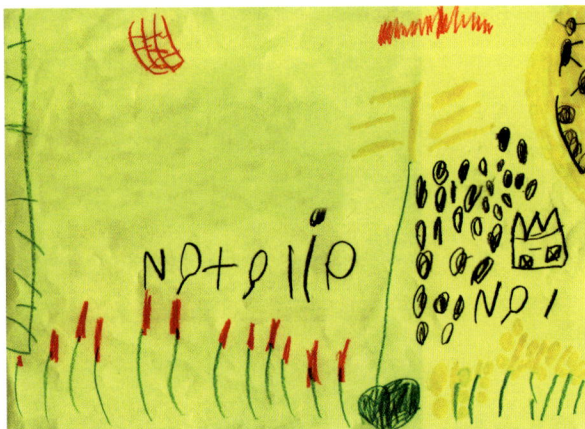

Natalie drew this garden and then said "We've got more red flowers than yellow ones".

Green level

Age 4.5

In practical activities and discussion begin to use the vocabulary involved in addition, subtraction and comparing numbers

49

If a child

Then they may have reached these objectives

If a child	Then they may have reached these objectives
Plays games involving dice or spinners and collecting objects Discusses whether or not they have more or less than someone else Talks about adding or taking away objects to make a collection larger or smaller	In practical activities and discussion, begin to use the language involved in adding and subtracting Work as part of a group or class, taking turns and sharing fairly
Responds to a request to find out how many fir cones there are altogether by combining the two piles and counting them or by looking at the two piles and working the answer out in their head Responds to the question "How could we find out how many there would be if three went away?" by removing three and re-counting or by looking at the counters and working the answer out in their head Can say whether a number is greater than or less than another number	Use a range of strategies for addition and subtraction, including some mental recall of number bonds Sustain involvement and persevere, particularly when trying to solve a problem or reach a satisfactory conclusion

Hannah said at the end of the game that she had fourteen bricks altogether.

Grey level

Age 5.2

with two removed always leaves four so, eventually, they learn that 6 minus 2 is 4.

How children learn to combine two groups of objects and to "take away"

Children learn about addition and subtraction through meeting simple number problems as part of their daily life and by being encouraged to talk through how to find the solution.

Children's experiences of playing games that involve winning or losing a number of objects as they progress around the board or move along a track give them opportunities to be involved in doing lots of adding and taking away in a fairly short period of time. Playing in a group or family situation lets them see how adults or older children do addition and subtraction.

Many children begin to understand a notion of addition as they learn clapping songs, and finger rhymes which they have to act out first with the right hand and then the left and then both hands together.

An abacus helps children gain a practical understanding of addition and subtraction

This chapter is about children understanding the idea of adding and taking away in practical situations.

One way of children learning about addition is through practical experience. In everyday life, we add when we combine two sets of objects, such as opening a packet of six cakes and a packet of four cakes and putting them on a plate. Sometimes we then count to find the total; in general we find the total mentally. Experience shows children that six cakes and four cakes always make ten cakes.

In subtraction too, children learn by practical experience. They learn that removing a particular number of things from a group always leaves the same number of things. And again this helps them learn about numbers in the abstract. A set of six cars

Helping children learn about addition and subtraction

To help children learn about addition:

>> Provide plenty of practical experience – games as well as real addition situations – involving objects, people, pictures and sounds. Introduce all the relevant language to help children talk about what is happening.

To help children learn about subtraction:

>> Provide practical experience involving sets of objects, people and pictures where some objects are hidden or removed. And, again, model the relevant language for children to acquire for themselves.

How many do you think there will be altogether?

I wonder how many there are left.

Have you got fewer pencils than me?

There were three dinosaurs in the box and two have escaped. How many are still in the box?

I think five fingers and five fingers together makes…

If there were eight frogs sitting on a log and one jumped off, how could you work out how many were left sitting on the log?

Have you got more or fewer pennies than you started with?

>> Ask children to roll two different coloured dice together and collect that many counters. Then discuss which colour counters there are most of.

>> Ask children to dig up buried treasure from the sand tray with a friend and decide how many things there are altogether.

>> Encourage children to make a ten-bead necklace and decide how many of each bead they need.

Progression in addition and subtraction

- Child joins in number rhymes and songs about increasing and decreasing numbers of fish, birds, sausages, and so on

- Child responds to the instruction to take more counters, bricks, or buttons, or to remove some

- Child uses counting to find the new number of items in a small group after some have been added or removed

- Child uses counting to find the total number of items in two separate groups

- Child uses counting to find the number left when some have been removed from a larger group

- Child predicts results before they know the actual answer to an addition or subtraction situation: *I think it'll be 7*

- Child can answer questions such as *There are five bugs in the box and two have escaped; how many are left?*

- Child can mentally add 1 or 2 or subtract 1 or 2, to or from a number to 10 or 20

- Child knows all the number bonds up to 5 or more: *3 and 2 makes 5*

- Child knows that when a group of three or four beans is split up, the total is still the same

Mathematics provision

Important words and phrases

add, take away, leave

make, sum, total, altogether

How many more to make...?

How many are left/left over?

How many are gone/hidden?

enough, not enough

double

more, less

count on

Two hands (outside)

Resource the outdoor area with large flowerpots, a container of pebbles and some small spades. Encourage the children to put some spadefuls of pebbles in each flowerpot and discuss adding more pebbles or taking some out. Develop the play by using large dice to decide how many spadefuls of pebbles to add.

River ducks

Fill a long, plastic window-box with water and float five plastic ducks on it. Help the children to construct a barrier of plastic water-weed that will separate the ducks into two areas. Develop the play by encouraging the children to make waves with their hands or blow down a plastic tube or straw to move the ducks into a different section of the river and then to talk about how many ducks there are in each section.

Water delivery

Set up a water bottle delivery service role-play area. Resource the area with empty plastic bottles and cardboard bottle carriers. Encourage the children to fill the carriers with empty bottles and deliver them to customers. Develop the play by adding wine bottle stacking systems for the children to fill.

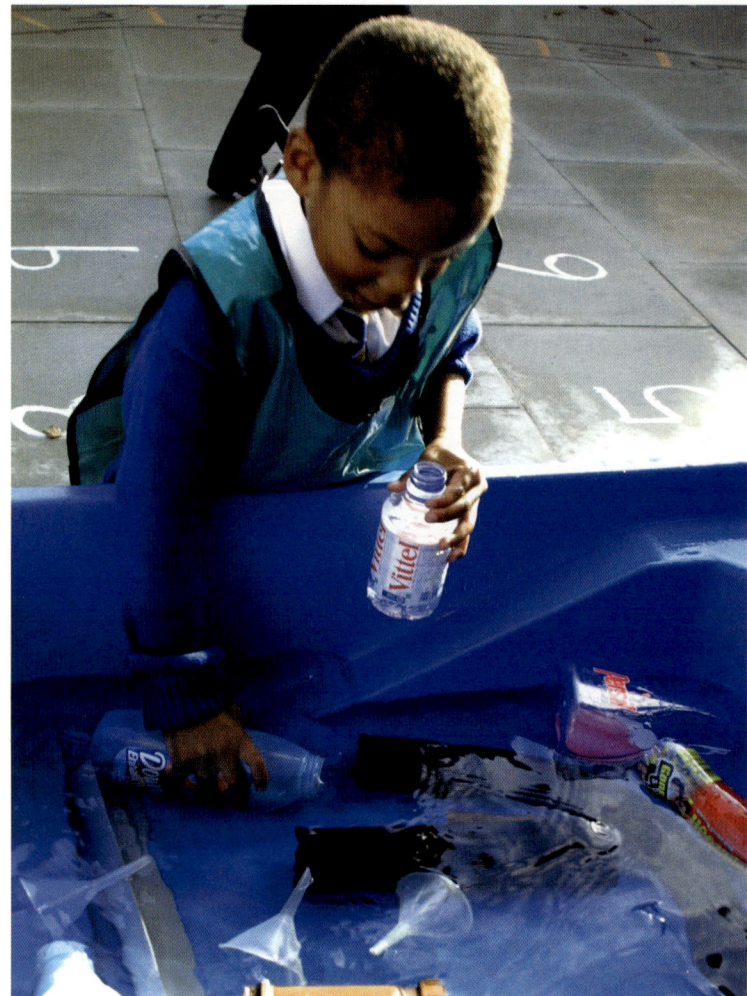

Trams

Use two shoe boxes decorated to resemble a two-carriage tram and make a queue of small-world characters waiting for the tram. The children decide how many should go in each carriage. Develop the play by adding more characters and another two-carriage tram.

Take some away

Provide a set of small, lidded containers and fill half of them with different objects. Leave the other half empty so that the children can remove some objects from one container and put them in an empty container.

Adult-led activities

Snap

Put two cars underneath each of two upturned small pots and under a third pot put one car. Move their positions to shuffle them. The children take it in turns to lift two pots together. Call "Snap" if the pots with two cars underneath are lifted up. Extend the activity by adding two more pots with three cars under each.

Chips for everyone

Play this game with a small group. Give everybody two paper plates then take it in turns to take one scoop of chips (counting sticks) from the pan and put some chips on each of their plates. Help the children decide if the two plates have the same number of chips on them or not. If two plates have the same number of chips they can have sausages; plates with different numbers of chips have a burger. Extend the activity by using a dice to decide on the number of chips each plate gets.

I think there are more chips on this plate. What do you think?

Magic purses game

Each child has a purse and there is a bank of pennies on the table. Everyone puts four pennies in their purse. A magician puppet says how many pennies to take out of the purses and then guesses how many are left in each purse. The children empty their purses and check. Extend the activity by encouraging the children to guess what the magician puppet is going to say.

How many do you think are left?

How many did we take away?

Domino adding

Play this dominoes game with a small group. Share out a set of 0–12 cards and lay a set of dominoes face-down on the table. Children lay the number cards face-up in front of them. They then take it in turns to pick a domino, count or add its spots and give it to the child who has that number card. Go on like this until all the dominoes are gone. The person with the most dominoes wins. Extend the activity by arranging the dominoes in lines according to their totals.

Do you have more or less than John?

How many does that make altogether?

Bear numbers

Play this game with a small group of children, in pairs. Put five bears on a tray with a 5 number-card in front of them and give each pair ten bears. Shuffle a pack of 0–10 cards and give one to each pair in the group. Pass the bear tray to each pair in turn and ask them to replace the card on it with their card and either take bears off the tray or put some on the tray to match the new number card.

Are there enough bears on the tray?

Escape

Show the children ten zoo animals and put them in a box labelled "animal house". Secretly remove some animals and explain that some have escaped. Show the children the animals that remain in the animal house and discuss how many have escaped.

Extend the activity by giving the children number fans to show how many animals are still in the house.

How many are gone? How many are left?

Opportunities through the day

Music area

Resources

Instruments that make distinct sounds (drums, tambourines, chime bars…)

Chalks and boards

Activities

Together use two different instruments to make up simple five-beat tunes, such as two beats on the drum and three beats on the tambourine.

Find a way to record (score) the music that has been made and display it for other people to try.

Look at the scores and guess which five-beat tune is being played.

Did you use your fingers to count the beats?

What do you think is the best way to score this music?

Small-world area

Resources

Flat tray to be a campsite

Trees and cars

Small boxes to be campsite buildings

Pieces of thin card

Five small-world family characters for each child

Activities

Make two tents by folding pieces of card in half or into thirds and deciding which of the five characters should sleep in each tent. Build a campsite and record how many characters are sleeping in each tent.

Make larger tents that will hold up to ten characters.

How many will there be in each group?

Is it possible to have the same number of people in each tent?

Outdoor area

Resources

A collection of cardboard boxes

A soft ball tied to a string, attached to a washing line

Easel and paper for scoring

Activities

Build a wall with cardboard boxes and swing the ball at the wall twice. Each time, count how many boxes were knocked down. Record the total on a score board.

Use the boxes to build a tall tower and demolish the tower by swinging the ball and finding out how many boxes are left standing after each swing.

How did you find out how many "bricks" there were?

Do you know a way to work out the total?

Creative workshop

Resources

Paints, crayons, felt-tip pens

Hand cut-outs

Sticks and plasticine

Small pieces of card

Activities

Children decorate two hand cut-outs to look like the hands are wearing gloves, using paints and pens. They attach the hands to sticks and then fold back some of the fingers on the hands. They use a felt-tip pen to write a card saying how many fingers can be seen.

Paint hands and print with them, then cut out the prints to make a five-and-five-fingers display.

How can we find out how many fingers are folded back?

Are there different ways to make five fingers folded?

Assessing children's development

If a child	Then they may be on this step
Joins in number rhymes and songs Comments that they and a friend "both have the same" when each child has two pieces of apple	Compare two small groups of objects, saying when they have the same number Show curiosity
Responds to the instruction to take one or two more bricks, or to give one or two coins to a friend Counts up to three or four objects, even when these are not all together: for example, two cherries on a plate and another cherry on the table Can help you count four bears, and say there are still four bears, even when you move them around	Show an interest in number problems Separate a group of three or four objects in different ways, beginning to recognise that the total is still the same Adapt their behaviour to different events
Counts the paint brushes in the jar, in order to find the total number when some more have been added Counts the paint pots on the table in order to find the number left when some have been removed	Find the total number of items in two groups by counting all of them Use own methods to solve a problem Show confidence

Akida threw the dice and removed three cars from the lorry, then he drew this.

Blue level

Age 3.7

If a child	Then they may have reached these objectives
With five counters can tell you how many they would have if you gave them three more With six counters can tell you how many they would have left if you took two of them away Can find out how many bears there are in two houses by counting both sets	Relate addition to combining two groups Relate subtraction to taking away Use developing mathematical ideas and methods to solve practical problems Maintain attention and concentrate
Responds to the request to find out how many there are altogether by combining two lots of objects and counting them Responds to the request to take away six and find out how many are left by removing six objects from a set, and counting what remains Solves imaginary problems set in familiar contexts, such as "If three more people went in the car, how many people would there be?" Seems to "just know" some number bonds: for example, that a domino whose sides have two spots and three spots must have five spots altogether	Use a range of strategies for addition and subtraction, including some mental recall of number bonds Sustain involvement and persevere, particularly when trying to solve a problem or reach a satisfactory conclusion

When she was decorating biscuits, Polly said "I'm going to have three red and five silver balls, that's eight altogether". She also checked the biscuits the others had made and commented on whether or not they needed to add any more silver balls.

Grey level

Age 5.2

they have. Combining both these bits of knowledge and understanding enables a child to know that if you add (or take away) an object the total count is the next number (or the previous number) in the sequence. Number tracks, number lines, and washing lines with number cards pegged on them, all help to present a model of numbers in a sequence for children to become familiar with. Going forward on the track, children will see that the next number is always one more and by going backwards along the track, that the next number will always be one less.

How children learn about one more and one less

Young children can understand finding one more and one less, providing the idea is introduced in a way that is relevant and makes sense to them. Children often begin to develop their knowledge of calculation through meeting addition and subtraction situations in stories and everyday life.

It is through their play experiences of counting out quantities that they gain an understanding of what one more and one less might be. If children are involved in counting-on and counting-back games and activities, they will also use the language of "more", "less" and "fewer" as they play, especially if you introduce a dice or spinner which indicates "count back one" or "count forward one". Using a track where some spaces are marked "take one more" or "give one more" and the children are encouraged to keep a running total as they play will also support their growing understanding of the language of calculation.

This chapter is about helping children understand the idea of "one more" and "one less" in lots of different situations.

The earliest stages in knowing about addition and subtraction are focused on the simplest situations: those where you are adding "one more" or taking away so there is "one less". These experiences can be related to the introduction of a 1–10 or 1–20 number track.

As children become more knowledgeable and more efficient at saying the number sequence, they begin to be able to identify the number before and the number after most numbers up to 10. At the same time they are also becoming more expert at counting real objects so they begin to understand that the last number they say in the count describes the number of objects

Helping children learn about one more and one less

>> Use the words "more", "less" and "fewer" as you discuss what children are doing.

Would you like more dough or more sticky tape?

You might need less paint on your brush

Why don't you put fewer bricks in the basket?

>> Play games where children add or remove one object from a collection, such as taking another bead or putting back a brick. Sometimes count the changed set to establish that there is one more or one less than there was before.

>> Provide games and activities using number tracks and washing line numbers

Counting out quantities helps children understand what one more and one less might be

where children deal with one more and one less in an abstract way (in that they are using numbers rather than objects). Draw attention to the next number of the track being one more than the number before.

>> Make use of opportunities that occur through the day. Putting away games and equipment provides situations where you can deliberately make sure that there is one beanbag fewer than there should be or one too many pencils in the tin.

Progression in learning to find one more and one less

- Child responds to the request to take more or give more of something but without paying attention to the quantity

- Child can respond appropriately to the request to take one more of something

- Child can count the two toys in a boat, and say that if one more got in, there would be three

- Child recognises that when some biscuits are removed from a plate, there are now fewer than there were before

- Child can count the two toys in a boat, and say that if one got out there would be one left

- Child can look at a number track and say the number one more or less than 3 or 5

- Child can use fingers to solve problems such as *Suppose you had five pennies and you dropped one down a hole. How many would you have left?*

- Child says the number one more or one less than, say, 4 or 9, when asked

Mathematics provision

Important words and phrases

as many as

more, fewer, less

most, fewest, least

one more, one less

make, altogether, How many?

next to, before, after

How many will there be when one more… ?

And another one

Put together an interactive table display of lines of elephants, ducks, pattern blocks, bead strings, number cards, and small cars, and encourage children to "add one on" to one of the lines. Develop the activity by reversing the procedure and having a "take one away" display.

Special offer

Ask the children to help set up a pound shop with a "buy one, get one free" offer. Put together pairs of objects to which the offer applies. Use pound coins to pay for them. Develop the play by suggesting that the shop puts together another shelf of goods which offers three for the price of two.

The one more snake (outside)

Resource the outdoor area with a collection of long scarves and encourage children to play snakes by arranging themselves in a long line, holding one end of each of the scarves the children in front and behind them are holding, and calling for "one more" as they wind their way round the area, getting children to pick up a scarf and join on the end of the line.

Room for one more

Develop a role-play area into a tour bus; resource with scenic posters, timetables and itineraries. Set up a coach with a ticketing system and six numbered seats. Suggest that the coach driver sells tickets for the seats and alerts passengers through a microphone as to how many seats are still available for the tour. Develop the play by recording a description of the journey for the passengers, using "one more" and "one less" terms and provide props to illustrate, such as sheep in fields and houses that the coach might be passing.

Nature plates

Put out a pile of empty paper plates and some natural objects, such as fir cones, shells and leaves. Suggest that the children take two plates and stick objects on the plates, making sure that one of the plates has one more object on it than the other. Develop the play by providing pegs and string for the children to make a "one more than" number line, using the decorated plates.

Adult-led activities

Give and take

Play this game in a small group. Each child has a collection of six small-world characters. They take it in turns to give one of their figures to the person sitting next to them. Develop the activity by introducing a small room-setting with six figures. Set up the room setting by taking furniture from a dolls' house and placing it in the middle of the table. Give the children a spinner that says "add one figure" or "take one figure away" and ask them to add or take away figures from the room according to what the spinner says.

There's one more person in the room now. How many does that make?

I've got it

Play this game with three or four children. Give everyone four plastic elephants and ask the children to close their eyes. You then say "and one more is" and add an elephant to one of the sets of four. Ask the children to open their eyes and decide who got one more elephant. Support the children in taking turns to be the "one more" giver.

Extend the activity by starting with five elephants each and having one taken away.

Have you got as many as Hassan or less than him?

Penny drops

Everyone listens, watches and counts as you drop between one and five pennies into a tin. Display a number card to show the number of pennies you dropped in. Now drop in one more penny and ask everyone to show with their fingers how many pennies are in the tin. Change the number card to show the new amount. Extend the activity by taking a penny out of the tin.

I wonder how many there will be when we add one more.

One more spot

Use a set of dominoes to play. Ask the children to find the dominoes that have one spot on one side. Put all the one-spot dominoes in a pile and show one at a time with the single spot hidden. Discuss how many spots there will be when you add one more.

Extend the activity by sharing out all the dominoes and asking children to count all the spots on their dominoes. Then set challenges such as "thumbs up" if you are holding a domino with one more spot than three spots, or one more spot than five spots.

Clap and stamp

This is an activity to play with a large group. Show a number card with a number less than 6 and whisper the number. Everyone then has to clap once more than the number on the card and then stamp once less than the number on the card.

How many stamps did that make altogether? Is that one less than 5?

Circling

Give everyone in the group a paper circle and tell them to count out ten plastic bears onto their circle, from the tub of bears in the centre of the table. Then take it in turns to spin the "one more and one less" spinner and either put one bear back in the tub or take another bear out. Have five spins each and then ask the children to work out whether they have more or fewer bears than when they started the game.

Extend the activity by asking children to record their results.

Can we tell who's got the most bears?

Opportunities through the day

PE area

Resources

Hoops

Soft foam balls, bean bags, felt balls

Made soft balls from rolled up socks, bath puffs, balloons

Containers to collect balls in

Activities

Suspend hoops from a washing line and practise in pairs throwing three soft balls through the hoops and then one more ball. Take turns to be the thrower and the fetcher. Discuss choosing three other soft throwing objects that are the same and one more that is different.

Do you all have the same number of things?

How many would you have if you gave one to your friend?

Science area

Resources

Balances

Conkers, fir cones, stones

Soft toys

Activities

Make Teddy balance the fir cones. Discuss what happens when you add more fir cones or take some fir cones off. See if the same thing happens when you balance Teddy against stones.

What happens if you put one more on?

Do you need more or fewer to make it balance?

Outdoor area

Resources

Stepping-stone pathway or drawn track

Large spinner

Large 1–6 dice

Collection of soft toys

Activities

Line up the soft toys at the start of the track.

Throw the dice and jump Teddy that many along the track. Then spin the "one more/ one less" spinner and Teddy must either jump back one or jump forward one. Choose another toy to jump along the track; keep throwing the dice, spinning the spinner and jumping along the track until one of the toys gets to the end.

When you jump backwards one space on the track what does that mean?

Creative workshop

Resources

Flower heads

Thin strips of card

Glue

Clingfilm or tacky-back material

Activities

Make bookmarks by sticking flower heads onto thin strips of card and covering with clingfilm material. Use different numbers of flower heads on each bookmark – some with more and some with less.

Make bookmarks using other natural materials such as leaves or seeds.

Make daisy chains and discuss which chain has more.

If you take one away, is the line longer or shorter?

Can you explain how you found out which line had more?

If a child	Then they may be on this step
Talks about the need for "more" of something: "I need more juice" Takes more of something (cake, sand, water, paper) when asked to do so	Compare two small groups of objects, saying when they have the same number Have a positive approach to new experiences
Talks about "one more" in the context of a game or activity where pencils or beads or biscuits are being given out Responds to the request to take one more counter, acorn, or domino, or to put one back Counts out two or three objects when asked to do so, then adds one more when asked, and can count the total	Show an interest in number problems Demonstrate flexibility
Adds 1 to (or subtracts it from) a number in the context of a rhyme or game Points to the correct number on a number track when asked to show which is one more (or one less) than, say, 5 or 2	Say with confidence the number that is one more than a given number Sometimes show confidence and offer solutions to problems Find one more or one less from a group of up to five objects Display high levels of involvement in activities

When we were singing *An elephant went out to play*, Marisa shouted "It's one more, it's one more elephant".

Yellow level

Age 3.5

If a child

Then they may have reached these objectives

If a child	Then they may have reached these objectives
Closes their eyes and tells you the number one more than or one less than, say, 7 Looks at a number track and asks their friend if they can say the number one more or less than 7 or 9	Find one more or one less than a number from 1 to 10 Continue to be interested, excited and motivated to learn
Closes their eyes and tells you the number two more than or two less than, say, 12 Solves imaginary problems set in familiar contexts, involving adding or subtracting 1. For example, "If the prince got eaten too, how many people would be left on the ship?"	Use a range of strategies for addition and subtraction Sustain involvement and persevere, particularly when trying to solve a problem or reach a satisfactory conclusion

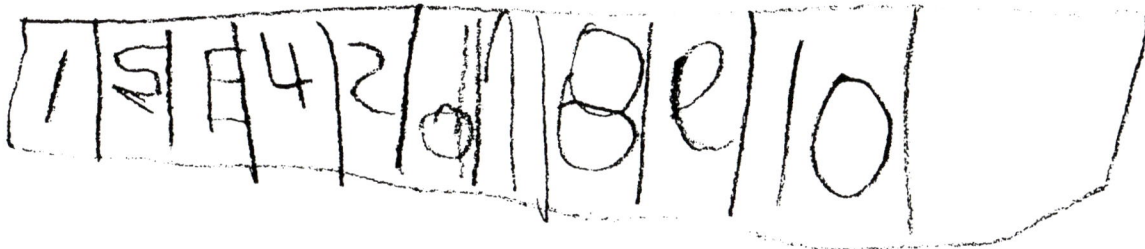

Joseph played putting plastic numerals on a track. While he was doing that, he asked himself questions and answered them. "5 is after 4… What's one more than 9? It's 10". He decided to draw the track with numbers on later.

Grey level

Age 5.1

65

"I've done four squirts of water, how many more do we need to make ten?"

This chapter contains ideas for encouraging children to compare and combine numbers and to solve problems involving addition and subtraction in practical contexts.

In the Foundation Stage, mathematical problems are often just everyday events with a mathematical aspect: making sure that everyone has a biscuit; working out how to check that none of the teddies is missing; or deciding the best way to stack the large blocks, for example. Children taking part in these activities are using the maths they know to help them find solutions and are sometimes learning new facts and ideas on the way.

The important point about problem solving is that it involves choices, so children have the opportunity to reason and make decisions.

Children's problem-solving strategies and skills develop through investigating, working on and finding solutions for a wide range of different practical problems. Some will have quick solutions while others will take much of the session time to solve or may even need to be revisited during the course of a week.

It can be helpful to see problem solving as involving two kinds of mathematical understanding: one is learning about some aspect of mathematics such as counting and the other is developing the skills of mathematical reasoning and decision making.

How children learn to solve practical problems using calculations

Children learn to solve practical problems by first recognising that there is a problem and understanding what the problem is. For example, how many wheels do we need to make three cars? They then learn to see the possibility of a solution: knowing how many wheels there are on one car.

Children progress in problem solving by being systematic to some degree, in this case, setting out four wheels and then another four and then another four.

They then begin to see connections: holding up four fingers and realising that another four fingers is 8 and linking it to the car-wheels solution and realising that what they did yesterday with the straws, for example, is relevant to today's problem with the wheels.

Finally, children need to be persistent and try different approaches: such as involving more children and more fingers.

Helping children learn about solving practical problems

>> Create an atmosphere where exploration and "having a go" is seen as more important than getting the right answer.

>> Provide a rich and interesting environment, with plenty of varied activities, and don't make things too easy for the children.

>> In your planning include both set-up problems and everyday problems that occur as part of normal activities and involve some kind of calculating with numbers – planning and preparing parties or picnics (real and pretend); playing dominoes or Pairs; or growing things (amaryllis, beans…).

>> Practise seeing the problem-solving and maths potential in everyday activities, and posing the problem in a way that appeals to – and challenges – the children.

>> As always, talk with children about what they are doing, and help them to try their own approaches to solving a problem. Acknowledge and respond to children's questions and comments and sometimes turn their comments around to form simple challenges:

How can I find out how many there are now?

I wonder which pot has more…

Let's agree how to decide who has won the game.

Progression in solving practical problems

● Child attempts to tackle problems without much awareness of the likely outcome, for example, doles out sweets randomly rather than dealing out one at a time

● Child begins to use mathematical skills and knowledge previously acquired – knows how to find which player in a game has more dinosaurs, up to about 5

● Child begins to be more thorough and systematic: for example, deals with an extra counter by saying *We must both have two. Put that one back*

● Child begins to use more sophisticated mathematical skills and knowledge: for example, uses a calendar to work out the days left until the weekend

● Child solves harder problems, in unfamiliar contexts: for example, works out that to have ten conkers they need to collect another three

If the children need help, ask open questions or provide prompts:

What have you tried so far?

I remember when we did something like this before. You did...

At the end of the task, you might sometimes recap with the children the problem-solving process:

Let's tell the class how you shared out the raisins. First you... Then you... And at the end you checked by counting how many each bear had.

Mathematics provision

Child-initiated play

Birthday cake factory

Use a long table as a birthday cake production line. Resource with different shaped cakes cut from painted slabs of foam-chair filling. Provide cake decorations, ribbons, birthday numbers and "Happy Birthday" slogans. Use candle holders and candles to match the birthday number. Develop the play by keeping a record of how many different age cakes have been made. Or declare a candle shortage and work out how many cakes can be decorated with that many candles.

Buy a brick (outside)

Set up an outdoor builder's yard and sell large plastic bricks for £1 each. Discuss how many bricks children would get for £5. Extend the play by constructing a builder's wall display: "Build this wall for £10", "Build this wall for £8". Encourage the children to collaborate by pooling their bricks and building walls together.

Inside/outside

Collect together a range of small boxes and containers on a table top and resource with ten farm animals, ten dinosaurs, ten plastic teddies and other collections of ten small-world characters. Children choose a box and the dinosaurs and put some inside and some outside the box. They then choose another box and the farm animals and put some animals inside and some outside the box. They carry on playing with some inside and some outside.

Table for four?

Turn a role-play area into a café with tables seating different sized groups. The children can queue in friendship or family groups to be seated at an appropriate sized table. Waiters can serve people as well as making sure that there are the correct number of chairs and settings per table, adding extra ones or removing them where necessary. Waiters can use order pads to write down orders and numbers in their own way.

Develop the play by presenting a problem: the café has to be reduced in size as the road outside is being widened. Will the café still be able to seat groups of two, three, four and five?

Is there space for any more?

Provide a selection of trays from inside sweet and chocolate boxes and cut them up to give trays of different sizes, for example with two, three, four, five and six sections. Put out collections of small, interesting objects on the table alongside the trays. Invite the children to explore the items and place them into the trays.

Develop the play by asking children if they have space for any more. Put items in some of the spaces and invite children to fill the trays up.

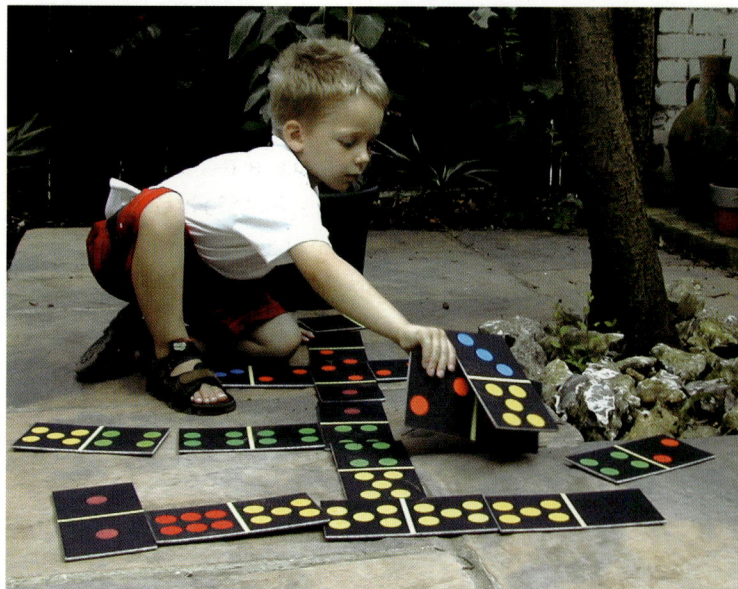

Adult-led activities

Teddy toasts

Arrange two teddies on a table with a plate each and ask the children to share out the six toast squares so that the teddies each have the same amount of toast to eat. Extend the activity by arranging for a third teddy to join the group so that the toasts will need to be redistributed.

Do both teddies have the same amount of toast? How can you be sure?

Follow me four

Resource the group with a lace each and either a box of plastic cotton reels in a range of colours or large wooden beads to share. Ask everyone to thread some cotton reels on their lace and then pass the lace to the person sitting next to them, who must add more reels or take some off until there are four reels on the lace. Extend the challenge by giving everyone a number tag to put on their lace to indicate how many reels should be threaded on it or taken off it.

How many more do you think you need to add?

How many does that make altogether?

And the total is

Play this game in pairs with a colour dice, a 1–3 dice and lots of coloured counters. Children take it in turns to have two throws of each dice and to collect the counters and then to decide how many they have altogether. Extend the activity by re-sorting the counters into colour groups and then finding out how many there are altogether.

So that's two red counters, add on three green ones. How many is that?

Collecting collections

On the table, spread a collection of sorting material, such as dinosaurs, shapes, pegs, plastic fruit and bears. Give each pair a small collecting pot and tell the children what collection to make, such as four bears with two the same colour or six pegs with three red ones or three dinosaurs all different.

Extend the activity by asking the children to suggest a collection for everyone to make or to describe the collection they have assembled.

How many more do you need?

How did you make your collection?

Ribbon pots

Give pairs of children three small, empty containers and some small objects, like pegs, counters or plastic bears. Ask them to put a few objects in one of their pots and tie a ribbon around it. Now ask them to take the other two pots and put more objects than are in the ribbon pot in one and fewer than are in the ribbon pot in the other. Discuss with the children how they decided what to put in each pot.

I wonder if there are enough counters in this pot.

What do you think you need in this pot?

Domino scores

Play this game with a small group and two sets of dominoes. Share out the dominoes and then roll two 1–6 dice and say the numbers and the total they make. If anyone in the group has a domino with the same numbers as the dice roll, they score two counters. Anyone with the same total as the dice roll scores one point. Carry on rolling the dice until everyone in the group has scored at least two counters.

Who thinks they should score two counters this go?

Opportunities through the day

Water tray

Resources
Transparent containers
Pebbles
Elastic bands
Dinosaurs and plastic lids

Activities
Together, put ten pebbles in each of the containers and slide an elastic band around them. Fill the containers to the top with water. Discuss making the level of the water rise and fall by adding or taking some pebbles out. Try and make the water in the containers level with the elastic bands.

Float dinosaurs on lids inside the containers and rescue them by making the water level rise.

I wonder how many there were altogether.

I wonder if we need to add one or take one away.

Cookery area

Resources
Two different flavoured packets of jelly
Small plastic pots

Activities
Together, make up the jellies and decide how to fill the same number of pots with red and yellow jellies.

How will we know we've got the same number of each colour?

How many have we got altogether?

Creative workshop

Resources

Make a bucket of papier mâché: cut a newspaper into strips and mix four cups of flour and one cup of water. Leave the mixture to soak then stir into a mash

Knitting needle or pencils for hole making

String and threaders

Two colours of paint

Curtain pole

Activities

Together take handfuls of the mash, squeeze out any water and make it into sausage shape beads. Make a threading hole in the long beads and paint some one colour and others another. Thread strings of ten beads using both colours. Discuss how many of each colour to thread on each string. Tie the strings to a curtain pole to make a bead curtain.

Have we got the same number of each colour?

How can we find out how many there are altogether?

Outdoor area

Activities

Five soft juggling balls

Easel, paper and pens

Hoops and ten bean bags

Activities

Throw five juggling balls in the air and count how many are caught and how many fall on the ground. Discuss ways of recording the results.

Throw the bean bags into the hoops and decide how to record how many landed inside. Discuss making a chart of how many are inside and outside the hoops.

I wonder how we can find out how many there are altogether.

Do you think there are more inside or outside the hoops?

If a child	Then they may be on this step
Comments that there isn't a paintbrush in each paint pot	Show an interest in numbers
Says that they haven't got enough dinosaurs in their box yet	Use number language in play
Puts pegs in a pegboard, trying to fill all the holes, and says they need more pegs	Show willingness to tackle problems and enjoy self-chosen challenges
Chooses to play with simple number puzzles and equipment and comments on it to an adult	Show curiosity about numbers by offering comments or asking questions
Answers a practical problem such as "How many teddies can fit in the pram?"	Show an interest in number problems
Talks about who has won the most counters so far	Take the initiative and manage developmentally appropriate tasks
Uses fingers to work out how many frogs would be left if two jumped off the log	Show increased confidence with numbers by spotting errors
Counts the spoonfuls of flour as they are put in the bowl and says "There aren't enough, you need another one"	Sometimes show confidence and offer solutions to problems
Picks one domino at a time and counts the spots; asked about one domino says "Five dots there and one there makes six dots"	Use own methods to solve a problem
	Display high levels of involvement in activities
	Persist for extended periods of time at an activity of their choosing

Avtar has played with the wooden numerals all this week and these are his favourite numbers. His "best" number is four.

Yellow level

Age 4.1

If a child

Then they may have reached these objectives

If a child	Then they may have reached these objectives
Fetches a calculator to help solve the problem of how many children are left when three are away	Use developing mathematical ideas and methods to solve practical problems
Suggests a method for sharing the fruit pieces between members of the group	Select and use activities and resources independently
Compares their tower with their companion's and says "I need four more blocks to make my tower the same"	Is confident to try new activities, initiate ideas and speak in a familiar group
Plays a number game, and works out how many more counters they need to reach 10	Use a range of strategies for addition and subtraction, including some mental recall of number bonds
Estimates that if the ten scones were shared between two plates there would be about four on each plate	Sustain involvement and persevere, particularly when trying to solve a problem or reach a satisfactory conclusion
Persists with the problem of making as many different sticks of four cubes as possible, using just two colours	

I have got the most pesis. teat bus not moen teat I have the most big hows it moens teat t yost the litl ist pesis I have 159 pesis in my hows Emma's hows had 92 pesis.

Carla describes the house she built using small construction material.

Grey level

Age 5.3

About the maths

Use language such as "greater", "smaller", "heavier" or "lighter" to compare quantities

This chapter is about providing children with opportunities to use words that describe measurements.

Comparing quantities, and measuring are complex skills. Comparing lengths or weights of objects against each other or against a measure, such as a tape or a gram weight, can be a complicated process. Sometimes we only need rough measurements and sometimes it is important to be more accurate. One of the skills children will learn is knowing when accuracy matters.

Measuring is something we do all the time; so there are lots of words we can use as comparison: big, small, wide, narrow, tall and short, for example. Young children need to play at measuring to have the opportunity to use as many different words as possible.

While children are comparing the length, weight, volume or capacity of objects, they are also beginning to gain an understanding of the conservation of measures: that length, weight, and so on, don't change arbitrarily, even though the appearance of an object might change. In other words, the child needs to eventually know that they still have as much dough – the weight is the same – whether it is in a lump or rolled flat. And that their height stays the same whether they are in a big hall, where they feel small, or in the play house, where they feel big.

How children learn to talk about comparing quantities

Children learn about comparing and using the language of measures as a result of playing with and exploring a wide range of materials and objects in lots of different situations.

Children initially compare things according to less formal measures: "These cups look the same", "This book is nicer than that one". This helps them to develop the general idea that comparing things is one of the things you can do in life.

A child's interest in measures often arises through contrasts: big and little bears, fast and slow cars, building high and low towers. At other times they will compare three or more things: putting Goldilocks' three bears in order of size, for example.

Children usually first gain an understanding of length by directly comparing two objects. The longest of two pencils or ribbons, for example, could be found by putting the two items next to each other, relying on a combination of trial and error and estimation to find out. A similar development of children's understanding of weight happens as they directly compare two objects: "this feels heavier". It is much later that they begin to make the distinction between weight and size and begin to compare weight, using a balance.

Children also develop an interest in measures by watching adults and copying: they like to use a tape measure and "read off" the number; they may try to "measure" water in a jug with a ruler. Although they don't fully understand the use of these measuring instruments, playing with them links what they do with the adult world.

74

Helping children learn to talk about comparing quantities

>> Talk about lengths, distances, weight and time without measuring them: talk about what a long way it is to the park, how heavy a box is to carry, or what a short time it took to tidy up.

>> Read stories about tall giants, long caterpillars, small mice and things that happened a long time ago or yesterday. Involve children in the stories by encouraging them to act them out.

>> Compare two things directly, one against the other: find which bead string is the longest, stand the teddies next to each other and see which is the tallest. See which bowl holds the most by filling one with rice and tipping it from one to the other.

>> Discuss the importance of lining up the ends in order to work out which of two things is longer.

>> Introduce measuring tools: centimetre tapes, rulers, simple balances and spring balances, jugs with measures and litre containers, sand timers and stop watches. Using real measuring equipment gives children the opportunity to rehearse being measurers.

Progression in comparing quantities

- Child uses hand movements to indicate size, and similar words, such as big or little, to indicate size or weight without comparison

- Child is developing a sense of size, and experiments with fitting objects into containers or clothes onto dolls or teddies

- Child uses sight to estimate and judge size and fit more or less accurately

- Child begins to appreciate that some things can be large but not heavy and tests weight by lifting objects

- Child selects from a range of words, such as "thick" or "thin", to describe an object

- Child is likely to distinguish between the vocabulary of weight and the vocabulary of size. For example, when building, talks about "tall", when using the balance talks about "heavy"

- Child begins to understand and use comparative words, such as "taller", "shorter" and "heavier"

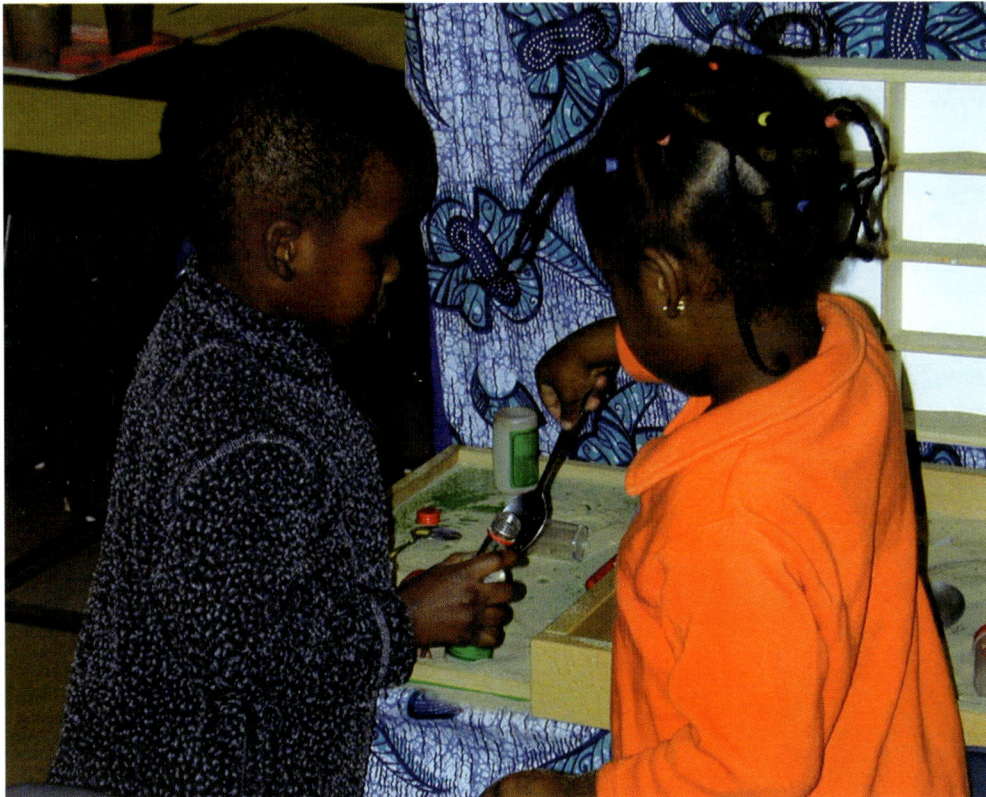

Children learn to estimate and judge size and fit more or less accurately

Mathematics provision

Important words and phrases

long, short, tall, high, low, wide, narrow, deep, shallow, thick, thin

weight, weigh, heavy, light, balance

full, empty, half full

more, less, shorter, longer

about the same as, just over, just under, too much, too little

today, tomorrow, yesterday

The public weighing station

Set up a weighing area and resource with a range of weighing equipment, such as large bucket-balances, kitchen scales, stand-on scales and any other weighing machines that will give the children an opportunity to weigh large and small items.

Introduce a block and tackle system for really heavy objects.

Develop the play by adding pricing: weighing heavy objects costs 2p, lighter objects cost 1p. Ask the children to build a "Speak Your Weight" teddy weighing machine and take it in turns to be its voice.

Ball sorting (outside)

Resource the outdoor area with two buckets, one labelled "large" and the other "small", and a collection of large and small balls. The children can throw or sort the balls into the correct bucket. Extend the play by introducing a medium-sized bucket and encouraging the children to describe why they are putting a particular ball into a particular bucket.

Diary day

Create a special events daily diary, from A3 paper, that children can contribute to by "writing" about an important event or attaching a drawing or photograph of a happening during that day. Develop the play by helping the children make individual diaries and calendars. Encourage the children to read the large diary and comment on what happened yesterday or last week and to use it as a reference point, to see what happened last Monday, for example.

Sleepovers

Resource an area with a range of different sized suitcases, bags, briefcases and trolley bags, as well as a selection of nightwear, jumpers, wash bags and small toys. Suggest that the children pack up a suitcase or bag to take on a sleepover. Develop the play by introducing sleeping bags, small blankets and a quilt.

Lots of lentils

Put out a tray with tiny containers, such as dolls' house cups, film cannisters, mustard spoons or bottle lids, along with a tub of lentils. Children can fill and empty containers with the lentils. Extend the play by adding pricing: lentils cost 1p per mustard spoonful. Find out how much each cupful is worth.

Adult-led activities

How big!

Provide a collection of pairs of objects that are similar but are different sizes, such as a football and a tennis ball, a small teddy and a large teddy, a small crayon and a large crayon. Discuss with the children the differences in each pair and then, together, sort the pairs into two sets of large and small objects. Extend the activity by giving children one of the large objects and asking them to find a similar object that's even bigger.

Stretching high

Tape a roll of paper to the wall and ask everybody to put a fingertip in some paint and then stretch as far up the wall as they can and press on the paper to make a fingerprint (the idea is to make a line of fingerprints across the paper). Write the children's names next to their print. Extend the activity by discussing whose fingerprint is the highest up the wall.

How far up the wall can you stretch?

How will we know who can stretch the furthest?

Vote for heavy

Provide three different objects for the children to hold, such as a ball of wool, a bag of pebbles and a potato. Give each child a voting disc (made from card) with their name on. Suggest that the children handle the three items and then decide which object is the heaviest by putting their voting disc next to it. Count up the votes for each object and then help the children use weighing balances to find out which weighs the most. Have a second vote after the weighing, in case anyone wants to change their vote. Extend the activity by asking children to vote for the lightest or by changing one of the objects.

How did you decide which object to vote for?

Hold the pebbles and the potato. Which feels heavier to you?

What happens when you pick up something heavy?

Footsteps

Cut out footprint shapes from newspaper or magazines. Encourage the children to make a footprint line between two different places, such as the book corner and the sand tray, or the book corner and the door. Extend the activity by deciding which footprint line was the longest.

The ribbon game

Play this game with a small group. You need a bag of about fifteen ribbons of various lengths. Pick five or six ribbons in secret and show only their ends. The children take turns to pick one of the ribbons. Together, you compare lengths and the longest ribbon wins its owner a counter. Return the ribbons to the bag and start again. Extend the activity by introducing a shortest/longest spinner to decide whether the person with the longest or shortest ribbon wins.

How can we find out who is holding the longest ribbon?

Does it matter whether or not we hold the ribbons next to each other?

Guess my weight

Give each pair a set of 1–20 number cards. Pass a small teddy or another soft toy around the group and ask them to estimate, in bricks, the weight of the teddy. Put the toy in the bucket balance and then ask each pair to show a card for the number of bricks they guess will balance the teddy. Encourage the children to count the bricks onto the balance. As they get closer to the final result, give them an opportunity to change their guess. Do this several times with different toys.

I guess that it will take ten bricks to balance Teddy. Is anyone guessing more than ten?

Why did you think that the little car would take fewer bricks to balance than Teddy?

What happens to the balance bucket when you put in something heavy?

Opportunities through the day

Creative workshop

Resources

Paper, water spray and paint

Eye droppers and tissue paper

Activities

Spray water on a piece of paper to make it damp and then drop a blob of paint on the paper and see how far it spreads. Put the blobs in order of size.

Use eyedroppers to drop paint on tissue paper and discuss the size of the drops.

Is that the largest you've made?

Which one do you think is the smallest?

Water tray

Resources

Large jug of water and collection of small containers

Glitter

Pebbles

Thick plastic freezer bags

Activities

Add glitter to the water to make a magic potion and find out how many containers you can fill with a jugful of potion. Discuss how many containers you would need to fill the jug half full.

Pour a container of potion into a freezer bag and ask the children to hold it in their hand and decide how many containers of potion a giant could hold.

Can you hold it all in your hands?

How will you know when it is half full?

Construction area

Resources

Large plastic building bricks
Wooden blocks

Activities

Build the tallest tower that you can, decide whether or not it is taller than anyone in the room and discuss how to reach the top of the tower. Use measuring tapes or ribbons to find out how tall the tower is.

Go for a "tall walk" and take photographs of tall buildings and cranes nearby and display them in the construction area.

Which one did you decide was the tallest?

Does anyone know how to use measuring tapes?

Outdoor area

Resources

Wheelbarrow and spades
Small and large buckets
Trolleys and handcarts
Bags
A small axle pulley and line (from a builders' merchants) or a washing line and pulley

Activities

Transport a pile of sand or compost from one area to another. Fill up different sized buckets and decide whether or not they are too heavy to carry.

Set up a washing-line pulley system to transport heavy buckets or use an axle pulley to transport the heavy buckets.

How can you tell if the bucket is heavy or not?

Which bucket is the lightest?

Assessing children's development

If a child	Then they may be on this step
Brings you, when asked, the "big one" or "small one" of two toy animals Has an undeveloped sense of size, trying to fit, say, a small dress onto a large teddy Can say whether it is fair or not when one child has a lot more juice than another	Use size language such as "big" and "little" Have a positive approach to new experiences
Puts the big plates in one pile and the small plates in another pile Makes statements using "than", such as, "This is curlier than that" Tells you which of two dolls is taller Predicts (accurately or not) that the sand in the jug will fit in the bucket or that the blue pot will fit in the red one Comments that the bucket of water is very heavy	Match objects by recognising similarities Adapt their behaviour to different events, social situations and changes in routine
Puts two laces side by side with their ends together when asked to find which is longer or shorter Makes a simple cloak for a doll and uses comparing words to describe it: for example, says "The cloak is too short" Distinguishes between weight and size: says that the little tin of beans is heavier that the big cereal packet Sequences several story pictures, using words such as "first", "second" and "last" Programs the floor turtle to move so many units forwards	Order two items by length or height Cut material, paper or ribbon to size Order two or three items by length Order two items by weight or capacity Instruct a programmable toy Operate independently within the environment

Conor said "It's a very big pig".

Yellow level
Age 3.11

If a child	Then they may have reached these objectives
Deals with imaginary comparisons: for example, "When the baby gets bigger, the clothes will be too small" Makes fine comparisons between things that are not very different: for example, "This mug's got more juice in than that one" or "Her tower is taller than mine" Talks about time or speed, saying, for example, "I want to finish before dinner" or "I was quicker than he was"	Use language such as "greater", "smaller", "heavier" or "lighter" to compare quantities Respond to significant experiences, showing a range of feelings when appropriate
Puts three things in order: for example, orders three bears by height, then finds where a fourth item fits into the order Counts in order to compare when measuring. For example, counts how many marbles fit into two different boxes, then announces which is bigger Watches you squash flat one of two identical dough balls, and says that they can make them the same again Says it is still fair when they watch you give them and a friend the same amount of drink and then pour theirs into a different shaped mug	Know that counting can help them compare size, capacity or weight Understand that the length of something does not change if you bend it Sustain involvement and persevere, particularly when trying to solve a problem or reach a satisfactory conclusion

light

ALex

heavy

Alex said "The red bag is very light because I can lift it high and the yellow bag is too heavy to lift up".

Grey level

Age 5.4

About the maths

This chapter is about introducing children to pattern and helping them describe and create patterns themselves.

Pattern is fundamental to mathematics. A key idea is that a mathematical pattern is usually not just an arrangement but involves a rule or mathematical relationship. Exploring pattern develops a sense of regularity and order, which children need in order to understand and recognise mathematical rules, solve mathematical problems and make generalisations.

When they make patterns, children are learning to apply rules. To be able to repeat a sequence pattern of blocks of colour, or of shapes, numbers, sounds or movements, children must identify the implicit rule in the sequence. For example, a bead necklace has the unit: red, blue, blue, green, and the rule "repeat sequentially". To make growing patterns, you decide on the unit and you have to apply the same rule again and again to form an increasing or decreasing sequence. When singing and enacting *Five little ducks went swimming one day*, for example, you have to remember the unit "one little duck" and the rule "take away" each time the rhyme comes round again. Creating symmetrical patterns requires a different set of rules to those for following a sequence: so, to make a mirror-image of red, blue, blue, green, you start with the green and repeat in reverse.

How children learn about pattern

Children have an intuitive idea of pattern. When playing with building blocks, for example, children often make symmetrical patterns unconsciously. They line toys up in order, they paint regular stripes, they have a sense of "balance" in design. As children develop, and with appropriate help, they begin to recognise, then copy, extend and create patterns of increasing complexity. For example, they begin to recognise not just simple alternating patterns, such as drum, triangle, drum, triangle, but more complex repeated patterns such as drum, drum, triangle, drum, drum, triangle.

Gradually, children learn how to discuss and describe their patterns, using a wider range of vocabulary. They extend their understanding by making sequences of repeated patterns in more than one direction, such as across, up, down, across, up, down, or this way, that way, this way, that way, or one, two, three, turn, one, two, three, turn. When they become aware of the patterns around them, young children become very interested in them and begin to create their own patterns.

Helping young children learn about pattern

>> Point out and talk about patterns around you, or in books: look at wrapping paper and wallpaper patterns. Discuss decorative patterns on posters and boxes.

>> Point out repeating patterns in the daily routine:

After fruit time there is always a story.

Sing songs where there is a pattern, such as the same line or chorus repeated.

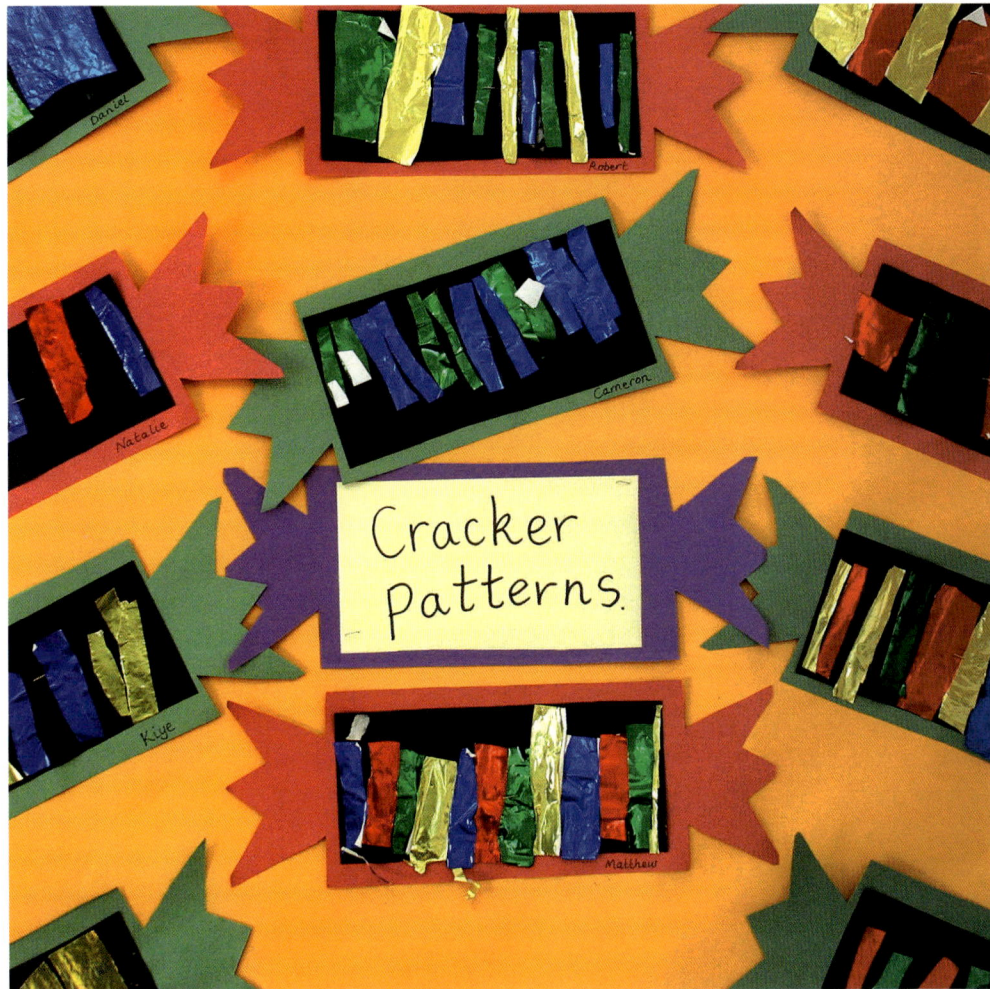

As they become aware of patterns around them, children begin to create their own

Progression in talking about, recognising and recreating pattern

- Child makes seemingly random arrangements of marks with paint or crayon, or uses beads, buttons or shapes and refers to the finished article as their pattern

- Child makes "splodge patterns" with paint and folded paper, and talks about sameness

- Child begins to make their own simple, occasionally repeating, pattern using threaded beads

- Child continues a pattern started by someone else, using blocks, shapes or colours

- Child discusses a repeated pattern on material and identifies a feature of it

- Child makes or copies a growing or decreasing pattern

>> Provide a computer with a suitable drawing program and when children make a pattern of any sort, describe it to them and identify the features that you particularly like.

>> Point out patterns in action songs or dances or make up action patterns.

>> Point out musical patterns and make up sequences of sounds.

Help children recognise growing and decreasing patterns:

>> Read stories and sing songs where there is a pattern of numbers going up or down. Or make a staircase pattern with bricks, dominoes or square tiles and ask children to continue it.

Help children recognise symmetrical patterns:

>> Play with plastic mirrors; make butterfly pictures; point out objects that have two sides that are the same, such as kites. Use print-making and peg patterns as opportunities to identify symmetry.

Mathematics provision

Important words and phrases

pattern, repeat, repeating pattern, symmetrical

first, second, third… last

size, bigger, smaller, the same as, copy

sort, make, build, draw

fit together, match, shape

Collecting patterns (outside)

In the outdoor area, encourage the children to go on an environmental pattern-collecting expedition. Children can collect objects that have interesting patterns on them, such as feathers, seed heads, fir cones and flowers. Take photographs of patterns that they find, such as spider webs, paving stones and tree shapes. Provide clipboards for drawing patterns that they see and soft crayons for making rubbings of tree barks, brick patterns and drain covers. Develop the play by putting together an exhibition of patterns collected, drawn and photographed.

Mirror play

Set up a table against a mirrored wall or a wall covered with silver foil. Resource it with small building blocks as well as different shapes and sizes of safety mirrors. Hinge two mirrors together to make a reflective angle and three mirrors to make a triangle shape. Add kaleidoscopes, both those with ready-made shapes and plain ones where shapes can be inserted. Encourage the children to build small constructions and look at the reflection in the wall mirror and then use the hand mirrors to look at different angles. Develop the play by changing the materials that can be reflected, every day.

Table patterns

Create a pattern table by making pattern lines or circles with small world objects, shapes, bead strings or plastic animals. Include some patterns made with 3D shapes. Every day start new patterns for the children to continue. Develop the play by encouraging children to start their own patterns.

Design centre

Set up a design consultant's office in one area. Resource with wallpaper pattern books, sheets of patterned wrapping paper and lengths of material with simple patterns, such as tartan, checks and lines, or spots. Display pattern blocks and printing blocks and ink pads. Discuss with the children the role of designers and pattern creators. Give the children the opportunity to discuss their "design needs" with the consultants. Invite designers and artists in to show their skills.

Computer design

Set up an art software package on the computer. Suggest that the children design a "screen saver" pattern. Display the results by cutting out a frame from a cardboard box to give the effect of a computer monitor.

Adult-led activities

Pattern clap

Together, practise clapping loudly, clapping softly, clapping quickly and clapping slowly and clapping with two fingers together. When the group is proficient at hand claps, introduce the idea of pattern clapping, such as "clap hands twice loudly and twice softly, twice loudly, twice softly" and so on. Extend the activity by starting the clapping pattern and saying what the pattern is as you are clapping, and encouraging the children to say the pattern as they join in the claps.

Saying patterns

Give out two different sizes of bears to a small group and help the children to sit in a circle holding their bears in an "every other one" pattern. Pass by each child saying what the pattern is: "small bear, large bear, small bear, large bear, small bear…". Ask the children to start saying the pattern and to see how fast they can go round the circle. Extend the activity by choosing different objects to hold, such as red cars and green cars or triangles and circles.

Copy me… Now let's say the pattern together.

Pass the pattern

Make a pattern, using objects from a feely bag. Put a collection of two kinds of objects, such as fir cones and conkers or counters and small bricks, into a cloth bag. Ask the children to take it in turns to pull the right object out of the bag to continue the pattern. For example, teaspoon, brick, teaspoon, brick, teaspoon. Extend the activity by asking the children to put some different objects in the bag to make patterns with.

Can you carry on the pattern? How will you do that?

Pattern jumping

Make a track using three different types of stickers, six times each, in a pattern. Use a blank dice or spinner with the stickers repeated twice. Ask the children to take it in turns to throw the dice and move their counter along the track to the next place that that sticker appears. Develop the activity by using the same track and jumping backwards along it.

Is the square sticker always after the round one?

People patterns

Work with a large group to create line or circle patterns. Start the pattern: one child standing, one sitting, one standing, one sitting… and ask the rest of the group to join in the pattern. Start another pattern with children facing forwards, backwards, forwards, backwards… and ask children to describe the pattern that they're making. Invite some to join the front of the line, still keeping the pattern going. Extend the activity by making patterns of two and one, such as two children touching ears, one child touching their knees, two touching ears… again invite the rest of the group to join in.

Can anyone tell me the pattern we're making now?

Pegging patterns

Give the children small pegboards and a large supply of pegs and ask them to create a pattern using every hole in the pegboard. Discuss the different ways the patterns might be created. Such as starting at the outside edge of the board and putting the pegs in a spiral or putting in the pegs diagonally, or in lines or in squares. Extend the activity by giving the children squared paper and pens to record their patterns.

What pattern did you make?

Opportunities through the day

Creative workshop

Resources

Plastic chopping board

Paints and paint rollers

Cotton reels, plastic shapes and combs

Activities

Make a pattern print by using a paint roller to cover a plastic pastry board in different stripes of colour, then use the ends of cotton reels or other print materials to create a design. Before the paint dries, press the paper on the board to take a print of the design.

Which part of your design did you invent first?

I wonder if the print is the same as your design.

Outdoor area

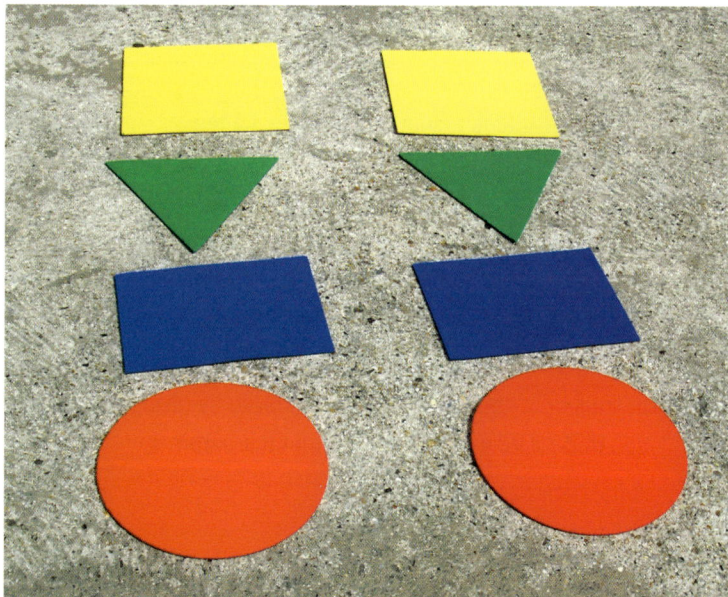

Resources

Collection of chalks in various colours and sizes

Collection of different coloured, textured, or patterned floor and lino tiles

Activities

Make an outdoor art gallery of patterns. Talk to the children about pavement art and ask if any of them have seen patterns or pictures drawn on the pavement.

Draw a large rectangle in the outdoor area and explain that you're going to make your own pavement art and that everyone will draw a part of the design. Children choose chalks to create their designs.

Use some tiles to make the first part of a pattern. Invite children to continue or copy the pattern.

What else could we use?

How could we try another way?

Music area

Resources

Percussion instruments (at least one per child)

Activities

Make a pattern using different parts of your body, for example: stamp, stamp, clap… stamp, stamp, clap. Ask children to watch and join in when they can. Speak the pattern as you do it to help some children. Invite children to help make up different patterns.

Make a musical pattern: each child chooses an instrument. One child makes a pattern and the other tries to copy it: tap, tap, tap, tap… bang, bang, bang, bang.

Help children line up to make a pattern: one child stands, next child sits, next child stands, next child sits...

Can you help me say the pattern?

I wonder what would happen if we repeated the pattern.

Malleable area

Resources

A quantity of dough made by mixing together two cups of flour, one cup of salt, two cups of water and two tablespoons of oil, over a low heat, until it forms into a ball. Add a handful of sawdust if making snakes or five drops of food colouring if rolling shapes.

Small beads, buttons, counters

Activities

Roll a family of snakes. Choose from the beads, buttons, and so on, to make a pattern along the back of the first snake. Use the pattern again on each snake to show that they belong to the same family.

Make a row of dough balls that get bigger and bigger. Invite children to make a ball to fit into the row.

I wonder what we should put next.

Can anyone make a row like mine?

Assessing children's development

If a child	Then they may be on this step
Shows interest in a pattern on paper, a box or a tablecloth Arranges objects neatly, perhaps in a line, but not in any order or pattern Enjoys playing with pattern blocks Points to "the one with the pattern on" when shown two posters or tablecloths, one plain and one patterned	Show interest in pattern Have a strong exploratory impulse
Attempts to make a pattern, using objects or crayons Puts a set of three or four objects, such as nesting pots, in order of size Talks about a set of three or four nesting dolls that you have put in order of size; puts them back in order when you disrupt the arrangement Copies a simple alternating pattern, using objects or crayons Extends a simple alternating pattern started by someone else	Recognise and copy simple alternating patterns Extend and create simple alternating patterns Demonstrate flexibility
Creates or copies a pattern, using objects or crayons, and, when asked, describes it: "It's red, red, blue, red, red, blue" Looks at a symmetrical pattern and talks about what is the same on each side Puts a set of four or more coloured rods in order of length; spots what is wrong when you move one of the objects	Recognise and copy more complex repeating patterns Extend and create more complex repeating patterns Make growth patterns Show awareness of symmetry Display high levels of involvement in activities

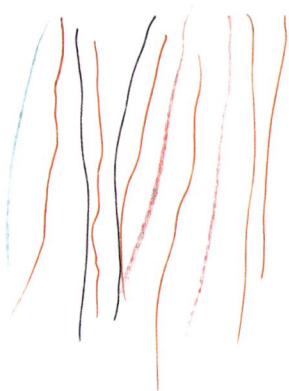

"Here's my pattern. I used the red pen and that one and the others".

Blue level
Ali, age 3.11

If a child

Then they may have reached these objectives

Puts pieces of number jigsaw in numerical order	Talk about, recognise and recreate simple patterns
Extends or copies a pattern started by someone else involving three or more colours or shapes	Continue to be interested, excited and motivated to learn
Describes the "rule" of someone else's pattern: "It's white bead, blue bead, red bead"	
Makes simple symmetry patterns with pattern blocks	
Makes a repeating pattern on the computer, or continues someone else's pattern	Use mathematical language to describe solid (3D) objects and flat (2D) shapes
Discusses simple symmetry patterns made with folded paper and scissors or paint and predicts what the opened-out shape might look like	Take into account the ideas of others
Positions a mirror on a picture so as to lengthen the tree or turn two dots into four dots	
Uses a squared grid to make patterns that go downwards as well as sideways – even if inaccuracies creep in	

Muddassir printed his design very carefully, waiting to use the cylinder to complete his pattern.

Grey level

Age 5.1

About the maths

This chapter is about providing children with opportunities to use words describing 2D and 3D shapes.

Everything we can see or touch has a shape. Mostly these shapes are too complex to describe, except very roughly: the shell is a bit round; the stairs are straight and they go up at an angle. Some objects have particular names to describe their shape. It is important to make available a variety of examples of different 2D and 3D shapes, such as equilateral triangles and tetrahedrons, squares and cubes, so that children can generalise their properties. It is also important to explore the relationship between 3D and 2D shapes and to look at how the shapes of some faces of an object determine the shape of the other faces.

How children learn about solid and flat shapes

Children learn about the differences between shapes by playing with them, building with them, drawing around them, combining them, making pictures with them, printing with them, rolling with them and by talking about their experiences with adults, who can help put these experiences into words.

Children learn most about shapes by handling lots of different ones, small and large – by climbing inside large boxes and holding small boxes in their hands. Children need a wide range of experiences where they focus on the differences between manufactured and natural objects, as well building their own constructions and using dough to make their own shapes.

Children will learn about the properties of shapes by playing, building and investigating with them and putting shapes together in different ways. Rather than just learning the names of shapes, children need to learn about what shapes are like; what shapes can and can't do; and which shapes fit together and which shapes don't.

Children need to handle both regular and irregular shapes. For example, they need to play with equilateral triangles and with irregular triangles in order to generalise that the concept of triangle includes any 2D shape with three straight sides.

Helping children learn about solid and flat shapes

>> Spend time opening out and remaking shapes with children: demonstrating and talking about how a 3D shape unfolds into a 2D shape that looks quite different.

>> Use blocks to construct different shapes and draw them to show how they fit together. Describe what they look like. It helps children to hear words such as "straight", "round", "corner" and "flat" when adults are describing something that they have built.

>> Provide children with an extensive collection of 2D and 3D materials for exploring and building with. This should include large objects, such as blocks, cardboard boxes, wood and crates, and smaller ones, such as sets of small bricks, construction kits and shaped blocks. Sometimes mix the two different types or sizes of construction material together.

>> Introduce tetrahedrons and triangular prisms; squares and cubes; circles and cylinders, so that children can generalise ideas and properties about 2D and 3D shapes.

To support children learning about the properties of 3D shapes:

>> Provide equipment for playing with, for climbing inside, and for sliding, rolling and stacking.

>> Provide modelling materials such as damp sand, dough, clay and modelling clay.

>> Post shapes into posting boxes, either bought ones or home-made ones.

>> Search for corners and put a teddy in every corner.

>> Sort out the pasta and find all the spirals, then look for some more spirals in shells and sunflowers.

To help children identify and talk about 3D shapes:

>> Help children sort shapes; describe them, using everyday language, and point out ones that are the same.

To help children learn about 2D shapes:

>> Provide play mats marked out with various shapes for children to fill.

>> Complete different types of jigsaw puzzles and fit together construction pieces.

>> Use chalk to draw shapes in the outdoor area and play "hopping round the lines" or "jumping inside the shapes".

>> Fill plastic water bottles and squirt the water using big, circular hand movements, or draw shapes on the outdoor walls with a bucket of water and a large brush.

>> Walk along in straight-line crocodiles and then in a curve or zig-zag.

>> Use skipping ropes to create straight lines and circles.

Progression in describing shape and size

- Child plays with and builds with a variety of 3D shapes

- Child uses 2D shape material to make pictures

- Child begins to show a sense of what shapes will and won't fit or balance when constructing towers, bridges or houses

- Child can hold an object and describe some features, such as smooth, pointy or round

- Child can make a collection of objects and say why one in particular can't be part of the collection

- Child can find another shape "like this" when asked

- Child recognises simple shapes (squares, circles, cubes) by sight and begins to name them

One way children learn about 3D shapes is by playing with them

Mathematics provision

Child-initiated play

Important words and phrases

shape, round, flat, straight, curved

roll, stack, slide, pile

2D, circle, triangle, rectangle, square

3D, cube, cuboid, sphere, pyramid, cone

corner, face, side, edge, end

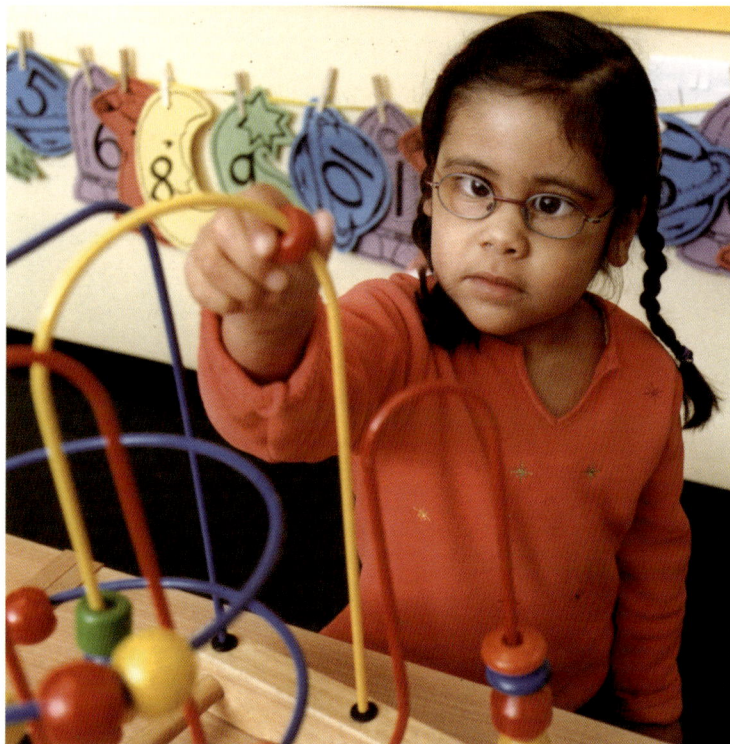

Airports (outside)

As part of a topic on travel or holidays, resource an outdoor area with a quantity of milk crates and recycled materials, such as large cardboard boxes, so that the children are able to build an aeroplane large enough for them to sit in. As the plane is being built, discuss with the children how the shapes of the building materials will fit together, as well as how passengers will enter and leave the plane. Develop the play by providing seating as well as cabin crew dressing-up clothes.

The torch light museum

Develop a role-play area as an "Unusual Objects Museum" by covering a space with a thick blanket and, underneath, resourcing with a display of different objects, such as a broomhead, a rugby ball, a saucepan and a construction arrangement built from large blocks. Provide some torches for the children to use in the museum so that they can explore the objects and the shadows that the shapes make. Develop the play by providing clipboards for the children to draw and identify what they have seen; make a guide book for the museum.

Architect's office

Turn the construction area into an architect's office. Display pictures of building exteriors and interiors, plans and elevations. Include a list of requests from clients: "an office block", "a bungalow", "a school", for children to build. Extend the play by providing easels and paper for children to draw the buildings and the plans and elevations.

Box-packers Incorporated

Set up a role-play area as a box-packing station. Resource with cardboard boxes of different shapes and sizes and a selection of contents that need to be packed. Provide address labels and a wheeled cart for delivering the parcels. Display some large maps of the area and a list of charges for delivering different sized packages. Provide the packers with overalls and caps.

Adult-led activities

Look for the shape

Show a small group a collection of circles, such as lids, counters, wheels or play biscuits. Discuss the features of each and then ask the children to find another circle in the room that they can add to the collection. Extend the activity by giving each child a paper circle and some bingo pens to use to print circles inside the circle

Can you see any circles in the room?

I wonder if the base of this tin is a circle.

I spy

Collect together a selection of 2D and 3D shapes, including everyday objects, and ask the children to guess what object you've "spied". Keeping adding information about the object until someone guesses. Extend the activity by showing part of a shape and see if children can say what it is by looking.

I spy something without any corners and it rolls very easily… how did you work out it was the ball?

This time I spy something shiny… how did you know I spied the teaspoon?

Creating caterpillars

Collect together some cut-up egg trays and sheets of newspaper. Give each pair of children a coloured stocking or half a pair of opaque tights and some small elastic bands. Ask the children to crumple the newspaper into balls and fill the stocking with them. Use the elastic bands to separate the "caterpillars" into segments. Make small slits in some segments to insert the egg tray compartments as feet. Discuss which caterpillar is the roundest, longest, thinnest, and so on.

Do you think any of the caterpillars are the same size?

What did you notice about this caterpillar?

Guess what's in my hand

Put four small-world objects or different sized and shaped bricks or flat shapes on a tray. Choose an identical object to one of those on the tray and put it in a cloth bag, without the children seeing. Ask the children to take it in turns to feel in the bag and identify what object on the tray they think it is. Remove the object from the bag and see if it matches. Extend the activity by putting replicas of all four tray objects in the bag and asking the children to remove a particular one without looking.

How will you know if it's a triangle in the bag?

I wonder what the shell will feel like.

Which of the bricks do you think will be long and thin?

Pairs

Provide the group with a box of different shapes: both regular and irregular, and small and large. Ask the children to find two shapes that are exactly the same. After discussing the shapes that they matched together, suggest that they now find two shapes that are nearly the same. Extend the activity by inviting the children to sort the shapes into sets.

Can you find another square?

How is that different from this one?

Inside out

Give each child a small cardboard box to open out. Discuss with them how to identify the longest edge and draw a line along it and then cut along all the other edges. Play refolding and opening and closing the box. Extend the activity by asking the children to draw along all the inside edges, decorating the inside of the box and refolding to show the new box design.

How do you know that's the longest edge?

What shape will it make now?

Opportunities through the day

Creative workshop

Resources

Paper napkins
Coloured inks in small bowls
Newspapers

Activities

Help the children double-fold a paper napkin into a square and discuss corners and edges. Dip the folded corners quickly into ink or food colouring. Press the napkins between newspapers. Unfold the napkins and peg them up to dry. Try folding napkins into triangle shapes and dipping the edges.

Fold sheets of paper in the same way as the napkins and discuss the corners and edges. Cut off the corners and unfold to see what shapes have been made. Compare with the patterned napkins.

How can we find out how many corners the shape has got?

Outdoor area

Resources

Torches
Plastic bottles and sticky tape
Squeezy plastic bottles

Activities

Use torch light to trace some straight and curved lines onto a shady wall. Use the torches to follow existing lines in the playground.

Make three holes in a vertical line in a small plastic bottle. Cover the holes with sticky tape. Fill the bottle with water, remove the tape and start drawing circles on the ground.

Fill a squeezy bottle with water and draw shapes on a wall.

Can you tell me about the shape you've made?

What other shapes can you see?

Sand tray

Resources

Shallow tray of damp sand
Five plastic 3D shapes
A collection of hollow containers

Activities

Use three different shapes from a collection to make an imprint in the damp sand and then decide which three they were.

Make lots of "sand pies" from hollow containers and arrange them on a tray.

Choose a hollow container from a collection and make a sand pie. Discuss which container must have been used.

Can you show me how I can make one like yours?

Do you think that this shape will fit into the hollow?

Science area

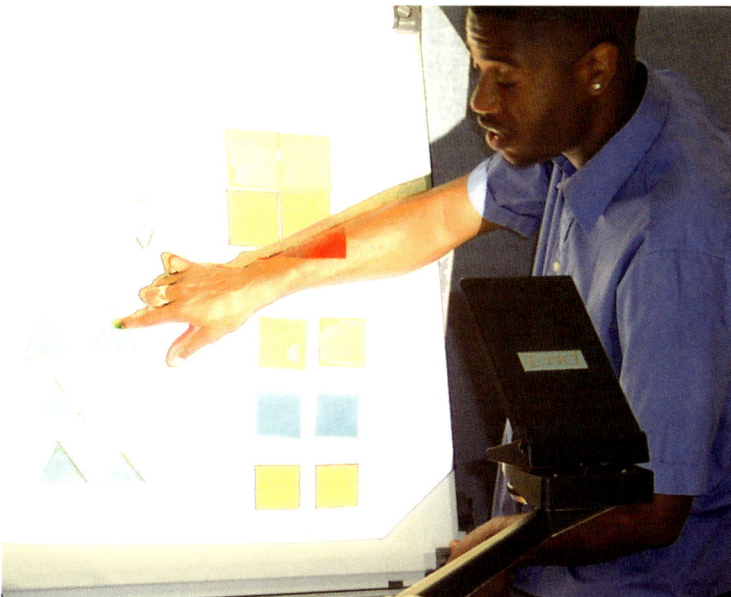

Resources

OHP
Sheets of paper taped to the wall
2D shapes
Pens

Activities

Invite children to choose a shape to place on the OHP. Project this onto the paper and discuss with the children what they can see there. Discuss corners and sides and compare with the original shape. Draw around the outline of the projected shape and cut it out. Try fitting the smaller shape inside the larger one.

Enlarge shapes on the photocopier, cut out and compare.

What happens when you put two shapes together?

I wonder if you'll make a different shape next time

Assessing children's development

If a child	Then they may be on this step
Makes an arrangement with flat shapes, or builds with blocks or other objects	Show an interest in shape and space by playing with shapes or making arrangements with objects
Comments that the pictures of the sun and moon are alike	Show awareness of similarities in shapes in the environment
Matches identical shapes when they are in the same orientation and the same size: points to the two shapes in a row that are both squares standing on their bases	Use size language such as "big" and "little" to talk about shapes
Points to the "big ball" in a picture of two different sized balls when asked to do so	Have a strong exploratory impulse
Chooses blocks according to their shape when building towers or other constructions	Show interest by sustained construction activity or by talking about shapes or arrangements
Talks about their construction when it is finished	Use shapes appropriately for tasks
Chooses a round shape when they want something to roll down a ramp	Begin to talk about the shapes of everyday objects
Separates out a set of shapes that is mixed up with others	Show increasing independence in selecting and carrying out activities
Talks about the shapes of kitchen rolls, ice cream cones, balls, hoops... but may not always use the correct words	
Can tell you what they plan to make, then keep working at this construction or picture	Sustain interest for a length of time on a pre-decided construction or arrangement
Chooses appropriate shapes when making constructions, pictures or patterns, and can talk about their choice	Match some shapes by recognising similarities and orientation
Matches identical shapes even when they are in a different orientation: for example, finds the two half-moons	Show curiosity and observation by talking about shapes, how they are the same or why some are different
Matches same shapes in different sizes: for example, finds the three circles of different sizes	Choose suitable components to make a particular model
Chooses a triangular sticky shape and cuts the corner off it to make a hat for their picture of mummy	Adapt shapes or cut material to size
	Begin to use mathematical names for "solid" 3D shapes and "flat" 2D shapes, and mathematical terms to describe shapes
Use terms such as "pointy", "flat", "round", or "straight" to name or describe shapes	Persist for extended periods of time at an activity of their choosing

If a child

Then they may have reached these objectives

Puts together all the "ones with corners" or "ones that roll"

Can talk about the shapes of solid or hollow objects, and about flat shapes, using words such as, "flat", "curved", "circle", "straight", "square", "corner", "end", and "slide"

Can talk about the shapes of everyday objects, using words such as "flat", "curved", "circle", "straight", "square", "corner", "end", and "slide"

Use language such as "circle" or "bigger" to describe the shape and size of solid and flat shapes

Be confident to try new activities, initiate ideas and speak in a familiar group

Sorts a set of flat or solid shapes, putting together triangles, squares, pyramids or cubes, and talks about what they are doing

When asked, sorts a set of shapes: putting together all the shapes that are not triangles

Can point to common 2D shapes and 3D objects when asked: for example, a circle, triangle, rectangle, star, cuboid or sphere

Matches a Poleidobloc by putting together two or more smaller shapes

Can tell you which flat or 3D object you are thinking about, when you describe one of a collection visible to you both

Use mathematical language to describe solid (3D) objects and flat (2D) shapes

Sustain involvement and persevere, particularly when trying to solve a problem or reach a satisfactory conclusion

Ayesha said "My bike has got circles [draws round wheels with finger] and straight bits like the handles, and these strokes [points to wheel spokes] they're straight and they go inside the circles, and see where they cross over, that makes me go really fast".

Grey level
Age 5.6

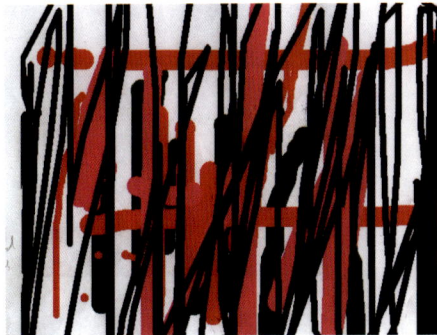

Gretel said she'd done a straight line picture on the computer.

Green level
Age 3.9

This chapter is about helping children learn to talk about where things are.

The whereabouts of an object is always described in relation to something else: the pan is on the stove, the school is next to the shops, the balloon is above the tree, the station is in square C5 on the street map.

Instructions on how to get somewhere include direction words: left, right, up, down. Instructions on how far to go include measuring words: one step, a minute's walk, ten metres away. Identifying the position of objects and places eventually includes measurement and scale. In order to really define, for example, where on the shelves the bricks are, you need two pieces of information: the third shelf up and the fourth pigeon-hole along from the left. Having two location references can increase the accuracy of directions. Think of plans, charts and treasure maps that are printed on a square grid to give two lines of reference, or coordinates.

How children learn about position and direction

The kinds of experiences that children need to understand position, movement and direction include all the activities that they enjoy doing, such as running and pedalling in all directions, climbing to the top of the frame and sliding down again and again, crawling through the tunnel, crouching underneath the table, getting inside boxes and cupboards, and just lying on the floor.

They also learn about position from small-world play as they decide where in the farmyard to put the horse, where to put the people in the house, and how to arrange the

Collaborative working enables children to talk with each other about what they're working on

cars on the play mat and the dinosaurs in the sand tray.

When the adults around them provide the language to describe what the children are doing and where they are putting different

objects, it supports the children in extending their language and knowledge of position and direction.

Progression in describing position and direction

- Child makes arrangements with materials such as bricks or small-world objects

- Child begins to follow simple instructions involving positional language such as "under" and "on top of"

- Child talks about arrangements made with materials such as bricks or small-world objects

- Child begins to use simple positional and directional information to find hidden objects

- Child draws a simple map or picture showing two objects in particular locations

- Child uses more complex positional and directional clues to find hidden objects

- Child describes a simple journey

- Child instructs a programmable toy

Helping children learn about position and direction

>> Provide activities and games in which children are asked to put themselves in particular places: in front of, behind or beside a friend; between two chairs. Ask them to provide a running commentary on how they or a friend are negotiating an obstacle course or climbing equipment.

>> Set up play scenes with small-world equipment then talk with children about where to put various objects. Take turns with a child: the child tells you where to put an object then you tell the child where to put the next one. Make model gardens and use shallow trays and sand to create dinosaur worlds.

>> Play "hide and seek the teddy" by putting Teddy in a secret place and searching for him. The finder has to describe where he was found. Search for the "magic shell" and say when children are close or far away when they are looking for it. Draw maps and go on walks, take photographs on the walk and recreate the journey.

>> Encourage children to practise putting things away in the top drawer, in the far cupboard or on the shelves near the bookcase.

To help children learn about movement and direction:

>> Provide activities in which children move themselves in different ways and in different directions – round the mulberry bush, following the leader, dancing, or using hoops and balls.

>> Set up situations where children give instructions to other children on how to travel around the outdoor area. Use computer toys that need directional instructions.

>> Install a computer program where children can paint and draw using a moveable paintbrush. Build a walkway where children have to follow footprints or a rope.

Mathematics provision

Important words and phrases

over, under, underneath, above, below

top, bottom

on, in, outside, inside, in front of, behind, front, back

before, after

beside, next to

forwards, backwards, sideways

close, far, opposite, between

Driving round town

In the outdoor area provide a large play road mat, or paint roads on to a plastic ground sheet. Mark out a level car park with individual car spaces. Provide large toy cars and diggers to give the children experience of movement, direction and position. Develop the play by using display shelving as a multi-storey car park and encourage the children to park their vehicles in both car parks.

Building the tunnel

Encourage the children to convert the construction area into a tunnel-building site. Use the large bricks to build tunnel walls and provide a piece of material to be the tunnel roof. Resource the area with construction hard hats and goggles. Have site plans available and a rest bay for construction workers. Develop the play by providing a programmable robot toy, such as a Roamer, to carry messages through the tunnel between the building teams. Write messages on sticky notes and stick them on the robot. Show the children how to programme it to move forwards and backwards through the tunnel.

Circuit-training commentators (outside)

In the outdoor area, construct a small circular course that includes apparatus the children can climb on and over as well as a tunnel to crawl through and a box to get in. Include hoops to climb through as well as a line of cones to zig-zag through. Extend the play by providing hand-held microphones for the children to talk through to give a commentary on the circuits that others are doing.

And now they are crawling through the tunnel.

Everybody has climbed over the frame.

Climbing frames are a useful tool in helping children understand position

Adult-led activities

Hunt the teddy

Cover a table with boxes, lids, polystyrene cups and other recycled materials. Hide a smallish teddy somewhere on the table. Take it in turns to be the hider and searcher. As the child looks under boxes and inside cups you and the other children give clues about where to look for the hidden teddy.

Teddy's inside something.

You're very close to Teddy now.

Teddy's next to a round container.

Scene shifting?

Play this game in pairs. Make up two small boxes containing six small-world figures that are the same. Give each child a similar shoe-box lid to which you have stuck four objects, such as a red brick, a plastic tree, a blue circle and a dolls' house chair. Ask the children to take it in turns to explain to each other where to put each of the characters. When the scenes have been completed, look at both boxes and compare and discuss the two scenes.

Can you put the wizard next to the brick?

Shall we put the duck on the blue circle?

Under the sea

Give each child a piece of blue felt to represent the sea floor and a collection of shells and sea creatures to arrange on their material. When the children have arranged everything, tell them that you are going to make up an "under the sea" story and they have to rearrange their creatures to match what's happening in the story.

All the crabs were huddling under a shell.

The fish were all swimming together.

Along came a large lobster and sat on top of some seaweed.

Going to school

Ask the children to make a 3D board game: on a table arrange some bridges and tunnels, made of plastic construction material, along with trees, houses and a school. Use small card squares as paving stones to connect all the features and to make a track. Ask the children to put some small-world figures in different places on the track. Take it in turns to throw a 1–3 dice and move any of the figures along the track to the school.

Which tree will you put the dinosaur next to?

Will the blue bear go under the bridge to get to the school?

I wonder how many of the characters go through the tunnel on the way to the school.

In its place

Put together a tray with six objects on and play a version of "Kim's Game". Children look at the tray and discuss how the objects are arranged. The children close their eyes while you change the position of one of the objects. The group open their eyes and decide which object has moved. Extend the activity by swapping two objects around.

Has the cat moved? Wasn't it in front of the dinosaur?

Can anyone remember where the spoon was last time?

I don't remember the cotton reel being on top of the box, do you?

Simon Says

Play "Simon Says" with a group. Explain to the children that everyone follows what the leader says and does if they start their instructions with "Simon says...". Otherwise they ignore the instruction.

Simon says put your hands on your head.

Simon says put your hands behind your back.

Simon says put your little fingers under your feet.

Opportunities through the day

Outdoor area

Resources

Ladders

Planks, heavy duty plastic crates

Climbing frame

Activities

Together devise a climbing circuit where the children's feet don't touch the ground.

Take photographs of the children using the circuit and discuss what they are doing. Make a photo montage and use positional words.

Encourage the children to go round the circuit using overs and unders as many times as they can. Play "Freeze" and ask everyone to say whereabouts on the circuit they are.

Can you describe which way you went?

What would have happened if you had gone underneath?

Role-play area

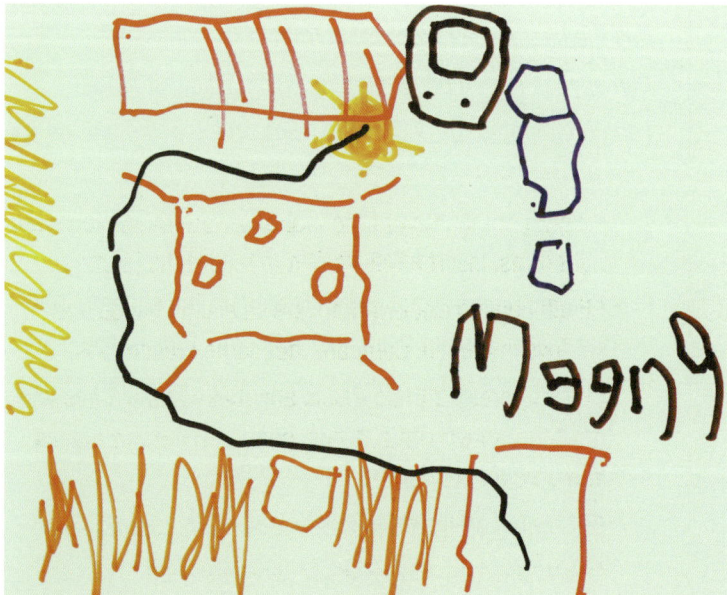

Resources

Small, brightly wrapped parcel

Activities

Play "Hunt the Treasure" by hiding a parcel somewhere in the home corner and encouraging children to search for it. Use positional words as clues.

Ask the children to draw picture maps of where the treasure was found.

How did you know where to find it?

Can you explain where you found it?

Woodwork area

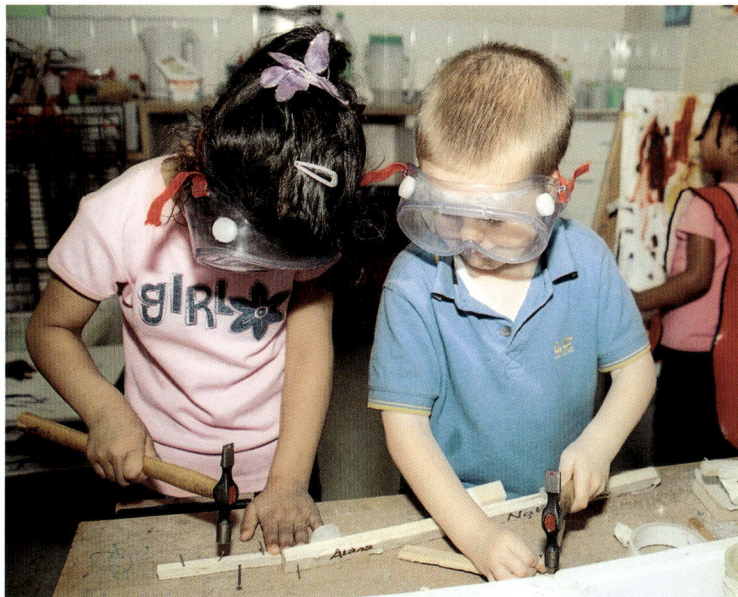

Resources

Woodworking tools
Balsa wood and sticks
Offcuts of wood
Cardboard frames

Activities

Make a big picture without using paper. Saw and arrange some blocks, shapes and sticks and nail together.

Discuss the position of the different features in the picture. When the picture is finished enclose it in a frame and take a photograph.

Use blocks of one shape but different sizes to create a modern building feature.

Where will you put that piece?

What else did you manage to fit inside?

ICT area

Resources

Roamer programmable computer
Range of clockwork toys
Elastic bands
Paper and pens

Activities

Programme the Roamer to make forward movements and right turns. Insert a felt-tip pen to record the journey.

Attach pens to clockwork toys with elastic bands and set toys in motion. Compare the journey recordings.

Children pretend to be robots and make straight line and right-turn movements. Attach pens to children's ankles to record the journeys.

Did you go on different routes around the room?

How will we remember which way you went?

Assessing children's development

If a child	Then they may be on this step
Arranges flat shapes, or builds with blocks or other objects Describes where something is, using words imprecisely, for example, "on" to mean "above" or "beside" or "near to" Follows simple instructions such as "stand on the rug" or "look under the chair"	Show an interest in space by making arrangements with objects Observe and use positional language Show curiosity
Talks about where things are in a picture or small-world scene Points out something they want you to look at, using language such as "here", "there", "up" and "down", and corrects you when you look in the wrong direction	Show interest by talking about arrangements Adapt their behaviour to different events, social situations and changes in routine
Describes the movement of an object (toy aeroplane, doll, ball) using language such as "up", "in front", "behind", "between", "forwards", "backwards" and "sideways" Describes a walk or journey they have taken, using the language of position and direction Talks about how things move: car wheels, an aeroplane, a jointed doll, using the language of movement and direction Follows two or more instructions such as "go under the ladder then through the hoop" Programs the floor turtle to move along a path	Sustain interest for a length of time on a pre-decided construction or arrangement Find items from positional/directional clues Describe a simple journey Instruct a programmable toy Operate independently within the environment

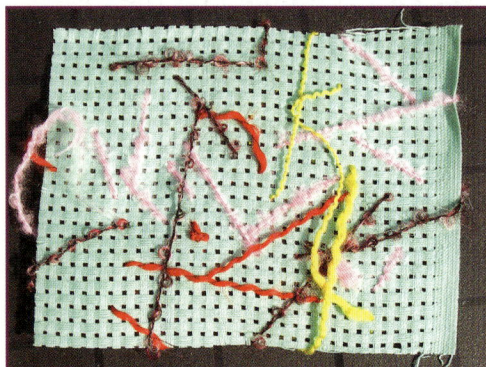

Shauna described how to sew her design: "You put the needle up and then it goes across and then you go down".

Grey level

Age 5.2

If a child	Then they may have reached these objectives
Sends you in the right direction to find an object they have hidden around the room or outdoor area Describes two or more movements of an object using language such as "first it went up in the air then it went behind the curtain then it went in the basket"	Use everyday words to describe position Form good relationships with adults and peers
Follows a wide range of instructions about where to position a doll: in front of, or beside the tree, between two other dolls... Follows a wide range of instructions about getting through an obstacle course: climb over the bench, cross the mat, go round the skittle and along the next bench... Gives instructions to other children: go around the stool, step into the hoop, jump onto the mat… Sort and talk about things that turn, roll or slide	Use mathematical language to describe solid (3D) objects and flat (2D) shapes Sustain involvement and persevere, particularly when trying to solve a problem or reach a satisfactory conclusion

"Daddy is climbing on the roof."
Yellow level
Abbie, age 3.2

About the maths

How children learn to solve practical problems using shape, space and measures

Children learn to solve practical problems by first recognising that there is a problem and understanding what the problem is. For example, how can we find out whether Teddy weighs more than Frog? They then learn to see the possibility of a solution: you could put Teddy on one side of a balance and some conkers in the other.

Children progress in problem solving by being systematic to some degree, in this case, putting conkers on or taking them off the balance one at a time.

They then begin to see connections: realising that putting on more conkers makes the balance go down not up and realising that what they did yesterday with the bricks is relevant to today's problem with the conkers.

Finally, children need to be persistent and try different approaches: such as balancing Frog and Teddy against each other.

This chapter gives ideas for problem solving relating to shape, space and measure.

In the Foundation Stage, mathematical problems are often just everyday events with a mathematical aspect: making sure that everyone has a biscuit; working out how to check that none of the teddies is missing; or deciding the best way to stack the large blocks, for example. Children taking part in these activities are using the maths they know to help them find solutions and are sometimes learning new facts and ideas on the way.

The important point about problem solving is that it involves choices, so children have the opportunity to reason and make decisions.

Children's problem-solving strategies and skills develop through investigating, working on and finding solutions for a wide range of different practical problems. Some will have quick solutions while others will take much of the session time to solve or may even need to be revisited during the course of a week.

It can be helpful to see problem solving as involving two kinds of mathematical understanding: one is learning about some aspect of mathematics such as counting and the other is developing the skills of mathematical reasoning and decision making.

Helping children learn about solving practical problems

>> Create an atmosphere where exploration and "having a go" is seen as more important than getting the right answer.

>> Provide a rich and interesting environment, with plenty of varied activities, and don't make things too easy for the children.

>> In your planning include both set-up problems and everyday problems that occur as part of normal activities and involve some kind of shape, space or measures – sorting and tidying up the home corner, wrapping up presents, or building and constructing.

>> Practise seeing the problem-solving and maths potential in everyday activities, and posing the problem in a way that appeals to – and challenges – the children.

>> Build on an existing activity, change an aspect of it and see if the children can rise to the challenge:

You've arranged three bulbs beautifully in that pot. Now can you arrange four bulbs in this bigger pot?

>> Talk with children about what they are doing. Encourage different children to try different approaches to solving the same problem, and talk about these. Acknowledge and respond to children's questions and comments and turn their comments around to form questions:

Kieran has packed the blocks back in the box. Do you want to have a try? You might find a different way to do it.

This is a new puzzle. Where shall we start?

Yoko says it won't fit in. I wonder why it won't fit.

Yesterday you made a pattern with two colours. I wonder if a pattern with three colours would work.

If the children get "stuck" or need help, ask open questions:

What have you thought of so far?

What could we try next?

Can you use this to help you?

Sometimes, at the end of a task, you can go over the problem-solving process with the children:

You were trying to build a tower as tall as the house. First you used those big blocks, but towards the end they were too big, so you used some smaller blocks, didn't you? Now your tower and the house are both exactly the same height.

Progression in solving practical problems

● Child tackles problems with only slight awareness of the likely outcome: for example, piles blocks randomly in the box rather than fitting some of the flat surfaces together to save space

● Child begins to use mathematical skills and knowledge previously acquired: for example, packs square blocks in rows rather than placing them together randomly

● Child begins to be more thorough and systematic: for example, checks each skirt in turn when trying to find the right one for the teddy

● Child begins to relate a problem to others they've solved: for example, remembers to turn a shape around to see if it fits in another way

Mathematics provision

Child-initiated play

Important words and phrases

Measure, size

enough, not enough

long, short, tall, heavy, light

shape, pattern

make, build, draw

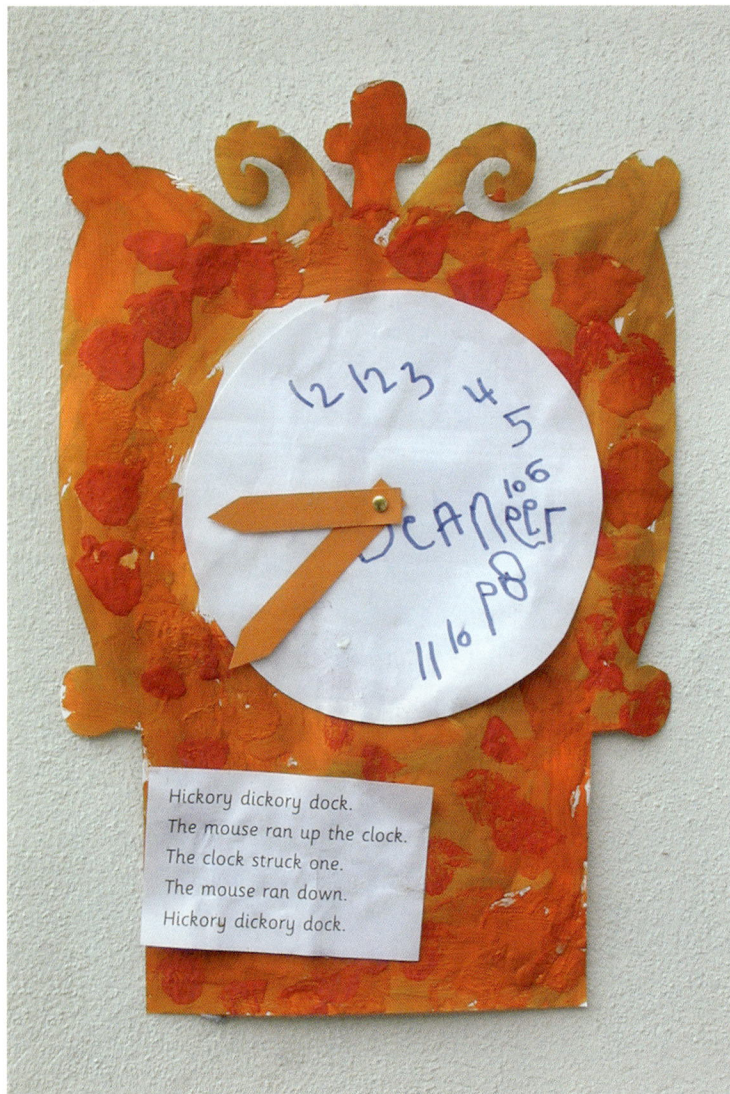

Hickory dickory dock.
The mouse ran up the clock.
The clock struck one.
The mouse ran down.
Hickory dickory dock.

Mending clocks

Resource the role play area as a watch- and clock-repair centre. Provide real clocks and watches that need to be mended. Show how different alarms work and listen to the "ticks" of some working, non-digital clocks. Supply cogs and wheels as well as small tools that can be used for repairing clocks. Provide some materials so that children can make their own pretend watches and clocks. Develop the play by providing a working wall clock so that customers can check the right time and a "speaking clock" booth that children can use.

A picnic for the bears

Provide a blanket in the outdoor area for the bears to picnic on. Indoors, resource a bears' house with three different-sized bears and a selection of plates, cups and cutlery as well as dough food, and a large picnic basket. Encourage the children to pack a picnic basket for the bears and then take it outside and lay out the bears' picnic. Develop the play by providing more picnic fare in three different sizes and discuss which of the bears should have the largest plate, and which the smallest plate.

Decorating

Decide that the walls of the home corner need redecorating and provide the children with wallpaper and flour paste. Provide measuring tapes and rulers and discuss measuring the walls and the wallpaper lengths. Show the children how to paste the wall and press the wallpaper on to it. Extend the play by providing lengths of muslin material to cut as curtains for the windows.

Obstacle course (outside)

In the outdoor area create an obstacle course. Give the children some large arrow markers and ask them to work out a route round the course and indicate the way with the arrows. Develop the play by adding more obstacles and encouraging the children to change the route and re-position the arrows. They could also draw a plan of the new route.

Adult-led activities

Face mobiles

Make face mobiles by arranging sticky paper shapes on a card circle to make a face and using wool for hair. Punch a hole in each one. Thread ribbon through it and suspend it from a wire circle. Extend the activity by using triangles or squares as a face.

Which shape are you going to use for the mouth?

What would happen if we punched the hole next to the nose?

I wonder if this ribbon will fit through the hole?

Wrapped up

Use tin foil to cover three items, such as a small, round box, a telephone and a toy bus, making sure that the features of each are shown through the foil, then remove the objects. Place the objects and their foil wrappings together and ask the children to decide which object each wrapping came from. Extend the activity by giving each child a small piece of foil and a plastic shape to wrap; show the children how to outline their shape with their fingers. Put the wrapped shapes and a set of identical shapes on the table and decide which shapes match each of the wrapped ones.

Shopping bags

Give each pair of children two carrier bags and a selection of shopping items and ask them to pack the bags so that each bag weighs about the same. Discuss with the children the best way of solving the problem.

When you hold the bags in your hands, do they feel the same weight or does one of the bags feel heavier or lighter?

What could it be?

Provide some photographs of different objects from unusual angles: from below or directly above, for example, and display these photographs and the objects. Ask the children to pair them up. Extend the activity by photocopying some everyday objects for the children to identify.

That seems to be round. I wonder which of these things it is.

Can you find the photo of the tin?

Would it help if we turned the cup upside down?

Box makers

Provide the group with some construction material and set them the challenge of making a lidded box which will hold just ten marbles.

Sabrina's made a long, thin box and Hugo's made a chunky one. Shall we see if they both really do hold just ten marbles?

Scavenger hunt

Give each child a small box and suggest that the children see how many different things they can find to put in their box, before it is full. After a box has been filled up, place the contents onto a small tray so that the children can compare the contents of each box.

Which box had the most things in?

Which box had the largest object in?

Which box had the fewest things?

Opportunities through the day

Cookery area

Resources
Sliced bread
A range of sandwich fillings
Pastry cutters
Menu cards

Activities
Make sandwiches using different fillings. Use pastry cutters to cut the sandwiches into different shapes. Write a menu and invent a way of showing the shape of the sandwich and the filling it has.

How can we cut them to make different shapes?

I wonder how we can show how we did it.

Graphics area

Resources
A quantity of small cards all the same size
Name list
Washing line and pegs

Activities
Make first name labels using a card for each letter and suspending them from a washing line. Discuss how to find out which name is the longest and which is the shortest. Decide if any of the names are the same length.

How can we find out which one is the longest?

Do you think there's a way we could check what we've done?

Science area

Resources

A teddy in a box
String and a bulldog clip
Bucket and pebbles
A plank to act as a ramp

Activities

Set up a ramp with teddy in the box at the lower end and the bulldog clip at the other end. Tie one end of the string to the box, thread it along the ramp and through the bulldog clip. Attach the bucket to the other end of the string. Find out how many pebbles you need to put in the bucket to pull the Teddy up the ramp.

What do you think will happen next?

Can you remember what problem we have to solve?

Malleable area

Resources

Make a quantity of sand foam by diluting three spoonfuls of bubble bath with one spoonful of water, then stirring sand into the mixture with a rotary egg whisk.
Small yoghurt pots and mousse containers and spoons
Combs and sticks

Activities

Use the foam to fill up the yoghurt pots and mousse containers and decide how many spoonfuls of foam it takes to fill each of them. Discuss which type of container holds the most.

Use the combs to draw shapes and patterns in the foam.

Can you think of a way of recording what we do?

Does it matter which way we do it?

Assessing children's development

If a child	Then they may be on this step
Fits simple puzzle pieces where they belong, even if this is done by trial and error rather than by comparing shapes Uses words such as "square", "round", "big", "heavy" and "pattern", even if incorrectly Chooses to play with flat shapes, building blocks, or other equipment for arranging objects in space, and sets their own tasks	Use mathematical language in play Show an interest in shape and space by playing with shapes or making arrangements with objects Show willingness to tackle problems and enjoy self-chosen challenges
Talks about patterns or other shape work that is on display Tackles simple problems, using some sort of system, but doesn't necessarily stick to it: for example, puts away some of the blocks in neat rows, but then puts the rest in anyhow Says something about the methods they use: for example, says that they are putting blocks "like this" (on end) to make a taller tower Tackles a simple task, such as collecting all the brick shapes, or separating the big bean bags from the small ones	Show interest by sustained construction activity or by talking about shapes or arrangements Use shapes appropriately for tasks Begin to talk about the shapes of everyday objects Take initiatives and manage developmentally appropriate tasks
Uses mathematical knowledge and skill: for example, finds a suitable size and shape of fabric scrap to use as an apron for the puppet Shows signs of having a plan: for example, collects the blocks they need before they start building Shows signs of being systematic and organised: for example, puts all the cups away with their handles in the same direction	Show curiosity and observation by talking about shapes, and how they are the same or why some are different Choose suitable components to make a particular model Adapt shapes or cut material to size Display high levels of involvement in activities

Benita decided to use the pattern blocks to draw around. She said "If you put shapes together, you can make other shapes. Look: add a square and now it's a diamond." She said she was going to make "an all round pattern that's the same".

Pink level

Age 5.9

If a child	Then they may have reached these objectives
Finds a way to solve a simple problem: for example, punches two holes together in order to thread thick laces through the card	Use developing mathematical ideas and methods to solve practical problems
Suggests a mathematical tool to use for a task: for example, offers a ruler to help solve the problem of moving the computer into a smaller space	Continue to be interested, excited and motivated to learn
	Select and use activities and resources independently
Uses a computer program to make their own repeating patterns	Use mathematical language to describe solid (3D) objects and flat (2D) shapes
Finds a box from which to make a house for a doll	Sustain involvement and persevere, particularly when trying to solve a problem or reach a satisfactory conclusion
Explores patterns made by folding and cutting paper or card	
Suggests what to try in response to "What could we try next?"	

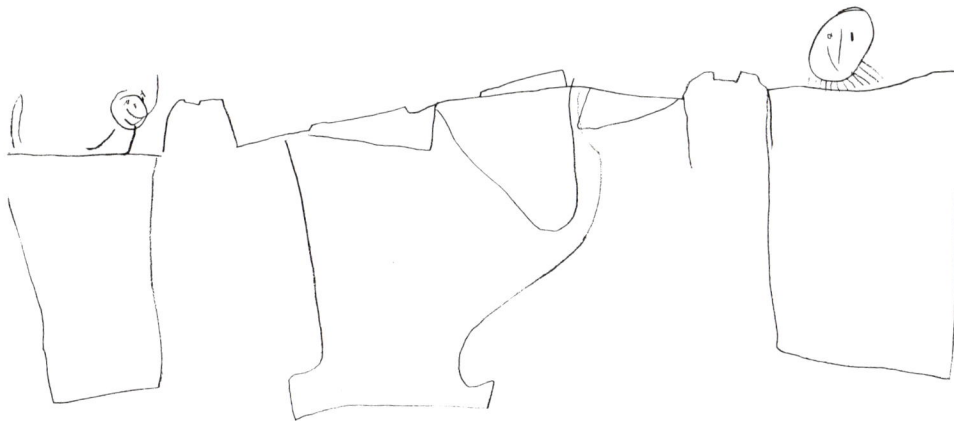

Sean found two toys that balanced. He tried several different weighings before he was satisfied.

Grey level

Age 5.6

So far in *Starting Out*, we've provided you with all of the elements you need to help children become mathematically competent and confident. Planning is what brings those elements together – get your planning right and successful learning and teaching is within your reach. Effective planning will help you and the practitioners in your team provide your children with a broad and balanced curriculum that is appropriate for each of them: you'll need to plan for the children who will need additional support to reinforce their understanding as well as for those who are more advanced and who will need further challenges. Providing daily opportunities for the children to rehearse and revisit their developing mathematical concepts, skills and knowledge is an ideal starting point for planning.

Number in everyday routines

- Counting how many children are in each group, or are using the sand and water trays

- Deciding how many children will work on the computer or play the new board game

- Looking at the calendar, writing in birthdays and holidays, counting how many days to the picnic

- Making sure that all the numbers are still in the right order on the washing line

- Singing a number song during fruit time; reading a book about number in story time

- Playing "I spy numbers"; talking about numbers in the environment

Calculations in everyday routines

- Discussing how many children are there when one child in the group is away

- Singing songs and rhymes that count in 2s or 5s at music time

- Putting two 1–3 dice and some counters on the games table, instead of a 1–6 dice

- Using the weather chart to decide whether there were more sunny or rainy days last week

- Deciding whether more children have chosen apples or bananas at fruit time

- Keeping a running total "and one more child arrives, so now there are… altogether".

- Finding out if the numbers of lunchboxes and children having packed lunch are the same

Shape, space and measures in everyday routines

- Using positional words by saying who is sitting next to, behind, or in front in circle time

- Putting away the big blocks on the shelf; fitting small blocks into the box, trolley or container

- Measuring and deciding on the height of the shelf, to make sure that everyone can reach it

- Using the cones to make a track for the bikes to use outdoors

- Looking at the clock and deciding whether it is time to clear away

- Sitting in a circle shape, a triangle, a straight line, or a wavy line

- Discussing which equipment is heavy to carry and which is light

Essentials of planning for the Foundation Stage

- Include clear goals for children's learning but take account of their interests and enthusiasm too.

- Provide opportunities for children to work collaboratively, as well as individually; and to share and negotiate, and reflect on their learning.

- Build-in time for, and encourage, children to talk about what they are doing and have done, and to listen to each other. Identify the questions that you might ask them.

- Plan for a stimulating context for learning maths: provide opportunities for meaningful child-initiated play and adult-led activities and aim for a high level of involvement by the children.

- Identify and maximise the mathematical learning opportunities across the different areas of your setting, both inside and out, so that children experience maths across a whole range of activities.

- Remember that many everyday activities are mathematically rich and can be included in your plans. When you do include them, make sure that the experience isn't always end-product-driven but is also about the process.

- Some activities will start inside and will continue in the outdoor area. For example, work inside on small motor skills and then build on this by throwing beanbags into crates outdoors.

- Make sure that activities are challenging enough for children to work on them for an extended period of time.

Exemplar plans

The following pages (116 to 119) hold four exemplars of planning in the Foundation Stage. These exemplars come from real practitioners and represent good practice in a variety of planning styles. The way you plan will reflect your team, your setting, your children and your strengths, so take what applies to you from each of the plans and interpret it in your own way.

- A termly plan – this creates a framework of learning objectives across the whole curriculum, using the stepping stones as guidance

- A medium-term plan – this identifies activities and experiences that will support the maths learning in the termly plan

- A short-term plan – this details the mathematical problem solving that happens in the different workshop areas of a Reception class

- A learning plan – this is a planning method that supports an individual child's interests and enthusiasms across the whole curriculum

Exemplar plans

Learning intentions for FS1

Areas of learning	By the end of the Spring term, most children will
Personal, social and emotional development	• Show increasing independence in selecting and carrying out activities • Have a sense of self as a member of different communities • Express needs and feelings in an appropriate way • Demonstrate flexibility and adapt their behaviour to different events, social situations and changes in routine • Show care and concern for others, living things and their environment • Take initiative and manage developmentally appropriate tasks
Communication, language and literacy	• Listen to stories with increasing attention and recall • Question why things happen and give explanations • Use a vocabulary that reflects the breadth of their experience • Show awareness of rhyme • Handle books carefully • Ascribe meanings to marks • Draw lines and circles using gross motor movement • Manipulate objects with increasing control
Mathematical development	• Recognise groups with one, two or three objects • Count objects by saying one number name for each item • Represent numbers using fingers, marks on paper or pictures • Separate a group of objects in different ways, beginning to recognise that the total is still the same • Observe and use positional language • Talk about the shapes of everyday objects • Order two or three items by length, weight, or capacity
Knowledge and understanding of the world	• Describe simple features of objects • Talk about what is seen and what is happening • Join construction pieces together to build and balance • Comment on and ask questions about the natural world
Physical development	• Move in a range of ways, such as slithering, rolling, crawling, walking, running, jumping, skipping, sliding and hopping • Move freely with pleasure and confidence • Demonstrate the control necessary to hold a shape or fixed position • Understand that equipment and tools have to be used safely • Construct with a purpose in mind, using a variety of resources
Creative development	• Make constructions, collages, paintings, drawings and dances • Sing a few simple, familiar songs • Tap out simple repeated rhythms • Play alongside children who are engaged in the same theme • Describe experiences using a wide range of materials

This plan identifies the learning intentions for a nursery class across all the areas of learning.
These learning intentions have been mapped onto a weekly provision chart.

Exemplar plans

Mathematical development of half-termly theme

Theme: Outdoors

TERM: Spring

Class: FS1

Curriculum Area: Mathematical development

Learning intentions	Activity
Recognise groups with one, two or three objects	Number games using found objects, dice and number tracks
Count objects by saying one number name for each item	Stone collecting, sorting and counting
Represent numbers using fingers, marks on paper or pictures	Keep a growth diary for Primula pots Catkin drawing
Separate a group of objects in different ways, beginning to recognise that the total is still the same	Hiding objects under two flower pots; counting and recording results
Observe and use positional language	Making tracks and following trails
Talk about the shapes of everyday objects	Nesting and stacking flowerpots Shape walk
Order two or three items by length, weight or capacity	Making different sized bird nests using found materials
Use mathematical knowledge to solve problems	Bulb planting Making a bird feeder Painting a collection of Ladybird designs

This nursery class plan identifies the mathematical learning potential in a half-termly theme of "Outdoors".
Similar plans can be written for all the learning areas for that theme.

Exemplar plans

Intended maths weekly timetable for FS2
Learning to use mathematical ideas and methods to solve practical problems

Workshops	Monday	Tuesday	Wednesday	Thursday	Friday
Art workshop/ technology area	"What proportions?" colour mixing $\longrightarrow$	Add water jugs and coloured ice-cubes	Design a patchwork quilt	Make a bed to fit the bear $\longrightarrow$	
Construction area	What's the tallest tower you can make with ten bricks? $\longrightarrow$	Add mirrors	What's the widest bridge you can build? $\longrightarrow$	Add small cars and ramps	Add play people and road system
Book area/ Role play	Read *It's the Bear!* by Jez Alborough and decide on different picnic food	Collect together bear picnic food $\longrightarrow$	Add plates, cups, cutlery and baskets	Setting up a vote for our favourite name for a bear	Read *Where's my Teddy?* by Jez Alborough and decide where to look for a lost teddy
Maths workshop	How many hugs will three bears make if they hug each other in turn? $\longrightarrow$		How many objects balance a bear?	How much tea in a teapot?	How many outfits can a bear make from three scarves and three hats?
Graphics area/ICT	Fill in a bear information sheet on the computer	Make a counting book for bears	Set up and take a photo of a bear picnic	Draw Teddy, using the computer	Make an address label for a bear
Outside area	How many bears can you fit on a truck?	Fill an egg box with bear souvenirs	Design a teddy footprint trail $\longrightarrow$		Organise a real picnic

This plan gives an overview of the Reception-level maths provision in the different workshop areas of the setting.
It was used in a week when the learning focus was mathematical problem solving and investigations.

Individualised plan with areas of learning

Name: Georgia

Child's interest: Connecting/enclosing/tieing things with string or wool

Curriculum area	Learning	Provision/activity
Personal, social and emotional	Include others in play Show curiosity	Message boxes and letters to friends
Communication, language and literacy	Begin to use talk to create imaginary situations	Join in singing 'Wind the bobbin up' Read Spencers spaghetti
Mathematical development	Use maths language: under/on, inside/outside Measurement words: long/short Connecting counting words Shape vocabulary	Using string to measure distances Threading and counting bead strings Tracing round 3D shapes using finger tip + chalks
Knowledge and understanding of the world	Use computer program Examine and look at objects Use books to find out about things	Electric circuits ICT colour magic Look at information books on wool and string
Physical development	Travel using over, under, through Use equipment Develop small motor skills	Follow my leader Dance Ring o Roses Hammer and nails to make own pin board
Creative development	Exploring different media Using lines to enclose space	Spider web pictures Painting with string Sewing design using binka Making a torch using a circuit

This plan links the learning intentions, and their provision, to a particular child or small group.

The focus of the plan comes from the child's interest or schema.

The Foundation Stage team will usually work on this schema for up to three weeks, to provide for a diversity of needs.

Assessment activity

Number as labels and for counting

This activity is for use with children who have reached the end of the Foundation Stage. It will support you in summarising and confirming your ongoing observational assessments of each child's mathematical development. We identify the maths assessment points during the activity, as well as the linked personal, social and emotional development assessment opportunities.

Dinosaur exchange

This assessment activity is for up to four children and takes the form of a game played on an unnumbered track.

Mathematical development; key scale points

Number as labels and for counting

>   **NLC4** Says number names in order
>
>   **NLC5** Recognises numerals 1 to 9
>
>   **NLC6** Counts reliably up to ten everyday objects
>
>   **NLC7** Orders numbers, up to 10
>
>   **NLC8** Uses developing mathematical ideas and methods to solve practical problems

Personal, social and emotional development; key scale points

Social development

>   **SD4** Works as part of a group or class, taking turns and sharing fairly
>
>   **SD5** Forms good relationships with adults and peers

Resources

A tray with 60 counters

An unnumbered track to 20

A box of 40 dinosaurs or other small counting equipment

A 1–3 dice

Two shuffled sets of 1–9 number cards

Introducing the activity (and the success criteria) to the children

Explain to the children that you will be looking to see how well they play the game together and if they take turns fairly. Say that you will also be noticing the children that are good at counting and the way that they solve any number problems.

Activity	Success criteria
Ask the children to each put a dinosaur on every space of an unnumbered 1–10 track.	*Does the child say the number names in order when they are counting out the dinosaurs? (NLC4)*
Tell the children that they need to take ten counters each from the tray.	*Do they count ten counters from a larger amount and realise that the last number they say is their total count? (NLC6)*
Explain that to play the game, they should take it in turns to roll the dice and remove that many dinosaurs from anywhere on the track. They need to replace each dinosaur that they take with one of their counters.	*Do they systematically solve the problem of exchanging a dinosaur for a counter? (NLC8)* *Do they understand when it is their turn to roll the dice and waits patiently, joining in any discussion about the game? (SD4)*
After everyone has had three turns, discuss how many counters each child has and how many dinosaurs. Give each pair of children a shuffled pack of number cards. Suggest that they work together to put the cards in order and then find the two numeral cards from the pack that show the number of dinosaurs in their collection.	*Can they put the 0–9 cards in order? (NLC7)* *Do they talk and work together to put the cards in order? (SD4)* *Do they choose the correct numeral cards to match their collections of dinosaurs? (NLC5)*

Assessment activity

Calculating

This activity is for use with children who have reached the end of the Foundation Stage. It will support you in summarising and confirming your ongoing observational assessments of each child's mathematical development. We identify the maths assessment points during the activity, as well as the linked personal, social and emotional development assessment opportunities.

Bears at the bus stop

This assessment activity is for up to four children to play as a game on the mat or as a table-top activity.

Mathematical development; key scale points

Calculating

C4 Relates addition to combining two groups

C5 Relates subtraction to taking away

C6 In practical activities and discussion, begins to use the vocabulary involved in adding and subtracting

C7 Finds one more or one less than a number from 1 to 10

C8 Uses developing mathematical ideas and methods to solve practical problems

Personal, social and emotional development; key scale points

Disposition and attitudes

DA7 Is confident to try new activities, initiate ideas and speak in a familiar group

Social development

SD4 Works as part of a group or class, taking turns and sharing fairly

Resources

One shoebox lid or polystyrene tray to be used as a bus

Four "bus stops" (try attaching sticky notes to pencils stood in an interconnecting cube)

A box containing 40 bears (ten bears for each child)

A 1–3 dice

A six-sided blank dice marked "on" on four sides and "off" on two sides

Introducing the activity (and the success criteria) to the children

Explain to the children that while they are playing the game you will be asking questions to see if they understand and can do adding up and taking away. Say that you will also be looking at how well they play the game together and if they take turns fairly.

Activity	Success criteria
Give each child a bus stop and two bears and ask them to add more bears from the box until they have ten bears each. Tell the children to arrange their own bears in line as in a bus queue.	*Does the child add enough bears to their line to make ten altogether, either by counting out eight or by repeatedly adding bears and recounting? (C8)*
Ask the children to take it in turns to roll both dice and either put bears on or off the bus depending on what they roll on the dice.	*The child shows by their actions in adding bears to the bus that they have some understanding of addition (C4)*
	The child shows by their actions during the game – removing bears from the queue or the bus – that they have some understanding of subtraction (C5)
	Do they understand when it is their turn to roll the dice and contribute to any discussion about how to play the game? (SD4)
During the game, ask the children questions such as "When you have put three more bears on the bus, how many will there be altogether?", "How will you find out what the total number of bears on the bus is?" and "How many bears will be left at the bus stop if you put two bears on the bus?"	*Do they use words such as "altogether", "add", "more", or "take away" when explaining what is happening during the game? (C6)*
	Can the child explain how many there will be altogether on the bus? (C4)
	Can the child predict how many bears will be left at the bus stop? (C5)
Play three rounds of the game and then ask everyone to count how many bears they have left in their queue. Ask each child "If I give you one more bear, how many will you have then?"	*Can the child respond appropriately to questions such as "What if we add/take away one more bear"? (C7)*
Ask the children if they can suggest a way of working out the difference between the number of bears they had at the beginning of the game and the number of bears they have now.	*Can the child suggest a way of finding the difference between the number of bears they started with (ten) and the number of bears they have left, either by calculating the answer mentally or by using fingers or moving bears to show how to solve the problem? (C8)*
Ask the group to suggest ways they could put all the bears back in a queue, so that there is the same number of bears at each bus stop.	*Does the child join in with solving the problem of putting equal numbers of bears at each bus stop, by talking and listening and making suggestions on how to do it? (DA7)*

Assessment activity

Shape, space and measures

This activity is for use with children who have reached the end of the Foundation Stage. It will support you in summarising and confirming your ongoing observational assessments of each child's mathematical development. We identify the maths assessment points during the activities, as well as the linked personal, social and emotional development assessment opportunities.

Keep the pattern going

This assessment activity encourages children to discuss and analyse as well as predict the patterns that they are making.

Mathematical development; key scale points

Shape, space and measures

SSM4 Talks about and recognises simple patterns

SSM5 Uses everyday words to describe position

SSM6 Uses language such as "circle" or "bigger" to describe the shape and size of solids and flat shapes

SSM8 Uses developing mathematical ideas and methods to solve practical problems

Resources

Large, plain coloured piece of paper (A1 size)

Counters of three different colours

Two different flat 2D shapes, such as triangles and squares, and 3D shapes, such as cubes and cylinders

Introducing the activity (and the success criteria) to the children

Tell the children that you are going to start making some patterns on the paper and that you want to see if they can carry them on. Say that you will be looking to see who is good at pattern spotting and who can say when the pattern is going wrong.

Activity

Activity	Success criteria
Arrange three different patterns in lines across the paper: one using coloured counters, another 2D shapes and the third 3D shapes. As you are putting out a pattern, ask the children if they can predict what colour or shape you are going to pick up next.	*Can the child "speak" the pattern by saying "triangle, square, triangle, square…" or add to the pattern? (SSM4)* *Does the child offer suggestions as to how the pattern might continue or respond to another child's suggestion or ideas? (DA7)*
Ask the children to continue patterns by following your directions, such as "Put the red square next to the blue square".	*Does the child use positional language such as "next to", or "between"? Or do they respond appropriately to requests to put the red counter next to, or between? (SSM5)*

Remove a section of one of the patterns and ask the children to find out which pieces of the pattern are missing.	*Does the child explain how they solved the problem of the missing part of the pattern? (SSM8)*
Suggest that the children now make their own designs and patterns. When they have finished, ask them to describe either their pattern or the pattern that their friend has made.	*Does the child identify shapes, such as a circle, or a property of a shape, such as corners, that they are using in the pattern? (SSM5)*

Weighing bags

This assessment activity is organised for pairs of children in order to show their expertise at weighing.

Mathematical development; key scale points

SSM7 Uses language such as "greater", "smaller", "heavier" or "lighter" to compare quantities

SSM8 Uses developing mathematical ideas and methods to solve practical problems

Resources

Pair of balancing scales

Small plastic sandwich bags or detergent nets and a selection of small items, such as conkers, marbles and plastic cubes

Spinner with two divisions saying "heavier" and "lighter"

Some plastic £1 coins

Introducing the activity (and the success criteria) to the children

Explain to the children that while they are using the balances you will be looking to see how careful they are at weighing, whether they know how to weigh objects, and if they can tell whether objects are heavier or lighter than each other.

Activity | ### Success criteria

Activity	Success criteria
Give each child a bag and ask them to choose some objects to put in it, then use the balance scales to weigh their bag against their partner's and decide which bag is heavier and which is lighter. Ask the children questions such as "How will you know which is the heaviest bag?"	*Does the child use the language of weight, such as "lighter" or "heavier" when comparing their bag with their partner's bag? (SSM7)*
When the children have weighed the bags, spin the lighter/heavier spinner and decide which bag-owner has won the spinner prize of a £1 coin. Keep changing the contents of each bag, weighing, and spinning the spinner to find a winner, until each child has won two coins.	*Does the child help solve the problem of how to identify which bag has won the spinner prize? (SSM8)*

What to provide

Lots of interesting and inspiring things to count: beads and buttons, feathers and shiny jewels, small-world people and animals, tea sets, conkers, acorns and shells

Games such as dominoes, number lotto and pairs, as well as board games that use a number track or show numerals

Collecting games, games with moveable objects, and game boards and grids with spaces to fill up with objects

Number jigsaws

Plastic or wooden numerals – use them as labels announcing the results of a count or as props when singing number rhymes

Tactile numbers: wooden, raised, feely and card, as well as peg numbers and calculator digits

Lots of different dice: small and large, with spots or numerals, and for indoor- or outdoor-area play

An abacus and strings of beads; pegs and pegboards

Picture books about numbers and stories that involve counting, as well as illustrations featuring animals, people, houses, cakes and cars that can be counted. Counting books, rhyme and song books, and tapes

Counting cubes that can be joined together, as well as structured counting material, such as Numicon

Some but not all of the interlinked plastic counting material, such as linking bears, elephants, dinosaurs, giraffes and paper clips

Real-life measuring equipment that shows numerals, such as tape measures, scales, measuring cylinders, clocks, watches and calendars

Large floor and wall number grids, floor number lines and number tracks – both indoors and outdoors. Large number tiles and number friezes up to 10, 20 and 100

What to provide

Table-top number tracks and lines and numbered carpet squares that can be arranged as a track or a grid

Large calculators and wooden, plastic and magnetic numerals for keeping running totals

Dice and spinners with beads, counters or pennies, together with small containers and dishes, for "taking away" and "all together" activities

Dominoes and number cards

A collection of empty film containers with two dice in each for playing instant addition games

Portable whiteboards, chalk boards or flipcharts for recording game scores

A selection of board games

A collection of objects that belong together, such as cups and saucers, keys and locks, pots and lids, plastic eggs and egg cups, glasses and straws

Shopping games, price labels, purses and real coins. A tray of objects that each cost £1 and a supply of notes and £1 coins to rehearse giving change

Resources for children to invent their own games of rolling the dice and collecting objects. Where children seem ready for it, offer a dice or spinner that shows "take 1, take 2, put back 1" so that they sometimes lose

Two-colour counters or beans for number-bond activities, and interconnecting counting cubes

Set rings

Grids, eggboxes, and chocolate-box trays that show empty spaces to discuss "how many more to fill it up?" ideas

In the outdoor area, a number track and giant dice and spinners

Beanbags and hoops, balls and buckets, and quoits and sticks

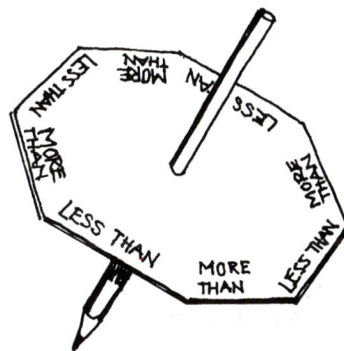

What to provide

Shape and space

Big blocks, tunnels, and bridges in wood, plastic or foam

Construction equipment in two different sizes and a selection of small construction material

Attribute blocks, other flat shapes; sets of 2D and 3D shapes that tessellate

Poleidoblocs and pattern blocks; 3D solid shapes and construction straws

Road mats and cars and lorries; play mats with small-world animals and objects

Jigsaw puzzles, shape dominoes, pegs and pegboards

Feely bags and posting boxes

Lacing boards and laces, and threading laces and beads of different shape, size and colour

Collection of patterned fabrics, wallpapers and wrapping paper

Sticky paper shapes, fuzzy felt and small plastic mirrors

Plastic mirrors, some hinged together with tape

Measures

Balances, scales and spring balances; compare bears and teddy bear counters to use as weights; real weights up to 1 kg

Measuring elephants or linking giraffes

Plastic cotton reels, counters and squares to use for area

Ribbons, flexible number lines, tape measures and rulers, height chart, metre rule

Containers: standard and non-standard

Sand timers, stop watches, clocks